THE DYING TRADE

DAVID DONACHIE

The Dying Trade

MACMILLAN
LONDON

First published 1993 by Macmillan London Limited

a division of Pan Macmillan Publishers Limited
Cavaye Place London SW10 9PG
and Basingstoke

Associated companies throughout the world

ISBN 0–333–57494–X

1 3 5 7 9 8 6 4 2

A CIP catalogue record for this book is available from
the British Library

Phototypeset by Intype, London
Printed and bound in Great Britain by
Mackays of Chatham PLC, Chatham, Kent

To Tom Preston

PROLOGUE

Drunk he might be, but William Broadbridge knew he was in the wrong part of the port. The only light he could see was the thin strip of pale night sky directly above his head. The moon hadn't risen sufficiently to penetrate this dank and stinking *carruga*, an alley so narrow that two men would struggle to pass each other. That very lack of width allowed him to support himself while he tried to make sense of where he was and what was going on. He peered into the darkness trying to identify the source of the scuffling noises, hearing a quiet, oddly familiar, yet seemingly disembodied laugh as he staggered forward. It must be imagination, for there was no one to be seen. It was the creaking sound of the straining rope, followed by a strangled gasp, that made him look up. The feet were kicking violently, but they were not aimed at him. The crack on the head from one polished toe not, in itself, enough to cause him to collapse. But it combined with the effect of drink and the mere act of looking up. He fell heavily against the stone wall and slid down into an untidy heap.

He was not out for long. Enough time for the moon to traverse far enough in the sky to send a shaft of silver light down one dirt-streaked wall. That light, and the fluid dripping on to his tricorn hat, sped his waking. Broadbridge sniffed loudly, aware, even in such a noxious port as Genoa, of the overpowering smell of human waste. He looked up, ill-advisedly, since another drop of urine parted from the polished toe, this time missing his hat and landing square in his eye. His angry shout reverberated off the walls of the alleyway as he struggled to his feet. He looked up again, this time with more caution. The body, closer now and fully lit, wore the full-dress uniform of a British naval officer, a senior captain judging by the twin epaulettes. It swung gently in the slight breeze, turning this way and that as though it could not settle. The eyes seemed to start from their sockets and the tongue, clasped between his clenched teeth, had been bitten through in death's agony, adding blood to the mixture of fluids staining the hard-packed earth below. The man was dead, and in his death he had voided himself, as all men do.

Broadbridge turned to get away, kicking the gold-braided hat as he did so. In one swift movement he picked it up and ran unsteadily towards the well-lit quayside, trying desperately to quell the pending upheaval in his stomach. Vaguely he registered his proximity to the looming bulk of the Customs Fort, with the added tinge of unease caused by the thought that he shouldn't be anywhere near the place. He managed to get his head over the low harbour wall before he was sick, retching noisily, ignored by the guards standing duty under the torches which lit up the fortress gates.

Eventually he pulled himself upright, wiping his sleeve across his mouth, cursing the burning sensation in his throat. He looked at the hat, still in his hand, fingering the gold that covered its edge. Then he turned it over, and peering inside he saw Howlett clearly marked on the name-tape sewn inside. With a swift movement he flung it out into the harbour. William Broadbridge wanted nothing to do with the Navy, nothing to do with murder, and nothing whatever to do with a man called Howlett.

That damned Customs Fort. He knew now that he'd turned the wrong way on leaving Ma Thomas's tavern. Not that he'd wanted to leave. William Broadbridge would much rather have stayed in that overheated, smoke-filled place, with a full pot of ale to drink, a wench on his lap, and a winning bet on the fight that would be taking place in the pit at the far end of room. But it was not to be. His tankard would stay as empty as the pockets of his blue broadcloth coat. Silently he cursed under his breath, damning God, the devil, and his fellow men, and wondering where in the world his next penny would come from.

The quayside became busier and brighter as he made his way north, away from the Customs Fort towards the area near the centre of the bay called the Madelena, with its teeming bawdy houses and taverns. He wiped his brow to remove the sweat caused by the warm night air and tried to adjust his eyes so that each image passing before him was singular, instead of the double he was seeing now. And he roundly cursed the citizens of Genoa, as though his poverty and his ability to focus could be laid entirely at their door.

That was the theme which dominated his thoughts as he staggered along. This cursed place, bankers to half the known world, bursting at the seams with gold, none of which he could get his hands on. A city state, a thriving port, and a so-called republic that was really just a swindle perpetrated by the rich upon the poor. The waterside tenements, rising up from the narrow alleyways into the sky till they nearly met at the top, crowded together with the warehouses, left little room for traffic of any sort. Yet beside a building teeming with ragged, hungry, and filthy inhabitants, amid the stink of crowded and deprived humanity, you could find an intricately carved doorway that would lead to a secret and spacious *palazzo*. Behind the buildings that bounded the port the new palaces of the rich, built cheek by jowl in glaring display, vied in size with the numerous churches and cathedrals of an earlier age.

Men spoke of revolution, of emulating their French cousins and setting up the guillotine before the cathedral in the Piazza San Domenico, so that the aristocrats and bankers who controlled their miserable lives could be brought to justice. Yet the advent of Jacobinism merely added another strain of conflict to a city at perpetual war with itself. Men fought ancient feuds, with Guelphs and Ghibellines still ready to carry their loyalty for Pope or Emperor to open conflict, even if the true cause was lost in the mists of time. Freemasonry flourished despite the efforts of friars and Jesuits to stamp it out. Business rivalries overlaid all this, with families pitted against each other in a bewildering series of shifting alliances. Few wealthy men ventured out into the streets without an armed escort to protect their person, and they took care to build their houses and *palazzos* with barred windows on the lower floors that made a surprise attack impossible.

Broadbridge, still cursing the city and his luck, bundled people

3

aside. He was in the Soparipa now, the arcade that ran under the sea wall, each arch a stall or shop with the vendors loudly crying out to shift their wares. The smell of exotic spices filled his nostrils, which did nothing to assuage his raging thirst. The hungry, adults and children alike, wandered about or sat listless where they could. Some, with more food inside them, sought to beg from him. Perhaps they would seek to rob him. The Englishman laughed at the thought of some dip stealing his purse. They were welcome to it, for its only value lay in the leather it was made of.

Little of the great wealth of Genoa permeated down to these wretches, who stood to gain something from any revolutionary upheaval. He swore at them in turn, for as a true-born Englishman he'd have no truck with turmoil unless, of course, it smacked of profit. Broadbridge sucked in a great breath of air as he emerged on to the quayside again, though to call it fresh would leave out mention of the stench of the port. He swayed through the crowds which parted uncertainly to avoid him, and fixed his bleary eyes on the entrance to Ma Thomas's place. Dry-mouthed and with a still-burning throat, he debated returning to his ship. But the problems there were, if anything, worse than those he faced here. The tavern was full of people. Folk with money to spend. Perhaps, at this late hour, one of them would be far enough gone, or so flush with a successful wager, that they would stand him a drink. And you could never be sure that there wasn't a soul inside just dying to invest in William Broadbridge. After all, he'd been lucky once. Perhaps he could manage the same good fortune twice. Volubly he reassured himself that for William Broadbridge something would turn up. Something always did!

CHAPTER ONE

It had been a mistake for the Ludlow brothers to attend the ball given in honour of Admiral Hood. Yet what excuse could they give to such a close family friend? You could not say they were being ignored, since all the proper forms were fully observed, and the officers of the newly arrived fleet, unaware of what was about to take place, were agog to hear about the action they had just participated in, a battle in which the *Magnanime* of seventy-four guns had engaged two Frenchmen of equal strength, though they studiously avoided any allusion to the other events which had resulted in a number of dead bodies aboard the ship.

But those based here were giving them a wide berth, lest by association they would be thought to be taking sides. Gibraltar was, in all respects, a garrison town. The Governor was an Army officer. Those posts in the administration not filled by officers of the Army or the Navy were filled by civilians who depended on the military for their very existence, and aware of the quarrel and its possible outcome the civilians were taking their cue from those in uniform.

The Admiral had stopped by and had a word, and for a brief moment they were at the centre of a busy throng. But the guest of honour could not be expected to expend his time on them, and Hood had passed on, circulating round the room in the company of the Governor, exchanging a word with everyone in turn. A number of ladies glanced in their direction, for the Ludlows were a handsome pair. But with strict orders from their husbands or fathers, none dared approach within ten feet.

James turned to his brother, having listened to him explain the recent action for the twentieth time. 'I think we could decently leave, don't you?'

Harry took a glass of punch from a passing servant. 'Let's wait till the Admiral leaves. It won't be long. He's not overfond of this sort of gathering.'

James frowned slightly. 'Do you think he knows?'

'I doubt it. If he did, he would likely forbid it,' said Harry.

'He surely cannot forbid you.'

'Duelling is illegal. Especially for serving officers. He could most certainly stop Clere.'

'I should think there are any number of people in this very room who could stop Clere.'

James had raised his voice so that a fair number of the people close by could hear him, including a knot of officers standing in a group by one of the tall windows. Some of them turned sharply at the sound of his words, flushed with embarrassment or anger.

Harry knew that James was indulging in a touch of family loyalty. He'd spent the last two days trying to persuade Harry that he was being foolish. Indeed, that his opponent wasn't worth the effort. But Harry took what James had done at face value, adding a small laugh. 'Hush, James. We can't fight them all.'

Hood, at the other end of the room by the double doors, was just taking his leave. Seeing the Admiral finally depart, a lieutenant detached himself from the group by the window and walked towards them.

'Mr Ludlow,' he said, stopping in front of them and addressing James. 'My principal wishes me to inform you that an apology is still possible.'

James just shook his head. He didn't even bother to ask Harry. Despair he might, but he knew his brother too well for that.

'Then I must inform you that Captain Clere has chosen swords for the encounter.'

'Thank you, Lieutenant,' said James stiffly. 'We shall see you at dawn.'

The man turned on his heel and walked away. With a sudden

show of anger, Harry flung the contents of his glass down his throat
and stalked out of the room, followed by his brother.

At dawn, the top of the Rock was a beautiful place to be. The sun
would rise in the east, clear across a thousand miles of sea, catching
the tip of the mountain and bathing it in light, while the town below
remained in darkness. Indeed, they had walked up in darkness and
in silence, for all that had to be said had been tried. Harry could
have declined this encounter with no real loss of honour, for Captain
Clere, who had engineered the challenge, had been drunk at the time.
It seemed to Harry that Oliver Carter, late captain of the *Magnanime*
and his old adversary, whose body now lay in the cemetery, was
going to cause him as many difficulties in death as he had in life.

Clere stood with his second silhouetted against the first hint of
light in the morning sky, the false dawn that came when the sun had
yet to clear the rim of the Earth. The effect was grey and morbid.
The surgeon stood off to one side, fussing around, not sure whether
to sort out his instruments or the two swords he was holding under
his arm. The sky was lightening quickly, as the new sun lay just
below the horizon. They stood watching as it rose, turning the night
sky from blue through grey. The red rim of the emerging orb added
a slim line of bright orange to the very east.

'I suppose one last appeal to reason would be a waste of breath?'
said James softly.

'It would only be putting off the day, James. If I decline this
challenge, I only open myself up to others.'

'You do that anyway, brother. It is not good to have a reputation
for going out. There are people who love this sort of thing, and will
challenge you for mere sport.'

'One thing at a time. Let me survive this and I promise you I will
worry about the rest.'

James spoke again, the light from the east now strong enough to
show the anger on his face. 'Someone could have stopped him, Harry.'

'The good of the service, James. He might have been behaving
like a drunken oaf. It may be that none of his fellows esteems him
very highly. But our actions have not endeared us to his fellow
officers. Call it partly envy if you like. But while they don't feel

strongly enough to challenge us themselves, they are quite prepared to let Clere have his chance. Besides, to interfere may expose them to the same threat. He has quite a reputation for his temper, I believe. A hard man to control. All that about Carter being his friend is so much eyewash.'

'All the more reason for you to decline,' said James.

'You have the flask, Pender?' Harry used this question to his servant to avoid answering his brother. Pender passed him the flask containing coffee laced with brandy. Harry took it, and allowed himself a small sip, before passing it to James. 'You may need this more than I, brother. Watching a duel is much more disturbing than taking part.'

James just shook his head, and Harry passed the flask back to Pender with the injunction to help himself. His servant did so gratefully, giving an exaggerated shiver as he did so.

The formalities had started as soon as the first edge of the sun tipped over the horizon. The surgeon approached both parties, giving them the option to withdraw. Once refused, cloaks and coats were removed, and with their white shirts taking on the colour of the blood-red sun, now just clearing the horizon and steadily turning gold, the two combatants joined the surgeon in the centre of the open space. Quietly he ordered them to abide by the rules of the engagement.

'For the last time, gentlemen,' he said, 'is there no way to avoid this encounter?'

Both shook their heads. Harry looked at Clere, seeing him for the first time without wig or uniform coat. The hair was long, mouse-coloured, straggled, and thin. His face bore the marks of many physical encounters, including a nose that had been on the receiving end of a fair number of heavy blows. His blue eyes were opaque and lifeless, and the lips, which always seemed to have an superior smile, were now tightly pursed together, evidence of the tension he was feeling. And the shoulders seemed hunched without the benefit of his epaulettes. Like this, Clere was an altogether less imposing figure. Harry felt himself relax. Now that he was finally going into action, the knot of fear, always present in the period of waiting, evaporated. He felt alive, able to see and think with absolute clarity, and the grin he gave Clere as they took up the 'on guard' position caused a look of fear to flash across the man's eyes.

8

Harry knew then that he was in the presence of an opponent who talked a good fight, a man who intimidated people by his sudden loss of temper and the violence of his language, a man who was now afraid, for on this occasion his passion had carried him to the point of a proper duel, and with a dangerous opponent. He didn't want to be there any more than Harry Ludlow, yet he could not withdraw for fear of losing face.

The sun was full up now, bathing the grassy slope that capped the mountain in a brilliant light, and making the carpet of long grass sparkle as it caught the tiny drops of morning dew. Below them the sea had gone from black to grey. Soon, as it reflected the light from the sky, it would turn to blue. The swords scraped together as the surgeon commanded the duel to commence. Clere tried to circle round, forcing Harry to face the low, blinding sun. Harry declined and thrust at his unprotected side. Clere parried and started to swing his sword to cut at his opponent. But Harry Ludlow wasn't there. In defiance of the proper rules of swordplay, he leapt past Clere and gave him a might whack on the buttocks with the flat of his blade. Clere gave a strangled cry, spinning round swiftly. Harry's sword sliced right through his flapping shirt, swept in an arc to push Clere's sword away, before he darted round to the back again and fetched him another mighty blow on the arse.

Clere staggered forward, propelled by the force of the blow, and Harry followed through, hitting him again and again, driving him on like a beast of burden. Every time Clere tried to turn to face him, Harry plied to with his sword, smashing down his opponent's blade to check him, before getting behind him again. Half his eye took in the astonishment on the faces of Clere's party as he alternately whipped his adversary with the flat of his blade, or slashed another slice out of his now tattered shirt. And they winced as their man's cries of pain rent the morning air.

He had no doubt that Clere would have put up a decent show in a proper contest, fought according to the rules. No doubt the man would have taken a wound and chose to carry on, even have died, rather than face the humiliation of being thought a coward. For Harry the choice was simple. To kill him or debunk him. He could see no point in the former course, for it would, to him, be tantamount to murder. Inelegant it might be, but this was a course that appealed to him more than the futile taking of a life.

Another blow to the buttocks, followed by a foot jammed into the back of his knees, forced Clere to fall forward. Harry waited for him to struggle to his feet before commencing again. The cries got louder, turning to screams as Harry's sword fell heavily on a part already bruised. The air resounded with the sound, the loud smack as the metal made painful contact, interspersed with the increasingly rare sound of blade upon blade.

Clere fell again, his breath coming in great gasps. Harry stood back, allowing him to rise. He moved like an old man, the pain he was feeling obvious in his eyes.

'Damn you, Ludlow. Stand still and fight,' he gasped.

Harry lunged forward. Clere raised his sword and managed to parry a few blows before Harry was through his guard, his sword on the man's chest. Clere had a look of defiance on his face, daring Harry to finish things and run him through. But Harry just leapt past him again and started on the same tactic of beating him. Clere went down several times, struggling to his feet more painfully on each occasion, his breath coming in great gulps. There was a look of despair in his eyes now, mirrored in the faces of his party, as they saw how fresh his enemy was, hardly even perspiring as he danced around, always out of reach of Clere's flailing sword.

It could not go on, and Harry, realizing that Clere would never give up, thrust forward with ease and put his blade through the fleshy upper part of the man's sword arm. A great spurt of blood came from the wound as Clere dropped his weapon. He clasped his other arm across his chest, his hand seeking to stem the flow of blood, and looked defiantly at Harry.

'Go on, sir. Finish it off.'

Clere was a victim of his tongue to the last. He could not see a way to withdraw and would not acknowledge that honour had been satisfied. Harry lunged forward again, his sword aiming straight for a point just under Clere's rib cage. He saw the look of terror in his opponent's eyes, just before they went glassy and blank.

The surgeon, standing behind Harry's opponent, rushed forward as Clere slid to the ground, turning him over and looking to stem the wound in the man's chest. He spun round startled, looking at Harry, who was standing, breathing easily, in the golden light of a full and sunlit morning. When he spoke, it would have been easy for the surgeon to mistake the target, for the distaste was evident in his voice. But it wasn't aimed at the comatose naval officer. Harry Ludlow was angry with himself, both for being here in the first place, as well as for the manner in which he'd behaved.

'Tend his arm, Doctor. I didn't touch his chest. He just passed clean away from fright.'

Harry walked back to where his brother and Pender stood. He took the flask his servant offered and allowed himself a deep swallow before saying anything.

'It's always seemed to me, brother, that the last word one should use at the conclusion of a duel is satisfaction.'

CHAPTER TWO

'Damned stuff and nonsense,' snapped the old man, looking directly at Harry Ludlow from under his thick grey eyebrows. 'I can't think what your father would say to hear you talk like this.'

'Perhaps it would be better not to discuss it at all, sir.'

James Ludlow, Harry's younger brother, looked at the two men and tried to suppress a smile. Both faces held expressions of politely masked displeasure. The older man sat at the head of the long table, set across the great cabin of the *Victory*, with the two brothers on his right and left. His dark blue coat was covered in sparkling decorations, with the red sash of the Order of the Bath across his snow-white waistcoat, evidence of his success, many years before, as a fighting sailor. And for all his years ashore, both at the Admiralty, in the House of Lords, and in attendance at the court of King George, Hood's language had lost none of its salty flavour. He was a man accustomed to silencing opposition, be it on a quarter-deck or in an oak-panelled debating chamber.

Harry Ludlow, despite his regard for Admiral Hood's age and reputation, did not enjoy being talked down to. He had spent too many years in command of his own ships to relish the tone of avuncular disapproval which had been an ongoing feature of their voyage aboard the flagship.

'I will discuss at my table any matter I please.' Hood, perhaps being a mite sharper in his response than was strictly polite, tried to stare Harry down.

'Then you will very likely find yourself dining alone,' snapped Harry, returning the stare, and the tone of the Admiral's observation, in full measure.

Hood'd face started to show real anger, the mouth hardening, his nostrils flaring, and the eyebrows seeming to thicken as they joined above his nose. But he suddenly leaned back in his chair and laughed out loud. He was a tall man, with a long raw-boned face, a big nose, and a high red colouring, set off by his thick grey eyebrows. Handsome in his youth, he'd aged well, seeming much younger than his years. Yet he had the kind of hearty, heaving laugh that with his ruddy complexion made one wonder for his health.

'You always were a gamecock, Harry, even as a nipper. I recall your father tellin' me how often he had to stretch you across a gun and thrash you.'

He dropped his voice to a clearly audible whisper.

'None of this lot would dare talk back to me. They agree with everything I say, sane or stupid. It makes for a dull voyage.' He looked down the long dining table at the assembled officers, senior captains amongst them. None even dared to catch his eye.

Hood sat back in his chair, the bony red face adopting an air of polite enquiry as he turned to his left to address his other civilian guest.

'What about you, young James. Do you share the Ludlow family temper? Or are you more of your mother's sort?'

'I do think, milord, that the last person to cast an opinion on their demeanour should be oneself. After all, if it manifests itself as a high opinion, it's self-aggrandizement, and if a poor one, it's likely to be false modesty.'

The thick eyebrows twitched as Hood looked at James. He saw before him a slim, fair-haired young man with a lively, handsome face, elegantly dressed, perfectly at ease. Neither exalted company nor an elegant setting would dent James Ludlow's self-assurance. He was a man at home in graceful society, a well-known artist, sought after for his portraits. He was also known to have a sharp tongue, and, it seemed from recent events, a mercurial temper. A man well able to look after himself. Yet it was not the bulldog temperament of his elder brother. The likeness in the two was evident. But with Harry there was a girth lacking in James, a physical presence, plus a life-long sailor's colouring and want of refinement.

Hood adopted a mildly disapproving air, though the bright blue eyes, twinkling merrily, belied the effect. 'No, I think not. You're not like Harry at all. I don't see your father in you, as I do in him. Tell the truth, you seem like a bit of a cold fish to me, James Ludlow.'

His guest held the old man's eye, unblinking. 'And I dare say that you imagine yourself as a jovial old cove, full of wit and bluff charm.'

There was a second's silence. It was Harry Ludlow who was now suppressing a laugh. James had a wry grin on his face now, but everyone else stared at their plates, anticipating, indeed wanting, the coming blast.

'Insolent swab. Whole damned family the same,' said Hood gently, his face relaxing into a wistful smile.

The cloth had been drawn, and the port was making its rounds. Pender sat in the pantry with Hood's steward, eating as well as those they had just served. It would be a foolish servant who didn't instruct the cook to prepare enough food, with a respectable quantity left over. Likewise with the wine. Having sipped fine clarets and burgundies, they were now treating themselves to a rich plum duff, and a fair quantity of an excellent Marsala.

'You don't know the half of it,' said Crane, the Admiral's steward, through a mouthful of food. He was as tall as his master, but thin as a rake, stooped from years in cramped quarters. He moved in a very fastidious way, his bony fingers elegantly and methodically wielding a knife and fork. The long doleful face was dominated by a large pointed nose, surmounted by sunken eyes. As he bent slightly to his food, he reminded Pender of a heron feeding in a marsh.

'Then I'd be obliged if you'd fill me in.' Pender lacked the refinement of the other man. He had a tendency to stab at his food with his knife, the fork poised useless in the other hand. But then he'd only recently had the chance to become acquainted with such surroundings, whereas Crane had been doing the job, afloat and ashore, for decades.

The old servant popped a morsel into his mouth. 'Thick as thieves they was, and always looking to advance each other's chances of a plum.'

Pender was fascinated by the background of the Ludlow family.

He'd picked up bits here and there about the two brothers who now employed him, from things they'd said, and from general lower-deck gossip. But Crane's memory could hark back to before James was born, to the friendship of Hood and their father, Admiral Sir Thomas Ludlow.

'There was a good case against that bastard he challenged,' Crane continued, munching steadily. 'Evidence that he had provoked young Harry Ludlow to a duel. If he'd saw fit to apologize to the court, your master would still be a serving officer. Still, the sod got his come-uppance in the end, eh?'

Crane's calm manner, and his stuck-up air of superiority, offended Pender. 'He damn near did for both of them second time round. It was touch and go, I can tell you.'

The other man sniffed loudly. 'So you say.'

It was obvious Crane believed he was exaggerating. What a pleasure it would be to tell the parchment-skinned bugger how wrong he was. To tell him the unvarnished truth about life aboard the *Magnanime* and the actions, never mind the preferences, of the ship's premier, Bentley. The despicable way that the Ludlows' ship had been sunk. Of how that old feud with the *Magnanime*'s captain had seemingly led to murder. Or the accusations laid against James, with evidence so strong that he was set to hang, for certain. Crane wouldn't eat so steadily, nor look down his nose with such deliberate scorn, if he informed him of the assistance that he himself had rendered. But Pender bit his tongue. Such a tale might require him to explain his background as well, to say where he acquired certain skills that helped Harry Ludlow prove his brother's innocence. A thief, especially a good one, does not go boasting, lest he's determined to hang himself.

Crane missed the look in Pender's eye. He thought the youngster cocky, mistaking his assured air for bravado. And lacking a sense of humour himself, he couldn't fathom the jokey way Pender went about his duties. To Crane, the lad was no proper servant. He was wrong about most things regarding his fellow-diner, but not about that. Just a few weeks before Pender had been a common seaman.

'It is sort of insultin', you know, Harry. I am not the only one who stood ready to help you. Indeed others spoke out, risking a rebuff on your behalf. Not only did you damn yourself out of your own mouth, but you threw our offers of assistance back into our faces.'

Not even the eminent Lord Hood would have wanted to utter such words in the presence of others. He was seated on the row of velvet-covered locker-tops by the sternlight of the *Victory*'s main cabin, still wearing his wig, but down to his shirtsleeves on this warm Mediterranean evening. The sun, sinking in the west, streamed through the seven windows that stretched across the rear of the great cabin, its rays flashing off the silver and the highly polished furniture. James sat in a captain's chair half-way across the room, hidden from view, his brow furrowed as he concentrated on the sketch pad balanced on his crossed knees.

'Reinstatement is not something I can ask for,' said Harry, his eyes fixed on the straight white line of the flagship's wake, which stretched into the distance across the smooth blue sea.

'Damn me, you won't get it if you don't. I should have insisted in sitting on that court martial myself.' He gave Harry a glare that had made the most senior officers in the Navy tremble. 'I like to have seen you refuse to apologize to me.'

Harry allowed himself a slight smile. 'I seem to recall that you were rather busy.'

Hood, second in command to Admiral Rodney, had just assisted his superior to rout the French fleet under the Comte de Grasse. The Battle of the Saintes had left both Rodney and Hood with other preoccupations. The trial of a junior officer for challenging his superior to a duel, expressly forbidden by the Articles of War, could hardly have distracted the attention of someone in that position, regardless of the nature of their relationship.

'All you have to do is apologize. Even now. Then we can petition the King.'

Hood's head snapped round angrily as Harry said an emphatic 'No.'

James looked round the side of his sketch pad. 'I dare say that Harry has in mind the fact that he will have to behave like all the other officers aboard, and forgo the pleasure of insulting you if he dons a King's uniform again . . .'

Hood opened his mouth to reply but James, his head now back behind the pad, cut him off. 'And I would be obliged if you would keep your head still. The hope is that this sketch will form the basis of a portrait. If you keep bobbing about it will end up like a Gillray cartoon.'

Hood, his thick grey eyebrows quivering, glared at the back of the pad. 'All I'm saying is this, James. That if your brother had good cause not to reapply for his commission, I would esteem it a kindness to be told. After all, the man he challenged is now dead, and in circumstances which cannot harm your case.'

'Will that become public?' asked Harry.

'Lord, no,' said Hood emphatically. Then his face darkened. 'It's bound to get about in the service, of course.'

'Then I don't see how it can help,' said Harry. He left out that regaining a commission in such circumstances might be equally demeaning.

'I can't abide pessimism in you, Harry. It's positively unnatural in a man of your stripe.' Hood paused, his ruddy face assuming a look of concentration as he marshalled his thoughts.

'So I must blacken his memory.'

'What's the matter with that? You couldn't abide the fellow when he was alive. Damn it, man, you put a bullet in Carter and sacrificed your commission rather than retract. All you'll be saying is that he was as bad a first lieutenant as he was a commander. That puts the offence of your challenging him to a duel in a different light. Believe me, if you can get the Court to see him in bad odour, then you are as good as back in the Navy. Take my word for it. That bunch of gossiping *arrivistes* that surround the King love nothing more than a reputation to blacken.'

There was appreciable bitterness in his last words. Hood himself had just been involved in conflict with those very forces, a battle he'd lost. 'King's mad of course, so a lot depends on the Prince of Wales. If you can stop him whoring for a moment, you might catch his ear.'

'That, my dear Admiral, is *lèse-majesté*,' said James, with deliberate irony, poking his head round the pad again.

That brought a flush to Hood's already ruddy cheeks. 'If you can find anyone with less majesty than that family, I'll be surprised. Royalty! They're not fit to be yeoman farmers.'

'Especially "Black Dick" Howe?' James raised an amused eyebrow.

'Don't bait me, you young brat. But it may be that the King gets his habit of talking to trees from trying to converse with his bastard cousin. Are you acquainted with Lord Howe, Harry?'

'I was introduced once.' Harry smiled. 'He didn't say much.'

'He never does. Talking to him is like talking to this.' He rapped his knuckles on the wooden bulkhead, and frowned, then sniffed dismissively. 'Corruption, pure and simple.'

Lord Howe had pipped Hood, then serving as the senior naval Lord of the Admiralty, to the command of the Channel Fleet. Hood knew, as did anyone with tactical sense, that in this new war with Revolutionary France the Mediterranean was a sideshow. The real naval battles would take place closer to home. That was where the true glory lay.

Harry couldn't resist a little baiting himself, after the drubbing he received for his intransigence. 'I have heard that he is a competent commander.'

'He damned well better be,' snapped Hood, with a gratifyingly apoplectic response. 'Or His Britannic Majesty, Cousin George, the third of that name, may find himself in deep water! He might find himself living next door to his French cousins in exile, or back in Hanover where the brood was sired.'

There was a great deal more in this vein, with a good deal of arm waving, as Hood vented his spleen on those who'd thwarted his ambitions. James, having surrendered any hope that his subject would remain still, used the gamut of expressions to effect a goodly number of less than flattering sketches, including one with the mad King George, portly and goggle-eyed, addressing the Admiral, drawn in the guise of a furious oak tree. Harry was merely pleased that the conversation had moved on from his concerns to those of their host.

It had been good fortune for them that their father's old friend had put into Gibraltar before they left. They'd been forced to stay longer than they would have wished, called upon by the Navy to participate in the investigations which had followed their arrival. Everyone had been shocked at their tale, but instead of being grateful to them for exposing wrongdoing, most naval officers had tended to cold-shoulder them. For one, they did not much favour privateers. Worse than that, as a breed they were painfully sensitive about their collective and personal honour. Harry's actions might have exposed serious wrongdoing, as well as solved more than one outright crime.

But he had brought the entire service into disrepute in the process.

And the Ludlows had not raised their standing when it emerged that they'd brought ashore a fair quantity of gold, the proceeds of an action against a French merchantman, who had, in turn, taken it off a Spanish ship. No one aboard the *Magananime* had even had an inkling of its existence, supposing, when Harry regaled them with the tale, that the specie had been shipped home in one of his previous captures. Nor did he or James let on once they were ashore. The agent of this further piece of approbation was the banker whose offer of purchase Harry declined. Gold in Gibraltar took its price from Spain, a country which offered notoriously low value when trading bullion. So the brothers elected to ship it home. Offended, the banker breached his normal rules of discretion.

In a small place like Gibraltar, word got round quickly. To have taken a quantity of gold was bad enough. To be a 'damned' privateer was worse. To be wealthy enough to delay before turning it into ready coin enraged certain people further. It was then easy for such types to cloak both envy and dislike in the mantle of their love of the service. Most had kept their distance, reserving their unflattering remarks for each other, rather than aiming them at the Ludlows. But a few of the naval officers were less restrained, especially when drink and braggadocio had loosened both their manners and their tongues. The challenge which Clere engineered was inevitable.

They had been seeking to book a passage home to England, always assuming that Harry survived the impending encounter with Captain Clere, when the *Victory*, at the head of ten sail of the line, had been sighted from the top of the Rock weathering Algiceras Bay. All thoughts of business, deadly or dull, were put into abeyance as everyone went down to welcome the fleet. Hood welcomed Harry and James aboard like his own sons. To the subsequent chagrin of his officers, he offered them a passage to Genoa, from where they could take the land route home through Austria, Germany, and the Netherlands. Harry had demurred, preferring a sea passage. But James, fired by memories of his Grand Tour, and the thoughts of the artistic splendours of Italy and Vienna, had prevailed.

Hood's regard for the Ludlow brothers forced a certain amount of official respect from the *Victory*'s officers. But their disapproval, once they'd been fully appraised of recent happenings, was never far from

the surface. And Harry had not raised himself in the general esti-
mation by his unorthodox humiliation of Clere. Finally losing his
temper one day, he asked James loudly, in the hearing of all the
officers on the quarter-deck, how they would have stood if he'd just
killed the bastard.

To the general relief, it would be a short voyage. Hood was making
for Toulon, to reinforce the ships already there, Spanish and English,
blockading the great French Mediterranean port. But, unless the
situation had changed in the mean time, he'd be forced to victual his
ships at Genoa, and Harry and James would transfer to whichever
ship was next due to take on stores.

CHAPTER THREE

Harry held up the white hose stocking, pointed to the very obvious repair, and smiled at Pender. 'They are, without doubt, repaired, I'll grant that much. Though the stitch is more suited to a bolt of number-seven canvas than a gentleman's stocking.'

'I reckon my talents don't lie in that direction, your honour. All a matter of upbringin', no doubt.'

Pender, sitting astride the great gun that occupied half the cabin, was smiling too, unabashed by this seeming rebuke. He was a small man with a lively dark-skinned face and a ready smile. And he had a way of addressing those in authority which undermined them, without them being quite aware of how it had happened.

'Indeed they don't,' said Harry. Pender had been allotted to him as a servant aboard the *Magnanime*, and it was plain from the first day that sailoring was not his true profession. His success in his true field of endeavour meant there were any number of hands waiting to lay themselves upon him to answer for his previous actions in England.

Hence his haste to join the Navy. Harry, desperate for ways to aid his brother James, had sought Pender's help, which had been forthcoming in no uncertain terms. Now, having been an inexperienced member of the King's Navy, he had taken to the role of Harry's servant with great enthusiasm. And he had been an almost unqualified success. The one thing he couldn't master was the art of sewing, surprising in a man with such nimble fingers.

Harry had engineered his release from the King's service, and the instructions to Harry's brother-in-law, Lord Drumdryan, guardian of the Ludlow family wealth, to seek out Pender's dependants and take them under his protection, had been sent off in the first mail packet leaving Gibraltar after the *Magnanime* limped into port.

'You'll be lookin' forrard to having your own ship again,' said Pender.

Harry shot his brother a quick glance to see if he'd heard, before giving Pender what he thought was an imperceptible shake of the head. Since they were sharing a berth there was little room, though, being one of the wardroom side cabins, it had the benefit of daylight. James was lying on his cot, his back to the casement window, apparently engrossed in a book by John Evelyn, who'd travelled in the part of Italy for which they were headed. Harry was therefore surprised when he spoke.

'Am I being excluded from something?' James turned towards the silent pair and snapped his book shut, trapping his thumb to maintain the page.

Harry Ludlow was the picture of innocence abused. 'What makes you say that?'

'An unnatural silence, Harry. Plus the fact that Pender seems intent on making himself so busy that he will avoid eye contact with me.'

'I do have work, Mister James.' Pender had a hurt tone that had fooled many a sheriff's man.

'You have not answered Pender's question, Harry.'

Harry now assumed a perplexed look. 'What question?'

'Now I know something's afoot.' He opened the book again, and began to read it. 'By the way, Lord Hood's clerk was looking for you earlier.'

'Indeed?' Harry did not attempt to hide his suspicion. He looked like a man who'd seen his watch on someone else's waistcoat.

'Nothing important, I gather.' James yawned, increasing the tension in the cabin. 'The fellow just wanted to know if you had made up your mind. Seems the Admiral is interested.'

Harry, on the other side of the gun, looked pointedly at the stocking, still in his hand. 'Made up my mind? About what?'

'About buying another ship, and continuing your privateering in the Mediterranean.' James looked up from his book again, his face devoid of expression. 'Instead of going home as we originally intended. After all, brother, you don't lack funds.'

Harry flushed guiltily, his hand rubbing his coat involuntarily, to check that the oilskin pouch containing their letters of credit was still there. James observed this, aware that the sums named therein considerably outweighed the value of their gold.

'It's as well that those fellows in Gibraltar knew nothing of our true financial position. If they had we'd have been stoned like Christian martyrs.' He followed this observation with another studied yawn. 'I believe I posed a question. Or was it Pender?'

Pender busied himself even more as Harry gave a grudging reply. 'It was only a thought. Nothing's decided.'

'Really. Fellow had some charts of the Ligurian Sea, and was full of talk of the situation in Leghorn, which, if I'm not mistaken, is just down the coast from Genoa. Talkative cove, the Admiral's clerk. He was telling me all about the place. He seemed quite sure of your plans, though he doubted that you would persuade the Admiral to reissue your exemptions. Strange that you didn't see fit to mention any of this to me.'

'I am still investigating the possibilities, which I may say I'm entitled to do. There are any number of obstacles. But regardless of all else, any thoughts I may harbour would all come to naught if I can't safely crew the ship, so getting those exemptions back would be vital.'

There was truth in Harry's words, but also a grain of dissimulation. They did not explain his eagerness to be at sea. Prior to his previous voyage, his brother-in-law had sought to persuade him that it was folly, using cogent arguments that a man with his responsibilities should not be chasing around the oceans trying to earn money he didn't need. Arthur, while happy to look after Harry's affairs, none the less saw telling the truth as part of his duties. He was ably supported by Harry's sister, though her concerns were emotional rather than practical. If he went back to England, he knew he would have no end of trouble getting afloat again. Arthur would seek to emesh him in politics and business immediately. His sister would load him with concerns about their estate. There was no point in saying any of this to James, who had no time, and even less regard, for their brother-in-law. Ignoring Arthur was a long-standing habit with James. He would not comprehend his brother's reservations.

'Pender,' said James, smiling. 'Do try and stop inventing little tasks. You sound like a ship's rat scrabbling about.'

'Sorry, your honour,' said Pender softly, addressing Harry. 'Sort of let the cat out of the bag.'

'Of course it's really none of my concern, Harry. After all that has happened these past weeks, I can understand your reluctance to have me sail with you again.'

'That's unfair,' snapped Harry.

'I know.' His brother laughed, closing the book on his thumb again. 'But I do so enjoy catching you out. Now pray tell me what you have in mind.'

Over the next few days, Harry spent much time in the great cabin with Hood, seeking to persuade the Admiral that the loss of his hands from the *Medusa*, all of them exempt from naval service, was just as much a matter for compensation as reimbursing him for the loss of his ship. Hood was unmoved, despite Harry's oft-repeated argument that without having his hands exempt from the press, he might as well not bother to search out a crew, since any naval vessel, coming across his ship, with him flying under a British flag, could whip off as many of his hands as they cared to.

'A fine state of affairs for an Englishman,' cried Harry, with a dramatic flourish of his arm. 'To have to run from the ships of his own country.'

Hood merely laughed. They both knew the tricks of the trade, like having your men dress in odd costumes and speaking gibberish when asked any question about their past. Legally, a man could only be taken out of a ship if he volunteered, or could be positively identified as a deserter. But they also both knew that legality counted for little in the middle of the ocean, far from any authority other than the barrel of a cannon.

'Perhaps you have chosen the wrong game, Harry,' replied Hood, eyebrows raised, and with a humorous twinkle in his eye.

'Does that mean that the answer is no?'

24

Hood shook his head. 'It means that I've yet to make up my mind.'

Their rendezvous with the rest of the fleet off Cape Sicie was attended by endless discharging of signal guns as the various admirals, Spanish and English, exchanged courtesies. But that was all the polite behaviour in evidence, for when the man being relieved, Admiral Hotham, came aboard the *Victory*, any pretence at good manners evaporated. Such a meeting was rarely a happy occasion. The incoming commander would always question the activities of his predecessor, probably in writing for the sake of his own skin, while the man relinquishing command would be on edge to smoke an insult to his name or reputation.

But this time the participants excelled themselves, for Samuel Hood not only held that Hotham's actions had been unworthy, but he also implied that they'd been positively criminal. He had, in Hood's view, used the ships of the King's Navy to enrich himself. Stiff formality was the tone of their first exchange. But once Hood had read the reports and had words with some of the more efficient senior captains, he used his superiority and prestige to blast Hotham. Being intimate with Hood, and with the older man seeing no cause for discretion, Harry and James were quickly apprised of the situation.

'You'll find precious little to line your pockets in these waters now, Harry,' he snapped, banging a fist on his polished desk, before turning angrily to stare out of the sternlights at the distant shore. 'For that scrub Hotham has used the fleet to sweep the Mediterranean clean.'

'I gather from your clerk that he's initiated no action against the enemy,' said James, who had seen in this man a source of useful information, and cultivated him accordingly.

Hood spun round and gave him a sharp look, but he let the remark about his clerk pass, concentrating instead on the matter uppermost in his mind. 'None that can shoot back. All his targets have been merchantmen.'

He waved his arm in the direction of the French coast. 'There are thirty sail of the line in Toulon, most with their yards uncrossed. Damn it, they're not even ready for sea. We could destroy them at their moorings.'

'It's not an easy place to attack, milord,' said Harry. It wasn't that he sought to support Hotham. But he was more aware than James of the traditional disputes between high-ranking officers.

'Nobody says it is, Harry. But Hotham hasn't even tried. Damn near every ship has been detached on a cruise, and with the war so young they've scooped the pool. They're all cock-a-hoop with the money they've made, and who can blame them?'

'I suppose that Admiral Hotham has also done well?' asked James.

The huge hand hit the desk again, even harder. 'He's had his eighth all right. He's made more money than anyone.'

Hood looked at James to make sure he understood that a commanding admiral received an eighth of the value of any prize taken by the ships under his command. He needn't have worried. He was addressing the son of a commander who'd secured his fortune in the West Indies from just such an avenue, whilst simultaneously receiving the thanks of Parliament for his endeavours.

Hood threw himself angrily into a chair. 'I had an inkling of this in Gibraltar when I was told the number of prizes he was sending in. If he'd shown the slightest inclination to attack the French as well, I'd be after a peerage for him. God only knows what the neutrals think.'

'Surely you can find that out,' asked James. 'Do we not have a representative there?'

Hood looked surprised, as though what he was about to say was something the brothers should have known. 'Our man, Lord Fenner, died before I left Portsmouth. We haven't yet got a replacement, though I harried the government to send someone out with me.'

The ruddy face closed up again, with Hood's voice positively growling with anger. 'To cap it all, we've just had word from Genoa that our victualling agent, Gallagher, the only man we have *in situ*, has decamped, taking the funds for the purchase of our stores with him. There a whole cargo of guns missing it seems, including carronades. And it will be me that has to account for it.

'Look at this!' His voice rose even more and his huge hand thumped the desk again, before reaching out to pick up a letter. 'If you doubted Hotham's bared-faced thievery, this would convince you. I've got here a petition from the English privateers in Leghorn, asking that the activities of the Navy be curtailed.'

'Will they be?' asked Harry anxiously, for he still had hopes of sailing from the port that had long been home to British privateers.

'Of course they will,' Hood cried, quite forgetting he was talking to a privateer. 'We're here to make war, not line our pockets!'

There was no chance to talk to the Admiral for several days, with a spate of conferences aboard the flagship as Hood sought to turn the combined fleets back to their original purpose. Captains were questioned for offensive ideas that might confound the enemy, their previous attitudes and actions called to account. Just as ruthlessly their logs, muster books, and accounts were thoroughly examined. *Hannibal*, the last ship to return from Genoa, received more scrutiny than the others, and Hood tried to collate a picture of what was going on. What he heard didn't please him. With no ambassador at present in the Republic, and as Hood put it, 'damned little influence', he was given good reason to wonder at the security of the arrangements. Over the last century, Genoa had usually sided with France in the wars between the Bourbon monarchs and the British. At best they'd assumed a neutrality which favoured the French.

This had less to do with brotherly love than with geography. The French nation, the most powerful in Europe before the Revolution, was less than a day's sailing from their city. For a French army an attack on Genoa required less than a week's march. The only thing that had changed was that some of the most powerful Genoese magnates, fearing for their heads and the safety of their banks, now inclined towards Britain instead of France. Fear of the 'Terror' was greater than fear of attack.

At a last private meal before the brothers transferred to the *Swiftsure*, a frigate on its way into Genoa to take on stores, Hood raised his glass to wish them God speed and good luck. Harry took both with a pinch of salt, considering that the Admiral had not yet answered his request for exemptions. But he did have some information that he thought might be of interest.

'Seems that there's a bunch of privateers running out of Genoa itself,' he said, cracking a pair of walnuts between his huge hands.

'That's unusual,' Harry replied. 'Sardinians yes, but not English. They usually stick to Leghorn.'

'Damn it, Harry,' cried Hood, eyebrows raised. 'What's usual these days?'

'Surely that proves their neutrality now?' asked James, thoroughly bored by the lengthy discussions of naval tactics and the politics of the region. He was about to steer the conversation back towards a discussion of various Genoese painters, but the old man snorted derisively, and cut right across him.

'Genoese neutrality is governed by money, not morality. Mind I dare say that the locals don't relish the prospect of the kind of France that we're dealing with now.'

'I'll wager they still do business with them if they can. A Genoese would trade with the devil for profit. I imagine their sole objection to revolutionary France is that they might not pay their debts.'

Hood let out a great laugh, slapping his thigh, his face flushing with pleasure at the sally.

'Damn me, Harry, you've hit the nail right on the head, and no mistake. The whole damned place is one counting house. And as for reliability, *Hannibal*'s captain tells me that Tilly, the French chargé d'affaires, is walking about the place bold as brass with an armed escort. And damn me if there isn't a French warship, with a full crew and a detachment of marines, sitting in the middle of the harbour, flying their new-fangled flag.'

James, still smarting from being interrupted, showed a rare degree of interest, not to mention a dash of mischief, at the mention of the French ship.

'They are, I'm given to understand, being credited with the murder of Captain Howlett.'

The laugh died in the Admiral's throat. Hood treated him to an icy stare. 'How do you know about that?'

James held his ground as best he could. 'It's common gossip.'

'It's not even common gossip that Captain Howlett was murdered, James,' said the Admiral coldly. 'Neither the circumstances or the suspicions are in the public domain.'

'Circumstances?' asked Harry.

Hood looked at both brothers in turn, before answering Harry. 'You might as well have it from me, since James here has, no doubt, had it from my far too loquacious clerk.'

James blushed slightly, but made no reply, as Hood continued, giving a brief description of the victim and the few facts he had concerning his death.

'The story put about was the Captain Howlett was murdered for gain.'

'But that is not the case?' asked Harry, with a quick glance at his brother, who'd not bothered to tell him about this.

'No. He had his watch and chain still in his waistcoat, and a purse full of gold in his breeches when he was cut down.'

'Cut down?'

'From a makeshift gibbet. They used a warehouse hoist to hang him. He was neither robbed, nor, it seems, harmed in any other way. The only thing missing was his hat.'

Harry sat forward eagerly. 'Who are they?'

'According to the locals, they were cut-throats and robbers. When Howlett's premier, having identified the body, pointed out that his captain still had his valuables, they changed their tune.'

'To the French?'

Hood shook his head. 'No. They came up with some cock-and-bull tale of deserters from Howlett's ship taking revenge, which is damned nonsense since he was no flogger. Truth is, they're not too interested, and with no ambassador it's near impossible to change their minds.'

Harry had that look of naked curiosity in his eye that James recognized. 'This chargé d'affaires is one thing. But a French ship . . .'

'Suspect, don't you think, Harry. I have written to the Council of State, demanding a more thorough enquiry, but I don't hold out much hope.'

'Have you had a letter from the Genoese privateers too?' asked James, deliberately changing the subject to try and deflect his brother's obvious interest. Hood looked blank, for the conversation had moved on. James had to repeat himself to remind the older man. 'The Genoese privateers, complaining about the lack of opportunity for profit.'

Hood was almost dismissive, betraying a seeming lack of interest. 'I have not. They're doing well by all accounts. Perhaps they're a more enterprising bunch. They're inclined to longer voyages than the captains in Leghorn, I'm told.'

'Perhaps I should sail from there myself,' said Harry.

That concentrated the older man's mind, for his response to Harry's observation was much sharper. 'Then have a care if you do, Harry. The French are busy trying to smoke what we're about. I never thought that would extend to cold-blooded murder.'

A silence followed this, as though the Admiral was going over the murder in his mind's eye. Harry waited several seconds before breaking it.

'Are you so sure they're to blame?'

'Not positive,' replied Hood. 'But sure in my own mind. It was meant as a warning to the rest of the Fleet. Who else but the French would want to warn us? And then there's the small matter of impressin' the locals. They're a dubious crew, I can tell you. The balance could tip from backing us to backing the French in the space of an hour. The neutral Republic of Genoa is neither truly neutral nor truly a republic. It's run as a business venture by the leading families and they are always at each other's throats. Anything to make more money. As you said, Harry, some of them are bound to be in league with the French, Revolution or no. That French ship wouldn't be sitting in the harbour otherwise, with a glass trained on whichever ship we next send in.'

Hood raised his eyebrows, as though what he was about to say had just occurred to him. But James had the distinct impression that the Admiral had formed this particular idea somewhat earlier. 'If you do decide to tie up there, perhaps you could keep your eyes open on behalf of the Fleet, for it would be good to know what they are about.'

'Are you asking us to spy on them?' James could not disguise the distaste in his voice.

Hood frowned, fixing James with a stare that had made captains tremble. 'Offends you, does it, James Ludlow? Well, let me tell you that we are as blind men without that someone does it.'

'It is the Navy's business . . .'

'I'll speak plain to both of you,' said Hood, with a slightly foxy air that belied his words. 'I need to know what's goin' on ashore, not only in Toulon, but in Genoa as well. I don't intend to sit here, off the coast, and just parade up and down. I tell you no secret when I say that I intend to bring the French to an action. That means I've either got to lure them out, or go in after them. Which is it to be?'

He spread his arms and shrugged his shoulders, leaving his own question unanswered. 'But I do know this. I can't do a damn thing if my back is not secure. Even if I do find another anchorage, it will be an age before it's ready. Imagine if I commit myself to attacking the enemy, only to find that Genoa is no longer secure, and has even changed sides. I'd have to fall back on Gibraltar and leave the Mediterranean to the French. It might not mean much to you, but Tilly marchin' about as if he owns the place and that French ship sitting in the harbour, able to murder our officers without redress, worries me.'

'Couldn't you take matters into your own hands?' asked James.

'Don't tempt me. Nothing would give me more joy than to send a frigate into the harbour at Genoa with orders to blow it out of the water.'

'What is it?' asked Harry, betraying a trace of eagerness which pleased the Admiral.

'Ship-rigged sloop,' said Hood, smiling. 'Never do. Play right into the hands of those who are against us.'

'Naturally. Though it galls me, as much as you, to think of it sitting there unmolested,' said Harry.

A slight smile flicked across the edges of Hood's mouth but he suppressed it, fixing Harry with an enquiring look. Harry opened his mouth to respond but his brother cut across him, uncowed by the Admiral's look of impatience.

'I did not allude to any act of violence. I merely suggested that you should go to Genoa yourself. You certainly have the prestige to demand a proper explanation.'

Hood's voice was flat, emotionless, as he replied. And he addressed his words to Harry, not James. 'I doubt I could spare the time.'

'Of course,' Harry replied, before lapsing into silence.

'Have you forgotten what happened the last time you sought to do the Navy's work for them, Harry?'

Harry bristled slightly, not relishing being checked before Admiral Hood. But he'd picked up the prevailing train of the older man's thoughts. He knew as well as James that the old fox had partly engineered this bit of the conversation, just as he knew what was being proposed.

'Your remark begs the question, brother. Would I do the same again?'

'Well?' asked James.

Harry tried to make light of the situation. 'I cannot say for certain.'

'I can.' James Ludlow's voice held no trace of banter. 'You would not be able to resist it.'

Hood cut in. 'You showed a sharp mind saving your brother, Harry. If I could prove that the French were responsible, perhaps that would shift them and force the Genoese to make up their minds, once and for all.'

'He may have saved me, Admiral, but it was nip and tuck. We were both within a hair's breadth of the gallows.'

Hood was unimpressed. 'All I can say in response is that if you aid me then I'll feel obliged to do everything in my power to help you.'

Harry leant forward eagerly. 'Meaning that I'd get my exemptions?'

Hood nodded as James spoke again, sharply this time. 'Harry!'

Harry chose to laugh, taking the sting of implied criticism out of his brother's tone.

CHAPTER FOUR

The voyage, given a fair wind, would have been accomplished in a day. With the breeze dead foul it had taken three. Hood's orders suspending independent cruising had angered the officers aboard the *Swiftsure*. Most of the other ships in the Fleet had been given their chance before Hotham was superseded, had taken a prize or two and made some money. Not *Swiftsure*. Having to transport, at the express wish of the Admiral, two privateers who would later hunt at will added insult to injury.

It was therefore with some gratitude that they first saw the great sweep of the mountains behind the city. James sniffed the breeze which blew steadily off the land, seeking the odours of Liguria so eloquently described by Evelyn.

' "The particular joys of Italy in the natural perfumes of orange, citrone, and jasmine flowers," ' he intoned.

'How very poetic, brother,' said Harry, a telescope to his eye.

'Alas, not my words.' He reached into his pocket for his book, flicked it open and read from it. 'Evelyn was quite lyrical about the whole place, Harry. There's much here about fragrant orchards and sumptuous villas. Indeed he names it a coast full of princely refinements.'

'Then he must have come upon the place by land.'

'No,' said James, flicking to another page, with some difficulty, for the wind was strong. 'He's quite clear about arriving by sea.'

Harry dropped his telescope, turned to James, and smiled broadly. 'Then I think he's allowed himself a unusual degree of licence. I've never been in a harbour that smells like that in my life.'

James sighed, closing his book. 'It would be fair to observe that you lack a poetic soul, Harry, though I own you know more about seaports than me.'

Harry put the telescope back to his eye, ranging round the coastline from Mount Fasce, which towered over the southern side of the city, right round to Cape Mele, now well behind them on the port side. He was still smiling, though his voice had a less humorous tone.

'Just because I've yet to meet the flower that can overpower the odour of drying fish. And let me observe that if you approach this landfall after a heavy fall of rain, it has a quite singular smell which bears no relation to jasmine.'

The shout of 'all hands about ship' rang out yet again, for they were still beating up into a stiff breeze, and the men of the *Swiftsure* rushed to their allotted tasks that would bring the frigate round on to the opposite tack. They let fly the sheets, releasing the great yards, and hauled them round as the quartermaster put down the helm. The ship came round, ropes were hauled taut and made fast. The shouting died away as the sails fully took the wind and the Ludlow brothers crossed the foredeck, once it was clear of sailors, to resume their close observation of the approaching shore.

Both the city and the harbour were soon visible to the naked eye, with the Lanterna lighthouse jutting some three hundred feet into the air above the Capo di Faro. This mole pushed out from the shore forming the western tip of the harbour. To the south-east another, newer, mole, shaped like a bent elbow, stretched out from the rocky landscape. Ever since they'd made the decision to take this route Harry had spent time studying the maps and charts of the region. He now occupied a fair amount of time pointing out the fortifications that surrounded the town, especially the forts on the surrounding hills. James, with a less martial turn of mind, used Harry's glass to search for the many palaces, gardens, and villas mentioned by Evelyn.

Inside those stout city walls stood a jumble of houses pierced by numerous church spires, plus the odd square tower. The mass of shipping in the outer roadstead, and the harbour, testified to the wealth of the Genoese Republic. Genoa stood to profit greatly from the war. Once a rival to Venice, this great Mediterranean entrepôt had lost most of its former glory and all of its island possessions in the Levant, suffering, like the rest of the Italian peninsula, from the rise of the Ottoman Empire, and the rivalry between Habsburg Austria and Bourbon France.

Harry was alone by the weather shrouds as the frigate tacked for the last time, setting her bowsprit straight towards the harbour, heading for her anchorage. He craned his neck to look up at the great Laterna lighthouse, which would have been blessed by many a sailor seeking a landfall on a foul night. Then he turned to look at the port. His eyes automatically took in the ships anchored at their buoys. Fat merchantman in the main, with the odd warship, of an old and obsolete style.

Close in to the northern area of the port lay the sleek schooners, barques, and small xebecs of the men who roamed the inland sea for profit. Some of the ships could be the property of local captains. The Sardinians also used Genoa as a base. But English privateers sailing from here was an entirely new departure, and it revealed the fading importance of their usual haunt, Leghorn. Money would be the motive. It stood to reason that if you took a prize you must land it, and its cargo, somewhere. But Genoa had the highest tariffs of any port in the Mediterranean, which was normally a good reason for foreign privateers to give the place a wide berth.

Leghorn had always favoured the English in that respect, granting special privileges so as to concentrate the trade there, plus a flag to sail under, if required. Perhaps Genoa, seeing money going elsewhere, had decided to follow suit. For privateers spent well, masters and crews alike, and given normal luck they had the money to do so. The Mediterranean was a busy sea, and the French depended on a great deal of trade with North Africa and the Levant to sustain themselves. The pickings could be rich.

James came up the companionway on to the quarter-deck. Unsmiling, the officer of the watch raised his hat. The officers aboard the *Swiftsure* showed even greater reserve than those aboard the *Victory*. Yet you did not lightly condescend to a man who held two parliamentary seats in his control, even if he was a damned privateer. Besides that, word would have come across with the Admiral's barge that these two 'passengers' were much cosseted by Lord Hood. It would be a foolish man who sought to casually insult someone with such connections.

But while they were polite, they could not mask their innate dislike of the breed, nor the circumstances of their presence. The Admiral's clerk had not been discreet, and, apart from all that had gone before, it had soon become common knowledge on the flagship that Harry was intent on acquiring another ship to continue privateering. With the trip taking three days instead of one they were, of course, invited to dine in the ward-room. But it was a sad affair with little conversation, plus the very minimum of hospitality in terms of food and wine.

Harry had sold his stores in Gibraltar, so he was in no position to lighten the atmosphere with a generous contribution. James was of the opinion that such a state of affairs was fortuitous, since he could see no point in expending anything on this set of officers, since they clearly resented their presence. Dinner with the commander, Captain Barnes, again forced on all concerned by the uncommon length of time it took to make their landfall, had been even less of a pleasure, since he only held the command of the *Swiftsure* on a temporary basis, standing in for the regular captain who, as a Member of Parliament, had decided to stay in London to see the session out. Barnes had no money to spare for personal stores, and he entertained rarely. But good manners dictated that he expend some of the little he owned on these two. And it was plain that he also, perhaps more than his subordinates, had little regard for them.

James, hating hypocrisy, had, on both occasions, taken some advantage of this confusion, effusively praising the ship, its crew, and the abundant hospitality in such fulsome terms that those with any wit knew he was baiting them. He did so now, hailing the officer of the watch and engaging him in a genial conversation that was patently one-sided. Harry, more conscious of the sensibilities of naval officers, of the lack of funds which prompted their dislike of privateers, felt the need to intervene, and request that he desist.

'If you cannot think of another reason, James, cast your mind back to the way the last naval officer we encountered at sea blew us out of the water. If you continue in your present vein, then any one of these officers, meeting us at sea, will be tempted to emulate him.'

'I would be so pleased if one of them checked me. It is plain we are not loved, and I, for one, could not care less. Why can they not speak their mind? Faces like masks, and fixed smiles. This rigid politeness grates upon my nerves.'

'This is not some gentleman's club, James,' said Harry sharply. 'These men are justified in the care they take. As I've had occasion to point out to you before, exemplary manners are a necessity at sea, even if they are forever breached. And I find you wanting in manners yourself to take advantage of them so.'

James smiled slightly. 'Is that the rebuke of an elder brother?'

Harry was as aware as anyone that being ten years older gave him no power over James. They were in all respects equals, and, unusually for brothers, good friends.

'Rather that than that you should behave badly. You would scold me if I let you continue, and I'm damn sure you would openly rebuke me if I were at fault.'

The smile spread. 'That is very likely true.'

Pender, who'd come on deck with James and was now standing a little way behind them, spoke out of the corner of his mouth. 'Admiral's bargemen made out you was practically Sam Hood's own sons. Couldn't wait to pass their message through the gunports as we came alongside. I had that from the ward-room steward. And to cap it all there's a story goin' the rounds that the Admiral has stopped their prize-takin' capers to favour you.'

'No wonder they don't like us,' said Harry.

'That's not the worst of it. Every man jack aboard knows that your strongbox is full of captured gold. It's not just the officers that's mad at us, it's the hands as well.'

'Ah,' said James, tilting his head back and biting his lip. 'I shall be silent from now on.'

Harry adopted a mocking tone, knowing they could be overhead, and indicated the approaching shore. 'Too late, brother, your reputation with these people will always be that of a base creature.'

James timed his pause to perfection, allowing Harry's words to take effect, before replying, 'I shall bear my mortification easily, brother.'

Heads that had shown signs of a nod, stopped abruptly.

Commands were being yelled from the quarter-deck as the *Swiftsure* reduced sail. The breeze had been full of the scent of the land, though it bore little relation to Evelyn's elysian description. It consisted of a burnt smell of baked earth, mixed with the odours of wild rosemary and thyme, still with the tang of the sea. But it had changed abruptly as they entered the harbour to the unpleasant odours that one would find in any great seaport.

'There are some sleek craft here,' said Harry, calling his brother's attention to the ships he'd spotted earlier. James scanned the harbour, looking from one ship to another, without being able to identify the fast from the rest.

'See, over there.' Harry pointed his finger and James followed his gaze. Several boats were tied up close together. Even James recognized that they were of a more graceful shape than most of the other vessels. Harry reeled off their details. Schooners, two- and three-masted barques. Ketch-rigged sloops, chasse marées. James was soon hopelessly lost, not knowing to which ships Harry was referring. He turned, and was pleased to note that Pender looked equally perplexed.

'I wonder of any of them are for sale,' said Harry finally.

'I hope that is something that can wait till tomorrow, brother. I, for one, am looking forward to some of the comforts associated with being ashore, like a solid surface beneath my feet.'

'A lubber to the last, James.'

'And proud of it, brother.'

Harry suddenly flung his arm out, his action causing more than his brother to look in the direction he was pointing. They saw, emerging from behind a cluster of merchantmen, a sloop, with the tricolour flying stiffly from the sternpost. Awnings were rigged over the deck and poop, making it impossible to determine what was happening aboard. But Harry had no doubt they were under observation. The side of the *Swiftsure* was soon lined with officers and men, naked in their curiosity at the first real sight of their enemy.

'Better see to our things, Pender. I must ask Barnes for the use of a ship's boat.' He turned to James. 'Let us hope that your wit, or ship's gossip, does not leave us to seek out the services of a Genoese bum boat.'

Pender went off down the companionway.

'It's beautiful, Harry,' said James, waving his arm to take in the great arc of the mountain and the harbour within.

'I was going to bring Caroline to Italy,' he continued. The smile disappeared from Harry's face. 'She used to get so excited when I described it to her. The palaces, the colours, the temperament of the inhabitants.'

He turned towards his brother, his face stiff, masking the pain he felt. 'But it was not to be, Harry. Our stupid convention maintains that she must stay with her dull and drunken husband. Did you know he was nearly penniless when he wed her? Now he has control of her portion, he's spending her money in the same reckless way that he dissipated his own. She would have so enjoyed this.'

Harry didn't lack sympathy. But he did wonder how his brother would have explained to Lady Caroline Farrar some of the exploits he had undertaken in this selfsame Italy while on his Grand Tour. James had spent most of his time in Venice, simply the most dissolute city in Europe, gambling, drinking, and doing his very best to seduce as many women as he could in the time available. He had even smuggled himself into one of the Venetian music schools, set up to teach orphan girls to play a musical instrument. Supposedly places of virtue, they benefited from a Latin lack of hypocrisy, with tutors, most of whom had taken holy orders, living openly with some of the girls they taught. But being full of young women nominally under the care of the Church, they were extremely difficult places for an outsider to enter.

He put these uncharitable thoughts aside. 'That's the first time you've mentioned her openly since we left England.'

James sighed gently. 'Yes. Surely that marks an improvement. But I cannot say that it truly feels like it. Perhaps when he has run through another fortune he will be less careful of his matrimonial honour.'

'Best not to dwell on it, James.'

'Dwell on it!' James laughed. 'Not a minute of the day goes by that I do not think of her. Still, enough of this melancholy.' He pulled himself up, rubbing his face with his hands. 'It makes for poor company. It strikes me, Harry, that if we are going to hang about in these parts, we had best inform Arthur. You know what a fussy old woman he is.'

'Good idea,' said Harry. He did not continue, since he saw no point in getting into a discussion about their brother-in-law, Lord Drumdryan. James disliked Arthur, seeing him as a penniless usurper lording it in the family home. But then James had first encountered him as a young boy. He'd never quite got over the fact that his beloved sister, Anne, who had raised him after the death of their mother, had married in the first place. To have gone and married a man who saw it as part of his duty to interfere in James' upbringing had guaranteed a clash of personalities.

Harry, while keen to avoid him, had nothing but gratitude for Arthur's industry. He did all those things that Harry should have undertaken as his father's heir, not only leaving him free to pursue his own pleasures, but managing affairs in such a way that the family patrimony increased, in terms of both wealth and power. And having met him when fully grown, he had a chance to appreciate Arthur's mordant wit. Added to which, much as he loved his sister, he did not hold her in the same high esteem as his brother.

But James had the right of it. He must inform his sister's husband if they intended to stay any time. For Arthur, on the basis of Harry's last letter, sent from Gibraltar, would be expecting them home. Harry did not doubt that, left to cope, Anne's husband would continue to manage their affairs in the same exemplary fashion he had shown hitherto. Arthur would meet with the great on their behalf, and lacking wealth himself, would take great, and justified pleasure, in doing so.

'When you do write, you must take care to send him my warmest regards.' James's voice held the same tone of wicked irony that he had used to address the officers of the *Swiftsure*.

Was it those barbs and rumours coming home to roost, or really the requirements of the service? Barnes, who had come on deck to see the ship anchored, smiled coldly at Harry's request for transport. No boat would be available to take them ashore, every one seemingly pressed to help load supplies. Harry could do nothing but nod, and walk away.

Noisily the crew went through the drill. Soon the *Swiftsure* was anchored head and stern, rocking on the slight swell. As if to rub home the insult one or two of the ship's officers had gone off as soon as they were at single anchor, leaving their fellows to complete the task. The other ship's boats were put to work, but the suspicion of deliberate malice hung in the air.

They had to wait on deck surrounded by their luggage, strenuously containing their impatience, hoping for a wherry. But they were fully occupied. Even the victualling agent, a portly fellow who spoke thickly accented English, complained about the time it had taken him to get out to the ship. Women piled aboard, gabbling away in Italian, and throwing meaningful looks at those working on the deck, before going below. The watch on duty, fully occupied in the loading of stores, plied to with a will, waiting for the chance to get down to the sweating and heaving main-deck, and enjoy the pleasure they had been so long denied.

'I imagine it's getting crowded down there,' said James, as he watched several vendors and yet another boatload of women come aboard and disappear below.

'You should have a look,' said Harry. 'It will be quite a sight.'

'I wouldn't if'n I were you,' said Pender, who had come on deck looking slightly bemused. New to the Navy, he had never seen what it was like in a ship when the captain was lax about letting women aboard.

'I ain't seen nothing like it in my life,' he continued. 'They're putting more strain on the hull than a full gale. It's a wonder the barky don't sink.'

'Isn't that what happened to the *Royal George* in the year '80?' asked James.

'It's never been officially admitted as the cause,' said Harry.

The *Royal George*, a second-rate of ninety guns, had been at Spithead, fresh back from a cruise, and the hands just paid. The carpenter had informed the captain of a leak below the waterline and, with the ship sitting in a dead calm water, he asked for that it be heaved over so that he could come at it. This had been achieved by the shifting of stores and guns to produce a list to starboard. Then someone had spotted some shoals of mackerel in a frenzy, no doubt being preyed upon by bigger fish and trying to escape. The smooth surface of the water to starboard had erupted, with a hundred square yards of leaping fish. All the visitors aboard, men as well as women, unused to such a sight, had rushed to the side to look through the open gunports, already close to the waterline. No exact toll had ever been established, but as well as the crew of seven hundred men, it had been reckoned that when she capsized she had somewhere in the region of seven hundred women on board, proper wives some of them, but mostly the local women that had themselves rowed out to every newly arrived ship. The *Royal George* went down like a stone. Some two hundred souls were plucked from the water, including the carpenter and his mates.

'Does the Admiralty ever admit that it or its officers can be at fault?' asked James.

Harry smiled. 'The Admiralty, never. The officers? Rarely. And they hang or shoot them when they do.'

James thumped the bulwark impatiently. 'How long before we get a boat?'

'We'll have to wait till the watch on duty have had their fun before any of them become available. And then they will only take us ashore if Barnes tells them to. After what Pender says, I doubt they'll volunteer.'

'Then I may as well go and see this phenomenon.'

James strode to the companionway and went down to the main-deck. The scene that greeted him was astounding. Traders had set up stalls between the guns, selling all manner of things, including trinkets which the hands were being encouraged to buy for the whores. Food and drink were freely available, and all the while, over guns and mess tables, in full view of their uninterested companions, some of whom were reaching over their recumbent mates to buy various articles, sailors and their consorts were engaged in every manner of sexual congress. The noise was like that of a city street, with men and women singing and laughing, the traders crying out to sell their wares, voices raised in praise and anger, and over it all the grunts and cries of ecstacy, real or imagined, from the copulating couples.

No stranger to the low life of London, where you could add to this picture people begging and dying, horses, dogs, and all manner of animals with their attendant filth, the scene still made a deep impression on him. Men were outrageously drunk, staggering around carrying flagons of the local spirit, spilling as much as they consumed. Not an officer to be seen anywhere, which surprised him, since this mob would be of precious little use when the time came to resume their duties.

Those officers still aboard were, of course, gratifying their own wants, be it with a bottle or a doxie, though in a more private setting.

He was tempted to get out his sketch pad and record this mayhem, thinking that should he ever be tempted to paint the last days of Sodom and Gomorrah then this before him, with a very slight change of costume, was the perfect setting. A sailor being sick by his boots finally turned him away, and took him back to the quarter-deck.

CHAPTER FIVE

Harry was talking to Captain Barnes, who seemed to have consumed a fair quantity of the local wine himself. The victualling agent stood impatiently to one side, sheaves of papers in his fat hands.

'You must wait, sir. For the business of the Navy takes precedence over that of a private citizen.'

As James approached he could tell that Harry was angry, just as the Captain's swaying frame left him in no doubt that the man was very drunk. Barnes should have provided them with a boat as a matter of common courtesy. It had nothing to do with relationships with admirals, their luck in the matter of captures, nor with their choice of profession. He knew that, even if his brother had chosen to play down the slight. It smacked of petty revenge, though he could not help a twinge of guilt for having deliberately made matters worse. And it seemed that Harry had put aside his pride in order to ask the man again. No wonder he was angry.

'It is an interesting interpretation of the duty of the Navy to fill the ship full of drink and women.'

Barnes stiffened at this rebuke. But his reply, intended to put Harry in his place, lost most of its force by being slurred. 'You're no longer a serving officer, sir, perhaps you have forgotten the responsibilities attendant on that.'

Barnes turned to include James in the conversation, giving him a drunken leer. 'Must let the hands have their fun, Mr Ludlow. Then they will go to work with a proper will.'

Harry smiled grimly. 'You do not fear that when the ladies depart, Captain, a fair number of your crew will go with them?'

Barnes did not see the fat victualling agent nod vigorously at these words.

'We will lose a few, for sure,' he replied, putting his hand on the bulwark to steady himself. 'But we'd lose those anyway. They'll find it mighty hard to make do ashore, here in a foreign port. Even if they do run, we'll have them back in a day or two.'

Harry glanced quite deliberately at the section of the port with its barques and schooners tied up to various buoys. Barnes did not follow his gaze, and Harry decided it was not his place to point out to a serving naval officer that with the presence of a number of English privateers in the harbour, not to mention a French warship, he had precious little chance of getting back any man who chose to desert.

'Barge putting off from the fort,' cried a midshipman.

Harry turned to look as Barnes, ignoring the pleas of the victualling agent, still vainly waving his papers, peered towards the main harbour. This was dominated by the round fort, bristling with cannon, at the base of the mole. An over-decorated barge, with a huge colourful pennant flapping at the stern, and smart, liveried sailors at the oars, was racing towards the *Swiftsure*. Someone important was paying them a call.

Harry looked back at the Captain, forcing himself to smile. 'It may well be quite late before we get ashore, Captain Barnes. I wonder if I can beg one indulgence that you will be happy to grant?'

Barnes stiffened in the way drunken people do, suddenly wary.

'You may not be aware that I'm carrying a certain amount of specie.'

Barnes' face stiffened, then showed the slightest flicker of distaste, as though the possession of money was somehow bad form.

Harry indicated the sea-chests and boxes piled in the middle of the deck, with Pender perched on top. 'Since we will be going ashore in a strange port, quite possibly in darkness, I wonder if you would be kind enough to let me leave my valuables, and our sea-chests, aboard the *Swiftsure*. I can send for them in the morning.'

The proper response would have been for Barnes to insist that, being delayed to such an extent, they should all spend another night aboard ship. But he merely nodded, acceding to Harry's request, without even acknowledging the hint that had been implicit in it, before turning away and heading for his cabin.

'Do remind me to curb my tongue,' said James, as Barnes walked back to his quarters. 'A little respect would have gone a long way.'

Harry laughed, causing the retreating captain to hesitate slightly. He then spoke loudly enough to be heard all over the deck 'Curb your tongue, brother. For what? And as to respect. There's precious little worthy of respect on this deck.'

'An interesting idea, Harry, yet not unique to you. I have often observed that people who give advice rarely follow it themselves.'

James made a dumb show of sudden realization. 'But if you're trying to get the Captain to sling us off the ship, I'd rather be a touch further inshore.'

'Pender,' snapped Harry, looking hard at the approaching barge. 'Get our dunnage off the deck. Ask the wardroom steward to let you stow it in the lieutenant's storeroom. A chain round the casket again, with the lock secured to an eyebolt.'

Pender nodded, rushing to obey as the whistles blew and a guard was mounted to welcome the visitor in the gaudy barge. Several officers and midshipmen, in a worse state than their captain, lined the deck to receive him, and the poor victualling agent, still ignored, was pushed aside to stand, with the Ludlows, out of the way. Harry looked down at the barge as it glided alongside, noting that the crew's livery, as well as the gilding on the boat itself, appeared a good deal less gorgeous close to. Yet it was clearly the conveyance of someone important, for he had an escort of soldiers as well. Harry glanced at the marines lined up on the quarter-deck. They, at least, were sober and properly turned out, their white belts stark against the bright red of their uniform coats.

The object of all this fuss was sitting in a velvet-covered armchair at the rear of the barge, immaculately attired in a coat of dark blue silk, his face hidden by a large tricorn hat fringed with short white feathers. A junior officer leapt aboard to apprise them of their visitor's rank, and Barnes was sent for immediately. The Captain came on deck still hauling on his full-dress uniform coat.

'Who have we here?' said James, looking over the side.

'A senior officer, I imagine,' replied Harry, looking at the flag at the rear of the barge. It bore the red crossed shield of the Genoese

Republic, and the right to fly that on any boat implied the presence of an admiral at least.

Sure that all due ceremony was being observed, the junior officer indicated that the important visitor should come aboard. The man left his chair and climbed the ladder on the ship's side with practised ease. Pipes blew, and as he swept off his hat, in a salute to the quarter-deck, Harry was at last able to see his face.

Middle aged and dark skinned, even for an Italian, with jet-black hair tied with a red silk *queue*. He had a full face, and the skin, severely cratered, bore the unmistakable signs of smallpox, the marks even more pronounced on his prominent nose. Barnes raised his hat to return the salute, and welcomed his guest aboard. The visitor spotted the victualling agent, and called him over. They exchanged a few rapid sentences in Italian. Harry thought he saw the visitor's head turn in their direction. Barnes spoke sharply to the victualling agent, who had pulled a sheaf of papers from his pocket, before taking his newly arrived guest off to his cabin. The victualling agent walked towards them, papers in hand, looking somewhat crestfallen.

'Custom demands that he offer his visitor some refreshments,' said Harry. He was wondering what prompted him to apologize for Barnes, especially to his brother.

'Then he'd better confine his offer to his guest,' said James. 'Or the conversation will be one-sided.'

Harry abruptly introduced himself to the victualling agent, now standing quite close. The man was slightly thrown, his mind on other things as Harry continued. 'And this is my brother, James.'

'Santorino Brown.' The plain English surname made the first name seem outlandish. He was used to a surprised reaction to the coupling of these names, since the brothers barely had time to react before the man had added that his father was English, his mother Genoese.

'It must be a fine occupation, victualling agent to the British Fleet,' said Harry, in a hearty tone perfectly suited to addressing a total stranger.

'This ship my first, Signor.' Something in the genial look of the Ludlow brothers' faces must have made him aware that they were different. Or perhaps he had understood the lack of regard for Barnes, for he'd observed Harry's last conversation with the Captain. Whatever, he wanted to confide in someone. He spoke softly leaning

47

forward to avoid being overhead. 'Are British officers all so difficult?'

'Captain Barnes has abused you most shamefully. Signor Brown. Yet I do sincerely assure you that he is the exception.'

James graced Harry with a rather jaundiced look at that remark, but he said nothing to contradict him.

'Your first ship, Signor Brown?' said Harry. 'Have you not had the responsibility for others?'

The word responsibility threw the poor man completely. James, more patient than his brother, explained.

Brown responded with a very Latin gesture, throwing up his hands. The words tumbled out, something of a mixture, with the odd French word thrown in. Too many words, delivered too quickly, for either Harry or James to interrupt his tale and tell him they already knew.

The previous agent, a natural-born Englishman, had absconded, and not only had he disappeared but the funds entrusted to him for the purchase of stores had gone too. And here he was on a British ship for the first time, faced with a captain who was not only drunk, but seemed incapable of informing him of what it was he required in the way of stores.

Once afforded the opportunity to speak, he did not stop there. He had cattle waiting to be slaughtered and salted. A water hoy ready to come out and fill the *Swiftsure*'s casks so they need not be shifted out of the hold. Bakers ready to bake biscuit, a warehouse full of wine and fresh vegetables, and a dockyard ready to provide spars, cordage, and sails as required. How could he, a poor landsman, be expected to know if the ship needed such things? And all must be signed for, and checked aboard. Pender returned, and taking no part in the conversation, he stood aside, amused at the looks of polite enquiry the brothers were forced to display as they listened to this tirade.

Santorino Brown could not have spoken for less than five minutes, the whole thing accompanied by a multitude of increasingly violent gestures, before Harry finally ran out of patience and interrupted. 'Signor Brown, spare us, for this is none of our concern.'

Brown clasped his hands together, and his animate face suddenly collapsed. The apologies poured out in the same uninterrupted flow. Harry stepped forward, a look of deep concern on his face, grabbed the portly Italian by both shoulders, and shook him firmly. It was

48

obviously a language the man understood, for he fell silent, returning Harry's look with an agonized one of his own.

'My friend,' said Harry. This reassured the man even more. Pender couldn't help himself. His laugh rent the air, and he was treated to a look from Harry that would have felled a lesser man. Pender swallowed quickly, but it was not easy for him to contain himself, for beyond Harry he was looking straight into the face of James Ludlow, who was in worse straits than he, and he was only saved from a grave piece of insubordination by the fact that James was so incapable of holding back his laughter that he had to turn away and lean over the side of the frigate.

'Perhaps you can be of service to me,' said Harry, giving Pender another glare. 'Should I require stores, I shall most certainly come to you.'

Brown was not the man to let a sympathetic ear down. He threw open his arms. 'Signor.'

Harry was somewhat at a loss for what to say, since his intervention had been spontaneous, and in some way related to his own need for stores should he sail from Genoa. But it took little reflection for him to realize that he would open himself up to something worse than he had already endured, if he hinted that he needed supplies. Instead, he turned, and indicated the privateers' ships in the northern part of the port.

'I believe the gentlemen over there, my fellow countrymen, are doing good trade. Do you supply them as well?'

Brown looked confused, and Harry had to explain that he was alluding to the English privateers. No smiles accompanied growing comprehension. Instead his face took on a worried look, and he shook his head.

'It is business I not care to get.'

Harry was intrigued, despite his fear of another pleading litany from Brown. 'Why, Signor? I hear they are doing well, and all ships need stores.'

'They their stores obtain from contractors different, Signor. Me even approach them would mean . . .' He ran his hand, flat across his throat.

'Beside,' he continued, shrugging his shoulders, 'I know not where they get money from to buy.'

Harry probed further, and slowly, with many corrections, it emerged that the English privateers landed no cargo and sent in no captures for sale in Genoa. Yes they had money, so they were successful. But what they captured, when, and where they took it was a mystery.

'How can this be, Signor Brown? Your Republic is not known around the world for commercial generosity.'

'They pay, Signor. But not Republic.'

'Who?' asked James, curious in spite of himself. It was an obvious question, but patently an unwelcome one, for Santorino Brown shook his head violently, waved his papers as if to indicate a prior duty, and moved away.

Harry watched his back as he retreated, clearly intrigued by what he'd heard. James gave the side of the ship another impatient thump, before pulling his book from his pocket. He flicked from page to page, looking up every so often, as if to relate some landmark to what he'd seen on the page. Harry trained his telescope on the French sloop. A tall angular man, dressed entirely in black with a tricolour sash around his waist appeared from under the shade of the awning. He seemed to be staring straight at the telescope in Harry's hand, as if seeking to etch his face in the mind of the man watching him. The lips were thin and colourless, the skin grey, and the eyes hooded. The face was not so much lifeless as souless. The image of Captain Howlett, swinging on a rope, came into Harry's mind, and he wondered if he was looking the man who had instigated it.

He had every intention of getting his exemptions from Hood. But, in truth, he was at something of a loss to know how to go about it. Questions abounded, yet who to ask them of remained a mystery. Enquiries about Genoa and the patterns of power and authority tended to get more byzantine the further you looked. And what was the point of asking if you could not be sure that the reply was genuine? Few in these parts openly declared any of their allegiancies, for to do so casually could see your throat cut. All would be secret, with no man prepared to divulge too much, either about his business dealings or his party.

He didn't even know if the Admiral had the right of it. And if someone with Hood's pre-eminence couldn't get an honest answer out of the locals, what chance did he stand? Harry looked at his brother and smiled to himself. James hadn't mentioned the matter since their talk with Hood. He had a point, of course, when he said it was none of their business. But Harry was curious. Worse than that, he was also anxious to reclaim his exemptions. James knew well that this represented a dangerous mix, and his deliberate silence on the subject was an attempt to defuse it.

Harry swung his glass back to the northern part of the harbour. He was not precisely sure which of the ships were English and which belonged to local captains. They flew no national flags. The victualling agents' words echoed again in his mind. They brought nothing into Genoa, ships or goods. Then he smiled fully, earning a enquiring look from his brother, who'd put his book aside when he'd observed the object of Harry's attention. They must have someone in their pocket. Someone powerful. So powerful that they could evade the local excise duties. If anyone knew what was going on in this part of the world, these English privateers would. Their survival would depend on it.

'You have observed something that pleases you, Harry?' asked James.

Harry debated whether to share his ideas with his brother. But he decided against it. For one, it was a thought half formed. Besides, James would only seek to dissuade him. 'You know me, brother, I'm always content to be looking at ships.'

Harry and James were still in the same place, half a glass later, when Barnes reappeared with the Genoese admiral. The obligatory tour of the ship would now take place. The only non-naval personnel on deck, and obviously gentlemen by their dress, Barnes could not avoid an introduction, which he carried out in heavily accented French.

'Admiral Stefano Doria, allow me to present the Ludlow brothers, Harold and James.'

Doria gave a slight bow, but his dark brown eyes never left their faces. 'Welcome to the Republic of Genoa, gentlemen. Your first visit?'

'It is, but my brother has been to Italy before.'

'By land,' added James.

Was it that response which prompted the next question, for the eyes narrowed slightly. 'Might I enquire if your visit is for the purposes of pleasure or business?'

'Pleasure certainly. But possibly business as well,' replied Harry.

He would have preferred not to say, but the presence of Barnes made any other reply impossible.

'You bear a famous name, Admiral Doria,' he said quickly. Barnes had looked set to say something and he wanted to change the subject. Barnes either by accident or from malice, spoke anyway.

'These are the two I was telling you about, Admiral. They intend to purchase a ship, and no doubt join that nest of privateers that plague your fine harbour.'

If Barnes had hoped to see his tone of disapproval mirrored in a fellow sailor's face, he was disappointed. Doria smiled, showing even white teeth, which contrasted strongly with his dark-skinned face.

'Then I hope I may be of assistance to you, gentlemen. Please feel free to call upon me for advice.'

'You are most kind, sir,' said James.

'We live by trade, Signor Ludlow. That is why you will be made welcome. You may call upon me at the Customs House.' He indicated the round fort that the barge had come from.

'Thank you,' said Harry. Doria nodded and walked off with Barnes.

'A prescient fellow,' said James.

'I wonder. I think he asked Satorino Brown about us when he first came aboard. And who knows what Barnes has said.'

As they were rowed away from the ship, they could see that things had slackened very little on the lower deck. The ports were open, and through them, quite clearly visible in the well-lit interior, the hands continued with their pleasures, though more sparingly since most of them had long since run out of money or the ability to remain upright.

Doria's barge was way ahead of them, well lit as it raced back towards the fort. All around them boats full of laughing women were being rowed along in the most lubberly way, with much screeching and derisive laughter at what Harry surmised were the physical shortcomings of the *Swiftsure*'s crew. He could also hear, quite clearly over the still water, the clink of coinage, fruits of the day's labours.

Their boat, rowed by two silent and swarthy Genoese boatmen, swiftly left these doxies and their craft behind, leaving the ring of light created by their lanterns. They seemed to be heading for a darkened part of the harbour between the fort and the dockyard, a part occupied by fishing boats, rather than the bustling well-lit quayside to the north. Harry spoke to one of them, pointing where he wanted to go. First the man tilted his head, as though deaf. Harry repeated his injunction and the man shrugged, rowing all the time and carrying them closer inshore. Harry tried in French with the same result, pointing energetically. James intervened with a few words of Italian, badly spoken, but seemingly enough to convince the man of his proficiency in the language. He was thus treated, for his pains, to a uninterruptable barrage of the local dialect, which seemed to be neither truly Italian or French, accompanied by many gestures from the oarsman's shoulders. This sufficed to bring them right through the bobbing boats and they were delivered alongside the quay, which was in pitch darkness, still protesting. Pender had used a lantern to load the boat, and was fortunate to have it still. He lit the way up the steps as the two boatmen unloaded the single sea-chest they had brought with them. Harry had already paid the men, and once he was ashore they immediately dropped their oars and, with powerful strokes, headed out into the harbour looking for more custom.

'Follow me,' said Harry, taking the lantern out of Pender's hand and setting off along the dark quayside towards the better-lit area in the centre of the port. The only sound was their footsteps echoing on the cobbles, and it was only by pure luck that Harry was looking in the right direction when the first of their assailants rushed into the arc of light cast by the upheld lantern.

CHAPTER SIX

Harry swung the lantern as a pure reflex, catching the leading attacker a sharp crack around the head, and plunging them all into darkness at the same time. He yelled to the others, and as the light went out he saw that Pender'd had the sense to drop to his knees. James, shocked and unprepared, stood open-mouthed, his hand fumbling for his sword. Harry lunged toward him, careering into another assailant intent on skewering his brother. His sword was out, and he threw it in front of James's silhouette, faintly outlined in the moonlight, to protect him against any other thrusts. He heard a grunt behind him, and the curse that came from Pender told him that he had successfully dealt with his first adversary.

Shadowy figures milled around the trio, now standing together with weapons in their hands, facing what they hoped was the whole number of their enemies. Even in the faint moonlight, there was no making out their features. Harry realized that their faces were blackened, that they were numerous, and that they were silent. A very professional bunch of cut-throats. And that silence meant that they were intent on murder as a prelude to robbery. No offer was made for them to hand over their valuables as a way of avoiding a worse fate. The best escape would have been to jump into the water, but Pender lacked the ability to swim.

'Come on you no-good bastards,' yelled Pender at the top of his voice. 'Shout, your honour. If we don't attract someone's attention we'll never get out of this.'

Harry started yelling, shouting *Swiftsure*, which would attract men from the frigate. It was just possible that Barnes had posted some guards ashore to catch deserters. Both his shouts and Pender's were met with total silence. Several of the shadowy figures lunged forward, and in unison the brothers and their servant swiped at their heads causing them to hesitate. Harry knew that such a defence could not be sustained for long. They must attack. He rushed forward, calling for the others to assist, and had the satisfaction of feeling his short naval hanger make contact with something. Pender was not so lucky, tripping on the cobbles in the dark, and going down heavily.

Harry stood over him, sword up, as their attackers backed off again. No shout or cry had accompanied the wound he'd inflicted, which made him doubt his success. He yelled again, encouraging James to do likewise. Pender had picked himself up from the ground and he joined in. Without warning, or a word of command, their attackers came on, seeking to involve them in a general mêlée in which they could separate the trio and deal with them one by one. Harry grabbed Pender, preparing to drag him to the edge of the quay. If he kept hold of the man when he jumped perhaps he could save him from drowning. For if they stayed on this quayside, outnumbered, they were most certainly going to die.

He stopped moving, but carried on shouting, as he saw a glimmer of light in one of the narrow alleys that ran from the quayside up into the town. The light grew brighter, and he increased the sound, bellowing his lungs out as he lunged and parried at the footpads who were trying to club him to the ground. He heard a gasp of pain by his side and Pender went down again. Suddenly a whole group of men holding lights came on to the quayside. They hesitated for a moment, taking in the scene before them, then they rushed forward to assist. Their still silent attackers turned to meet them. Harry saw that they were indeed blackened up, and that both their clothes, as well as the scarves wound round their head, were black. It was little wonder one could barely see them in the pale moonlight.

Equally extraordinary was the professional way, without a word of command being spoken, in which they melted away from this group of rescuers. They seemed to just disappear out of the area of light, and individually and in pairs they shot up the numerous alleys. In a few seconds, Harry, James, and Pender were left looking into the faces of their rescuers. Not one of their assailants could be seen, not even those that must have been hurt in the assault.

'Allow me to thank you, gentlemen,' said Harry in French, hoping that these local people might understand that better than his appalling Italian.

'Ain't you English?' asked the man at the front, a thick-set individual, seemingly the leader of the group.

'Indeed we are,' said Harry surprised.

'Thank Christ for that then,' said the man. 'Wouldn't want to go a-rescuing no Jean Crapaud.'

James spoke up, a mite breathlessly. 'Pray, sir, whom do we have to thank for our deliverance?'

'More light there,' the man commanded, and all those behind him edged forward lifting their lanterns. Some of the party, seeing the Ludlows in the increased light, hastened to try and hide behind their fellows. Harry thought he recognized one of them as a member of the *Swiftsure*'s crew. No doubt there were others, but his attention was elsewhere. Pender, now standing again and swaying unsteadily, had a nasty cut above his eye. Blood ran down his cheek dripping on to his white shirt.

The man addressing them was a squat, barrel-chested fellow with a round flat face made more so by the nose which seemed crushed against it. Obviously not a man to take the sun, his countenance was bright red, set off by purple broken-veined cheeks. He was dressed, like Harry, in a good quality blue coat with gold edgings, and a tricorn hat. In his hand he held a long club. Behind him a sea of half-lit faces, most hiding, but one or two leaning forward eagerly to see what they had come upon.

'William Broadbridge, master of the *Dido*, at your service.' He gave a slight bow. 'By your tone, and your attire, I seem to be addressin' someone of quality.'

'Harry Ludlow, Captain Broadbridge. My brother James Ludlow, and my servant.'

This caused increased scuffling at the back of the Broadbridge group. Harry ignored them and turned back to see if Pender was all right. As soon as the light fell on his servant's face, a voice came out of the crowd. 'By Christ, Pender, what the devil are you doing in these parts?'

'Who's that?' snapped Pender, gently pushing Harry aside and peering at the sea of shaded faces. One man pushed further forward.

'Don't say you don't know me, Pious. Carey Sutton.'

'Bugger me,' said Pender. 'I thought you was in Botany Bay.'

'I was on my way, Pious, old lad. But then one of His Majesty's ships in Gibraltar was a bit light on hands, and we was given the chance to volunteer.'

'Be quiet, Carey Sutton,' snapped Broadbridge. 'No wonder you was had up, with your babbling tongue.'

'They're off the *Swiftsure*,' said a voice from the back, causing Broadbridge to start with alarm.

Harry spoke quickly, taking Pender's arm as the man swayed again. 'You have nothing to fear from me, or my brother, Captain. We are not in the Navy. And what you are about is none of our concern. Let me thank you again for your timely arrival. I fear we would have been hard put to survive if you hadn't happened by.'

'I dare say,' said Broadbridge, gruffly. His tone had become less friendly. It was obvious that he was suspicious of them. 'Who were those fellows?'

'I've no idea, Captain. I thought perhaps you would know.'

Broadbridge merely shrugged, but in reality he wasn't listening to Harry. One of the sailors behind him was busily whispering in his ear, and his eyes expanded at what he was hearing from that source.

'Cut-throats and robbers, of that I'm certain,' said James. 'And a professional crew the way they were got up in black. I fear they must have had an arrangement with the boatmen to bring their victims to this lonely spot.'

Broadbridge coughed noisily as Harry picked up the conversation.

'If I could further presume upon your kindness and ask for directions, indeed an escort to some inn, I would gladly stand a round of drink to convey our thanks. Not that they'll run to a decent tavern in these parts.'

'Why that's all you know, Mister Ludlow.' Broadbridge's face had a cunning look as he spoke. You could almost see his mind working. 'You come along with us, and we will show you to a place as good as any at home, and one that serves a tankard of ale as good as any brewed in England itself. And if you wish it, a place to rest your head for the night. Indeed you may take it, sir, that I insist.'

'Why that is extremely good of you, Captain,' said Harry. He hadn't missed the look in Broadbridge's eye as the sailor told him all about the Ludlows. At the very least they were being taken to a place where they could be kept under observation.

Again a slight bow. 'If you will follow me, gentlemen.' He peered at Pender, still being supported by Harry. 'And you, whatever your name is. I should get some'at round that wound, you're drippin' blood everywhere.'

James, standing on the other side of his brother, had not noticed the extent of Pender's cut. He whipped out a fine cambric handkerchief, folded it into a bandage, and wrapped it round the man's head. As soon as that was done, Broadbridge ordered a couple of his men to pick up their small overnight chest and they set off along the quayside, their rescuers in front and behind them. James, holding one of Pender's arms, leant forward and spoke softly to Harry.

'What were you on about back there, when you said they had nothing to fear?'

Harry responded quietly, speaking out of the corner of his mouth. 'I would say that Captain Broadbridge is short of hands. He was out trying to collect any deserters. There's more than a couple of *Swiftsure*'s in this party.'

'Would that have anything to do with us being dropped off in that deserted quay, your honour?' asked Pender.

'Very likely. If Broadbridge had any sense he would have bribed the boatmen to land anyone from the ship there. It's a perfect spot.'

James could not keep the surprise out of his voice. 'And our attackers. What of them?'

'I don't know. But if it's perfect for picking up deserters, then it's just as good for other things.'

'Like robbery?'

'More than that, James. They were too organized and numerous for casual robbers. Did you notice, not a word passed between them? They made no attempt to seize our baggage . . .'

Broadbridge, walking in front of them, had been in earnest conversation with some of the others in his party. Suddenly he dropped back to talk to Harry, interrupting his speculations. He ordered two of his men to take care of Pender, freeing Harry and James from the task.

'Might I be allowed to ask how you come to be in Genoa, Mr Ludlow?' he asked, and for the remainder of their journey, Harry obliged him, but omitting both the success that they had enjoyed and the fact that he was looking to buy a ship. James, walking alongside his brother, contributed nothing. But he did wonder whether his brother was being wise to leave out so many details.

After all, Broadbridge could hardly be unaware of what they had in mind, since it had been common gossip on the *Swiftsure*. It was also likely that he had been apprised of the amount of gold they were carrying. But nothing in his manner betrayed this, and he seemed quite well disposed towards them, cursing sympathetically under his breath about the 'bloody Navy' as Harry related their tale.

They left the darkened part of the port behind. The party was now walking along the brightly lit and bustling quayside to the north of the Customs Fort. They passed through the teeming arcade that ran under the sea wall and came back on to the quay, heading for a brightly lit section that seemed the busiest part of the port. Slender alleys ran between the tall narrow houses, all seemingly some kind of drinking or eating place. Given the warmth of the climate much of both activities took place outdoors. As a busy commercial harbour there would be plenty of loose coin around in the pockets of sailors and merchants. With the added business which war had brought, the place had the air of easy money.

Street urchins were accosting the men and noisily trying to sell their sisters. Others, darting round behind the men, were intent on relieving the prospective client of the means to pay. Whores of all shapes, sizes, and ages paraded up and down the quayside, mingling with the traders carrying baskets full of fruits and sweetmeats. A carriage clattered along the cobbles, scattering the men and women plying their wares, and obliging Broadbridge and his party to stand close to the water's edge. Harry and James caught a glimpse of several wealthy men in the carriage, and though he couldn't be sure, Harry thought he saw the uniform of a British naval officer.

The sound of steady marching feet behind them made them all turn and they, like the rest of the crowd, immediately cleared a space for the oncoming file of blue-coated marines. Each man had a musket slung over his shoulder and a tricolour cockade in his black hat. The man Harry had seen on the French sloop was in the centre of the party, easily visible from his superior height. He walked past looking neither left nor right and his carriage added to the air of superiority that hung naturally upon him.

Broadbridge cursed under his breath, then headed straight for the noisiest doorway on the quay. Drunks milled around outside and they could hear the sound of several fiddles being played inside, to the accompaniment of much singing, shouting, and banging of tables. The surprise was that English was the dominant tongue. Harry looked above his head at the swinging sign. The limner who'd painted it had essayed a portrait of a round-faced man, bewigged and with goggle-eyes. Underneath that he'd painted the name. The place was called the Royal George.

'Here we are, Mr Ludlow. A little bit of England stuck right here in the middle of all these Eyetalians. I venture to suggest that we go in by the side door, since the tavern is packed to the gunnels, and I reckon you want to see where you're to berth before thinkin' of enjoyin' yourself.'

Broadbridge led them up a narrow alley by the side of the building, as Harry, taking Pender's arm, called after him: 'I must see to my servant's wound.'

'Never fear, Mr Ludlow. I have a surgeon here, and if he be upright enough, he'll attend the wound.' Broadbridge stopped by a dimly lit door and turned to address the others. 'Carey, round the back, lively now, we don't know who's about.'

Sutton went off with Pender and the rest of the men, going past the side entrance and into the darkness beyond. Broadbridge led Harry and James through the door into a side parlour. The noise of the tavern pounded through another door at the rear of the room. An enormously fat woman sat at the table in the middle of the parlour. She had a bright red face, with blotched skin that looked as if it was swollen. The eyes were narrow slits, in between the jutting forehead and the huge cheeks. Despite the warmth of the night, and a fire burning in the grate, she was covered in a quantity of multi-coloured shawls. From the little Harry could see, there was no welcome in the eyes.

'Ma Thomas. We have here two gents looking for a berth, short-term like,' said Broadbridge, leaning over and talking to her in a friendly voice. The round face, which was already possessed of a permanent scowl, looked even angrier. The woman opened her mouth to speak, exposing toothless red gums. Broadbridge dropped his friendly manner as he cut her off.

'Now don't you start gettin' on your high horse and sayin' there's nowt, 'cause I knows there is. So you just be a-shiftin' your whores and bum-boys out of some of them rooms, and get it ready in double-quick time for Mr Ludlow and his brother, who I might say, are to be my guests.'

'Like fuck I will!' she spat in a lisping voice. 'How am I going to raise a crust if'n I don't get the use of them rooms? Fuckin' captains, you're robbin' bastards the lot of you. Left to you I'd be without a pot to piss in, nor a window to sling it out of.'

She stuck her huge fleshy forearms on the table and heaved herself to her feet.

'Guests!' she spat, then throwing her head back she opened her mouth and laughed, though it emerged as a cackling sound. 'Who the fuck do you think you be, William Broadbridge, comin' in here, all high and mighty, when you've yet to show your mettle? Not that I ain't shocked to see you upright, you drunken arse. You come and talk to me when you've a prize or two under your belt . . .'

'I am a shareholder here,' shouted Broadbridge. 'And I will not be addressed so by you!'

'Would it assist if we offered to pay, Mrs Thomas?' said James gently. Her eyes opened a fraction at being so addressed, since no one had called her Mrs Thomas for an age. James smiled graciously, and added a courteous little bow. She looked him up and down, her face showing just a trace of appreciation for such a handsome fellow.

'I fear we must throw ourselves on your good offices, since we have nowhere else to go, and we have just been involved in a most fearsome fracas. Because of that we have a wounded servant to attend to.' James then reached into the inside of his coat. 'It wouldn't be just if our sudden arrival put you out of pocket.'

Broadbridge opened his mouth to protest but James, still speaking gently, still smiling sweetly, continued without pause. 'I'm sure that a woman of your parts will take pity on a weary traveller.'

'Now there you be,' she lisped, responding to James' polite tone with the smallest of curtsies. 'If'n you was to go askin' polite like this gent here, instead of barging in and yellin' like the fuckin' swab you are, you might get some change out of old Ma Thomas.'

The noise from the tavern, which had been growing louder, reached a crescendo of shouting and whistling.

'You'll forgive me, sir,' she said to James, in a different, more refined voice, almost coquettish, 'but I must attend the paying out of the wagers, or else some poor bastard might get a knife in the ribs.'

She spun round and went through the door, moving with surprising grace for a person of her bulk. The noise rose and fell as the door opened and shut, though Harry glimpsed the crowded room, the rafters full of smoke.

'How I envy the way you have with the ladies, James,' said Harry, smiling. 'Why, you positively made her simper.'

'Damned woman,' snapped Broadbridge. 'Allow me to apologize for such an unseemly welcome. You will not pay, sir, and I insist upon it. If I say that you're my guest, then that is what you shall be, or my name isn't William Broadbridge.'

He made a dismissive gesture towards the door to the taproom. 'Pay no heed to her. She behaves as if she owns the place, yet she's only employed to run it for us, making what she can from our absence.' He jerked his head towards the closed door. 'And the gambling.'

'Us?' asked James.

There was a pause while Broadbridge debated with himself whether to answer the question. For the first time Harry got a good look at him. Pale blue eyes underneath thick sandy-coloured eyebrows only served to exaggerate his high colouring. In the full interior light the broken-veined patches on his cheeks stood out, even from the bright red of his face, as did the state of his nose, which was not flat as result of nature. Finally he spoke, but quietly, as though imparting a confidence.

'The privateer captains. Half a dozen, all told. We all have a share in the place, which when times are good not only gives us a decent berth, but returns a tidy profit.'

'The crews entertain themselves here after a cruise?' said Harry.

'They do, and that be what they are doing right now, having just come in two days ago.' Broadbridge smiled, looking at the brother intently, waiting for one of them to articulate the conclusion. It was James who obliged.

'So having paid them out anything they have coming in the way of profit, you then encourage them to spend it a place in which you have a share.'

'That be the way of it,' the older man replied. 'I have yet to see a decent return myself, since I'm new out here. I've had one cruise. Not trying to catch anything mind, more in the nature of workin' up the crew, so to speak.'

Harry said nothing, which must have worried Broadbridge for he continued breezily. 'Not that I would have turned anything away, mind. But it was not blessed with any success.'

'Was that because you're short of hands?' asked Harry.

Broadbridge shot him an angry look.

'Please, sir,' said Harry quickly. 'I do not mean to alarm you. But I have told you that I am a sailor, and in the same line of business as yourself. I would be making myself look very foolish if I didn't smoke what you were about tonight.'

'Who can ever have enough hands, sir? But let us say that I am burdened with other concerns right now.'

James looked towards the noisy room. 'There seems to be plenty of men available in there.'

Broadbridge bristled slightly, and by doing so betrayed the extent of his knowledge. 'Enough to man the squadron. Yet all the men are spoken for, and on the books of one of the other captains . . .'

The older man stopped suddenly, aware that he was giving the game away, telling Harry and James that he knew why they were here. He was saved from further embarrassment as the door opened and Ma Thomas came waddling back in.

'Now, gents,' she said, addressing James direct, after throwing a withering glance at her blustering shareholder. 'Since you, no doubt bein' of a more sober disposition than some drunken swabs, know how to go about addressin' a lady proper, I've a mind to accord your wish.' She flicked her thick stubby thumb towards the angry Broadbridge. 'Despite what this'n says I must and must not do. So if'n you will take a seat by this here table, I'll see which one of the rooms is free.'

'And free it better be, for I will not countenance them payin',' growled Broadbridge.

Ma Thomas put her hands on her hips and graced Broadbridge with a stony glare. 'Then they can bed down on the quayside, for all I care.'

'Do as I say!' shouted Broadbridge.

She ignored him, her eyes lighting on James, quite deliberately looking him up and down. Again that almost coquettish voice.

'Mind, there's more'n one way of paying, young sir. You can either dip your hand in your purse—' She rubbed her hands across the lower part of her huge belly. 'Unless you've a mind to dip your parts in here as payment in kind.'

James blushed to the roots of his hair. Harry had to turn away to hide the smile. Ma Thomas made no pretence at her humour, she threw back her head and laughed heartily, her gums exposed, and her entire body shaking and heaving as she waddled out of the room. But she could not leave without a parting shot at Broadbridge.

'If you're so worked up to give them a fuckin' berth, William Broadbridge, you put them up.'

'God forbid, Harry,' said James, looking after her. 'It seems that whatever I do with my tongue these days, it gets me into hot water.'

CHAPTER SEVEN

Growling to cover his embarrassment, Broadbridge suggested they go and look at Pender. He took them back out into the dark alleyway and headed towards the back of the inn. The rear entrance looked to be part of a separate building, with an overhead passage forming a bridge which led to yet another building just beside it. A lantern shone brightly in the window in the middle of the bridgeway, casting a good light on to the door. Broadbridge knocked carefully, using some form of pre-arranged signal, and Harry thought he saw a head bob up in the overhead window.

After a long wait the door swung open, creaking noisily. Harry knew this to be another precaution, an alarm to alert those inside against an unexpected invasion. The door opened directly on to a huge high-ceilinged room. It was obviously a sort of warehouse, the walls were racked for storage, with large wine barrels, and various sized bales stacked around the walls. Yet the place had an empty air, which only reinforced what they'd heard. If the men in the tavern had just returned from a cruise the place should be full of the spoils of their voyage.

Off to one side lay a small office, its light casting deep shadows across the warehouse floor. Carey Sutton stood by a desk holding a lantern over Pender's upturned head. Presumably it was the surgeon bent over him, a wispy-looking fellow with straight fair hair flopping over his eyes. He looked up as they entered, and the lamplight showed a long, gaunt face, with pale blue red-rimmed eyes sunk deep into his head throwing his nose into sharp relief.

There was no sign of the rest of the party that had escorted them, but that was no surprise. They would be up to all the smugglers' tricks, these men. And they were in the land of experts, given Genoese excise tariffs. Smuggling, especially to the locals, was a way of life. Each one of these close-packed buildings would in some way be connected to the next one, providing a warren of escape routes for both men and contraband. Perhaps some of these large barrels were empty, or the bales concealed hidden exits.

Pender was still groggy from the blow. If anything his condition had worsened; his face was chalk white and he looked as though he was about to vomit, his throat working to hold back the bile. The surgeon, who'd returned to his labour without addressing them, was busy stitching the gash together, talking to himself under his breath as he did so.

'How is he, Matty?' asked Broadbridge.

'Don't call me Matty!' The surgeon spoke angrily, but he had such a weak voice that his protest carried no force.

Broadbridge leant over and looked enquiringly at Pender's wound, then turned to the man called Sutton. 'Gather the lads, Carey. Time to go out again. An' this time we'll put a watch on the main quay. I shouldn't wonder if some of those *Swiftsure* hands are coming ashore dressed as women.'

Was it Sutton's surprised reaction, or the bluff, false-sounding note in his captain's voice? Harry felt instinctively that whatever Broadbridge planned, further hunting for deserters was not included. Carey Sutton handed the lantern to Harry, who moved forward to stand over his recumbent servant, before going out to collect his men.

Broadbridge, satisfied that Pender was receiving proper care, stepped back a pace, addressing Harry. 'I'll leave Sutton behind, Mr Ludlow. He will direct you to my room, which you may use until you find another berth.'

Harry wondered if Sutton's instructions would include keeping an eye on them, but he checked himself mentally. This was no way to respond to such a generous offer.

'Please, Captain, I fear we have inconvenienced you more than enough.'

'One Englishman to another, sir,' said Broadbridge with a pompous note. 'I shall bed down aboard my ship.'

Ignoring their further protestations, Broadbridge left, the door creaking noisily as he closed it behind him.

'How is he, Doctor?' asked James.

The surgeon lifted his head and fixed his deep-set eyes on Harry for an age, before turning to answer James. 'How would I know? All I've been asked to do is stitch up the wound.'

'It would help to know if that is all that's amiss,' said Harry, impatiently.

The surgeon's head wobbled as he replied, and there was an attempt at levity in his voice. 'A consultation, sir. Is that what you want? A general assessment of this man's health? I really think you should look at my scale of fees before you ask for such a thing.'

Harry snapped at him angrily. 'If you want paying, sir, say so.'

The surgeon ignored him. Patiently, taking great care, he finished his stitching and cut the thread with a small pair of scissors. He stood back to examine the work, and spoke without looking at either of the brothers. 'Was a time you would have thought twice about saying that, sir. Was a time when it needed deep pockets to consult Matthew Fairbairn.'

'There was a time when Matthew Fairbairn didn't lose patients through a lack of care,' said James quietly. The surgeon lifted his head and looked closely at James, as if trying to place him.

Harry looked from one to the other as James continued, his voice cold. 'Be so good as to examine this man. Then charge what you like.'

'Do I know you?' asked Fairbairn, peering at him.

'We've never met. But I know you by reputation.'

'Reputation. Surely that is the wrong word, sir. Am I not notorious?'

'Notoriety carries a certain amount of glamour, Mr Fairbairn. Perhaps it would be better to say you are infamous.'

Fairbairn shuddered like a man feeling the cold, then bent over to look at Pender again, more to avoid James' steady look than to examine his patient.

'All surgeons lose patients, sir. If they're poor, no one turns a hair. Good riddance they'll say, more like, and how much will Surgeon's

Hall pay for the cadaver. But lose a wealthy man under the knife . . .'

Harry, looking closely at his servant, had grown increasingly anxious at Pender's pallid countenance. 'Are you positive he doesn't require further treatment? A blow to the head can be mortal . . .'

Fairbairn interrupted him. 'Rest. That's all he needs. And if you're worried about him being groggy, you should know that he's had near a pint of rum. Some men cannot face the prospect of a needle in their skin.'

'Pender!' Harry was surprised. He'd seen him puncture himself enough times as he ham-fistedly tried sewing and stitching.

'Is that his name? I suppose he's as brave as lion. Not afraid to face cannon-fire. There are a lot of men like that.' He emitted a small laugh, one that was as weak as his voice. 'I can understand their reluctance to face the knife. But a needle!'

Carey Sutton was hanging around at the side entrance as they came back in, carrying Pender between them. Ma Thomas, now caressing a huge ginger cat, glowered at them. Carey told them that their 'dunnage' was already stowed in Broadbridge's room. He led the way through a maze of corridors, a candle held aloft, as the brothers transported the softly singing Pender. The inn was like a warren, with stairs leading in all directions, and seemed larger than the outside structure would indicate.

It was a plain, untidy room, with a single cot in one corner, a rickety desk with a jug and washbasin, and a single chair. Broadbridge's sea-chest was in another corner, and by adding their own, plus the chair at one end, Sutton had contrived to make up a second bed. As soon as he'd shown them in, he mumbled something about being wanted, and left. Harry guessed that he wouldn't go far.

'One of us is in for an uncomfortable night,' said James gloomily.

'There's no question about who would feel it least,' said Harry, knowing James' attachment to comfort. James smiled, equally aware that Pender, in his present state, would sleep happily hanging over a rope. But they laid him on the cot anyway.

'Never fear, I shall take the floor, James.'

Harry waited for a slight indication of protest from his brother, for the sake of good manners if nothing else. He waited in vain. The noise of a creaking floorboard made him turn round. Ma Thomas stood in the doorway, the cat cradled in her arms. She tried to smile, but with her fat red face she looked like someone squinting in strong sunlight.

'Well, gents, it would never do for you to spend the night alone.' She then bent all of her formidable personality to the task of providing them with a couple of 'good' girls to warm their bed.

'Thank you, no,' said James, avoiding her eye, as well as another invitation, by turning to indicate the small room. 'As you can see, we are in rather cramped accommodation.'

She frowned at this, as though she thought James was baiting her. Then she looked at Pender, fast asleep on the cot. Such consideration for someone so obviously not of their class led her to an erroneous conclusion.

'You don't look the type for boys, but if'n that be what you want, just say the word.'

'I'm sure you could provide us will all sorts of services, madam,' snapped James, 'but we don't require them.'

Again she gave the sleeping Pender a knowing look. Then she tilted her head to the side, hands on hips, in a rather fey gesture. 'Got each other, have we?'

Harry smiled broadly, as James completely lost his temper. 'No, madam, we have not, as you so indelicately put it, got each other.'

'You're not shy are you, cause of bein' related?' she said, her eyes taking in the small room. Then inspiration seemed to strike.

'Ah,' said Ma, holding up a thick finger, refusing to admit defeat. 'Virgins, is it?' She looked at the floor, her huge fat face taking on an air of worry. 'Now that would be a mite difficult to produce right off, but if you was to order 'em now, why they'd be warming your bed before tomorrow twilight.'

James threw up his hands in exasperation, leaving Harry to decline. 'Perhaps we avail ourselves of your services some other time, madam. For now, we have other things to attend to.'

'Then you come and see Ma Thomas, whatever it is you be after.' She aimed another toothless grin at James. 'Be sure you do.'

'We most certainly shall,' said Harry.

She waddled her way down the narrow corridor leaving James still blushing. 'God. What an awful creature.'

'You can hardly claim that you have not been offered such services before,' said Harry, turning to check on Pender, now snoring gently.

'Not with such determination. And if I'm going to indulge myself, I would not choose to do so in a place such as this. Why, it must be riddled with the pox.'

Harry looked around the room. 'Odd set-up here. Did you hear Broadbridge? The privateer captains own the place, and she runs it.'

James lay down on the makeshift cot. 'An odd set-up indeed. They seem to own the doctor as well.'

'Who was that fellow?'

'Fairbairn. I'm surprised you've not heard of him. He was the talk of the town two years ago.'

'I've spent too much time at sea, brother,' said Harry with a trace of impatience. 'I tend to miss such things.'

'Had a practice in Bath, became quite sought after, in fact. Fairbairn had been out East, and returned with some interesting remedies for the kind of ailments afflicting those who were taking the waters. Herbal potions and the like, and a novel curative involving the use of long needles.'

James looked at the bed, rose himself, and leant over the snoring Pender, looking closely at the stitching around his wound. 'I doubt that our friend here would find such treatment attractive. I must say he does a neat stitch. By all accounts he was good. Brought the Duke of Portland back from death's door, apparently, after he'd had an attack of the bloody flux. Suddenly, he was all the rage. Then he lost a couple of well-connected patients. I doubt he would have been in quite such a stew if he hadn't upset his medical contemporaries in the process. But it was the physicians who hounded him out in the end. You know how physicians like to look down on surgeons, as though they're a lesser breed. Fairbairn sneered at convention and combined the two, which caused much comment, even amongst his surgeon colleagues. Both sets of medical men like to keep their disciplines separate. It doubles the available fees.'

Harry poured some cold water from a large jug into the bowl below the mirror, peering at his grubby countenance as he did so. 'It's a long way from Bath. Was he brought low by drink?'

'Did I not refer to opium? I believe he acquired the habit of eating it in China.'

70

James looked around the room as Harry washed his face, his words echoing their earlier impression.

'It's a rum set-up here. I wonder what the rest of the place is like. By the way, you didn't mention to Broadbridge that you were in the market for a ship.'

Harry didn't answer right away, concentrating on his toilet. He felt a tiny twinge of annoyance at having to explain himself again. Since they landed in Gibraltar, James, once ashore, seemed to feel that the imbalance of equality that existed aboard ship no longer applied. And he was, of course, right. It occurred to him that the bond of friendship between him and his brother had stayed strong precisely because of the limited amount of time they'd spent in each other's company. It had survived on board ship because James deferred to Harry in all things nautical. Then he silently cursed himself for his arrogance. The problem was created by his bad habits, not James'. His brother welcomed conversation in a way that Harry just wasn't familiar with. He dried his face furiously.

'I doubt if I had to. He would have had all he needed to know from the men who'd run from the *Swiftsure*. After what he let slip downstairs about the hands, I'd guess he's well aware of our plans. But I feel no need to go volunteering the information.'

James frowned, immediately smoking Harry's reasons for playing his cards close to his chest. 'Does the nature of this set-up attract you?'

Harry dried his face. 'I don't know. I've yet to see it all. I suppose it would be in order to go and have a look.'

'What a strange way to put it, brother.'

Harry threw the towel playfully at his brother's head before answering. James caught it and proceeded to fold it neatly.

'We are not guests here, James, though we are not exactly prisoners either.'

'Prisoners?'

'Broadbridge is unsure of us. For all he knows we could have thanked him for his help and walked straight off to tell Barnes where his crew had gone. He has put us up here to keep us in view, that is, until he finds out more. And the fact that we are accommodated in the good Captain Broadbridge's own room means, for all my caution, he probably knows more about us that either you or I would wish him to.'

'The strongbox?' asked James.

Harry nodded. 'Mind you, with the number of crew that have got ashore, not to mention the officers, I dare say the whole port knows what we're carrying.'

'Could that explain why we were attacked?'

'It might, brother. It just might. Yet if you add what Lord Hood told us about Captain Howlett, and the French here in numbers, not to mention that ship in the harbour, then the possible explanations do tend to multiply.'

'Did you hear any French spoken?'

'I didn't hear a word of any language spoken,' said Harry.

As if acknowledging that it was a unsolvable mystery, he changed the subject. 'Pender seems to have settled in.'

His servant's snores were growing louder, filling the room. 'I hope he's fit tomorrow. There are questions that require answers. Pender can ask in places barred to the likes of us.'

James frowned. 'Would it surprise you if I said that I don't very much like the sound of that?'

'It is possible to be too cautious, James.'

'If I ever catch you displaying caution, Harry, I shall hasten to tell you.' James looked closely at his brother in the dim light from the single lantern. 'You have a smug air, brother, as if you are up to something.'

'I wonder that you don't see it, James. That despite our misfortune in being attacked as soon as we came ashore, we have fetched up in exactly the right place.'

James treated the room to a meaningful look. 'Perhaps for you, Harry. The right place for me would be better appointed, not to mention more spacious.'

'Do you remember what it was that Admiral Hood suggested we might do?'

James spoke cautiously. 'All I remember is being wary.'

'It sounded like a difficult task at first. After all, we don't know anyone here in Genoa, we don't speak Italian, and given what I've heard you'd have to be brought up in the place to make any sense of the politics. But our old friend the Admiral missed something. And that something makes the finding out what he wants to know a whole lot easier, if not downright simple.'

'Why is it that your air of certainty bothers me so, Harry?'

'Come along, James. A man of your intelligence should be able to smoke it now.' Harry, realizing he'd spoken harshly, spread his arms to indicate that it had something to do with their surroundings.

'I must be too tired, Harry, for I cannot see what you're driving at.'

Harry spread his arms wider. 'This.'

'The room, or do you mean the inn?'

'The inn, and the people in it. Do you not see the privileges it implies? You can't go creating something like this, in a city state like Genoa, without being under the protection of some powerful locals. I've told you it's a shock even to find them sailing out of here. That warehouse at the back was empty, James, and they've only just come in from a cruise. Brown, the victualling agent, said they don't land their cargoes here, and what I've seen bears that out. That smacks of a high degree of influence. I doubt they have it themselves. It's more likely someone who stands to gain by their presence. Whoever that is can hardly be a friend to the French, since he seeks to profit from interfering with their trade.'

'How do you know he profits by it?'

Harry laughed. 'If we find there's another reason, I'll be very surprised.'

'So you intend to question the people here to find out who this protector is.'

'Perhaps. But knowing who it is may not be necessary. At least not necessary for us to achieve the result we desire.'

James's frown deepened. 'This is what I most feared. I detect a desire to bring to justice the murderers of Captain Howlett.'

Harry frowned, and when he spoke his voice carried a carping tone. 'Would that be so terrible?'

James exploded at the criticism implied in such a rebuke. 'That's unfair, Harry, and you will oblige me by withdrawing what you imply. Any man with an ounce of decency would like to see justice done. But I have already said that it's none of our concern.'

James's temper was up, and his face flushed as he continued. 'Can I fill in the spaces you're deliberately leaving blank, for I'm not stupid. You say the men here have a powerful protector. This person, if he exists, and for reasons as yet unclear, will furnish you with proof of French involvement in the murder of Captain Howlett. We will put aside the fact that he's not done so already, though confounding the French would appear to be self-interest. Such proof, by your hand, can then be presented to the Genoese Council of State.'

James paused, his face talking on a look of mock alarm, made theatrical by his continued anger. 'They will be exceedingly shocked by this. After all, Genoa is neutral. They will, at the very least, censure the French chargé d'affaires. At your urging they will then order his ship out of the harbour. The murderer might not face the gallows, but the enemy will have been displaced. This, in fulfilling the best part of Admiral Hood's wishes, will allow you to claim your reward. Exemptions will flow and we will sail off to a prosperous future.'

Harry smiled to take the sting out of his brother's temper. 'Lord, James. I thought you had put the whole thing out of your mind, and here I find you've been mulling on it all along. What a deep cove you are.'

James was not mollified. 'Do you know what it is to over-simplify?'

Harry laughed loudly enough to disturb the sleeping Pender, who grunted and turned on his side, momentarily stopping his snoring. Harry put his hand on his brother's shoulder.

'I know, James. It's more complicated than that. But we have finished up at the very place I wanted to. And that augurs well.'

'Will anything I say make a difference?'

'You cannot be unaware of how much I value your opinion.'

James Ludlow looked long and hard at his brother. He shook his head, half amused, and half in despair. Harry chose to latch on to the smile. 'That's better. Let's go and have a look around.'

CHAPTER EIGHT

They made their way back through the warren of passages, the sound of revelry guiding them. Ma Thomas was not at her table, and the side vestibule was deserted. Harry headed for the door she had used when they first arrived. Another great roar greeted them as he opened it. They found themselves in large open room which comprised the tavern. Everyone seemed crowded into a smaller area than necessary, facing away from Harry and James. Encouraging, individual shouts were frequent, and yells of a more general nature, mixed with groans and bad-tempered imprecations, greeted some event they could not see.

'Dogs?' asked James over the noise.

'Cocks, I think,' said Harry, looking at the rafters and judging from them the size of the room. 'Can't see that there's space for a dog-fighting pit.'

Harry jumped on to a table, followed by his brother, both gingerly avoiding the tankards thereon. They looked over the heads of the spectators, but still they could see nothing but the eager, sweating faces of those on the other side of the pit. Ma Thomas sat on another table at one end, her feet splayed out and her elbows on her knees, watching with a keen eye. In one of her fat red hands she held a gold hunter, which she glanced at occasionally, timing whatever was going on.

'Ma Thomas seems to be judging the contest,' shouted Harry.

James spluttered, choking at this height from the dense smoke emitted by dozens of pipes. 'Then there'll be no argument about the result.'

Suddenly, to the accompaniment of a great roar from the crowd, a grey furry object shot up above their heads. Its body seemed to be jerking spasmodically as it fell back down to earth.

'What was that?' asked James, rubbing his smarting eyes.

Harry stood on tiptoe, straining to see further. 'A rat, James. They're having a rat fight.'

'What! How can one rat throw another that high in the air?'

'It's not rats versus rats, brother. It's rats versus a man, teeth only. I've only seen it done once in a pit and that was in the West Indies.'

Harry put his hands behind his back and leant forward in a dumb show, his voice loud to carry across the din. 'The fighter ties his hands behind his back, then gets on his knees and fights the rats like a dog. He should break their neck if he catches them right.'

'I don't believe it. Do the rats fight back?'

'Of course they do,' shouted Harry, again craning to see. 'Especially if they're hungry.'

'Rats are always hungry.'

'True.'

'Can they win?'

'The fight is timed, so if you can't kill them all in so many minutes, you lose. And, of course, if they get you in both the eyes, brother, which is the part they go for, then they have won.'

The crowd roared again, this time with deafening noise. James had to shout very loud to be heard. 'Look at him.'

A tall, well-built negro, his body glistening with sweat, stood up in the centre of the roaring crowd. He had a limp rat in his teeth and his face and shoulders were bleeding from a number of bites. Suddenly, he tossed his head, and the rat, neck broken, flew through the air into the arms of the eager crowd, to be held aloft as a token of gambling success. Someone untied his hands and gave him a cloth. He wiped his sweating and bloody face, then raised his arms in triumph. Most of the crowd roared. Those who had bet against him gave an underlying groan.

Ma Thomas stood up and held the watch out for all to see. 'Eight minutes near enough. Well inside the ten, and a fair contest.'

Another yell of approval accompanied this, and the rat fighter approached the table. From a pouch on the front of her voluminous garment, Ma Thomas produced several glittering coins. The man took his prize, and as he walked away the successful spectators pushed forward round the table, holding aloft their betting tally slips. Those who had wagered against the rat-fighter returned, some resigned, and some angry, to their tables. One of which was the one Harry and James had chosen to stand on.

They were treated to baleful looks from three sailors, battle-scarred and mean looking, as they climbed down. The table tipped slightly, upsetting a jug of beer, as James's weight came off it.

'Mind my ale, you no-good bugger,' said a swarthy individual, the tallest of the trio. He pushed James's shoulder at the moment he managed to steady to tankard. James fell back, tipping the contents on to the floor. Harry immediately stepped between them, facing the man. He was wearing a broad-brimmed hat decorated with rat skins, the lifeless eyes catching the glare from the multitude of candles around the walls. His face, which looked at first to be marred by smallpox, was really a mass of small scars, some barely healed. He looked like another rat-fighter.

'My apologies,' said Harry, one hand held up in a gesture of reconciliation, the other indicating the pit at the end of the room. 'But we didn't know what was going on.'

'Apologies,' mimicked one of the others, in a travesty of Harry's polite tone.

'You're not regular here. Who are you?' said the third one of this unsavoury trio, leaning forward and sticking his face close to James'.

'Guests of Captain Broadbridge,' said Harry, pushing his hand between them.

The rat-fighter looked angry and disbelieving. 'Guests. Of that no-account drunken bastard. An' you come in here an' tip over my ale.'

The brim of the man's hat was nearly touching Harry's face, with one of the rat tails swinging before his eyes.

Harry was clearly angry, but kept his voice friendly, still attempting to mollify the man. 'With respect, mate, I think you tipped over your own drink.'

The rat-fighter pulled his head far enough back to look Harry up and down. His eyes narrowed as he took in the cut of his cloth. He turned to his companions with an arrogant leer. 'I'm his mate, lads, d'ye hear.'

He turned back, running his fingers along the collar of Harry's coat as he pushed his face close again. 'Quite the gent, ain't we?'

Harry growled, fighting to keep the anger out of his voice, but it was James who spoke. 'If you tell us what was in your tankard, we will replace it.'

The rat-fighters ignored him. His fingers felt the cloth again, but this time taking a tighter grip, as if ready to tug it and throw Harry off-balance.

'Can't say I've ever had the chance to own such a fine coat. Now that don't seem fair, your bein' a gent and me just a luckless gambler. Happen my luck's set to turn. Perhaps you should pay a bit more than the price of one tankard of ale.'

'Mine looks as though someone's been at it,' said the man closest to James.

The third one reached out, picked up a tankard and drained it. He wiped his mouth with his dirty sleeve before speaking. 'An' mine's empty.'

Harry put one hand on the rat-fighter's chest and pushed very gently. His voice was soft too. 'Back off, mate. You've had our offer. Either take it or pass it up.'

Something happened in the rat-fighter's eyes, which went glassy. He looked like a man about to lose control of himself. His voice was as tense as his body, and as it rose drops of spittle shot out of his mouth.

'Don't you call me mate. I'm not your mate. I'm Ralph Beldeau, d'ye hear. An' I'm telling you I don't like you. Where I walk men get out of my path, or rue the day. An' you're in my way, you lily-livered sod. Now you get some drinks on that table, enough to ease my temper, or both you and this bugger with you will feel more than the edge of my tongue.'

The third man snarled, and he, in turn, pushed his empty tankard hard into Harry's chest. 'I'd shift to find my purse if I were you, mate, lest you end up head first in the harbour.'

He never saw the blow coming, but, catching him right under the chin, it lifted him bodily off his feet. He'd just hit the floor by the time Harry, in a flurry of movement, felled the rat-fighter with a straight jab, breaking the man's nose in the process. James threw the remains of the tankard of ale into the face of the other man, giving his brother time to turn to face him. Harry's foot caught him right in the groin and he doubled over, a great whooshing sound issuing from his mouth, and Harry's fists, clenched together, came down on the back of his head, knocking him to the ground to join his companions.

Harry Ludlow spun round to face the crowd, suddenly finding himself in a space cleared of people, his fists up like a prize fighter inviting all-comers. James, looking a great deal less threatening, emulated him.

'Belay that. I'll not have fightin' in here!' shouted Ma Thomas above the heads around her.

Harry, seeing that no one was coming on, dropped his fists, and called across the room to her. 'Then you should tell your customers to mind their manners. I'll not put up with a lack of respect, from anyone.'

'Why, it's Harry Ludlow!' yelled a voice from the back of the pit.

'Who's that?' said Harry, his eyes searching the room. The crowd had parted, revealing a table, slightly raised on a dais, close to the pit itself. The people at this table seemed to be better dressed than the others in the tap-room crowd, clad as they were, with one exception, in a variety of good-quality coloured coats. The exception wore a loose-fitting white shirt, and had his back to the room.

'Joe Crosby,' said a small man, crossing the sand of the pit and pushing through the crowd. 'Don't you recall, Captain? I did a trip to Calcutta with you in the year '90.'

He stopped in front of Harry and looked up at him, smiling. James looked at his brother, still breathing heavily. The smile was not being returned. Harry, always a sociable fellow with an old shipmate, wasn't happy to see this Crosby.

'What brings you out here, Captain?'

'Chance, Crosby. Pure chance. I was stuck in Gib and Admiral Hood was on his way here with the Fleet, so he offered me the passage.'

There was a loud buzz of discontent at the mention of Admiral

Hood and a fleet, and it wasn't because they were impressed. Privateers disliked the Navy just as much as the Navy disliked them.

'I heard tell you was privateerin' off the Girdone.'

'I was, Crosby. But I had my ship sunk under me.'

'The *Medusa*?'

Harry nodded. Two of Harry's victims had hauled themselves upright and, standing over the still unconscious rat-fighter, were murmuring in the background, as if set to try another bout. Crosby turned and snapped at them. Yet for all his hard words to them he still seemed able to grovel to Harry. 'You leave it be, Tinker. This be Captain Harry Ludlow, and if you mess with him again, it'll be an early grave you'll win.'

He looked down at the rat-fighter, whose bleeding nose was staining the front of his shirt, while at the same time taking Harry's arm. 'I should get Beldeau upright before he chokes on his own blood. Come away, Captain Ludlow. An' stay away from that bugger, for he's as mad as a rabid dog. Let's hope he forgives you for deckin' him.'

'Crosby.' A loud voice cut across the buzz of conversation. The small man turned quickly, looked once, and without any further bidding scurried across to the raised table. He stopped beside the man in shirtsleeves with his back to the room. The entire place fell silent. Crosby leant down to whisper in the man's ear, his head close to the long curly black hair that was all Harry and James could see. The hair jerked occasionally as Crosby was questioned. Once more, it seemed, they were the object of curiosity.

Slowly the man turned, and as he looked at them every eye in the room followed his, creating a tangible air of menace. Harry felt that one word from this fellow and the crowd would tear him apart. Steady dark brown eyes, slightly hooded. Black eyebrows, a dark complexion, and a slightly crooked nose. Handsome to say the least, and confident of his authority. He held Harry and James in his gaze for some time, imposing the silence, then suddenly the full red lips parted, treating the Ludlow brothers to a slightly mocking smile. The tension in the tap-room dropped immediately, allowing a buzz of conversation.

Crosby, responding to words that the brothers couldn't hear, rushed back to their side. He took Harry by the arm and led him towards the raised table. James followed. Behind the men seated at the table he could see the pit where the rat fight had taken place. Spots of blood stained the pale sand, and the bodies of three rats lay ignored.

'Allow me to name Captain Harry Ludlow,' said Crosby, addressing the man in shirtsleeves, who then looked enquiringly, and somewhat suspiciously, at James.

'My brother, James Ludlow,' said Harry.

'Brother,' said Crosby, looking more keenly. 'Why, the likeness is there right enough. Wonder I didn't smoke it right off. This here be Captain Gideon Bartholomew.'

'Good evening, gentlemen. Crosby has favoured me with my full handle, but I normally answer to Bart.'

The voice was low and compelling, with a hint of a colonial accent. The man stood up and signalled for some chairs. The speed at which these appeared testified once more to his authority. 'I would esteem it an honour if you and your brother would join us, Captain Ludlow.'

The other four men at the table sat silent, their eyes fixed on the brothers without a hint of welcome in their eyes. Harry looked from one to the other, gracing each with a small bow before sitting down.

'Since we are all captains here, Ludlow, it might be best to dispense with titles.' Bartholomew rattled off their names, each person acknowledging with a slight nod. 'Pilton, Freeman, Chittenden, and Frome.'

He swept the room with his hand. 'I shan't bother to introduce you to their entire crews. Though you seem to have met some of mine already.'

Harry glanced around the tavern, idly wondering if there was another room somewhere, for there were not enough men here to crew two privateers of any size, let alone five. Bartholomew treated Harry to another mocking smile, but his voice had an edge to it as he addressed his companions. 'Now that our sport is done, gentlemen, I'm sure you have other matters to attend to.'

Mumbled 'ayes' followed as they stood up and left. The tavern had returned to some semblance of normality, noisy, but with the crowd now dispersed at the various tables. Crosby, standing slightly away from them, waved his arm and a dark-skinned serving woman appeared. He directed her towards the table. She was like the rest of the place. False. A plump girl, she wore a mob cap and a low-cut gown designed to push her ample bosom up, the very parody of an English serving maid. But her smooth olive skin and jet-black hair spoiled the effect, as did her apparent inability to understand more than two consecutive words of the language.

Drinks ordered, Bartholomew treated them to another of his smiles. 'A privateer captain, Ludlow. Is your presence here a coincidence?'

Harry deliberately chose to misinterpret the question. 'It most certainly is. We are here as guests of Captain Broadbridge.'

At the mention of Broadbridge's name, a slight frown crossed Bartholomew's face, which disappeared quickly as Harry, in response to more specific questions, outlined how they had come to end up in the Royal George. The conversation took on the air of an interrogation. James, wholly excluded, noticed again that Harry volunteered nothing, waiting to be asked something before imparting any information of value. Crosby must have managed to convey a great deal in that brief whispered conversation with Bartholomew. Asked, he told Bartholomew how the *Medusa* had been sunk, but as with Broadbridge, nothing else. James watched the other man as he listened intently to Harry's replies.

Then he turned to look at Crosby, who was straining forward to hear what was being said. He was a small man in many ways. His head seemed small even in comparison to his body. He had lively brown eyes, and dry-looking skin, with patches where the sun had burnt it. His nose was slightly crooked, and he had a habit of grabbing it between thumb and forefinger, as if to ensure it was still there.

'So you're just on your way home?' asked Bartholomew.

Harry, ducking the point of the question, indicated his brother. 'James here wanted to revisit some of the places from his Grand Tour, and since we were offered passage here, it seemed the quickest route home.'

'So you won't be looking to set up here then?'

'Set up here?' said Harry, quietly wondering how fast gossip travelled in this place. James tried to keep all expression out of his face as Bartholomew shot him a look.

'The thought never occurred to me,' said Harry, leaning forward, pensive, trying to look like a man who's just had an idea. Crosby, who'd managed to get very close to the table by now, spoke out.

'Then I'm glad we've brought it to your mind. For if'n you was to set up here, Captain Ludlow, I'd be mighty glad to serve with you again.'

Harry spun round to look at Crosby. 'Why, if I do, Joe, you'll be the first person I'd want on my crew.'

If Crosby noticed the insincerity, he didn't bat an eyelid.

Nor did Bartholomew. He looked into his tankard with some distaste. 'This is a poor brew for a gentleman, Ludlow. If you'd care to join me in my rooms, I think I can offer you something better.'

The contrast between Bartholomew's rooms and the accommodation afforded to Captain Broadbridge could not have been greater. Nothing cramped here, Bartholomew had a sitting room, a bedroom, and a personal privy. The place was panelled in dark oak, aged over the years till it was almost black. The floor was the same, with twelve-inch boards, and Bartholomew had furnished it to match, with pieces that could have been out of any English country house built at the time of the Stuart kings. High-backed chairs and divans were laid out around a huge stone fireplace. And it was as if Bartholomew himself had adopted the same style. With his dark curly hair, worn long, and the open-necked shirt with a lace collar and cuffs, he looked every inch the Jacobean. In fact, quite the Cavalier.

'This wine is from a region to the north of here,' said Bartholomew, tipping the cane-covered bottle and filling three huge pewter goblets. 'I think you'll find it compares favourably with the better clarets.'

Harry picked up his goblet and took a deep draught of the wine, nodding his approval as he tasted it. James did likewise, but while Bartholomew hung on Harry's reaction, he seemed intent on ignoring James's, not even glancing in his direction to witness his appreciation.

'It is unfortunate that your first impression of Genoa should be one of unbridled licence,' he said, sitting down opposite Harry. Given the depth of the winged armchair, this cut him off from James's view. 'Did you glean anything about your attackers?'

'Only that they knew what they were about. For one thing they were dressed in black, and were hardly visible.'

'An odd thing,' said James. 'They didn't speak at all.'

Bartholomew leant forward so that he could see James beyond the side of his chair. His voice was as cold as his look when he replied: 'Why is that odd?'

James Ludlow was not a man to be treated so. Natural authority and grand surroundings were not enough to subdue him. 'If you, sir, cannot see something odd in that, then I am at a loss to explain it, for it is as plain as day.'

Bartholomew sat back, leaving James looking at the side of his chair, and addressed Harry. 'Nothing you have said identifies them to me. They could have been any one of a number of the gangs that plague this part of the world.'

'Perhaps they were not from this part of the world,' said Harry.

Bartholomew raised a dark eyebrow, inviting Harry to elaborate. 'Come, Captain Bartholomew. There is a French ship in the harbour. An officer of His Majesty's Navy was recently murdered in these very streets. I don't know if you are aware of that.'

Bartholomew gulped his wine, looking at Harry's dark blue coat before replying. 'You think they mistook you for English officers?'

'Or perhaps English privateers,' said Harry. He'd meant it as a joke, but he suddenly realized that his blue coat looked remarkably like Broadbridge's. Bartholomew nearly smiled, but it was only a fleeting impression that was soon replaced by a look of blank passivity.

Harry sat forward in his chair. 'In the opinion of those who ought to know, this officer, Captain Howlett, was murdered by the French. Why would they do that?'

Bartholomew did smile this time. 'I'm sure you're about to enlighten me.'

'Let us suppose that's true,' said Harry, keen to develop a recent thought, for if he could convince Bartholomew that he too was threatened, then he might be more forthcoming. 'What's to stop them trying the same thing on English privateers? After all, you will be doing as much damage to the French as our Navy. Perhaps more right now. And they could have well suspected that someone like Broadbridge would be out tonight, hunting for deserters.'

For once Bartholomew was startled out of his composure, sitting forward. 'Broadbridge was out tonight!' He recovered quickly, sinking back into his chair. 'I can see that he has not been entirely discreet.'

'It's not something I need Captain Broadbridge to tell me.'

'Captain Broadbridge?' James looked at Harry, wondering if he'd noticed the way Bartholomew emphasized the word 'captain'.

'He had sailors from the *Swiftsure* in his party when he rescued us. They recognized me, and I'm afraid I recognized them.'

'You were not tempted to inform the Navy of this?'

'I'm not tempted to meddle in affairs that are none of my business.'

James took a deep drink of wine to cover his smile. His brother, to his mind, suffered from an excess of curiosity, and like most people with a failing, he was entirely unaware of it.

'Not even for so lofty a patron as Admiral Hood?'

'Sailors run, Captain Bartholomew. You know that as well as I do. Though I might add that if it gets out of hand, you may find this place surrounded by marines one night. Hood is no more of a fool than you are. If his losses exceed the norm, he'll soon smoke where they are.'

There was a slight hint of steel in Bartholomew's voice as he replied, expressing the same thought which had probably troubled Broadbridge. 'He might have it from you.'

'I doubt it,' said Harry, sitting back and crossing his legs. 'After all, I could suffer myself.'

Bartholomew waved his hand dismissively. 'We sail under Genoese colours.'

That produced a humourless smile from Harry. 'I'm at a loss to know which court you'd apply to for redress, if the Navy took matters into its own hands.'

A silence followed as Bartholomew digested this. Then a sharp tap at the door had him swiftly out of his chair. He opened the door a fraction and had a quiet conversation with someone who remained outside. Neither Harry nor James could see to whom he spoke. Harry was left to mull over what he'd just said, sure that Bartholomew knew, just as he did himself, that you couldn't ever sail a ship, especially a privateer, without having aboard someone who'd deserted from the King's Navy. Not unless you wanted to crew your ship with landsmen.

Bartholomew finished his conversation, and after filling Harry's goblet, returned to his chair. 'Do I detect from what you've just said your intention to sail from these parts yourself?'

Harry avoided the real point of the question. 'I had not expected to find Englishmen sailing from this port.'

'Leghorn?' asked Bartholomew, smiling at Harry's nod. 'Tell me, sir. What did you make of Broadbridge?'

'Make of him?' asked Harry, slightly taken aback by the question.

James had stood up and lifted the bottle off the table. If Bartholomew was not going to offer him another drink, he felt he should help himself. This brought him back into sight of their host, and he answered for both of them. 'I have nothing but praise for him, sir. Both his timing and his hospitality are of the highest order.'

'We would not be here now, if it wasn't for Captain Broadbridge,' said Harry.

Bartholomew ignored James, and changed the subject back to the previous point. 'Does Leghorn still attract you?'

'I cannot say till I have been there and had a look.'

James, reseated, spoke up again, determined to be included in the conversation. 'According to our information, you are faring somewhat better than the good sailors of Leghorn.'

' "Our" information?' Bartholomew made the possession of information about him sound like a sin.

'Yes. The people in Leghorn petitioned the Admiral to curtail the Navy in its prize-taking. Here, you obviously didn't feel the need.'

Harry intervened. James was in danger of saying too much. 'It's all luck, James.'

'Nonsense, Harry,' said James sharply. It was bad enough Bartholomew ignoring him. He would not take it from Harry as well.

Bartholomew flicked back his curly hair. 'Your brother is right, Ludlow. It would be a foolish thing, merely to trust to luck.'

'I accept that you have to be in the right place, of course. But you can do that and still finish up empty-handed. I mentioned that very thing to Broadbridge.'

'I am a firm believer in making your own luck.' Bartholomew leant forward to top up Harry's glass. 'In the case of Broadbridge, I'm afraid he gets the quantity of luck he deserves and that certainly doesn't rise to the level we expect.'

There was a pause of several seconds. James broke the silence. 'Are you issuing us with an invitation, Bartholomew?'

He leant forward again, this time gracing James with his mocking smile. 'What we have here, sir, is a syndicate. The rules are that we share our "luck". That reduces the element of chance quite considerably. If however there is a weak strand in the cable . . .'

He shrugged and stood up, leaving James's question unanswered. 'However, we must not get ahead of ourselves. You have only just arrived. Look around, and if you like what you see, we may talk further.'

Harry wasn't finished. 'May I ask you, Captain Bartholomew, if you know anything of the death of Captain Howlett?'

'I had heard of it. But you would do well to heed your own counsel in these waters, Ludlow. I cannot stress how dangerous Genoa is. Murder on the streets is not uncommon.'

'I merely wondered if you incline towards the suggestion that the French were to blame?'

'I believe that he still had his valuables about his person.'

'He did.'

'Then it must be the French. There's not a local, rich or poor, who would do that.' Bartholomew laughed softly, without the slightest hint of humour.

CHAPTER NINE

'I wouldn't have Crosby aboard my ship if he was the last available sailor in port. He's a liar, a cheat, and though I couldn't prove it, a thief to boot.'

They were back in their room, having checked on Pender, who was now snoring fit to wake the dead. James was lounging on the makeshift bed staring at the ceiling.

'I observed that you were less than delighted to see him. That was quite an impressive display of fisticuffs, Harry. All that boxing at the local fairs has not been wasted. Not exactly gentlemanly behaviour, mind.'

Harry grinned. 'I've had more practice at sea, James. I haven't always had the luxury of a flogging to keep the hard cases in check. No matter how good a crew are, someone is bound to get out of hand, especially when they're in drink. And as for gentlemanly behaviour, I'm a dab hand with a marlin-spike from behind.'

'All your skills will be in demand, brother. We've been ashore for less than four hours, and already we've been in two scrapes.'

'It's a good job we left that strongbox aboard the *Swiftsure*. I don't think we'd have that now if we'd brought it ashore.'

'Damn the money. I doubt we'd be alive.' James dropped his eyes and looked at Harry. 'So, how does the plan proceed?'

'Plan?'

'I believe you tend towards the expression, "fine calculation of chances". Has it occurred to you that Admiral Hood may be entirely wrong?'

'More than once.'

'What does that do to the fine calculation of chances?'

'Could we adopt another expression, James? That one strikes a very jarring note.'

'Would that I could think of one that fits the bill, brother, but that would tax the limits of the lexicographer's art.'

Harry responded sharply, stung by his brother's irony. 'James. I want my exemptions. Hood can give them to me. I assure you that if it is in my power to shift that French sloop, shift it I will.'

'And the murder of Captain Howlett?'

'A means to an end,' snapped Harry.

'I doubt that's wholly true. But at least you have, in your nautical way, hoisted your colours.'

'What do you mean?'

'It's a bad idea to keep me in the dark, Harry. I know you are used to the solitary exercise of command, and it must come hard to you to share your thoughts with anyone. But be warned, as long as you exclude me, I shall exert a wholly negative influence on your efforts.'

'James.' He was stung by guilt, reaching over and touching his brother's arm affectionately. 'I thought you, of all people knew.'

'Knew what?'

'My fallibility, I suppose. This air of certainty is a habit, worn at sea. It's vital everyone thinks you know exactly what you're about.'

James favoured him with a look of mock alarm. 'Are you trying to tell me I've been sailing with a poltroon, a novice?'

'No. It's all experience. And luck. But I'm no different to most men. Often I have only the foggiest notion of what I'm about.'

'Even such candour, Harry, does not entirely reassure me.' But James was still smiling. He followed this with a yawn. 'I don't think Bartholomew was overly impressed with our theory.'

'Which one?'

'That the French were responsible. Mind, he strikes me as a man not given to over-reaction.'

Harry's mind was elsewhere. 'If Broadbridge bribed those boatmen . . .'

'He didn't actually say he had.'

'Pender could ask that fellow Sutton.'

James yawned again, and settled back on his makeshift pillow. 'It will have to wait until morning.' He nodded towards the comatose servant. 'Do you think we'll be able to sleep with that going on?'

'It won't trouble me,' said Harry, putting a chair under the door handle. 'But with the reception we've had so far, I think I need this.'

The sun was high up in the sky when they woke, though little of it filtered through the shutters. Pender stood beside the desk with a tray bearing coffee and bread, still warm and fresh from the bakery.

'How is your head?' asked Harry, sitting up and reaching for the beaker of coffee. His whole body felt stiff after a night on the floor.

'A mite sore, your honour,' said Pender.

'On the inside or the outside?' said James, yawning and stretching.

'Bit of both, Mister James.' Pender smiled and narrowed his eyes slightly to acknowledge the hangover. Then he shuddered. 'That needle, with thread hangin' off it.'

Harry got to his feet, stretching painfully, and making much of the aches so that his brother should feel remorse. James responded with a smile. He peered at Pender's bandage, as if trying to see through it.

'Rest assured he did a neat job, which did surprise me. From what I could see his hand was none too steady.'

'Have you had a look round?' asked Harry, sure that his servant would have done so.

Pender nodded. 'And I've had a good talk with Carey Sutton.'

'I seem to be the only one without a friend here already,' said James. Pender looked curious. 'My brother has found one of his old shipmates here.'

'A man called Crosby,' said Harry.

'I met him. Little fellow with a bent nose. You have him to thank for this.' He indicated the breakfast. 'He started asking about you, while I was talking to Carey.'

Harry stiffened slightly, but his servant just favoured him with a slight smile. 'From what Carey let slip, I don't think that we've got many secrets to worry about.'

'Is Sutton a friend?'

'Not close. But we've known each other, on an' off, for years. Let's say we've done each other the odd good turn, without ever needing to do each other a bad one. He knows me well enough to be sure that I won't split on him, or his mates.' Pender pointed to his bandaged head. 'I asked him about this, but he didn't have a clue who it might be.'

'How many of *Swiftsure*'s did they bring in last night?'

'Quite a few, though Carey wouldn't say exact. Funny thing, Crosby had a bit of a go at Sutton, asking him what the hell they were doin' out lookin' for hands, when they've got more'n enough already.'

'Then I'm damned if I know where they all are,' said Harry.

'An' then he starts on about Broadbridge goin' on a cruise. He and Sutton were yelling at each other at the finish.'

'Sutton sailed with him?'

'He did that, and a right bloody mess it was by all accounts. He didn't get very far, and he came back empty handed.'

'He told us he wasn't really trying. It was more a case of working up his crew.'

'Not accordin' to Crosby. They was after prizes all right. And since he didn't make anythin' he's stuck for a shilling, I think.'

'That must have been what he meant last night,' said James. Harry looked at him, trying to recall what his brother was on about. 'When you hinted he was short of hands, Broadbridge said he had other problems.'

'Anything else?' asked Harry, taking a refill of coffee from Pender, thinking that Broadbridge had painted a somewhat rosy picture the previous night.

'Chapter and verse. Nothin' like two blokes arguing to have 'em both let on more'n they should. Broadbridge wants to buy another boat. The one he's got is near useless for privateerin'. A right slab-sided barky with a rotten hull that leaks at anchor. Even worse at sea when the seams are workin', which is what made his cruise a waste of time. He wallowed up and down off Marseilles. They didn't see much, and what they did spot they couldn't catch. That's why I reckon he's hard up. I suppose he's sunk so much money into buyin' his share of this place that he's left himself short for the purchase. And all the while he's having to pay his hands so they won't just disappear. Poor bugger's in a right bind, it seems. Sutton reckons the man who heads the syndicate will bail him out. Crosby had a right laugh at that.'

'Bartholomew?' asked James.

'That's the one. Top dog with this bunch. And he and his mates are coining it. If Broadbridge can just get the loan, for which he can put up his share in this place, he can get to sea in something sound and set things to rights.'

'It seems straightforward,' said James. 'Especially if the other members of the syndicate have the money to oblige him.'

'It's down to Bartholomew. For all the syndicate is supposed to vote, it's usually what he wants that prevails. An' I had that from the pair of them. It's about the only thing they agreed on, so it must be right. A nod from him would do. Trouble is, if Broadbridge don't get that nod, he might go down completely.'

'He could always sell his share in the syndicate.'

'Harry!' said James.

'Just thinking aloud.'

James turned back to Pender. 'You said earlier that Carey let certain things slip about us.'

'He knows we're well heeled, gold included. He'll have got that from the deserters they picked up last night.'

'And a ship?'

'One secret tends to follow another.'

'Where's Sutton now?'

'Gone back aboard the *Dido*.'

Apart from the Ludlows, the tap-room was empty, with no trace of the activities that had taken place the night before. The dead rats were gone, and the sand in the rectangular pit was raked clean. The whole place had been scrubbed and the shutters were open, allowing a pleasant warm breeze to waft through the room, taking with it the smell of drink and stable tobacco, as well as the odour of the vinegar used to overcome it.

They sat at a table eating heartily, consuming quantities of the local sausage and great hunks of bread, and washing the whole lot down with pot upon pot of coffee. The residents of this tavern were

92

obviously not early risers, since no one else appeared. Harry, facing the harbour across the table, had a slightly glazed look, wrapped up in his thoughts.

James held his hand in front of his mouth and exhaled. 'We must find some parsley, Harry. The amount of garlic in this sausage is quite remarkable.'

'I confess, James, my mind was on other things.'

'Spare me more of your speculations.' James waved the remains of his sausage in his brother's direction. 'I feel we should call upon Captain Broadbridge to thank him, Harry. After all, he did save our lives.'

'A capital idea, brother.' Harry used his sausage to point towards the tavern door behind his brother. 'Though I fear we are too late.'

James spun round just as Broadbridge came through the door. Harry was already on his feet, still with a sausage and a hunk of bread in his hand. 'Good morning, Captain Broadbridge. I trust I find you well?'

'Well enough, sir. As well as any man can be on two hours' sleep.'

'You were out most of the night?'

'I was that, and to little purpose.' Broadbridge looked about the empty room, seemingly surprised that there was no one about. He called out for a bottle of wine, and as he sat down at their table, Harry caught a whiff of drink on his breath. This wine would not be his first of the day.

'We've not had a proper chance to thank you,' said James. 'And because of your generosity we were afforded a chance to get more sleep than you.'

Harry looked at his brother with something less than humour, longing to tell James that he was speaking for himself. Again Broadbridge looked around, as though someone he wanted to see must be there.

'We will, of course, find other accommodation today, Captain, but if we can leave our small chest in your rooms, I'd be much obliged.'

Broadbridge just nodded. His mind was elsewhere. When the door at the back of the tavern opened, he looked up keenly, but his face registered disappointment at what he saw, for it was only one of the serving girls carrying a bucket and mop.

'You have come ashore for a purpose?' asked James, seeing both the look and the disappointment.

'I have that. I arranged to meet Bartholomew here at ten of the clock. By my reckoning he's late.'

James pulled out his watch. 'Not by much, Captain, a mere five minutes, if this is correct.'

The man's flat face took on a slightly dissatisfied look. 'I'm told you met last night. Quite taken with you he was, Mr Ludlow, by all accounts, though he was no surer of your purpose here than I am.'

Harry was sick of all this pretence, quite putting his role in the subterfuge aside. 'I doubt that there's much about us that either you or Captain Bartholomew don't know. Thanks to certain people our every intention was the talk of the port.'

The older man's face betrayed just a hint of impatience. 'Yet you chose not to let on.'

James cut in. 'Captain Broadbridge. You saved our lives last night, and if anyone was to be privy to our plans it would be you. But as yet they are mere speculation.'

He raised his eyebrows. 'So you are not looking for a ship?'

'It is possible that we are,' said James.

Broadbridge sat forward, with his elbows on the table, adopting a more aggressive pose. 'Those I spoke to seemed pretty sure. And they was just as sure that you had the means to do so.'

It was Harry's turn to speak. 'If you are a sailor, sir, I need hardly tell you of the problems associated with gossip.'

'So you're not carrying gold?'

'Yes. But I doubt it is in the quantity that you have come to believe.'

'Believe.' He sat back, a slightly mocking smile on his lips. 'I do believe that it's been suggested that you sail from here. In fact, there was a hint that I turn in my share so that you could purchase it.'

Harry looked right into Broadbridge's pale blue eyes, wondering how something that had been the merest suggestion had gained sufficient currency to cause the older man a problem. True, he had remarked on it himself, but that was done in privacy. There was no malice in Broadbridge's eyes, more a look of enquiry, with a hint of disappointment at their prevarication. 'The truth, Captain Broadbridge . . .'

'Would be appreciated, sir.'

Harry bridled at this. Yet he held his anger in check, for he had the feeling that the man opposite wouldn't have mentioned it if someone had not already assured him that there was substance in his suspicions.

'My brother spoke the truth. Nothing is decided. I am in the market for a ship, but we only landed here on our way to Leghorn. Bartholomew suggested last night that we might sail from here.'

Broadbridge cut in, his voice angry. 'So it was him.'

'To call it a suggestion is to give it an importance it scarcely warrants,' said James. Broadbridge raised an eyebrow in disbelief. 'Mind, it would be foolish to pretend that the idea had not occurred to my brother. After all, it seems that the captains here are doing well, which we have been informed is not the case further down the coast. But if someone has implied that we have sought to dislodge you, sir, then they are lying, for that was never mentioned.'

Harry had not taken his eyes off Broadbridge since he'd sat down, and Bartholomew's question about the man came to mind. Taken with what he'd observed last night, what he saw before him now did not overly impress him. It had nothing to do with liking the man. He was a personable enough fellow, with a cheerful manner and a kindly disposition being his abiding traits, who had come to their rescue, and no doubt saved their lives. But he lacked authority. It was in his eyes and his demeanour. He had little control over his men, and none whatever over the likes of Ma Thomas.

Harry knew, more than most, that if there was one thing needed on the quarter-deck of a ship, especially a privateer, it was that quality of leadership that would cause men to obey you unquestioningly. It stemmed from ability. And ability came from experience. Broadbridge may have hidden depths, but if he did they were well obscured from Harry Ludlow, as near to a trained eye as it was possible to get. Harry had the impression that Broadbridge was no true blue-water sailor, and certainly not the stuff of the successful privateer. And for that reason, in spite of what they owed, he decided to go on the offensive.

'I believe you too are in the market for a ship yourself.'

'Who told you that?'

Harry fixed him with a glacial stare. 'It would be as well to remember that we are all the object of loose tongues. If you care to tell me that it is untrue, Captain Broadbridge, then I shall most

95

certainly take your word for it. I would esteem it a kindness if you would extend the same courtesy to my brother and I.'

Harry decided that a lie would benefit all concerned. 'No one mentioned you last night except me, and that was only to inform Captain Bartholomew that we were the recipients of both your good timing, and your most generous hospitality. If he has taken it upon himself to imply something else . . .'

'It wasn't Bartholomew.'

'Then whoever it was, I urge you to put it out of your mind, for I would say you have been practised upon.'

The older man's face cleared, and he leant forward again, relaxed this time, and took a great swig from his tankard. 'I owe you an apology, sir. I'm venting my spleen in the wrong place.'

'Would it be beyond the bounds of good manners to ask where it should be directed?' asked James.

'Bartholomew and I had words last night, and I dare say what I had to say to him did not endear me to him. I find myself strapped for funds. The *Dido* is a good enough vessel, but not a proper one for what needs doin', so I can see how the other captains would be reluctant to let me cruise alongside them.'

'They sail together?' asked Harry, mildly surprised.

Broadbridge nodded impatiently, as though the answer to Harry's question was obvious. Yet privateers almost invariably cruised alone. The very nature of the men who did such work mitigated against combination.

The older man frowned. 'All my monies are tied up in this place. Tell the truth I'm having trouble in feeding the hands. I must get to sea, and in the right kind of vessel. One voyage will set me to rights.'

To Harry this was just another manifestation of his lack of ability. His words echoed those of the previous night.

'You seem very sure, Captain Broadbridge. But let me tell you there is nothing certain at sea. Success requires a degree of luck. It would be folly to pin all your hopes on one voyage.'

Broadbridge smiled, and tapped the side of his flat nose with a finger, as if to say, 'that's all you know'. But if he had good grounds for confidence, he was not about to share them.

James gave Harry a quick look before speaking. 'If you are so strapped for funds, Captain Broadbridge, my brother and I would esteem it, as no more than your due, to offer you some assistance.'

'Why that is most kind of you, Mr Ludlow. And I won't pretend, hearing what I did, that approachin' you for some help did not come to mind. Why, rumour had it you was carrying the proceeds of a Spanish plate fleet.'

'Sailors love to gild the lily,' said Harry.

'They do that. I knew that the tale had grown in the telling, but when I returned here last night, I had half a mind to call.'

James gave Harry another look before speaking, and was pleased to see his brother respond with a nod. 'I hope that you will not take it as a blow to your pride if I say that the offer still stands.'

'It would never do, Mr Ludlow.'

'Why ever not?'

'It would be like presenting a bill for helping you.'

'I can think of many less deserving reasons, sir. When you came to our rescue last night, what prompted you to do so?'

'I heard you shouting, in English of course. It was plain you were in dire straits. Couldn't leave a fellow countryman in the lurch.'

James slapped his hand on the table. 'Then neither can we, Captain Broadbridge, even if his calls for help are more muted.'

Broadbridge's manner changed completely, his frown disappeared and he spoke rapidly, making interruption impossible. 'Then I can do no more than accept, sir. For not to do so would be an insult. A hundred guineas would see to my immediate needs, and if your offer still holds after that, then it will strengthen me in my negotiations with the syndicate. Nothing like another source of funds to concentrate the mind, I always say. And rest assured I will provide security.'

Harry looked at his brother, wondering if he had the same feeling that they'd just been caught in a trap. 'You refer to your share in this inn?'

'I do not, sir. Why, I have investments in abundance. Loath to part with them, of course, for they're worth a mint now and set to grow. I cannot take your help without putting something solid up to cover it.'

'You're too generous,' said James with biting irony. He too had the look of a man who'd just been stung.

'Nonsense, sir.' Broadbridge looked around with an exaggerated air of conspiracy, then spoke in a whisper.

'And to show how much I appreciate your kindness, I may be able to put you in the way of a good opportunity. For if you've got funds for investment, then I may be in a position to make you a pile. I believe that Bart and I finally struck a bargain the other night, so I doubt I'll need your help. But the thought of all that money doing nothing, why it's a disgrace, I say.'

Broadbridge leant even closer. He looked as though he was about to try and sell something. Harry spoke quickly to avoid it. 'I was given to understand you had a particular ship in mind.'

He fixed Harry with a distrustful look again, yet the merest novice could have guessed where the information came from.

'I do.'

'And you've been after it for some time, I gather?' said James.

'That's so, and many an obstacle put in my path, I can tell you. I had hellish difficulty in finding out who owned it, for a start. She's sitting out there in the outer roads. Has been for weeks, since she came out of the dockyard. I put out a number of feelers saying I was interested. Think they'd be glad to talk to me, but nothing has come back.'

'Captain Broadbridge. If you don't know the owner, how do you know it's for sale?'

Again Broadbridge tapped the side of his nose, and adopted a cunning air. 'I know now. It was just a case of unlocking the mystery.'

Broadbridge pushed himself back from the table, and treated himself to a hearty laugh. But he declined to share the joke with the Ludlows.

'You're sure she's the right type of vessel?'

'I am. And you can see from her lines she's a flyer. I shall strike a bargain on the spot if I can.'

Again he exposed himself, for no experienced captain would ever buy a ship before he'd had a chance to take it out to sea. Broadbridge might be lucky. But there again, he might make an expensive error. 'Captain Broadbridge, I have some knowledge in these matters. If you feel the need of a second opinion, I would be happy to cast an eye over her myself.'

Broadbridge's face closed up quickly.

'Mere curiosity, I do assure you, Captain Broadbridge, plus a love of ships.' But Harry knew he had said the wrong thing. And he was given no opportunity to repair the sudden suspicion he'd created in the older man's mind, for at that moment the door at the rear of the tap-room opened and Bartholomew entered, dressed as he had been the night before.

He paused when he saw them all sitting together, leaving them in no doubt that he considered such a gathering worthy of a second thought. Broadbridge stood up, and hurried towards him. Bartholomew nodded to Harry, with just a ghost of a smile, before turning his attention to Broadbridge. He gave the man approaching him a cold look, and they exchanged no greetings. His voice carried no hint of friendship when he spoke.

'I think we would be best to transact our business in my rooms.' With that, he turned and went back through the door.

Broadbridge came back to the table, rubbing his hands together. 'If you could see your way to that little loan, gentlemen?'

James and Harry had to pool their funds for that. Broadbridge chattered throughout, assuring them what a good friend they'd made in William Broadbridge. Once he had the money, he followed in Bartholomew's direction, calling loudly to Ma Thomas that he wished to settle his bill.

'Well,' said Harry. 'We're a hundred guineas lighter for that exchange.'

James, knowing that he was at fault, didn't reply. He drained the last of his coffee. 'What now, Harry?'

'Fetch Pender. Let's get our things ashore and safely stowed,' said Harry. 'After last night I shall demand an escort from Barnes.'

CHAPTER TEN

And demand is precisely what Harry did, in the man's cabin, at seven bells in the forenoon watch, and to a Barnes who was incensed by his tone.

'I would remind you that I command here.'

'And I would remind you, sir, that I am not someone to take such obvious condescension lightly. I do not take kindly to being left ignored on a ship's deck waiting for the first available boat, while the entire ship's crew indulge themselves in drink.'

'Mr Ludlow,' spluttered Barnes, half angry, half guilty.

'In drink, sir!' shouted Harry, making no attempt to moderate the level of his voice, even though the skylight above his head was open, and his words could be heard plainly on the deck. 'Not to mention all manner of other things. Left hanging about until it was dark, and nearly killed for your want of good manners, and I suspect more than a pinch of pure envy. It would be interesting to see how the ship's log looks when you muster the hands. Every officer drunk, and the crew going ashore in droves. You put your pleasure before your duty, sir.'

The shot struck home. Barnes must know by now how many sailors he'd lost, and sober, he must have realized that he had little chance of seeing them again before he sailed. And he would be called to account for it. It was not in Harry's nature to do anything to make his situation worse, but Barnes didn't know that.

The Captain spoke with as much dignity as he could muster. 'You may, with my permission, talk to the premier. If the needs of the ship have been met, you may instruct him to provide you with the cutter.'

The first lieutenant was no more pleased than his temporary master. He immediately set off to check the orders, and, looking somewhat crestfallen, emerged from the cabin to give the necessary instructions. Pender took charge of the line himself, not trusting any of the nauseous crew to lower their clothing, let alone the strongbox, into the boat. From the way they moved, slow and uncoordinated, the chest containing the Ludlow's funds would have stood a fair chance of being dropped right through the bottom planking.

Barnes had learned his lesson, and the cutter had a half-dozen fully armed marines aboard under the command of a senior midshipman. The ship could afford no more deserters. From the enemy sloop came the glint of a telescope being trained on the *Swiftsure*. Harry borrowed a spy-glass from a midshipman too young to refuse him and trained it on the French ship. The breeze had fallen away in the noonday heat, leaving the new tricolour hanging limp on the pole at the ship's stern. Whoever was watching them had set up a chair on the poop just in front of the flag, with the telescope on a tripod. Harry could only discern a silhouette, but he suspected it was the same man he'd observed yesterday. Then the silhouette stood up, and the deserted deck suddenly came alive with running figures, hastening to get a boat over the side. It hit the water just as Harry gave the order to shove off, and, once the occupants had piled aboard, set a parallel course across the harbour.

Someone on shore had a glass trained on the *Swiftsure* as well. As Harry's cutter fended off from the ship, the decorated barge put off from the customs fort, heading straight for them. Doria's aide was in the rear, lounging in his master's velvet chair as though it was his own. He hailed the cutter to heave to, and swung his barge in a wide arc to come neatly alongside. Harry, looking back, saw the French boat continue to shore.

'The Admiral's compliments, Mr Ludlow. He wonders if you might care to join him for some refreshments.'

The invitation was quite clearly an instruction, and Harry nodded to the midshipman to follow the barge back to the fort. The round tower, at the base of the massive mole, had a sea gate, and the barge glided under the raised portcullis, into the dimly lit tunnel, and alongside the dark, covered quay, followed closely by the cutter.

'I doubt you will need these men any more,' said Doria's aide, indicating the English sailors and marines. 'I suggest that they unload your property and return to their ship.'

Harry just nodded again, and he exchanged a glance with Pender. His servant was out of the cutter in a flash, calling for their things to be hauled on to the quay. Harry and James, having carefully thanked the midshipman, followed. They stood, saying nothing, until the gear was unloaded, and the cutter had backed oars and headed out through the sea gate. Some of the men from the Admiral's barge took hold of their sea-chests, carting them through a low door on the quayside. Pender, following, made sure that he had one end of the strongbox.

'If you will come this way.'

Harry and James, still silent, followed the aide up a short set of steps and through a heavy wooden door, leaving Pender to care for their property. Up another staircase, still stone, though less damp, to emerge into a large hallway with a tiled floor. James stopped for a moment to take a look at the elegant hangings and furnishings which adorned the stark stonework of the fortress. Heraldic banners hung from the ceiling, with intricate, colourful tapestries covering the walls. The aide, without pausing, crossed the hallway and held open the door to a small anteroom, waiting patiently for James to catch up.

'If you will take a seat, I will inform my Admiral that you have accepted his invitation.' With that he departed, closing the heavy door with a thud.

'Am I right in thinking we have been abducted, Harry?' asked James, walking across the small room and peering out through the narrow window. It overlooked the busy quayside, and had once been an embrasure for the firing of crossbows.

'More or less,' replied Harry, sitting down in one of the armchairs and stretching out comfortably.

'You don't seem in any way alarmed by this. After the events of last night I find that odd.'

'No, I'm not. First it is happening in daylight. And secondly, if

Admiral Doria wanted to abduct us, he would not do it in the middle of the harbour, and take a fair proportion of the *Swiftsure*'s crew as well.'

James continued to stare out of the window. 'So we have nothing to fear?'

'I didn't say that. But since I don't know what the threat is, or even if it exists, then I can do nothing about it. I see no point in fretting uselessly.'

James raised his eyebrows. 'You can say that, after all we've been told about this part of the world?'

'You're about to remind me how dangerous and unpredictable it is. I am only too well aware of that, just as I know that I've been in many worse places.'

The door opened and the aide, bowing, beckoned for them to follow him. They walked across the hallway, up a wide stone staircase which ran round the outside of the building. He stopped and rapped at a studded door set in the inner wall, opening it without waiting for a response. Up another few steps and they were shown into a large room at the top of the fort. It had a panoramic view of the harbour, and the lower parts of the city, from any number of narrow windows, plus several brass telescopes mounted on tripods with which Admiral Doria could survey his domain. He was obviously waiting for them, standing with his hands behind his back, and an enigmatic smile on his dark cratered face.

'Signori,' he booked, gesturing expansively, 'please come in. Can I offer you some refreshments?' Doria indicated a sideboard covered in fruits, cheeses, and cuts of meat. Bottles of wine, wrapped in damp cloths to keep them cool, beckoned invitingly. 'I am just about to dine myself, if you'd care to join me.'

'Delighted,' said Harry, walking past him. He made his way round a large oak table to one of the windows, bending down to look through the brass telescope which stood in the opening. It was trained on the *Swiftsure*.

Doria smiled at James, still by the doorway. The smile was not returned. 'It must seem like you've been placed under restraint. I did send to invite you while you were still aboard the frigate, but of course, by the time these fools had got the barge out you had loaded and put off.'

Harry, standing upright, indicated Doria's aide, standing silently beside James, waiting for instructions. 'This fellow didn't quite manage to make it sound like an invitation.'

Doria frowned, snapped his head in an impatient gesture to indicate that the young man should leave. The smile reappeared as his head disappeared down the steps and the door closed behind him.

'I fear I must take the blame. My nephew's terribly afraid of my displeasure. Certainly more than he is fond of proper manners. But it is an invitation. You are here as my guest. And if you do not believe me, feel free to go.' Doria made a gesture with his hand towards the exit.

'And leave all this?' Harry walked towards the sideboard. Doria beamed, first at Harry, then at James, and indicated with a broad sweep of both his arms that they should help themselves.

'My servant?' asked Harry.

'They will see to him, never fear.'

Harry, filling his plate, had an image of Pender, trying to eat with one hand, for he was sure that the other would remain round their strongbox. Doria, a burgeoning plate of food in his hand, led the way to the huge oak table. Having seated his guests, he poured the wine himself, before sitting down to eat.

Both Harry and James set to with a will. Doria watched them, making small talk and picking at his own plate, though he was more liberal with the wine, quaffing it down in great gulps, and encouraging the Ludlows to do likewise. He talked about the war and its effect on trade. How the increase in activity added to his workload. If he was waiting for his guests to quiz him about their presence at his table, he waited in vain. While polite in their responses, neither volunteered any statement or asked any questions. They merely ate their food, declined as much wine as they consumed, and waited. Doria finally ran out of patience, wiped his mouth with a large napkin, and leaning forward addressed Harry.

'I invited you here because I am anxious to assist you. Plus, of course I have my responsibilities. You are aware that there is a tariff to pay for the importation of gold into the Republic?'

'I was not aware of that,' said Harry quickly.

'It is a recent ordinance.'

'How recent?' asked James.

'Since the upheavals of eighty-nine. The French are fond of gold.

Naturally, with the trouble in the country, they seek somewhere safe to stow it. Somewhere safe, but not too distant.'

'Does a tariff not discourage them?'

Doria gave an elaborate shrug. 'They are not overburdened with choice, Signor. So it is, alas, the case. Besides, gold fetches a high price in this part of the world.'

'There are places where it fetches more.'

'Distance, Signor Ludlow, compounds the danger of complete loss. Only citizens of Genoa may import gold without a duty. You are, I believe, carrying a quantity of gold?'

It would be useless to deny it. Harry nodded. 'It is no great quantity.' Doria gave Harry the kind of smile that implied that he knew better.

Barnes must have told him everything, and probably exaggerated to boot.

'You said you wish to assist us,' said James quietly, looking at the Admiral through an upheld crystal glass full of white wine.

Doria looked from one to the other, frowning slightly at the look on Harry's face. Also he had the air of a man unsure of whom he should deal with, a man hoping that one or the other of his guests would speak so that he would know. Finally he put both his hands on the table and leant back to address them both. 'If I may presume a little, I would like to ask, what are your intentions?'

'That is still in the balance,' replied Harry testily.

James followed up swiftly, his words quite as sharp as his brothers. 'It may very well turn on the outcome of this conversation.'

The Admiral ignored the implications of that remark, and the unsmiling directness with which it was made. 'I mean for today, Signor Ludlow, not for the future.'

Now all three sat silently, Doria content to let them weigh up the relative merits of providing an answer. Finally Harry, having elicited a nod from his brother, spoke. 'To find a bank and deposit my funds, and if the price of gold is high enough, sell it.'

Doria face broke into a smile, and he tapped the ends of his fingers on the table. 'I thought so. And that is where I can assist you. It so happens that I am fortunate to have connections with certain business interests in the town, people whom I know will give you a good deal of interest on your funds.'

'No doubt they are traders in gold,' said James coldly.

Doria's smile spread, and his eyes twinkled. 'We are a trading nation, Signor, possessing little in the way of land and population. Therefore we must do our best in banking to supplement what we make with our ships. Mind you, I often wonder whether we aid our cause by taxing the importation of gold so heavily.'

James gave him a sardonic look. 'Only for foreigners.'

'Just the point I was coming to. For I think I can see a way to avoid such duty, but that would of course mean your taking my advice on where to deposit your funds.'

Again a long silence, but the game had to be played. He would not speak first now. He waited for one of the Ludlow brothers to move things forward.

'You mentioned some connections that you have?' asked Harry.

'Yes. With the trading house of Guistiani, who, I might add, also act as my personal bankers.'

Harry looked at James as he continued. 'As we came ashore last night, Admiral, we were attacked by a gang of men, whom I presume were intent on robbery. That is, after they'd killed us.'

Doria showed no trace of surprise or embarrassment. He didn't even blink as Harry stared hard at him. 'All the more reason to accept my protection. The city teems with thieves.'

Harry reckoned that he was sitting in the presence of one of the peers of the tribe. The man had not even pretended to be surprised at this information, nor did he enquire about the nature of the attack, where it took place, or ask for any description of those involved.

'It was wise of you to leave your things aboard ship last night. I remember remarking on it to Captain Barnes.' He smiled broadly at both of them, amused at their studied lack of movement. Then he threw his head back and laughed out loud.

'Suspicion is a natural emotion. So I will not pretend to be offended by the drift of your thoughts.'

'Caused by your complete lack of curiosity, Admiral,' said James.

'Ah! I see. I am to throw up my hands and imply that I am shocked that such a thing could occur. Ask, perhaps, for a description of your assailants.' Doria laughed again, before leaning forward again and looking intently at Harry. 'I see I'm reading your mind, Signor Ludlow.'

Harry returned the stare. 'Most accurately, Admiral.'

No smile now. Harry and Doria's eyes were locked together. 'I think any complaint should be levelled against Captain Barnes. He should never have let you go ashore, after dark, in the first place. Quite apart from the presence of thieves and vagabonds in the city, there is a well-armed French sloop in the harbour. The city teems with agents and sympathizers of the French government. You come ashore, quite obviously not common sailors, I assume in darkness, and you are surprised that you are attacked.'

He smiled again, then the smile suddenly disappeared, to be replaced by a grim look that embraced them both. 'Rest assured, gentlemen, that if I had wanted to rob you, I would have first ensured you were carrying something that made my efforts worthwhile.' The eyes were hard now, as was the tone of his voice. 'Then I would have made quite sure that no trace of you was ever found.'

Again suddenly, his face was lit up by that wolfish smile, which left you doubting if he was serious. Harry wondered what the price would be of telling this man to go to hell. Admiral Stefano Doria belonged to one of the greatest families of the powerful local aristocracy. As Harry had remarked, he bore a famous name. One of his ancestors, Andrea Doria, had been the greatest sailor of his age. If you looked out of the right embrasure you could scarcely miss the Palazzo Doria, with its spacious formal gardens running from the house down to a *loggia* that abutted the wharves where family-owned ships could tie up. To hold his present rank, and to have the control of the excise in the most rapacious port in the Mediterranean, argued a powerful man. Too powerful to insult.

'I assume that your assistance will benefit us in some way?' he asked gently.

'But, of course. It is a poor bargain that only benefits one party.' As Doria spoke, each point was emphasized by a gesture of his hands, in a very Italian way. 'Let us say you were to transfer your gold to my possession. Only nominally, of course. Then it would no longer be subject to an import tax, which would result in a saving of twenty per cent. I could then give you some of my own funds to cover the value.'

'That would be after we have established the value,' said Harry.

'Of course. Naturally I would have to charge you for the service I'm providing. I cannot be out of pocket, you understand, much as

I wish to assist a fellow sailor. But my charges would be somewhat less than those of the state. Say half of the normal duty. And, taking into consideration the events of last night, it would then be in order for me to escort such funds to a place of safety.'

Harry could barely hide the look of distrust on his face as he spoke. 'Which would be your personal bankers.'

'Quite.'

James cut in. He could see that Harry was about to let his temper get the better of him. 'So we would save ten per cent of the value.'

Doria nodded, but he could not fail to be aware that Harry was less than pleased. He looked at the older of the two, with an eyebrow raised, inviting whatever Harry was thinking to be openly said.

'May I ask a question?'

That surprised Doria, who was expecting an insult. 'Of course.'

'Who issues permission for foreign privateers to sail from Genoa?'

'The Council of State, Signor.'

Harry ignored the look his brother gave him. 'Would you be a member of that?'

'Not personally. But I have been known to advise them.'

Harry's face remained blank as he spoke. 'Then it would seem to be politic to do business with you, Admiral.'

Doria threw his arms wide again. 'Not with me, Captain Ludlow. With my bankers. It ill becomes men of our stamp to descend to mere trade. More wine?'

The coach, with four matching white horses, was drawn up outside the land gate to the customs house. Pender was already on the box, and he looked stoically ahead as Harry and James approached the conveyance. James climbed straight aboard. As Doria appeared through the gate so did his guards, and with a precision born of long habit they took up position in front and behind. Harry observed that their weapons were in no way ceremonial. No pikes or muskets, but rather short swords, clubs, and pistols. Last into the coach, he joined his brother, sitting opposite their 'host'.

'I am informed that permission to sail from this port is somewhat restricted.'

The smile deepened and he fixed Harry with a cunning look. 'That would rather depend, Signor, on who you ask and who you are.'

'But is it regulated?'

'Of course. But in the nature of things, such regulation must be to everyone's advantage.'

'The Republic's advantage being paramount?' said James, with an innocent air.

Doria's eyes twinkled, belying the attempted sincerity in his voice. Again his arms waved as he spoke, emphasizing the point with a grandiose gesture. 'How could it be any other way?'

Harry wondered. Doria would promise them the world to get his share of their gold. It could be that Bartholomew had gained his through providing a hefty bribe to whoever was in charge. But that did not explain his ability to avoid the customs duties.

'You would also, in your position, be aware if there were any likely craft available for purchase?' asked Harry. Doria nodded, but volunteered nothing. The coach turned, taking one of the few routes off the quayside wide enough to accommodate its width.

James posed the next question, deciding to indulge in a little mischief by beating Harry to the next subject. 'Tell me, Admiral, who dealt with the matter of Captain Howlett's murder?'

Harry stiffened, and Doria seemed unnaturally still. He didn't reply for quite a time, just staring at James, who'd turned to gaze out of the coach window, craning his neck in an attempt to see the tops of the buildings that crowded in on either side.

Doria spoke eventually. 'Since it happened in the area of the port, it fell to me to deal with it.'

'A terrible business,' said James languidly, without turning his head.

A small shrug. 'Such things happen in all ports.'

James finally turned from the coach window, his voice steady and his look calm. 'Rather more elaborate than normal, wouldn't you say? Or is it the habit here to string up your victims?'

Harry sat silently, aware that his brother, by his manner, was baiting their host. But he was asking the questions he'd intended to ask himself.

'Was the gentleman a particular friend?'

'No,' said James, 'I believe my brother met him some years back.'

'I wondered at your interest,' said Doria, almost implying that this line of questioning showed a want of manners.

That really set James alight. His voice became icy. 'I would like to bring to your notice, once more, that we were very nearly killed last night. And since that took place in the confines of the port, I find your lack of interest remarkable.'

Doria's skin was too dark to show a blush, but the narrowing of the lips told the Ludlows just as much. He tried to assume a blasé air, but it didn't come off. 'I had intended to enquire further, after we'd transacted our business.'

'Would it surprise you, Admiral, if I said we'd rather you did it before?' The accusation of greed before duty hung in the air, no less potent for remaining unspoken.

Doria obliged them, albeit reluctantly, asking questions, and nodding sagely at their answers. But Harry knew his mind was elsewhere. He was tense and his hand hovered near his sword as the coach made its way, with some difficulty, through the crowded narrow streets, with much shoving and shouting from their escorts before emerging into the more spacious boulevards of the city proper. The buildings now looked reasonably new, with fine stone fronts and carved lintels over the huge windows. But they were mixed in with ancient structures. They passed an imposing church, twin-spired with a central dome, in walls made up of black and white marble in horizontal stripes. It stood at the apex of a crowded piazza, its roof towering above them. Once past this landmark, Doria lost his tense look, his shoulders visibly relaxing.

He turned back to James. 'All in black, you say?'

James nodded, making his next point quickly. 'It strikes me as curious that they didn't exchange a single word.'

Doria just looked at him, waiting for him to provide the answer.

'It's as though speaking would have given them away.'

'How so?'

'What if they'd spoken in French, Admiral?' asked Harry, finally joining in. 'French may be common among well-educated citizens of Genoa, such as yourself, but it is hardly the language of local footpads.'

'I see that you share your compatriots' obsession with that French sloop.'

'Captain Howlett's death was meant as a warning, Admiral. I can think of no one else who would gain from issuing one. Can you?'

'I can, and I have already made my conclusions known to your Admiral.'

'Taken in conjunction with the attack on us last night . . .'

'Signori! Provide me with evidence of a connection, and perhaps I will take your suspicions more seriously.'

'Until then?' asked James.

'I will institute some enquiries. A dozen black-clad villains cannot run around such a crowded city without attracting some notice.'

There was little passion in those words. The Ludlows were left wondering how energetic he would be. But being able to say nothing that would force him to action they remained silent.

Again the tenements pressed closely on each side, until they once more emerged into an area of more imposing buildings. Each one occupied an entire block and Doria, noticing James' interest, named the owners as they rattled over the cobblestones. All the great names of the Genoese republic seemed to be represented in these few thoroughfares. Doria reeled them off, preceding each name with the word *Palazzo*, and pointing to the coats of arms that adorned the cap of each portico. Several Spinola palaces, Grimaldi, Fieschi, Visconti, Lecari, Gambaro, Pallavacino, and a modest nod to a palace of the extended Doria tribe.

'They are certainly imposing enough,' said James, his head bobbing from one side window to the other. 'Yet I wonder that the magnates of Genoa wish to construct their houses in such close proximity?'

Doria smiled, but ventured no answer.

James turned to Harry. 'I can envisage only two reasons. Either a fear of the mob, or the wish to outdo each other.'

'Since all the ground-floor windows are heavily barred, and those above are shuttered, I would choose the former,' replied Harry.

CHAPTER ELEVEN

The coach shuddered to a stop outside another substantial building. James put his head out of the coach window again, and saw their guards take up defensive positions on either side of the great oak doors. The building was older, more weathered than the others, with white and black horizontal stripes in the same pattern as the large church they'd passed. Doria informed James how this denoted wealth since, in times past, only the important families of the Republic were permitted to decorate their residences in such way.

The lack of windows on the ground floor made it look very forbidding. Indeed, with the size and thickness of the gates, and the narrowness of the windows above them, the place looked more like a fortress than a palace, harking back to an earlier age when open warfare was common in the streets of the Italian city states. Pitched battles were now a thing of the past, but the knife in the back, or the ambush of a poorly armed party, was still commonplace.

The oak door swung open and they pulled into a shaded courtyard with a fountain in the centre surrounded by trees. Liveried servants hurried to open the door and steps were produced. Other servants, under instructions from the coachman, and under the watchful eye of Admiral Doria, unloaded Harry's strongbox and carried it inside. Harry indicated silently that Pender should stay with the remainder of their possessions. The sudden laugh from a corner of the courtyard made him look towards the sound. A party of French marines lounged there, hats off, muskets leaning against the wall, taking their ease. Harry stared at them, trying to determine whether their presence represented a threat. If it did he was powerless to do much about it. He followed his brother inside.

James stood with his head back, looking around the vaulted hallway, lit, even in daylight, by huge chandeliers and guttering candles in sconces around the bare stone walls. Tall desks lined one side of the area, each one with a clerk busy at his labour, quill pen in hand. Messengers brought slips of paper from various rooms that surrounded this central area, all transactions being carried out in a funereal hush of rustling parchment and whispered instructions.

Admiral Doria's heavy footsteps echoing off the bare stone walls caused even the most conscientious of the clerks to look up from their labours. He made straight across the hallway and up the broad staircase, beckoning for Harry and James to follow. James noticed that the eyes of each clerk dwelt not on the Admiral, but on the chest being carried between the two servants following on behind, as though they were attempting to penetrate the stout wood of the brass-bound box and discover the value of the contents inside.

Doria, followed by the brothers, bounded swiftly up the stairs and on reaching the first floor, without a knock or any form of announcement, flung open the double doors to a set of elegantly furnished rooms. The contrast with the hall and stairway could not have been more marked. The walls and ceilings were a blaze of colour, with frescos edged by ornate gilded cornices. Nymphs danced, gods played and beasts gambolled, all overseen by a benign deity.

Doria didn't hesitate. He made his way across the carpeted room to another set of matching doors at the other end. These too were flung open and a buzz of conversation flowed out. Harry and James followed him as far as the doorway, stopping there to observe the scene that greeted them. They looked in upon yet another sumptuously appointed and decorated apartment. Well-dressed men, bewigged, in coats of every colour of silk, stood around in groups, while others sat on ornate couches engaged in earnest conversation. A fat, well-fed prelate, robed in the red of a cardinal of the Roman Church, stood surrounded by acolytes, his huge stomach ringed by a jewelled belt. All heads turned in Doria's direction and nods were exchanged as he crossed to the other side of the room, to yet another set of double doors. Harry and James were left standing in the second doorway, unsure what to do. The noise of conversation died as the occupants of the salon turned their attention to these strangers.

There was no welcome in the looks, neither was there malice. Just undisguised curiosity. No one made any attempt to welcome them. James, more sure in such surroundings than his brother, bowed slightly, and with a touch of Harry's arm led the way into the throng. Those nearest them moved away, as if fearing physical contact. This movement revealed one other person obviously not part of this society. He stood alone and still, with his hands clasped behind his tricolour sash, the gaunt grey face expressionless. Harry stared at him, once more struck by the natural authority of the man. Even being politely ignored by those around him, he dominated his immediate area. Seeing the stare, he favoured Harry with a slight bow and a chilling smile.

A servant sidled up to them carrying a tray bearing coffee and several varieties of sweetmeats. The babble of conversation resumed as the people in the room turned their attention back to their own business. Another servant, a rouged fellow in an old-fashioned wig, senior to the others by the cut of his livery, eased himself through the groups, bowed low, and beckoned for them to follow. Again the conversation faltered as they were led to the other set of doors, which opened to admit them. Doria stood in the inner sanctum by a large ornate fireplace. Tall windows overlooking the courtyard filled the room with light. Two men in plain black coats rose from behind matching Louis Quinze desks as they were shown in, and advanced to be introduced.

'The brothers Guistiani, Signori,' boomed Doria, addressing the Ludlows. Then he turned to the two men, and in a quieter tone, reversed the introduction. 'I bring these gentlemen to you on a personal recommendation. Please treat them as though you were transacting business for me.'

The words were certainly impressive, but somehow the delivery lacked conviction, as though in the presence of these two Doria was in some way diminished. The Admiral gave them a slight bow, then left the room.

'The Admiral's introduction was somewhat brief,' said the taller of the two Guistiani brothers, he too bowing slightly. 'Allow me a proper introduction. I am Giacomo Guistiani, and this is my brother Alfredo.'

The shorter one bowed also, but there was no servility in either of these acts of courtesy. Harry spoke for them both, since James seemed more intent on the paintings that lined the office walls. 'Harry and James Ludlow.'

'Admiral Doria informs us that you require our services.'

Harry was looking around the room too, but not at the walls. He was seeking the strongbox, which was nowhere to be seen. A slight frown crossed his face. James, having finished his inspection, turned to look at his brother, seemingly unaware of the nature of his curiosity. Harry pulled an oilskin pouch from the inside of his coat.

'I have here some letters of credit from my bankers in London.'

The elder of the Guistiani brothers raised his eyebrows, as if to question the fact that Admiral Doria was unaware of this addition to their available funds.

'Splendid.' Alfredo Guistiani was more businesslike than his elder brother, immediately holding out his hand to take the pouch. He turned away from the Ludlows to examine the contents. Simultaneously a side door opened and an elderly clerk, with the grey skin of a man who saw little sunlight, sidled up to the older brother, handing him a slip of paper. Giacomo glanced at it, and waved the clerk away, raising his head to smile at Harry as the man retreated through the side door. He reached behind him to his desk and picked up another slip of paper, passing it to Harry.

'The Admiral informs me that he is indebted to you for this sum, which, for convenience, we have calculated at the latest price we have from London.'

Harry looked closely at the paper, frowned, but said nothing. Then he looked at it again and the frown deepened and a flash of anger crossed his face. He passed the slip of paper to James, who, in turn, examined it. He too frowned as soon as he saw that the Admiral had, by using imaginative accounting related to the differing value of both bullion and the currencies, substantially increased the percentage of his gain. Harry indicated the papers that Alfredo Guistiani was still studying.

'I can appreciate currency fluctuations on letters of credit, Signor Guistiani. That is in the nature of things, and accepted by all as matter of some risk. But that strongbox contained gold, and the price of that, so close to a zone of conflict, tends to be high. It is also well known that gold has less value in England than it does on the entire continent of Europe. To set it at the English rate is to devalue it.'

Giacomo's face showed not the slightest flicker of reaction at the implications of what Harry was saying.

'It would also be true to say that this is not the only banking concern in the Republic,' added James, still frowning at the paper in his hand.

'That is true, of course. But I would be disappointed if a good friend like Admiral Doria were to deposit his funds elsewhere.'

The banker emphasized the word 'his', and the inference of that was as plain as a pikestaff. You have come to some arrangement with the Admiral. It's his money we've deposited. If you want to dispute the sum he has given you, take it up with him.

The smaller Guistiani, who had finished perusing Harry's letters of credit, quickly grabbed a pen and wrote on yet another slip of paper. Then he intervened, passing the paper to his brother. Giacomo looked at it, a slight flicker of his eyebrow showing that he was impressed. Had Harry not been angry, perhaps he would have admired the smooth way that Giacomo Guistiani executed a hundred-and-eighty degree turn.

'It was, of course a hurried affair. And once we have had it checked, the figure in your hand could well be revised.'

'Upwards,' said Harry coldly.

'As you so rightly point out, Signor Ludlow, gold, in times of trouble, tends to increase in value. And we do live in troubled times.'

Giacomo Guistiani smiled, and indicated that the Ludlow brothers should be seated. James declined, taking the opportunity to get a closer look at a large painting which dominated the wall above the mantelpiece. It was of Venice, Genoa's great commercial rival. James peered closely, looking not just at the content, but at the brushwork and colouring.

'Canaletto?' he said, without turning round.

'Security,' said Alfredo dismissively. 'For a loan to the Pope.'

Giacomo was looking at James' back. 'These funds, gentlemen. Am I to understand that they are for the purchase of works of art?'

James shot a glance at Harry before speaking, eyebrows raised.

His brother nodded, smiling. 'A proportion of the funds could be used for that purpose.'

'Ah. Admiral Doria mentioned that you wish to purchase a ship.'

Giacomo's brow creased, leaving no doubt that he regarded such an act as unwise. 'The harbour is full of such vessels, and one wonders if there is really enough profit to sustain them all, let alone the hands to crew them. I believe the situation in Livorno is even worse. In terms of investments, we could offer ventures with a higher potential return. For instance, we have one gentleman waiting to see us who needs to dispose of a cargo of alum. Given that his need for funds is acute, and the shipment is due at any time, it would seem a better use for part of these funds than privateering.'

'Or art?' asked James, finally sitting down.

'Who knows, Signor, with war in the offing, if works of art are a good investment,' said Alfredo mournfully.

'I don't see them in financial terms,' said James.

'Alas, we are bankers. Aesthetic values are a luxury we can ill afford.'

'Then all these works of art are pledges?'

Giacomo answered. 'No, Signor. Some of them are indeed ours.'

'So you do collect?'

'Of course. But some of those you see here have come by default. While they afford great pleasure, the method of their acquisition does not.'

James favoured them both with a slim smile. 'I imagine that my brother has a similar attitude to investments in cargoes of alum. But if you feel that you're unable to assist . . .'

'Please, Signor Ludlow,' said the older Guistiani, hand held high to stop James. 'It is no part of our duties to direct our clients. If you wish to purchase a painting, or a sculpture, so be it. We will happily do all in our power to introduce you to those who have artefacts to sell. As for a ship, then there is also someone in the next room who has a ship available.'

Harry's attention had wandered at all this talk of art. But the mention of a ship brought him back into the conversation. 'It would have to be the right sort of craft.'

'I think I can guarantee that. The price, however, will be high, since it has just come out of the dockyard after an extensive refit.'

'And commissions?' asked Harry, his caution doubled by the previous chicanery with the gold.

'They fall upon the vendor,' said Alfredo. 'The ship would seem perfect for the task you have in mind, though I cannot say that encouraging someone to prey on cargo vessels is something I would normally engage in.'

'Rest assured, Signor Guistiani, the ships of Genoa will be entirely safe.'

'Would that all your fellow countrymen showed equal restraint,' said Giacomo sourly.

Harry wondered if he was referring to Bartholomew. Was that how they made their money, preying on Genoese ships, like a parasite on a host body? He would ask, perhaps, when he knew this man better.

'I know of fellow countrymen of mine who would rather you didn't trade with their enemies.'

Giacomo smiled. 'Enemies, Signor? The only enemies we have are usury and poverty.'

There was an unmistakable trace of eagerness in Harry's tone as he spoke again. 'I would like to meet this shipowner.'

'Then please come this way,' said Giacomo.

Alfredo Guistiani returned to his desk, content to leave his brother to carry out the task while he got on with the business of running the various family interests. Again all the heads turned as the doors opened, but this time, instead of patent uninterest, the crowd of people looked towards the Ludlows eagerly, their status obviously enhanced by the presence of one of the banking brothers. Giacomo led them through the crowd, ignoring the keen, and occasionally desperate, looks of most of those he passed. He paused quite deliberately by the tall Frenchman, forcing Harry and James to stop.

'Mr Ludlow,' said Giacomo. 'Allow me to name Monsieur Tilly, the French chargé d'affaires to the Republic of Genoa.'

The man bowed slightly as Guistiani introduced them. Harry was struck by the lack of expression, even in the man's eyes. Yet he had the feeling that he was looking at someone who harboured a great deal of passion, but took great care to keep it in check. The fat cardinal was close by, yet it was this black-clad figure who looked more like a priest. Harry bowed in return and they passed on.

'A neat way to underscore the utter neutrality of a man of commerce,' said James quietly.

'No wonder Hood is worried about this place,' replied Harry, earning a frown from his brother.

A knot of gaudily dressed men, gathered round a chaise, parted to let them through, and Harry was startled to see a very beautiful girl, who could not have yet reached full maturity, sitting on the couch. Surprised, for this was definitely a salon for gentlemen only. A place of business, not society. And surely no place for such an innocent-looking creature.

Giacomo stopped before her, and she smiled engagingly as he bowed over her raised hand. But it was the man sitting next to her that he addressed. A small man, somewhat wizened, though not by age. His skin seemed translucent, stretched tight over prominent cheekbones and a small sharp nose, and he leant forward, both bony hands on his cane, staring straight ahead, as Giacomo Guistiani introduced them.

'Gentlemen, allow me to name the Count Alfonso di Toraglia and his wife,' he said, turning back to Harry and James, who were both staring with open admiration at the young girl. Of medium height, she was slim and graceful. Her jet-black hair was piled high on top of her head in a mass of curls, fixed by a flashing jewelled clasp in the manner that had become fashionable in Paris, after the wildest excesses of the puritan revolution had been succeeded by the more corrupt and worldly regime of the Directory. Likewise her gown, cut low and loosely worn, yet made of a material designed to enhance the appearance of a woman's natural figure.

Her skin was pale and utterly unblemished, and she had used only the lightest dusting of powder. Full lips, with a slight, ingenuous smile showing even teeth, and huge black eyes. She was returning their fixed look with one of deep curiosity. They started guiltily, in unison, at such a breach of manners, which would have been rude if the girl was this man's daughter, but unforgivable to his wife. But the Count seemed oblivious of the attention being paid to her. It was only when he failed to look at them as they mumbled their greetings that both brothers realized the Count was blind.

'Forgive me if I don't stand up,' he said. His voice was deep and rasping, yet warm and friendly. 'But I cannot do so without assistance, and it would be too much to put my friends to such trouble.'

'If you gentlemen would forgive us,' said Giacomo to those friends, 'we have some business to discuss.'

With murmured agreement the men who had been crowded round the couple drifted away. Servants appeared with three chairs, and they placed a small table bearing refreshments between them and the chaise. With the chairs on one side of the circle, and that chaise on the other, they had created an island in the middle of the room, an island the others present were careful to respect. No one came within ten feet of them.

'Now, Alfonso. These two gentlemen wish to discuss with you the purchase of that useless hulk of a barque you have sitting idly in the harbour.'

The Count smiled. It was a warm expression for all that it was thin and weak. The Countess laughed, flashing her teeth and her eyes, with the candlelight from the overhead chandeliers catching the sparkle from the jewellery in her hair. Underneath the fine blue silk of the dress her breasts moved, and Harry looked quickly at his brother to avoid staring, only to find himself looking right into his eyes. James made a slight tutting sound to convey his disapproval, before turning to examine the Countess himself.

'Permit me to say, Countess, that I will find it impossible to conduct any business,' he said. 'Why, I am quite dazzled by your beauty.'

The girl dropped her head, an attractive blush colouring her cheeks. Everyone else's expression became fixed. The Count's smile, now devoid of warmth, looked ghoulish. Harry did not know what to say. James could not be unaware that he had exceeded the bounds of good manners. But his brother lost none of his urbanity as he continued.

'I say that, madam, as an artist, a modest painter of the human form, and I would welcome the opportunity to become well enough acquainted with you, and your husband, to seek permission to execute a portrait. I hope that my expression of such admiration, which is nothing but the plain truth, causes no offence. It is in the nature of an artist to enthuse openly when he encounters perfection.'

Harry spoke quickly. 'My brother would be too modest to say that, in England, he is quite highly regarded.'

The fixed expressions had already relaxed, and the Countess was laughing. Harry's attempt to help was superfluous. James had deftly turned his apparent gaffe into an acceptable compliment. Harry felt a slight pang of jealousy. Was it because his brother could, so easily, manage such a verbal trick, something he could never achieve? Or was it because he realized that James would, by exploiting his artistic talents, get close to this girl?

The Count reached out at the sound of her laughter, waving his hand uncertainly until his young wife took it. He squeezed affectionately, a gesture that the girl readily responded to.

Her low voice, warm and enchanting when she spoke, did nothing to diminish her. 'What am I to say to such a raft of compliments, Signor?'

'Only that they are inadequate, madam,' said James.

The Count squeezed his wife's hand again, and sought to bring the conversation back on to the original subject. 'Giacomo thinks you know nothing of ships, my love, but he's very wrong.'

Guistiani bowed his head, smiling. The Countess looked first at him, then at Harry. She laughed again, and Harry realized that he had a sort of inane grin on his face.

The fan in her hand shot open and she held it up, as if to share a secret with the Count, but her words were clearly audible. 'No he doesn't, Alfonso. He's just teasing.'

James spoke, not seeking to disguise the tone of heightened amazement in his voice. 'You combine naval architecture with such beauty, madam. Truly, this is marvellous, and surely most uncommon.'

'She is my eyes, gentlemen,' said the Count. He was looking at a point between the Ludlows. 'Were it not for my dear Leila, I should be a pauper.' He lifted his stick and pointed it into thin air. 'People like Giacomo here would fleece me . . .'

'Nonsense, Alfonso,' said the banker.

The Count wasn't really smiling as he continued, though the words had a humorous ring. 'Never trust a banker, gentlemen, for they never fail as regularly as their clients.'

'That, Alfonso, is because they rarely gamble. Would that all our customers showed such probity.'

The Countess addressed James directly, referring to his earlier question. 'I know the value of ships, Signor. I have no need of anything else.'

The Count had not finished his attack on the banking fraternity. 'You need to have a care when dealing with the house of Guistiani.'

'Come, Alfonso. Giacomo is very patient with me. He goes to no end of trouble to explain things.'

'Madam,' said James gallantly. 'The patience of Job would be as nothing to the attention you deserve.'

James's sally, and the enthusiasm of his delivery, was perhaps a shade too gallant on such short acquaintance. It took the smile off the Count's face again, but it had his wife hurriedly putting the fan over her mouth to hide a smile. Because of that, or merely because they were now talking business, there was none of the jovial, joking tone of earlier when the Count spoke. 'Am I to understand that you wish to purchase the *Principessa*?'

Harry sat forward, glad to get back into the conversation. 'We have yet to see the ship, Count. It's too early to say that we wish to purchase her.'

'Oh, she is a fine ship, sir,' said the Countess. 'Dry and weatherly is the expression I have heard my husband use. And she is newly out of the dock with her bottom recoppered and cleaned. She will show a clean pair of heels to any other barque in the Ligurian Sea.'

The girl spoke with conviction, but her words had the air of a rehearsed recitation.

'If what you say is true, Countess, then the only obstacle to a bargain would be the price.'

Her husband cut in. 'We mustn't discuss that till you've looked it over.' He turned his head half towards his wife. 'Well, my dear. What do you think? Are these *Inglese* people we could do business with?'

She looked from Harry to James and back again, her beautiful face carrying an expression of mock doubt. Then, in a rather theatrical way, her face cleared, and she smiled. 'I would say so, Alfonso. Most assuredly.'

'Then Signor Ludlow, you have my permission to look over the ship.'

'I would, of course, wish to take her to sea, sir.'

'Very wise,' said the Count with a thin smile. 'Though I cannot furnish you with a crew.'

'I can muster a crew for a day's sailing.'

'You have a crew available?'

Harry spoke with some hesitation. 'Not yet.'

Toraglia's nose rose slightly and his expression seemed to show that he'd misread the reasons for Harry's delayed response. 'Never fear, Signor Ludlow. The words my wife used to describe the *Principessa* are nothing less than the truth. Once you've examined her you will be impatient to take her to sea. Send to me when you do and I'll arrange for someone to go out with you. Guistiani here will direct you to my house, which is outside the old city walls.'

'And if we decide to proceed with the purchase,' said Harry, glancing at the banker sitting beside him.

It was now Toraglia's turn to hesitate. When he did answer his voice was listless. 'Then you may come back to my house to discuss the terms. And now, Giacomo, be so kind as to call my chair. I grow weary.'

They all stood and exchanged farewells. Then the Countess led her husband out of the room.

James addressed Guistiani. 'Did my brother say something to upset him?'

There was a slight crack in the banker's voice as he replied. 'There was a time when Count di Toraglia owned a fleet. But this one was special. It was his first ship, the one he started with as a young man. To look at him now, you would not credit the man he was two years ago.'

The Ludlow brothers spent half an hour discussing the methods by which they could deposit and withdraw their funds. Giacomo Guistiani walked beside James as he escorted them out of the building, explaining the provenance of the frescos in the outer apartment.

'The artist was Perin del Vaga.'

'It is the first work of his I've ever seen,' said James, peering closely and touching the colourful surface lightly with his fingertips. 'Painted in the sixteenth century, was it not?'

Guistiani nodded as James continued. 'I am not overly familiar with Genoese artists.'

'Del Vaga was a Florentine.'

James smiled knowingly. 'A contemporary of Michelangelo.'

'There are further examples of his art at the Doria Palace at Fassalo. Indeed, many fine painters and sculptors have helped to decorate our *pallazzos*. If you are in the market to buy, and you're interested in local artists, they also have some interesting sculptures by the Schiaffinos, father and son, which I believe are for sale. If you wish I can arrange a visit.'

'I long to see some works by Magnasco. He was a native of Genoa, was he not?'

'Indeed. But there are no great collections. His works tend to be scattered, but I'm sure we can arrange some examples for you to view.'

'I'm always happy to view.'

Guistiani laughed. 'Then you are in for a busy time, Signor Ludlow. Genoa does not bow the knee to any other state where art is concerned.'

Harry had listened to these exchanges, consumed with impatience at all this talk of art and artists, while his whole being was taken up with his own cares. 'Let us look at ships first, for all love.'

James turned and favoured his brother with a wicked grin.

'Don't feel excluded, Harry. The Hollander Cornelius de Wael lived here for fifty years. He was contemporary to Rubens and much praised for his seascapes. There must be some fine examples of his marine works about. You, especially, will esteem him. He was excellent at painting battles.'

Harry refused to respond to this teasing remark. It was Giacomo Guistiani who spoke. 'That furnishes me with a thought. It would perhaps be an idea to commission a painting of the *Principessa* for Count Toraglia before it is sold. Who knows, with God's help, he may recover his sight.'

'You've stated more than once that he's particularly attached to it,' said James, fixing the banker with a quizzical look.

Guistiani smiled, immediately picking up the drift of the remark.

'It adds to the price, yes. But the Count wasn't exaggerating. It is the most excellent vessel. There's not a sailor in Genoa who would not confirm that.'

'How long has it been for sale?' asked Harry as they made their way down the stone staircase.

'He has pondered on it for at least a month. The Count informed me that he'd finally decided to sell it this very morning. Not that he was pleased at the prospect.'

'I felt that,' said Harry, who understood how a man could come to love a ship.

Guistiani shook his head sadly. 'What choice does he have? He is a very sick man. I believe he delayed in the hope of a recovery.'

'What ails him?' asked James.

The banker, walking across the vaulted hallway, glanced at his busy clerks before replying. 'Who knows, for we are sadly ignorant where the human body is concerned.'

He turned to Harry, so much broader than James. 'Two years ago, he was a match for you, Signor. Then he was struck down. It is a wonder he didn't die. Only the strength of his constitution saved him. But he lost his sight, and over the last two years he has shrunk to the frail specimen you see today. If it wasn't for the devotion of his wife, he would not still be with us. She alone keeps him alive.'

They stopped in the courtyard. Pender still sat, guarding the rest of their possessions. Doria and the coach, along with Tilly's escort, had disappeared.

'It is unusual for a banker to say this, but I would beg you to be gentle with him. Do not try to drive too harsh a bargain, for you will cause him great distress.'

'A tragedy,' said James, shaking his head. 'Especially with such a young and beautiful wife.'

'And how she has stood by him. She is a prize, Signori. Half of Genoa is waiting for him to die to claim it.'

CHAPTER TWELVE

Guistiani provided them with two servants and a litter for their sea-chests, plus a pair of armed retainers as escort, overriding Harry's protests by pointing out that they were still carrying substantial sums of money. James showed more appreciation of the dangers.

'If Monsieur Tilly feels he needs a file of marines every time he steps ashore, Harry, we would do well to emulate him. I think a refusal would be stupid.'

Harry had to concede the point. They were soon enmeshed in the old city again, leaving behind the open vistas where the rich had built their palaces. The crowds seemed to increase in contrary proportion to the available space and they made their way down through the teeming city to the harbour. One of their escorts obviously spoke some English, for he grunted unhappily as James made a less than flattering reference to Admiral Doria.

'An extremely careful man,' said Harry.

James stopped suddenly, his attention seemingly taken by a gaudy fresco on the wall of a church. But his words demonstrated that his attention hadn't wandered. 'Not only careful, Harry, rapacious too!'

Harry suppressed his impatience, and didn't speak until they had begun to continue their journey. 'I admire him for one thing, James. His caution. He saw us, and fed us, alone, without even the presence of a servant. Mind, that could mean his position is more tenuous than he would like us to think.'

'Do I detect a desire to test that theory?'

'No.'

James stopped again, his head back looking at a carved portico. It showed a knight, plainly St George by the cross on his buckler, rescuing a maiden from a dragon. Given the narrow thoroughfare, it was difficult to distinguish all the detail. In Genoa, hemmed in by mountains and with land at a premium, people build upwards not outwards, making dark and dangerous caverns of the streets. James spotted the odd building, fresco, or heraldic carving that engaged his interest, and, despite the crowds, he would insist on stopping for a closer look. That this annoyed their porters and guards and engendered signs of increasing impatience in his brother bothered him not one jot. These frequent halts were interspersed with their continuing speculations about the character of Doria. 'It still feels like robbery. Do you think he will investigate our attackers?'

Harry shrugged. 'He might.'

James frowned. 'I don't trust him.'

Harry took his arm to hurry him along. 'I hope that I didn't imply that I do.'

As they walked downhill to the port, the powerful smells of the city seemed to come together in one all-pervasive odour. The stench was now such that they had difficulty in breathing. James, gagging slightly, whipped out his handkerchief and covered his nose. They came to a junction where the alleyway they were using traversed one of the mule tracks that led from the mountains which surrounded Genoa down to the harbour. Being barred from the interior by this range meant that normal carriage by ox carts was impossible. Even the most sturdy oxen could not manage the gradients and the magnates of Genoa, for all their private wealth, could not agree to combine in order to pay for a proper road over the mountains.

As a result nearly everything that came in and out of the port had to be transported on the back of thousands of mules. To avoid their filth filling the whole town, they were confined to special routes. Needless to say the sheer quantity of mules made such lanes extremely noxious. The stench, on a warm day, especially in the dry season, was almost too oppressive to bear. Great clouds of flying insects buzzed around and the smell diffused through the town, filling the narrow streets and alleyways. The only relief was provided by a substantial fall of rain which washed the filth down into the port. This in turn made conditions in the harbour unbearable, since with the Mediterranean's very small tidal rise and fall, it could be days before the sludge drifted out to sea. All ports had their odours, but Genoa was truly special.

They passed over the mule track at a point where it had been swept, furiously brushing aside the hundreds of flies that investigated them. The sweeper, sitting on a stool, oblivious of the insects that covered his body, accepted his small coin from their guard without acknowledgement. Even through the cloud of insects Harry noticed the number of people who took advantage of their crossing to rush through the gap on the strength of their payment.

They emerged on to the narrow causeway which fronted the great warehouses that lined the inside of the harbour. The wharves contained a bustling mass of bodies going in all directions and they had to force their way through the throng, around mules, donkeys, carts and people. When the signal gun went off from the port all eyes turned seawards.

'Keep yer hand on yer purse,' snapped Pender, who'd been silent since they left the banking house. 'This is a dip's paradise.'

The signal gun went off from the fort again, and looking up Harry saw a succession of flags rising on the staff set at the highest point of the tower. People on the quayside were craning forward, though there was little to see. But their action at least provided the Ludlows and their party with a clear route to the inn.

Few tables were occupied in Ma Thomas's and little curiosity was shown as they entered. The exception was Joe Crosby, who had been sitting in a far corner. As soon as he spied them he rushed over to talk, his voice carrying a hurt tone, like a child afraid of abandonment, which matched the wounded look on his face. 'Captain Ludlow, wherever have you been?'

'About my own business, Crosby.' The sharp note in Harry's voice did nothing to dent the man's servile demeanour. 'I'm looking for Captain Broadbridge.'

'Not here, yer honour. He's on some private business.' Crosby aimed a sly look at Harry. 'And that on such a hot day, Captain Ludlow.'

'I take it that you know what he's about, Crosby?' asked Harry, trying to contain his distaste as he slipped him a coin.

'Indeed I do, Captain.' Crosby grinned and tweaked his bent nose, his voice rising to an insincere tone of surprise.

'Weeks he's been waiting. Weeks. There's a ship that he's had his eye on for an age. You might've spied her as you came ashore. She's moored in the outer roads. Broadbridge is afire to have her. Dare say he's not alone in that, mind, for she's a beauty, and handles as well as she looks, I hear. Try as he might, he hasn't been able to find out who owns the barky. Lo and behold, not more than half a glass ago, a messenger arrives from some local nob, just as we're settlin' down to a nice drink, to tell him that if he truly wants it, to come and have a look at it right off.'

'This ship,' said James, unhappily sensing the coincidence. 'Does it have a name?'

'It do,' said Crosby, tweaking his nose again. '*Principessa* she's called.'

There was a long pause. In the silence Crosby looked from James to Harry, trying to decipher their thoughts. He might be the lowest form of human life, but he was a survivor, and far from stupid. A slow smile spread across his face, and grabbing his bent nose, he began to nod slowly.

'Broadbridge couldn't have known,' said James, aware that his dilatory pace, and constant halts, had probably caused them to miss him.

'I can't see how,' said Harry, looking angrily at the ceiling. 'They must have sent a messenger before they ever spoke to us. As a way of doing business, it leaves something to be desired.'

'That's a trifle prudish, Harry. Two potential purchasers can only push up the price.'

Pender came in through the door at the back, having checked on their gear, trying to make sense of the expressions on their faces.

'God knows where he plans to get the money,' said Crosby, with a knowing air.

Harry spoke absent-mindedly. 'He struck a deal with Bartholomew.'

'He never!' said Crosby, genuinely amazed. 'He had money to stand a round, mind, an' that's not normal. Bart must be softer'n I thought. Don't suppose you know how much?'

They both wanted to get away from him. He seemed to exist on trading the scraps of information he gleaned from eavesdropping. Harry said nothing till they were on the quayside. 'It seems we have been humbugged, brother. And to think that I was going to ask Broadbridge if I could borrow some of his crew to put the damn thing through its paces.'

'It would have been some recompense for our loan. He may decide against it.'

'He wouldn't know how,' snapped Harry.

'There must be other ships in the harbour,' said James.

'I dare say,' said Harry glumly. Then his voice crackled with anger. 'I've a good mind to have a look at the damn thing anyway.'

'Whatever for?'

'Curiosity,' Harry replied. 'Besides, I'd like to know if it's as fine a ship as we've been led to believe.'

James looked at him closely, knowing it was more than that. Harry had not entirely given up hope. 'I don't think Broadbridge would appreciate it.'

Harry smiled. 'I shall, of course, have the decency to wait until he's finished his business.'

They passed the time as best they could, waiting for Broadbridge to return. James had Pender set up his easel on the quayside, and, under the protection of a hastily purchased straw hat, he sat down to do some sketches of the harbour and the waterfront buildings. Harry, sitting on a bollard, merely fretted at the inactivity, and tried to stay out of Crosby's orbit, though, for the price of another drink, he had him point out where the ship was anchored. What he saw pleased him, though he would not have called the *Principessa* a barque. He was well aware of the Mediterranean habit of applying that name to anything that had three masts and floated.

But this ship was different. Judging by the bare poles it had little of the fore and aft rig normally associated with the name, though it did have a boom for a lanteen sail abaft the mizzen. The masts themselves seemed out of true. With a telescope to aid him, he could see more of the lines of the ship: about eighty feet long, with a poop deck above the cabin and elaborate decoration around the sternlights and side casements; she showed six gunports on her side, which gleamed with fresh black paint. The *Principessa* was certainly sleek enough in appearance, with a low freeboard and graceful lines. He lifted his telescope and looked at the masts, which were raked slightly towards the stern. It was a matter of opinion whether such a disposition was an advantage or not. Any increase in speed might be offset by less stability in a blow.

Signal guns had been firing regularly from the Customs Fort, and the harbour had become a busier place because of it. Raising his glass once more Harry could make out the sails of a whole host of ships beating up towards the anchorage. Those who sailed best on a bowline were already making their way between the twin moles of the harbour mouth in ones and twos. But the rest of this fleet was strung out over miles of sea. Some of them might not be at anchor before nightfall. And being latecomers they'd probably have to anchor outside and wait for a berth. They wouldn't want to spend the night aboard. That could occupy every boat in the port, leaving him none with which to make his way out to the *Principessa*.

The sun had started to dip in the sky, and still nothing had happened when Harry's patience finally ran out. He stood up suddenly and called to Pender to organize a boat. His servant dashed off along the quay, and made his way to where his brother sat, oblivious of the sun on his back, entirely engrossed in his drawings.

'We can't wait any longer.'

James didn't look away from his work as he replied. 'We?'

'You, of all people, know the limits of my patience. I'm going out to have a look. You may remain here if you wish.'

A quick look at something then a flick with his charcoal. 'And Captain Broadbridge . . . ?'

'Will, I'm sure, be heartily glad to see us.'

James adopted an air of mock seriousness, his voice deepening theatrically. 'You can take nothing for granted at sea, Harry.'

Harry smiled for the first time in an hour. 'Do I sound as pompous when I am using those words?'

James finally looked at him, returning the smile. 'Certainly, brother. So pompous as to be positively sepulchral.'

Pender approached and he nodded vigorously to Harry's enquiring look. 'Come on, James, we have a boat.'

'Do I have time to put my things away?'

That wiped the smile off Harry's face. He looked angrily at the setting sun. 'Bear a hand, Pender.'

His servant set to and had the easel and the drawing materials together in a flash, carrying them up the side alley so that he could deposit them in Broadbridge's room. Harry stood impatiently, occasionally raising his telescope to look at the ships now actually beating up into the harbour, then again at the sun, his foot tapping on the cobblestones as he waited for Pender to return.

'What is he about, for God's sake?'

Just then Pender emerged. He was festooned with weapons. Three swords, three knives, and a brace of pistols. Harry, wholly out of character, positively snarled at him. 'What's all this, Pender? We're only going to look at a blasted ship.'

His servant was not a man to be cowed. Pender looked at him defiantly, and his words matched his mood. 'We've been here less than a whole day, Captain, and we was no sooner ashore than we was attacked. Then we was had up by that lot acting like pirates this mornin'. And if'n this is the sort of place that you can't walk across the town without an armed escort, then I for one don't feel safe going anywhere without these.'

Harry was quite taken aback at the depth of his feeling. Instead of being angry at being addressed so, he sought a gentler response, gesturing towards the armaments. 'Armed is one thing. This is an embarrassment. We really don't require them all.'

Pender was not about to be deflected. 'Well, they're here now, so we might as well take them along. And anyhow, we'll be returnin' in the dark.'

They made their way along the quayside. Pender indicated one of the slime-covered ladders on the harbour wall. Harry looked over. A jolly-boat swung empty at its mooring.

'I rented the boat, Captain, but not the oars. I thought we could row ourselves. Safer, like.'

Harry decided that there was no use in trying to calm his servant's fears. So he abdicated with as much grace as he could muster. They climbed down the slippery ladder, James coming last, and being much helped by his brother. Once settled they set off across the harbour, with Harry and Pender pulling powerfully. Harry kept glancing over his shoulder. Yet more of the lead ships in the convoy had entered the harbour, while the other filled the outer roads close to where the *Principessa* lay. They were busying themselves, making the journey more hazardous, as they backed and filled to avoid each other as they anchored. James looked up at the sky. The sun was dipping towards the horizon, and night came quickly in the Mediterranean.

'If you're planning a look at the ship, Harry, the sun's setting mighty fast.'

'I only need daylight to examine the hull and the upper decks. Once we're below, I'd need a lantern anyway.'

'I didn't fetch one,' said Pender.

'They'll give us one aboard.'

'That is, if they make us welcome,' said James.

Harry was frustrated by such carping. First Pender with his ridiculous armoury, and now James, still hinting that the whole thing was a mistake, or worse, a waste of time. The fact that he was pulling the oars made him sound even more impatient with his companions.

'Well, they must have made Broadbridge more than welcome. He's been there all afternoon. He was at the bottle at breakfast. If they've been plying him with a drink, as like as not we'll have to lower him down on a line from the yard, and fetch him back in the bottom of the boat.'

There was still no activity on deck, and even when he rowed quite close to, under the sweep of cabin windows that ran round the stern, there was no reaction. His inspection of the hull complete, they rowed alongside, and Harry deliberately, and noisily, bumped the boat into the hull by the ship's ladder, normally the cause of much abuse from anyone who cared for their ship. Still nothing, and Harry gazed up at the bare poles, stark and black against the darkening sky, a frown on his face.

'There's no one about, Harry. The ship's deserted,' said James.

'He must still be here. I've had my eye on the ship practically since he came out.'

'Then where's his boat, Captain?' said Pender.

He noticed his servant fingering his sword and smiled. 'Come now. He would have hired a boat to get out here. Mind, he'll have had a job getting one to pick him up again with all this shipping coming into the harbour. I'd say that Captain Broadbridge will be glad to see us, since we can at least offer him a passage back.'

He grabbed hold of the man ropes that ran up the sides of the ship's ladder and hauled himself aboard, then turned back to assist his brother. Pender followed and all three stood on the deck staring around them. Twilight now, with the sun set and the remaining light fading fast. And no sign of any lamps being lit.

'Pender, find a lantern. We'll be in the pitch dark in five minutes.'

'Beggin' your pardon, Captain. How am I to light it?'

'There should be a flint around someplace. Try the binnacle locker.'

Harry took the pistols off his servant and stuck them in his breeches. James followed Pender, walking past him, and tried the cabin door, but it was locked. He turned back and looked along the deck.

'No sign of Broadbridge, at all?' said James, gloomily, and to his brother's mind, unnecessarily.

'Nothing here, your honour,' said Pender. 'The locker's practically bare.'

'Let's look below.'

They made their way down the companionway to the lower deck, fumbling in the gathering darkness. Harry bade them stay still, while he ran his hands around the outer planking looking for a lantern. It was the slight scraping sound that alerted him, and he turned round and shot up the companionway, pushing James and Pender out of the way to rush back on deck. The boat was already a good way off, two men pulling like the devil. Harry could see the shape of Broadbridge's tricorn hat, and he yelled his name to call him back. But the boat rowed on, oblivious of his shouts.

'Damn,' said Harry, gazing towards the shore. The sun still lit the mass of the mountains, but the city was already falling into darkness. The harbour was beginning to fill with points of light, the lanterns of the various ships either at anchor, or on the way to one. None of them was close enough to hail, since those who had made their landfall early had taken the berths inshore, and those who hadn't had decided to stand off until dawn.

'I'm afraid Captain Broadbridge has stolen a march on us,

brother. He must have had a harder job getting a boat than we thought. Looks like we're here for the night.'

They stood, watching the darkness rise up the brown hills, turning them black. It was going to be a clear night, and the moon was beginning to rise, casting a bluish light across the deck. Finally Harry spoke.

'We might as well make ourselves comfortable. I suggest that the lock on the cabin door is best left to you, Pender.'

His servant's teeth actually did glow in the pale moonlight, and he slipped across the deck to kneel silently at the lock, pulling his instruments from his pocket as he did so. The speed of his entry showed just why so many people were eager to lay hands on him back in England. With an elaborate bow, Pender beckoned for the two brothers to pass through.

'What would we do without you, Pender?' said James, following Harry through the door.

'I dare say your brother would have made an unholy mess of the door, James. I reckon that both those pistols would have been aimed at the lock in a trice.'

'With the Count and his pretty wife demanding compensation for its repair, as well.'

Harry stopped just inside the cabin, James and Pender taking place beside him. Broadbridge, hatless, was silhouetted against the sternlight windows, arched back in the captain's chair with his head at a curious angle. Harry walked over to the desk and peered closely into the face. In the poor light his tongue looked black rather than the dark purple it must be.

'Light, Pender,' said Harry softly. 'And rip the place apart if you have to.'

Pender started on the footlockers by the stern windows, moving aside some of the chairs that lined the bulkheads as he did so. Harry didn't move, standing over Broadbridge's body, saying nothing. Without any bidding James joined in, searching the coach and the sleeping quarters on either side of the main cabin. It was he who found the match and flint, and an oil-filled lantern to go with it. He started to light them just by the doorway to the sleeping cabin, when Harry's hurried cry of 'belay' made him stop.

'Something tells me that a light would be a bad idea, James.'

James looked towards the silhouette at the rear of the cabin, still standing over the inert corpse. 'How so?'

Harry was momentarily surprised. Again that need to explain. 'I'm not sure I have the right of it yet. But the people who killed Broadbridge may come back. They've taken our boat, so they would have good reason to think we're stuck aboard. But there is just a chance that we could have hailed a passing boat and got off. That light would alert them, not only to the fact that we are still here, but that we are in the cabin.'

'Captain Broadbridge . . . ?'

'Is beyond any help we can give, James.'

'Captain's right, Mister James. Them bastards might not have just scarpered. They might have gone to get some of their mates. Captain Broadbridge didn't go natural.'

'Relock that door, Pender. Did you find any more weapons?'

'Nothing, your honour, there's a pile of flags, and there's this length of line which was lyin' on the deck, but apart from that the lockers are damn near empty.'

Harry looked up at the skylight. 'They can only come in here two ways.'

'You seem very sure they're coming back,' said James.

'Ask yourself why Broadbridge is dead.'

'How should I know? A drunken brawl?'

'Even with the lack of light in the cabin you can see there's been no drinking. And I touched him, James, he's been dead for hours. Guesswork, I grant you, but I suspect he was doomed from the moment he came out here.'

'They brought him out here to kill him?'

'Yes, though who "they" are is still a mystery. Why do it, and then having done it, why not heave the body over the side?'

'We had a watch on this ship all afternoon,' said Pender.

'True,' replied Harry. 'They could have shoved him over the other side, mind.'

James spoke impatiently. 'Not with all that shipping in the harbour, Harry. Someone would be bound to observe them.'

The three of them were feeding off each other's thoughts, piecing things together. Pender spoke next. 'They must have been waiting for darkness.'

Harry: 'But we happened along.'

Pender: 'Which puts us at risk.'

James: 'Surely they won't come back?'

Harry again: 'What worries me, James, is that they will come back, with a file of marines. I think in the interests of self-preservation, it falls to us to see Captain Broadbridge to a watery grave.'

'I find that a trifle barbaric, Harry. Surely he deserves a decent burial?'

'It's not something I would choose to do normally, James. But being found in a foreign port, the sole companions of a recently murdered fellow countryman, is an even less appealing prospect. Especially when you have a man like Crosby around. He would take great pleasure in swearing that we were rivals for the same ship. And I would suggest we be quick, for if these men are intent on returning, with or without someone in authority, then it won't be long from now.'

'We could deck him out in some of these flags, your honour. Be a bit more decent than just heaving him over the side.'

'Make it so, Pender.'

Harry started to go through the dead man's pockets while his servant set to laying out the flags. Aware of his brother's sensibilities, Harry sent James to keep a watch on deck, adjuring him to listen more than look, for he would be likely to hear anyone approach before he'd see them.

Wrapped in flags, they carried Broadbridge up on deck. Pender had found a length of halyard line under the flags, and the body, swathed and tied, had taken on the shape of an Egyptian mummy. Finally they lashed two rounds of shot to his feet. James turned to watch as the ghostly pair heaved the wrapped body on to the bulwarks. He heard Harry whisper 'handsomely now' as they lowered Captain Broadbridge into the water with the faintest splash. Pender leant over and did something James couldn't see, just before he finally let go.

James was still looking towards them when he heard another soft splash. He spun round and knelt to look out over the ship's rail. Harry must have seen this movement, for he hurried over to join him.

'Perhaps a fish,' whispered James, but Harry's hand pressing on his shoulder made him stop talking. Another soft splash, but no sound of voices.

'Muffled oars,' said Harry. He pulled James away and they made for the cabin door on all fours. Pender was already inside, and as they passed through he knelt down and fumbled in the dark, cursing softly as he hurried to relock it.

'They may be headed somewhere else, Harry,' said James.

'Let's assume they're not. Just for now.'

Harry was looking up at the skylight. It had wooden sides which projected about eighteen inches above the poop deck immediately over their heads, and was topped with a framed glass canopy, arched to catch whatever sunlight was going. Because of the sides, it was impossible to see the whole floor area from the poop. The only way to see the entire cabin was to look through the windows which covered the stern of the ship, a difficult task as they sloped inwards. Harry checked the catches that secured them, feeling that with their multitude of small glass panes they represented a difficult method of entry.

Likewise the two side cabins, though they had casements that ran further round to each side. These sloped outwards with the hull and the catches were easier to force. Of course, there was just a chance they wouldn't look, and be content with the cabin door, still locked and unmarked. But they might not, and if they searched the ship, they would most certainly come in here.

Harry whispered urgently. 'James, just inside the sleeping cabin. Keep out of sight so that they can't see us through the side gallery casements. Pender, you do the same in the coach. If they come in through the windows, get yourselves back in here and hold the doors shut.'

'That won't stop no one for long, Captain,' said Pender. 'And it puts us mighty close under the skylight.'

Harry looked around for a solution, his eyes lighting on the heavy, ornate desk that took up so much space in the cabin. 'Do you have any of that halyard line left?'

'A fair bit,' replied Pender.

'Right. Lash it to the door handles. If they come in through the side galleries, we can lash it to the feet of the desk. That should keep them out.'

Pender had his knife out, and cutting quickly he set to. Harry saw him glance upwards towards the skylight, as he finished one and darted across the cabin to complete the other.

'Our only hope is to cut down the number of ways to get in here. We don't know how many of them there are, but they can only come in through the door or the skylight one at a time. Now get down and stay out of sight. The best we can hope for is that they will think we have somehow hailed a boat and gone ashore.'

James ducked into the small sleeping cabin, Pender into the coach, a sort of office-come-guest-quarters on the opposite side. Harry pulled out the pistols and sat, wrapped in a dark flag, with his back to the heavy desk, both guns pointed at the locked door.

The *Principessa* dipped slightly to starboard from the weight of those coming aboard. Harry was not immune to the thought that he could be entirely wrong. But if there was an innocent explanation, he was at a loss to think of it. He was working on instinct rather than knowledge.

CHAPTER THIRTEEN

Mentally he'd labelled them as attackers. He had no doubt that they were just that now. There had been no lights on their boat as they'd approached with muffled oars, and no hailing of the *Principessa* to warn anyone aboard of their approach. At least he could put out of his mind the possibility of unjustified arrest. People intent on apprehending felons did not come aboard as silently as this. That at least increased the prospect that having searched the ship they might not even look in here.

Harry closed his eyes, hoping by his feelings for the motion of the ship to tell their position. And that was all he had to go by, for there was no sound at all. No voices, not even a hint of a whisper. A vision of the previous night's attack came to his mind. Then too there had been no sound, and he wondered if he was dealing with the same people. He experienced a slight tightness in his chest at the thought, for they were deadly, cold, and efficient. And here on this ship there was no chance of the sudden arrival of a rescue party. If it was them, and they were thorough, then they had only one hope. To make the cost of taking their lives prohibitively expensive. But if these men were not fooled by the precautions they'd taken, and not deterred by the death of their comrades, the three of them would die in this cabin, just like Broadbridge.

A shadow, thrown by the moon, flitted across the skylight. Harry crawled into the well between the two pillars of the desk, pulling the dark flag around him. He knew that he would be invisible to anyone looking in. It was at that moment that he realized his mistake. He'd been forced to cover two eventualities, and he had chosen the wrong one. Fearing arrest, he had disposed of the corpse. But the absence of Broadbridge's body, no longer in its chair, would be obvious to anyone looking through the skylight.

Whatever explanation these men put on this, they would be bound to try and investigate. Harry cursed himself for his haste. He should have left the body there until near dawn, and risked arrest. He waited for the exclamation that would accompany the discovery of the missing Broadbridge, sensing, rather than seeing, the head peering through the pointed canopy of the skylight. Nothing. Yet the ship lurched a trifle as one of their visitors moved with more purpose and less care than previously.

The metallic scrape of a key entering the lock, and Harry squeezed quickly out from under the desk and aimed his pistol at the doorway. He dived to one side, fighting the instinct to look up, as soon as he heard the glass break. Just in time. The cannonball that had been flung through it bounced with a great thud where he had been standing. As if that was the signal the door shot open and Harry, his balance aided by his shoulder, shoved hard against the side bulkhead, put a ball into the throat of the man who came rushing through the door. No cry accompanied the striking of the bullet, just an ethereal gasp.

His momentum carried him on, pushing Harry backwards, but the knife in his hand dropped as he collapsed on to the recumbent defender. It was fortunate that he did, for a boarding pike, aimed through the skylight at Harry, struck the dying man full in the back. James, at the first sound, had rushed into the main cabin. He stumbled slightly, tripping on the cannonball, and fell forward. His outstretched sword took the second man coming through the doorway, and the momentum of his fall pushed him back through the gap. He abandoned the grip on his sword, and instead threw all his weight on the door, slamming it shut. He turned his back to it, and as he did so his eye caught a movement, and he looked up.

The dark figure straddled the skylight, another boarding pike in his upraised hand, this one aimed at James. Harry still on the floor, still with the first assailant on top of him, had no time to aim. His pistol thundered out, lighting up the whole cabin by its flash. They could not see if they hit the man on the skylight, but more glass shattered, and he jumped back with or without a bullet in him, abandoning the pike, which dropped harmlessly into the deck, where it stood upright, quivering.

Pender dashed across the cabin and pulled the dead man off Harry, who struggled to get to his feet. James, his feet splayed out, was trying to hold the door closed. It was obvious that the weight on the other side was greater than his own, for with each silent heave it opened another inch. Pender threw himself at the door. Harry grabbed the captain's chair with its rounded back, and joined in. Heavier than James or Pender, his bulk forced it shut. He jammed the back of the chair under the handle, ordered Pender to secure the other doors, then grabbed at James to pull him to one side. They ended up in the furthest corner of the dark cabin, out of the line of the skylight.

Someone, perhaps the same man, was once more straddled across the broken skylight, in the act of throwing a third pike. He stooped his throw as Harry pulled James to safety, and shifted his aim to Pender, crouched by the leg of the desk trying to lash the rope that he'd attached to the door of the sleeping cabin. Harry yelled a warning, and without looking round to see which direction the danger was coming from, Pender dived under the desk, using the top as cover to finish his task.

James was sucking deeply, his breath coming in gasps, his upturned face glistening with sweat in the warm night air. Harry, now with his sword in his hand, realized, as a slight breeze wafted through the broken skylight, that he too was damp with perspiration.

'Pender, lash that other door while we distract him. James, dash to the other side and retrieve the pike from that fellow's back. I'll take out the one in the middle. With a bit of luck he'll try a throw at me and we'll have one each.'

'As long as I'm not required to retrieve the third from your back. It would never do to have a surplus.'

Harry laughed, softly, and then louder, for reasons he could not really understand. This affected James, who joined him. They stood, their backs to the wooden bulkhead, heaving with laughter. Pender's voice, slightly querulous came from between the pillars of the desk.

'If you gents know summat I don't, I'd appreciate being told.'

'Nothing, Pender,' said Harry, suppressing a grin. 'But let's hope that our laughter depresses our foes as much as it has elevated my brother and I. Ready?'

'Yes,' gasped James.

'Now.' Harry threw his sword into the corner opposite, where it landed with a metallic clatter. They launched themselves together, James jumping over the chair which held the cabin door shut and Harry rushing across the strip of moonlight that covered the centre of the room. The boarding pike, coming from above, was so close to his back that he could almost sense it scraping his spine. Had he hesitated to pull out the other one he would surely have died.

Instead he merely grabbed it at the top of its shaft and kept moving. His efforts didn't fully dislodge it. But it did swing down enough from him to reach out from the bulkhead and drag it right out of the deck. Without stopping he ducked down to retrieve his sword. A quick glance told him that Pender had carried out his allotted task and was now back in the well of the desk. He slid the first pike towards him, bounced off the wood at his back, and wrenched the third pike out of the floor and was back in his original position before the man on the skylight could rearm himself and take aim.

'Pender, did you fetch the means to reload these pistols?'

'Aye.'

'If I push them towards you with my pike, you should be able to retrieve them with yours.'

'I'm not sure as I can reload them in this light.'

'You might as well try, Pender. They are of precious little use as they are. Perhaps if you turn round the moon through the sternlight windows will help.'

First one pistol, then the other, scraped across the floor. Harry heard Pender cursing as he tried to manoeuvre in the confined space under the desk.

'What now, Harry?' whispered James.

'We wait.'

'I will find that harder than doing something.'

'No choice, brother. I don't know how many men we face. So I don't feel that it would be a good idea to go out on deck and engage them. All I do know is that they have no muskets, for which we must thank the Lord.'

James couldn't keep the disappointment out of his voice. 'So we are as badly off as we were when they came aboard?'

'Not so, James. We have held to our plans while forcing them to improvise theirs.'

James' voice became terse. 'You have a rare habit of calling something you've just dreamed up a plan, Harry. This may not be the moment to point out to you that it is a great failing.'

Harry laughed again. The *Principessa* lurched, as if in response to the sound. The laughter would make their assailants curious, and he hoped do nothing for their confidence.

'Guns are loaded and primed, your honour. Shall I slide them back to you?'

'Not a good idea, Pender. They'll very likely go off in the process. They'd be more of a danger to us than our attackers.'

'They must be having a little get-together, trying to decide which way to play it.'

As if to give a lie to his words they heard the sound of breaking glass from the sleeping cabin. The rope attached to the desk jerked suddenly, and as it stretched the door opened slightly, before slamming shut again. Glass tinkled on the other side, as another one of their attackers tried the coach, hauling fruitlessly on the door. The result was the same, except that Pender, forewarned, scurried across the floor, and as the door opened a fraction he fired a ball right through it, pointing his pistol upwards.

An odd inhuman scream and a great gurgling sound, as though the ball had lodged in the man's gorge, followed the crack of the pistol shot. The thud of the falling body, and the crash of the door slamming shut, were almost simultaneous. Pender didn't stop to congratulate himself, but rolled over swiftly, careering into the foot-lockers that ran along the rear of the cabin. The other pistol was aimed at the skylight as his body came round and he fired up through it. At that angle he had no chance of hitting anyone. But the sound of a gun, and the crash as the ball struck the skylight frame, served to distract any attacker while he returned to safety under the desk.

'I think another one of them laughs might do a power of good now, Captain,' he said, his voice resonant in the confined space.

'That's at least three we have accounted for, Harry. Surely we must have discouraged them by now?'

'How I hope that you are right, James. But just in case I'd better elaborate on their options. If they come through the skylight, they can only do so one at a time. In that event, I shall engage the first one. Pender, reload as quickly as you can. Both barrels through the skylight at once, aimed at anyone following. James, if he has his back to you, and he is close enough, kill him. Otherwise leave him to me. On no account are you to engage him.'

'Why not?'

'How much practice have you had with a boarding pike, brother?'

'None. But I doubt that I'll get a chance to explain that.'

'Do you have a chair by you?'

'Yes.'

'Then use that to defend yourself.'

'I . . .'

'There's no time to argue, James. Do as I ask. Keep your pike trained towards the door in case they try to come through there. With that chair in place I doubt they'll be able to smash it fully open. As soon as there's a gap, just shove the thing through it as hard as you can and hope to hit something. Keep jabbing to discourage them. Pender, keep your eyes on the sternlights. I don't think they'll be fool enough to try that route, but you never know.'

'What course would you adopt, Harry?' asked James quietly.

Harry, aware that he had been extremely brusque, answered softly. 'Depends on my aim, James.'

'I should think their aim is rather obvious.'

'Perhaps they'll try both at once.'

'And?'

'Then we each do what I have already outlined, though I doubt we'll keep them out completely. At that point, and I expect this will delight you, James, I fear we shall have to improvise.'

'You seem to imply an alternative course of action.'

'They might have sent ashore for some muskets, your honour,' said Pender.

'That's possible, but it's the other possibility that worries me.'

'What's that?' asked his brother.

'That is that they'll set fire to the ship, and stand off, waiting to spear us like fish when we jump into the water.'

'I'd be obliged if you say that more quiet, your honour. We don't want to go giving the bastards ideas.'

Silence. And no movement. It was plain that some kind of stalemate had been reached. Time passed slowly. On the opposite side of the doorway he could hear James breathing steadily and the occasional scraping sound as Pender moved his position. He was just about to remark that the situation was looking more promising when the top edge of the axe came through the bulkhead behind him. He jumped away quickly. Another axe crashed through the panelling just by the doorway, the blows raining on the wood, seeking to smash it through. Harry cursed under his breath at this unforeseen development.

The men swinging the axes knew how to handle them. There would be little to gain from working side by side to make a small hole in the bulkhead, since that would not get them to their quarry on anything like equal terms. Their idea was much more ambitious, and dangerous. They sought to remove one whole area of the cabin wall so that they could come at them as a body and overwhelm them. Harry stood still, his mind racing as he watched the axes do their work, knowing that the others were waiting for him to say something, waiting for him to vouchsafe them a method with which to counter this assault.

Crash followed crash, as the axes struck in an almost single continuous sound. The bulkhead was fixed and constructed of solid oak and there was still a great deal of work to do before it collapsed. No gap of sufficient size would open up through which they could thrust a pistol or a pikestaff. And was this merely a diversion? Would they, having got them to concentrate on the wall, drop behind them and attack in the rear as well?

'Damn,' Harry said aloud, but the expression was covered by the noise of the axes. He could come to no conclusion, given that it all depended on their numbers. Gingerly he backed into the centre of the cabin, his eyes fixed on the rectangle of starry sky above his head. He spoke quietly.

'Pender, the pistols, if you please.'

His servant scuttled out from under the desk and handed him the pistols, never once himself taking his eyes off the skylight. No head appeared. Once he had handed the weapons over, he lifted his pike into a position that would give him a chance of hurling it at anyone who poked their head over the rim.

Harry took the pike off him. 'Undo those lashings on the desk. See if you can find something else to tie them to.'

He stood there while Pender scurried about. Out of the corner of his eye he realized that his servant was tying the two doorhandles together with a fresh length of line, before undoing those attached to the desk.

'James. Out here and keep your eye on this skylight. Pender, the desk into the centre of the room.' Harry had to risk being heard, raising his voice over the sound of the blows to give his instructions. Swiftly he pulled out the drawers, tossing them, and their contents, all around. With Pender's help he dragged the desk into the middle of the cabin, positioning it below the skylight. Then he jumped on to the desktop and reached up, his hands easily gaining the point at which the wooden skylight surround connected with the poop deck.

He looked down. Pender and James stood, pikes ready. 'Put those aside for a moment, both of you. This desk top will separate from the two bases.'

'How do you know?' asked James.

Harry responded angrily, but answered nevertheless. 'If you can tell me how they got it into the cabin otherwise, brother, I'll be obliged. I'm going to jump up and try and get some purchase on the rim. As I do, lift the desktop to provide me with a platform to stand on. With your arms outstretched I should be able to see over the top.'

'And if there's someone there waiting for you?' asked James.

'If I shout "let go", please do just that.'

It was a gamble, and they all knew it. But with an unknown number of assailants on the other end of those boarding axes, doing nothing guaranteed their death. Harry leapt up in the air, trying desperately to get high enough for his arms to lock straight and take his weight. They didn't and he started to drop back. But the rising desk took his weight and lifted him just enough. He heard the pair below grunting at the effort of holding him up, and he knew that they would only be able to do so for a matter of seconds.

He heaved again, pushing the desktop down as he did so. But it was just enough to allow him to lock his arms, lift his legs, and take all his weight off the makeshift platform. James and Pender straightened their arms and held the desktop steady. Harry bent his legs into a crouch as it came up, then eased himself down to allow them to take the weight. The desktop remained rock-steady, and pulling out his pistols he slowly raised himself till he was standing upright.

He peered over the edge of the box which supported the glass canopy of the skylight, twisting quickly to see if there was anyone about. None of their attackers was on the poop, and he blessed his most uncommon luck. He'd fully expected they'd post a lookout there, as the most obvious place to keep an eye on the reaction of the prisoners to the assault on the bulkhead. Perhaps they weren't so numerous after all. The glass from the skylight was completely gone, barring a few jagged shards, and using the rim of the skylight box, he stepped gingerly on to the moonlit poop.

There was no sound, barring the relentless crunching of the axes. Pistols out ahead of him, he made his way to the companion ladder. The moon was full up now and its light illuminated the entire main deck of the *Principessa*, all the way to the naked bowsprit. The black guns along each side, with the small piles of cannonballs, gleamed dully where the moon struck their barrels. He looked over the poop rail, again surprised that no one stood guard. Perhaps this crew were not as professional as he'd first supposed.

Softly he made his way down the ladder, though the sound of the axes crashing into the oak bulkhead would have covered the approach of a herd of elephants. The poop deck extended out over the outer bulkhead of the captain's cabin, forming a canopy that provided some shelter for the doorway, be it from sunshine or foul weather. But it also cut out the moonlight, making it difficult to see, and he was almost at the bottom step before he could make out clearly the scene before him. Four men stood, feet splayed and hands on the bulkhead, heaving in a silent rhythm, trying to dislodge it. At each end the two axemen swung in that steady way, working up and down the ragged seam they'd already made in the thick wood. Calmly, taking careful aim, Harry shot one axeman in the head, then the other.

The exploding pistols, going off within a second of each other, made the others drop to their knees. Harry was at the top of the ladder before they recovered enough to try and pursue him. He threw the pistols through the skylight and jumped after them on to the upheld desk, yelling for them to let go. As it dropped from beneath him he reached out instinctively to grab the rim of the box to break his fall. His arm felt as though it was being wrenched out of its socket. He let go, landing awkwardly, and painfully, on the desktop, intending to roll sideways. As he landed he felt the hands grab him, hindering his movements rather than aiding them, and he pushed out blindly, trying to get away from the centre of the room, out of view from the top of the skylight. A shower of missiles followed him through the gap.

He heard the crunch of breaking bone, then the scream behind him, and spinning on his knees, he was just in time to catch his brother as he fell. Ignoring the agonized cries of pain, he dragged him into a corner, out of danger and another wound as more objects came hurtling through the skylight. Cannonballs, marlinspikes, even a small water cask. He could hear James gasping, as he fought to contain his need to cry out.

'Where are you wounded?'

'Shoulder,' replied James through gritted teeth. 'A cannonball, I think. Right arm's gone.'

James raised his head, looking towards the skylight, and the still cascading contents of the ship pouring through, thrown in a frenzied attempt to cause further damage. He fought audibly to control his voice. 'There is some danger, if this goes on, that this ship will sink by the stern.'

Harry nearly choked, since he was out of breath from his exertions, which made laughing difficult. But he couldn't help himself. James' voice had that languid tone of the bored man-about-town which he often used to such devastating effect. He heard Pender laughing too.

A sharp intake of breath, before James reverted to that urbane tone. 'Is it only the proximity of death that amuses you, Harry, or have you observed something out there that's responsible?'

'We must get some light,' said Harry. 'Are you bleeding?'

'I don't think so.'

'You should have let me be, James, and looked to save yourself.'

'So it seems.'

'The heat of battle. Now remain still.'

'Pistols reloaded,' said Pender. 'But that's the last of the shot.'

There was a lot of movement on the deck of the ship, interfering with gentle rocking motion as the waves ran underneath the counter. Harry felt the ship dip to larboard, and heard the scrape of a boat along the outer planking.

'It may well be sufficient.' The sound of oars thumping the ship's side as a boat shoved off convinced him. 'I think our visitors have had enough.'

'Shouldn't we pursue them?' said James, struggling to sit up. 'Perhaps with the pistols . . .'

'Just stay still,' Harry snapped, already on his feet. He was undoing the door to the coach. Pender, on the other side of the cabin, grabbed the line and wrapped in around his arm to keep it taut on the other doorhandle. Gingerly, Harry pushed his door open, sword held forward in case of attack. Nothing. He swung the door right back to trap anyone standing there, but it crashed into the wall behind. In the moonlight, streaming through the stern and side casements, he could see that the room was empty. Not even a body. No sign of the man that Pender had shot. He rushed to the side gallery windows and peered out through the thick salt encrusted glass. The boat was no more than a dim shape which quickly faded. The catch was undone and he threw the casement open. He could see them clearly now, slowly pulling away towards the inner harbour. Four men sitting upright, with two rowing, the rest of the boat full of huddled, immobile figures.

Pender hadn't moved, sensibly awaiting instructions. Harry shut the casement and walked back into the main cabin. 'I think that we can afford some light now.'

It was almost tangible, the way that the tension eased. Pender, now standing upright, hesitated for a moment, rubbing his hands over his sweating face, before he set to, finding the flint, match, and taper to ignite a lantern. The taper took the spark, and the flame began to rise. Harry grabbed the lantern and quickly knelt beside his brother. James' upper arm was at an odd angle, clearly broken.

'We must remove your coat, James. More light, Pender, if you can find any.'

Pender was kneeling over one of the drawers that Harry had thrown aside. 'A box of candles here, your honour. For the sconces on the wall, most like.'

Hurriedly he lit them, and as he did so the full extent of the damage done to the cabin was revealed. The bulkhead had great gashes in it, forming a rough rectangle. It had been close to collapse and could only have been a matter of minutes before it gave way. Paper and the various objects that had been on the desk littered the floor, mixed with the debris that had come in through the skylight. In the far corner lay the black clad body of the first attacker to try and enter the cabin.

'If you can sit up, brother.' Gingerly, Harry pulled James's coat open, and tried to ease it over his right shoulder. He stopped as he saw the pain registered in his brother's face. He pulled a knife out of his boot and started to cut the cloth from around the useless arm. Sharp as his knife was, he could not help snagging on the material, causing more pain. The linen on the shirt was an easier proposition, and as that fell away, he could see the bone protruding from under the skin.

'No blood,' he said gently. 'But I doubt that you will be doing any painting for a while. We need to get you to a surgeon.'

'Fairbairn?' asked James.

'No,' said Harry emphatically. He tried to tell himself that he wanted James out of danger, and that was true. But he knew it wasn't the only reason. Now, more than ever, Harry needed freedom of action. The freedom that came from operating alone. Perhaps he should say that straight out. Maybe James would understand. But even as he considered it, Harry knew that he'd never ask.

'There's Williams aboard the *Swiftsure*, that is, if she has not already put to sea. If not, then someone local. We must bind you up now so that you cannot move your arm. I could try to set it myself, but if there is a doctor near by it is best left to him.'

'These things are better done straight away, Harry. Even I know that.'

'True. But we have nothing with which to dull the pain.'

'You decide, brother,' said James. 'But if you feel you can manage it, go ahead.'

'Are you concerned about using it again?'

James positively snapped at him. 'Of course I am. For God's sake, I'm a painter.'

Harry called Pender over, and bade him hold James's shoulder steady. Then he put the wooden handle of his knife between his brother's teeth. 'Bite hard on this, and make sure your tongue is out of the way.'

James fainted with the pain, going limp, as Harry pulled on the broken arm. There was a slight grating sound as the two broken ends came together. Harry smashed one of the desk drawers, using the two sides as splints. He lashed his brother's arm to his side with the line that had been used on the outer cabin doors. James came to as he completed this, and Harry raised him up so that he sat with his back to the outer planking.

Having made his brother as comfortable as he could, Harry walked over to the body on the other side of the cabin and turned the man on his back. The eyes were wide open, black, and staring sightlessly in death. The mouth hung slack, exposing white teeth, stark against the dark lips and sallow, leathery skin. Blood oozed out of the hooked nose. That, with the skin and the dark patches under the eyes gave him the appearance of an Arab. Blood matted the front of his tunic, but against the black cloth it didn't show as anything other than a glistening stain.

'Harry,' said James. 'Have you observed his clothing?'

'Yes.'

'Would it be too singular an idea to assume that all Genoese cut-throats wear some kind of uniform?'

Harry turned to look into the open doorway of the coach. 'Just so. Just as it would be too singular, James, to assume that all such people take away their wounded. Remember last night. Not a word was exchanged between them, yet when Broadbridge and his men arrived they seemed to disappear. And they took the man I skewered with them.'

James patted the wooden slat holding his arm. 'Far be it from me to praise them, but is it not admirable to care for your wounded?'

'Yes. But in an emergency, I would expect them to abandon their dead. The man that Pender shot through the door. Do you remember the sound he made?'

It was his servant who answered. 'He was a goner for sure, your honour. I've heard that sound too many times to doubt it.'

'And I felt sure that the blow I struck last night was mortal. They left this fellow because they had no choice. But I'll wager that when we go out on deck, there will be no sign of the two I shot either.'

'You can't be sure you killed them, Harry, either last night or now.'

'Can't I, James? I was less than ten feet away from the furthest one, and within three feet of the nearest. I know I put a bullet straight into the back of his head. He was certainly in no condition to walk away.'

Harry was right. Leaving James in the cabin he and Pender went to investigate. The lanterns showed no shortage of blood on the deck, one pool of sticky gore not only on the planking but the axe the man had dropped when Harry shot him. There was also plenty of blood on the poop, a sure sign that the shots fired through the skylight had not been wasted. But no bodies.

'Let's take another look at that fellow.'

They made their way back to the cabin and looked down at the still body. Black breeches, black shirt, and filthy bare feet. And that large black bandanna around the head. Pender bent and started to search him. His single pocket held a clasp fisherman's knife and a few of the local coins. Pender looked up at Harry, who nodded. His servant removed the scarf first. The man had thick black hair, curled and matted where it had been compressed. Pender ripped the shirt open next, then cutting gingerly with the man's own knife, he sliced at the breeches.

'Harry,' said James hoarsely. 'What are you looking for?'

'I'm not looking for anything. But if there is some distinguishing feature, I would want to see it. If they are so careful to remove their wounded and dead, it must mean that there's something to identify them.'

'What kind of feature?'

'A tattoo perhaps. Something that might tell me if he was a sailor, perhaps even a French one.'

'There's nothing of that sort, your honour,' said Pender, lifting the man's arms to check. 'I think we best do the same as we did with Captain Broadbridge, and heave him over the side.'

It was when they turned him over to secure the lashings round his arms that they saw the scar. It was in the shape of a crescent, a new rising moon. Harry bent to peer at it, holding a lantern close, and he saw the deformed skin with the indistinct letters that ran down the side of it.

James struggled awkwardly to his feet and came over to look. 'There's your mark, Harry. Though what you expect to learn from a scar, I cannot tell.'

'Look closer, if you can.'

James put his good hand on Harry's shoulder and knelt down beside him. 'That's no scar, James. It's more like some kind of brand.'

Carefully they searched the rest of his body, but there were no more scars or marks of any significance. He was slipped over the side naked, with the two cannonballs lashed to his feet without even the small ceremony that had attended the earlier disposal of Broadbridge. As he was lowered into the water, Pender reached out to slash open the man's stomach.

For all the blood he'd seen that night, James, looking over the rail at this, gagged and pushed away. Pender looked at Harry, holding the other arm, but he just nodded and they let the assassin slip into the black water. Pender walked over to where James leant awkwardly over the side.

'You have to do that, your honour. Otherwise the body floats up in a few days if the cannonballs work loose. There's many a villain gone to the gallows for not remembering that.'

'Spare me the lore of the dark side of our lives, if you please.'

Harry joined them, a new note of urgency in his voice. 'Come, James. You must rest, while Pender and I make all secure.'

It could have been pain, but it was more like a flash of alarm, almost of fear, in his brother's face.

'I don't think they'll return. But you never know. So we'll berth in the main cabin till daylight. Pender and I will keep watch, then we can hail a boat and get you over to the *Swiftsure*.'

James was standing, head bowed, his good arm supporting his weight. 'I apologize, Harry. I'm obviously not cut out for this sort of thing.'

'Neither am I, James. After all, I'm just a simple sailor.'

Harry grinned at him, and James gave him a weak smile with his reply. 'Well, one thing I've learned, brother: when I'm around you, I am unlikely to die of boredom.'

CHAPTER FOURTEEN

James lay on the footlockers, with a makeshift pillow under his head, while Pender put the cabin to rights. They shifted the desk over and jammed it against the damaged bulkhead. Pender transferred the key left behind by their assailants to the inside of the cabin door and locked it. Then he retied the other door handles together, while Harry piled all the loose debris in the cabin in the centre, and jammed the pikes upright, facing towards the skylight. When they'd done all they could, they threw themselves on to the deck, their backs propped against the planking. Pender closed his eyes straight away, but tired as Harry was, he could not countenance sleep. For now all was secure, and the tension created by caution drained away, it allowed him time to think. It was like trying to build a house with half the bricks missing. Every question he answered generated a dozen more uncertainties.

James, who had been still all the while, spoke softly, wearily, with his eyes fixed on the deckbeams above his head. 'It is almost as if there is some unseen hand intent on our destruction.'

'Chance,' replied Harry quietly. 'We have had the misfortune to be in the wrong place at the wrong time.'

'Twice.' James did not need to elaborate on the unlikelihood of that.

Pender, for all his eyes were tight shut, wasn't asleep either. 'If this was chance, Captain Ludlow, I'd be more worried than I am already.'

'Is that what killed Broadbridge, Harry?'

Harry answered with a question. 'Who brought him out here?'

There was a long silence before Pender replied: 'The men that killed him?'

'Hark back to what Crosby said. A messenger came for him, saying that if he wanted to buy the *Principessa*, he should come along right away. Crosby said there was a boat waiting. That means he was deliberately lured out here to his death.'

'He didn't fall and break his neck,' said James impatiently.

Harry spoke gently. He knew James to be in pain. 'Please, brother, I'm merely thinking aloud.'

'Those two buggers that stole our boat, most like,' said Pender.

'There would have to be someone out here to look after the ship. You don't leave a valuable vessel like this unguarded in port. It would be gone in five minutes.'

'Captain,' said Pender, 'if'n there was one boat that came out, and one already here, why pinch ours?'

'There wouldn't be one for the guards. If they had a boat, they'd do precious little watching. What's to stop them going ashore when they please.'

'What about supplies?'

'They'd come aboard with sufficient to sustain them.'

'Then if we find out who had him brought out here, we have found his murderer,' said Pender.

James couldn't keep the surprise out of his voice. 'Count di Toraglia.'

'The message reached Broadbridge either before, or when we were with the Count and his wife.'

'Didn't Guistiani say he'd only just decided to sell?'

'Was he precise?' said Harry.

James pushed himself up on to his good arm. 'The timing is wrong. I don't think they sent a message at all, do you?'

Harry didn't reply. He was reluctant to entertain the notion of the Count's guilt himself, but he could think, at present, of no other explanation. Yet what the man stood to gain from the cold-blooded murder of a potential purchaser escaped him. If someone wanted to buy something of yours, you took his money, not his life. But there was no gainsaying the fact, even if Harry didn't bother to articulate it, that the men who had first attacked them in the cabin had made their entry with a key. Only the owner of the ship, or his hirelings, would have a key. How that connected to the attack made on them last night was even more of a mystery, but connected it was, for it had been undertaken by the same people.

'No,' said James emphatically. 'No one could sit there, as calm as they did, having just sent orders to kill a man. They would have tried to fob us off.'

'I don't know who this Count di Toraglia is, your honour, but Broadbridge knew this boat was goin' ages ago.'

James spoke again. 'He havered about selling it. The rumour must have been around that it was coming on the market. Broadbridge could have picked that up. I wonder how much time elapsed between the arrival of that message and Bartholomew finally offering to advance him the money?'

Harry didn't answer. His mind was racing furiously, trying to make sense of a dozen conflicting arguments. Why had the two men run when they'd come aboard? That didn't make sense. They could have stayed in the locked cabin, moving Broadbridge's body so that it couldn't be seen through the skylight. They had the key. How could they know that of the three men who'd come abroad, one of them was practised at picking locks? He got to his feet and grabbed the lantern off the deck. Pender stood too as Harry called to him.

'Lock the door the door behind me, just in case.'

Pender frowned and Harry looked at the skylight. 'I know the quick way in. If you hear me yell your name, please get those pikes from under the skylight before I come through.'

His servant unlocked the door and Harry slipped through, hearing the key turn behind him. He emerged on to the moonlit deck, moving purposefully towards the companionway which led below. The swell had increased and the *Principessa* creaked as she rode, hauled up and jerked by her twin anchors. Habit made Harry sniff as he reached the lower deck, and by instinct he registered, with approval, that the air held no odour of damp or rot. Devoid of the men who would normally sling their hammock here and with the minimum of stores aboard, the deck ran from the tiny manger at the front to a wooden bulkhead under the main cabin. Only the galley stove, the capstan, and the upper deck supports interrupted the clean sweep. The lantern was not strong enough to reach every corner of the space, so Harry made his way forward down one side, then aft down the other, till he came to the bulkhead that separated the officers' cabins from the rest.

He opened the door on to a small ward-room, with a stove in the middle and four tiny cabins, two each side. The two men lay trussed and dead on the table which occupied the centre of the room, their bodies cold to the touch. They were dressed in grubby shirts, breeches, and waistcoats. These, in the local manner, were gaily embroidered and decorated with coloured beads, which gave a macabre contrast to the looks of pain and suffering on their faces.

Unlike Broadbridge, they had not died without a struggle, for as Harry held the lantern over them he could see that their clothes were in disarray, and their faces bruised and cut. No surprise in these deaths. These men had been brutally overpowered. They were tied hand and foot, with several loops of rope around their upper body, and Harry knew just by looking at them that the corpses had been made ready to be slung over the side, very much in the manner that he and Pender had disposed of two other unfortunates tonight.

But Broadbridge had not been prepared for that. It was Pender who trussed him up. The late captain had been sat in his chair like a statue, stiff and cold like these two, as though he had been deliberately left, like the skeleton guarding a pirate's treasure. It smacked of the same display as Captain Howlett, swinging from his makeshift gibbet.

'He was there, at the Guistianis'. He could easily have overheard them talking about the *Principessa*. And last night, just after we were attacked, Tilly came marching by, bold as brass, with a file of marines.'

'I'm still left with the thought, why Broadbridge?' said James.

'Struck me as a touch headstrong, Mr James. Happen they thought no one else would fall for their lure.'

Harry answered James's next question before he asked it. 'Perhaps the French have someone in Ma Thomas's. A spy. Though with a gossip like Crosby I doubt it'd be necessary.'

'That is a very imaginative leap, Harry.'

'Can you not see the hand of the French in this, James?'

'I can see that there are other possibilities, perhaps too many for comfort.'

Harry started to pace up and down the available space, which, given their precautions, was not very much. 'When we came aboard and found his body we surmised that they hadn't slung him overboard because of the incoming ships. What if they'd never intended to put him over the side?'

'To what purpose?'

'To the same purpose as hanging Captain Howlett. To serve as a warning to the British sailors that they are not safe, even in harbour.' Harry increased the speed of his pacing. 'The people we fought tonight were the same crowd that attacked us last night.'

'Yes. But we both surmised that it was because they thought we were King's officers,' said James.

Pender was beginning to see what Harry was driving at. 'We were on the wrong track altogether. Go on, Captain.'

'I think they attacked us by mistake. Odd that I hinted as much to Bartholomew. I was trying to create the illusion that he and his compatriots were threatened, thinking that might get him to help me. Was I closer to the truth than I knew? Were they really lying in wait for Broadbridge? He was wearing a blue coat too. With the *Swiftsure* just arrived they might know he was in that vicinity, and what he was after.'

'He had a lot of men with him, your honour. Too many to attack.'

'Quite a number of them off the *Swiftsure*, Pender. As for his own men, he would have had to spread them along the quayside to catch those coming in. No point in standing together all in a bunch.'

'But they wasn't on the quay, they came down the alley from the town.'

'Perhaps he'd only just gathered them up.'

James was not finished with his devil's advocacy, needing for his own satisfaction to chase the very thought which came into his mind.

'Could that not imply that someone at Ma Thomas's tavern wanted him dead, hired these people to do the deed? They failed last night, and so they lured him out to this ship tonight.'

Pender cut in, with such certainty that his words brooked no argument. 'Not someone at Ma Thomas's. Why lure him out here to kill him, and two others as well, when you can knife him in his bed?'

'That would attract attention to the place.'

'That's naïve, James, if I may say so, even for someone like you. I doubt the customers of Ma Thomas's, or the lady herself, would have much trouble, or any qualms, about disposing of a corpse. No. The question you must ask yourself is who stands to gain from this death. Quite obviously the French would do all in their power to hamper the efforts of British privateers, to stop them interfering with their trade.'

After a long pause, James finally conceded Harry's point. 'There are things we may not know about, some form of rivalry. But it does increasingly look to be the work of the French.'

'I would guess that had we not happened along last night, Broadbridge and perhaps one or two of his hands would have been found at daybreak, hanging from a gibbet in the same manner as Howlett.'

'I doubt my brain can contain this, Harry. I yearn for some sleep. Perhaps things will be clearer in daylight.'

James moved slightly, and his gasp of pain was clearly audible.

'I'll take first watch, Captain,' said Pender.

Harry nodded, handing his servant his watch. But he didn't sleep, mulling over in his mind what he knew, and what he suspected. More importantly, what to do about it. If he could prove a connection Tilly would be obliged to hoist anchor and leave at the very least. Yet he was at a loss to know whom to approach in order to make something happen. Doria, he felt instinctively, would be useless, since he patently cared only for his pocket. The power structures hereabout were so fragmented as to baffle an outsider. Perhaps he could get Bartholomew to act. Whoever lured him and his compatriots here, and granted them permission to sail, might strongly favour the British cause, instead of doing it for the profits that the privateers brought. Thinking about Doria, and his pocket, and profits, made him wander off at a tangent.

How did Bartholomew avoid excise duty? He conjured up a memory of his own captures. That gave him pause. He could see a pile of cargo in his mind's eye, with cordage and sails, and all manner of items from barrels of turpentine to boxes of nails. But what of the vessel itself? If you took prizes, you captured ships. You could unload a cargo at any convenient bay, and with such a mountainous coastline there was no shortage of places hereabouts. And moving goods on mules in these parts excited no comment, since it was the customary form of transport. But you could not dispose of the ships themselves so easily, and they represented a major share, sometimes the best part, of the profits to be derived from privateering. Bartholomew must be disposing of his cargoes, vessels and all, somewhere else entirely, and only using Genoa as a place to victual.

And the lack of proper crews? He distinctly remembered Hood saying that they went in for long voyages. The longer the voyage, the more men you needed. Every ship you took had to have a strong enough party aboard to both sail the prize and cow the prisoners. With the size of crew Bartholomew and his acolytes took to sea, any reasonable success would leave them without sufficient crew to sail their own ships. And sailing in convoy? He would hate to do that, for it implied some sort of commodore. Someone would have to co-ordinate the actions of the various ships in the fleet, otherwise they'd be forever fouling one another's hawse.

And there was bound to be no end of arguments. It stood to reason that men who held command in such circumstances would not take lightly to having their actions either directed or questioned. And when it came to sharing out the booty, there would be endless disputes about who did the most to effect the capture in the first place. At that moment Harry knew that he could never sail with Bartholomew and his band.

Harry was off again on another tangent. They must drop off their ships and goods at another port, re-embarking their crews, then sail back to Genoa to spend the money. That meant that the place Bartholomew unloaded was not secure. He shook his head violently, forcing his mind back to the more immediate problem, searching for a solution.

With the clarity that often comes from thinking laterally, his mind cleared away the inessentials, leaving the core of the problem exposed. Nothing he could do, in the form of laying accusations, would shift that French sloop. It had to be the actions, or the disapproval, of someone much more powerful. Also, he doubted, without positive proof, impossible to refute, that even the eminent Admiral Hood could achieve as much. The chances of laying a hand on the actual person responsible posed insurmountable difficulties. Having exposed the nub of the problem, it seemed to require little mental effort to expose the solution. He recalled the conversation with Hood, and the suggestion that he should just blow it out of the water.

Harry stopped frowning, and smiled, half wondering if this was what Hood had been hinting at all along. The British Navy couldn't go near the French ship. Up until a few hours ago neither could he, for he lacked the means. But not now. Even if he declined the half-offered chance to join the syndicate, perhaps he could convince Bartholomew that Broadbridge's death was a warning to him and all his fellow captains. In that case it might be possible to persuade him to take some action, in conjunction with Harry, to remove the threat altogether.

Harry felt the blood begin to race through his veins as the outline of his proposed action took shape. He started guiltily. Was this his real reason for suggesting that James have his wound attended to aboard the *Swiftsure*? That his brother would then be away from him, and unable to question or interfere with his plans.

It was the old thrill, when an idea presented itself and the whole thing seemed to fall into place in a matter of seconds. It was all there now in his mind's eye. A blatant attack, guns blazing, was out of the question. Hood couldn't do it, and neither could he. But what was to stop him, with or without the aid of Bartholomew, from adopting the same tactics as the French, and indulging in a little activity at night? Harry had been given plenty of time to examine the sloop. She had no boarding nets rigged, so given enough people he could make her capture painless, and above all, quiet. It couldn't be done with a British ship in the harbour. But *Swiftsure* was due to sail tomorrow. There would be a gap of at least two days between her rejoining the fleet and another British warship coming in to revictual.

Given luck they could take her, cut her cable, and sail her out of the harbour, for all the world as though she'd set out on her own. A stage-managed capture, away from the sight of land, by a ship of the Royal Navy would be easy to arrange. Harry's smile increased in size, as he contemplated Hood's response as Harry Ludlow, having not only turfed the French out of Genoa, turned up off Toulon with their ship as a prize.

He took over the watch from Pender earlier than necessary, and had his servant let him out of the cabin again, ordering him to get some sleep. If he was going to go through with his plans he needed to know if the *Principessa* was a good ship to buy. As the sun rose over the mountains he set about checking the rest of the ship, half his mind on what he was examining, and the other half gnawing away at his scheme, looking for flaws.

To some it would seem ghoulish, to be looking over the *Principessa* now, given the recent deaths. It was even more ghoulish to contemplate the possible quality of Broadbridge's men. Sutton and his mates were now without a captain, and there should be enough real sailors aboard to make a start at forming an efficient crew. If they were of the right stripe he'd have no need to involve Bartholomew. And if he could accomplish his goal with what was to be his own crew, it would augur well for the future. A successful action, right at the beginning, would do wonders for their morale. It sounded as though they'd been on short commons under Broadbridge, both in the article of food and the opportunity for a bit of profit.

They'd had to watch the crews of the other ships flinging money about, and behaving as though Genoa was Fiddler's Green, which must have been galling. A capture, and a payment to go with it, would be all he needed to have their undying loyalty. He was standing on what seemed a dry and weatherly ship. Given a willing crew, all the rest he could manage. The more he thought on it, the better it looked. All Harry needed to square the circle was his exemptions from Hood, and as far as the Mediterranean was concerned he was sitting pretty.

CHAPTER FIFTEEN

The binnacle locker might be empty but in most other respects she was well found. The raked masts, with extra stays, seemed somehow to fit the whole shape of the vessel now he was aboard. The yards needed to hoist the sails on to these masts, all new timber, were stored amidships, raised on the booms that would normally have held the ship's boats. The sail locker was well ventilated and full of good-quality canvas. In her compact holds beneath the lower deck she had all the cables and cordage aboard that he would need to rig her. The magazine, not surprisingly, held no powder. But the shot lockers in the hold were full. Extra ballast, in the form of shingle, had been loaded to compensate for the lack of consumables such as water and food. He looked over the side, checking the state of the paintwork, and over the stern, noticing that the gudgeons holding the rudder were well greased.

The brass fittings gleamed and the decks were clean. There was a reassuring freshness about the ship, if you excluded the cabin and the tiny ward-room. He stood on the quarter-deck, by the wheel, looking for'a'd, and tried to image the *Principessa* in motion. The feeling that he had was impossible to explain. She just looked right, and it was easy, in his mind's eye, to imagine her heeled over with a fine spread of canvas aloft.

There was only one flaw. To Harry, with his naval background, the guns were a disappointment. The *Principessa* carried twelve four-pounders as her main armament, with popguns as stern and bow chasers. Accurate enough, and sufficient to scare a merchantman, they would be barely adequate in a proper fight with a determined enemy, and useless against a warship unless you had them by the score. Harry knew that if you stayed at sea long enough, taking prizes close to enemy harbours, one day you'd bite off something bigger than you could chew. A pair of long nines, of a decent calibre amidships on each side, and another two pairs set as bow and stern chasers, well handled, could make all the difference.

He took a telescope from the rack and made his way up to the cap. Harry quickly surveyed the approaches, now, at sunrise, full of ships making their way into the anchorage. He swung round to look at the crowded harbour. Some of those who had tied up the night before were being warped into the quayside to unload their cargo. Those two unfortunates in the wardroom would have been over the side without the presence of those merchant ships, and all they would have found, had they come out today, was a ghost ship with the single corpse in the cabin.

Harry swung the glass round to take in the entrance to Ma Thomas's tavern, but there was little activity there at this hour. He swept on, past Broadbridge's ship, the *Dido*, which at this distance didn't look impressive, to view the ships of Bartholomew's little squadron. Two barques, a pair of two-masted sloops, and a polacre. The decks were deserted. At this hour, on any ship of his, the hands would be up and at it, in true naval fashion, holystoning the decks and keeping everything shipshape. Back on deck, he gently woke his brother. He must get James over to the *Swiftsure* for Williams, the surgeon, to have a proper look at his arm. He brutally suppressed his feelings of guilt. Even with his vivid imagination he had trouble envisaging his brother stealing aboard an enemy ship, face blacked and dagger in his teeth, intent on knifing people in the dark.

He roused them out of the cabin with loud and unwelcome knocking, bidding his servant to tidy up the place and leave the door unlocked while he sought some transport. It took some time to hail a boat, Harry yelling furiously, and cursing frequently. James' face was drawn. Harry's knew that he must still be in considerable pain, but he was at a loss to know what to do about it. He also knew that if he said nothing James would question him about his plans, so, in between hails he set out deliberately to mislead him, for his brother's own good.

'I must check what we have only so far surmised. I must talk with Crosby, for one, and see if anyone caught sight of the men who took Broadbridge out to the ship. Anyway, even if I discover nothing, I must see Count Toraglia, then lay the matter before someone in authority.'

'Admiral Doria?'

'Yes, though I'd prefer it to be someone else, this is his domain. Not that I think he'll do anything. Of course, it is quite possible that Count di Toraglia will take the whole problem out of my hands, though I cannot say I relish burdening his pretty wife with such a matter. But it's his ship at the moment, so really he is responsible. Perhaps a word with Guistiani . . .'

Harry was so busy articulating his thoughts that he failed to notice the increasing gloom on his brother's face. 'What you said last night, Harry, about the French wishing to use Broadbridge as a warning—'

'Yes?'

'Does it not occur to you that having foiled that plan they will hatch another?'

Harry, who had been concentrating on these other matters, was surprised. 'I don't follow you.'

'Then you should, Harry. If we were involved by sheer chance before, that can hardly be true now, for we have scuppered their plans. As a warning, you, Pender, and I will do just as well as our late friend. I think we should all get out of Genoa as soon as possible. Let's lay our conclusions before Admiral Hood and let him sort this out.'

'I would not want to be seen to be running away.'

'I'm not suggesting that you make a habit of it, Harry.'

Harry didn't respond to that at all. James gave him a thin smile, and spoke with deliberate irony. 'It is so gratifying to see that my words are having the intended effect.'

Harry disliked the idea of deliberately lying to James. Avoiding questions and not informing was one thing, but barefaced falsehoods quite another. Yet he could see no alternative, for to do otherwise would enmesh him in the very net he was so pleased to have escaped, quite apart from the fact that James would insist on staying with him, increasing the risk to both of them.

'I see all this as easing the task at hand, James. Not complicating it. My best hope was always the English privateers. They will have no love for the Navy, so the death of Captain Howlett was hardly likely to move them. But Broadbridge was one of their number, and he's now dead. If I can convince them that they too are in danger, and that by aiding us they protect themselves, then we can bring matters to a speedy conclusion, while at the same time removing the threat to our persons.'

'Harry, you are still over-simplifying the whole thing.'

Harry nearly relented, for his discomfort was acute. But to outline his plans to James would not improve his standing in his brother's eyes. He would see it as being rash, whereas Harry saw it as making perfect sense. And given that James knew his intentions, nothing would get him out of Genoa, which would double the risk to James, and increase Harry's workload tenfold in having to look after him. He searched his mind in vain for a happy phrase, knowing he had to say something. When he did speak, he knew the words he used fell lamentably short of what was required.

'I don't really expect you to understand.'

'Then I thank God for it, for it passes all comprehension.'

Harry opened his mouth to speak, to try again, but James refused to give way, and there was a note of exasperation in his voice that was quite new.

'There are things we never speak of, brother, areas of our lives that we respect as private. But for once I feel I must breach that privacy. Hood practically told you that you could have your commission back. Yet you declined. Why? Because you would have to beg for it?'

Harry, who had been gracing his brother with a slightly patronizing smile, immediately frowned. 'I think that our respect for each other's personal lives is best maintained.'

'I cannot contain my curiosity. What is it you want, Harry? We lost a ship, and you damn near lost your life and mine, because of this sort of behaviour. You could have walked away from Captain Clere in Gibraltar without loss of honour. The man was drunk. And before you say that he was representative of the other officers, remember that I'm aware of how little you care for their professional disapproval.'

James rubbed his forehead with his fingertips, part exasperation, part pain. 'I can appreciate your reasons for avoiding a return to England, since I'm reluctant to do so myself. But there comes a point when the game isn't worth the candle. And now you are proposing to go nosing around in this place, talking to this person and that. To prove what, I pray? Something as plain as day; that a large part of the local oligarchy incline towards France, rather than England. The very best you can do is identify them, and that will achieve nothing. The very worst is get a knife in your ribs. Can it be worth it? Is it that you so love a fight that you put aside all common sense?'

Harry Ludlow was not the kind of man to be talked to like that. But he fought hard to keep the anger out of his voice. 'Your arm must be paining you badly.'

James softened his voice, almost pleading. 'I realize what I'm saying isn't welcome, Harry. Perhaps this arm is making me speak with less delicacy than usual, but I would dearly love an answer.'

Harry looked him right in the eye, his voice now gentle too. 'I can think of no answer that would satisfy you, brother.'

James gave him a half-smile. 'I didn't have in mind an answer that would satisfy me. I was rather thinking that you might find one to satisfy yourself.'

Pender, who had taken over yelling from Harry, finally secured a boat. As it came alongside, he looked suspiciously at the boatmen, easing the pistols which now resided in his belt so that they would know not to trifle with him. They returned his curiosity in good measure, for there was no doubting that their three passengers had been in a scrape. Harry's blue coat was stained with blood, and his face bore several bruises. Getting James down into the boat, with only one usable hand and no rope to hold him, took an age.

The *Swiftsure* was making ready for sea as they approached, though the hands seemed sluggish as they went about their duties, and the frigate was still surrounded by any number of craft, plying their wares through the open gunports. A marine guard at the entryport, musket raised, looked down suspiciously as they came alongside. But he must have recognized Harry, as he quickly lowered the musket, and called for the officer of the watch. Harry was half-way up the ladder before the midshipman's head appeared, and he ignored the look of anger as he came aboard without invitation.

'Mr Dalgliesh,' he said, recognizing the young man. 'My brother has sustained a broken arm, and he requires the attention of a surgeon.'

The boy looked at him blankly, not sure what to do, for he knew that neither his captain, nor many of the other officers, had much time for the Ludlows.

'Come along, man,' snapped Harry. 'We need a whip from the yard and a padded sling to help him get aboard.'

Barnes, told of the arrival of the Ludlows, came out of the main cabin, an irritated scowl on his face. 'What is all this?'

Harry explained, but he could see that as he did so, his words were having no effect on the *Swiftsure*'s captain. Just the opposite, for it was evident in the man's eyes that he was working up to a refusal, to a demand that Harry take his brother ashore.

'I can hardly think that you will refuse to succour a fellow Englishman, sir, especially one held in such high esteem by your commanding officer.'

The allusion to Hood held Barnes' words in check, allowing Harry to nail him with a threat, a particularly potent one to an acting-commander desperate for a ship of his own.

'For any man who failed to aid someone that Admiral Hood looks upon as a near-adopted son would answer at their peril for such a foolhardy action. Why, he'd likely spend the rest of his days on the beach.'

James was aboard in a trice, with Harry himself supervising the hands that rigged the line. Pender came up behind James, and the surgeon, Williams, brought on deck to see him aboard, hurried him down to his quarters. Harry followed, and watched as the surgeon undid his splints.

'Seems neat enough,' said Mr Williams, one of the few sober souls on an otherwise loose ship, forever trying, Bible in hand, to bring the worst cases to God and redemption. He'd been a sorry specimen when they'd first arrived in Genoa, standing on the poop, mournfully praying for the souls who were debauching themselves beneath his feet. Like most evangelical men, when not talking about salvation, his abiding trait was pessimism, and this applied to wounds physical as well as scars spiritual.

'But you never can tell,' he continued, dosing James with tincture of laudanum to dull the pain. 'Even the simplest wound can prove mortal. You need rest, sir, and you will require to be bled more than once.'

He turned to Harry. 'We sail upon the ebb, Mr Ludlow, which will be during the first dog watch. I will happily attend to your brother until then, but he must go ashore for further treatment. Would it not be best to take him right off and find a local man?'

'No, Mr Williams. I would want my brother taken back to the *Victory*, and put under the care of the Surgeon of the Fleet.'

'Harry . . .' said James, sitting up sluggishly.

'I know what I shall do, James. And please believe that I have listened to what you've said.' Harry smiled, and laid his hand gently on James's good arm. 'There's not another man alive I'd take such a wigging from.'

Williams was still fussing about with his instruments, providing a good excuse to avoid giving details of his plans once more. The laudanum was beginning to affect James. But Harry could not avoid that recurring feeling of guilt, for deep down he knew he would have said nothing anyway. Instead, he sought words to reassure James.

'Perhaps staying in these parts isn't on the cards after what's happened, but I must go ashore to sort out our financial affairs in any case. Leghorn will be a safer bet as a base, but I would still like to buy the *Principessa* if she's for sale at a decent price. As for you, I would rather you were in the care of Mr Williams here than someone we don't know. If you return to the Fleet, then I'm sure that Admiral Hood will insist that you berth with him aboard the flagship.'

'I would rather we stayed together.'

'That would be flying in the face of your own advice, brother. We have had two very close shaves, and you have already alluded to the degree of danger. I must stay a while. I will not risk exposing you to another attack bearing a broken arm.'

'Harry,' said James anxiously, obviously not convinced that his brother had been completely open with him. 'I know how impetuous you are. I would hate you to be the victim of another murder . . .'

'Murder!' said the surgeon, alarmed.

Harry was grateful for the surgeon's interruption. 'Nothing to concern yourself with, Mr Williams. I'm sure you're aware of the disorder in the streets of Genoa.'

'I am not, sir, for which the Lord be thanked. I have been saved the need to go ashore amongst these papist heathens. All my medicines have been brought out to me by Signor Brown, who I may add, is an excellent fellow, even if he has taken the wrong spiritual road. The price of the potions is higher, but it is not to be compared with the risk of imperilling my soul.'

James seemed to accept that he was wasting his time, just as he confirmed to Harry that he was not to be fooled by a breezy manner. 'I can say no more, brother, except to repeat that you put yourself at risk to no purpose.'

Harry didn't falter. The prospect of an end to this dissimulation raised his spirits. He was as hearty as Old King Harry of the six wives. And for once, he thought he was being reasonably truthful.

'Never, fear, James. I shall be with you long before you've had a chance to relish a little solitude. If, in the course of settling our business, I stumble upon anything, I shall note it. But I'll not waste any time seeking it out. I dare say I'll be on the next ship to victual here, and be back aboard the *Victory* before your arm is mended.'

'Are them pistols still loaded, your honour?' asked Pender as they were rowed steadily towards the inner harbour.

'They are, though I can't see that we'll have use of them in daylight.'

Pender gave him a wide smile. 'You never know, Captain. Remember the last time we came ashore in one of these.'

'True. And you may castigate me for my attitude of last night, if you so wish, for I fully deserve it.'

It was true. Without his servant's precautions they would certainly be dead by now.

'I've got to keep you in one piece, Captain Ludlow,' said Pender. 'Anythin' happens to you, I might have to go back into the King's Navy. But there's another reason I'm askin'.'

Pender's face clouded and he looked genuinely worried, 'I hired our boat off the roughest-looking bastard in the whole of this Godforsaken port. I dunno how he's going to take it when I tells him that it's gone.'

'What now, your honour?' asked Pender, casting his eyes around to see if anyone had observed them coming ashore.

'We must move quickly, Pender.' Pender's expression left Harry in no doubt that the reply was inadequate, and he knew he'd have to offer more.

'It would be mortal to have those two bodies discovered by someone else, Captain.'

'You're right,' said Harry. 'But first I must have a change of clothes. I cannot walk about the place coated in blood.'

Pender nodded, and they made their way along the quay to the inn. Ma Thomas's was a mess after another night of drinking and gambling, and as yet the place had not been cleaned up. Bodies lay everywhere, and despite the open shutters, the whole room stank of tobacco, drink, and unwashed humanity. Few were awake, and those who were showed little curiosity, content to nurse sore heads with fresh poison. Fairbairn was sitting hunched in the corner by the door to Ma Thomas's domain, at the only clear table in the place. Harry, passing by, paused, and with a deliberate air looked at the assembled bodies.

Fairbairn lifted a steaming cup to his lips, and for a brief moment the smell of stale rum was overborne by the smell of coffee. 'As you can see, Mr Ludlow, our little fleet is still celebrating.'

'Three nights in a row. It must have been a very successful cruise,' said Harry.

'Won't be long before they're skint,' said Pender.

The surgeon's words and movements were slow, yet every so often his body gave an involuntary jerk. 'So it would seem. But this is to be a short run ashore. Word is that they will be off in a day or two.'

Harry cursed under his breath, and sat down suddenly. He called to a serving girl to fetch them some breakfast, then turned back to Fairbairn. The surgeon's eyes roamed over Harry's face and coat, lingering for a moment on the bloodstain down one side. With a deliberate movement he looked past them to the anchorage.

'The good Broadbridge is not with you?'

Harry shook his head. If he was going to say anything, it would be Bartholomew who'd get the information first. The surgeon seemed to realize that Harry would say no more and he lapsed into silence, nursing his cup. But that didn't suit Harry Ludlow.

'They're off on another cruise, you say?'

Fairbairn nodded. 'Bart has a rendezvous to keep, I hear.'

Coffee, fresh bread, and more of the strong smelling sausage were placed before them, and after the exertions of the night they set to with a will. But Harry was trying to place this new information in the context of his intentions. He'd yet to see the material that he had to hand, so he might, after all, need Bartholomew's help. He had fully intended to string the man along. James had been right. Bartholomew had been toying with an invitation to join the syndicate the other night. Whoever came to the door had told him about the gold they were carrying. Broadbridge was a liability, and the man sitting in his room had come not only with money, but bearing a successful reputation. As long as he saw Harry as a potential investor in the syndicate he would be well disposed towards him.

Fairbairn watched him silently. Harry, sick of being examined, looked directly at him, forcing the surgeon to avert his eyes. In the daylight, with the sun streaming through the tavern windows, the dry grey colour of his skin was apparent. The stubble on his chin looked grey as well, rather than fair in the manner of his thin lanky hair. The lips, set in such a colourless face, formed a slash of red which glistened, for he was forever licking them, a sure indication of the nature of his habit. His eyes were red too, not just the rims, but the whites, and with the pale blue of his pupils he would have looked like a corpse if it was not for the constant small involuntary movements that racked his body.

Fairbairn was looking past Harry again, avoiding his eye. 'You went out to join Captain Broadbridge, I believe.'

The surgeon paused slightly before continuing: 'Crosby tells me that you are in contention for the same ship. Said you were in a high old temper when you found out that Captain Broadbridge was aboard.'

'If you go listening to Crosby, you're a fool.'

Fairbairn stiffened, then pointed to the huge bloodstain on Harry's jacket. 'I am a surgeon, Mr Ludlow. In the course of my duties I have often found that my clothes take on that colour. It is the bane of a medical man's existence.'

Harry responded sharply. 'I must say that I find the drift of your remarks impertinent.'

Fairbairn flushed. Harry wiped his mouth and threw down his napkin.

'And now, if you will forgive me, I must find hot water and a razor. It may seem fitting to you, sir, to appear at breakfast as you are. But I am accustomed to more careful society.'

Fairbairn smiled, unaffected by that remark. He long since given up caring about his appearance. Harry stood up. He didn't leave the table as his eyes were still locked with those of the surgeon. Pender raised himself, breaking the spell, and with his servant still munching a mouthful of bread, they made their way towards the rear of the tap-room, to the door that led to Ma Thomas's domain.

'Hot water, Pender, if you please,' he cried, proceeding up the stairs three at a time. Ma Thomas may have run a bawdy house, but it was nevertheless an efficient one. The water arrived in less than five minutes. Pender produced Harry's shaving kit, with soap and combs, hazel twigs for his teeth, and dusting powder for the wig he never wore, all together in a mahogany box inlaid with brass. Harry opened it, peering at himself in the mirror affixed to the lid.

No wonder Fairbairn had been curious. Besides the state of his coat, his face was covered in tiny abrasions from last night. He sat down in the chair while Pender worked up a lather, brushing it on to his chin when he was satisfied. Harry winced slightly as the hot soapy water found its way into the broken skin.

Pender had, up until now, kept his peace, aware that Harry would do what he wanted regardless of his opinion. But he could contain himself no longer. 'What happens now about buying that ship, your honour?'

Harry could have declined to answer that, since it really wasn't Pender's place to ask. Yet their relationship fell outside of that which normally existed between master and servant.

'I'll buy her if I can. And I'll crew her with the late Captain Broadbridge's men. And then we shall be off to sea again.' It was with an impish delight that he saw Pender's face fall at his next remark. 'Perhaps in the company of Gideon Bartholomew.'

Pender, not really knowing how his captain felt about Bartholomew, refused to be drawn, taking refuge in a generalized criticism.

'Don't give his hands much time ashore. Worse than the bleedin' Navy.'

Harry laughed, narrowly avoiding a mouth full of soap as Pender jabbed the brush in his direction. It was beautifully done, for you could never say it was deliberate. 'Never fear, Pender. Bartholomew's not my sort either. A rendezvous, Fairbairn said. I wonder where that is? He seems to have some golden touch when it comes to the taking of prizes. That can only mean one thing.'

'He must know where to look,' said Pender.

'I'll say. He was looking in the right place when those sailing out of Leghorn were writing to Admiral Hotham complaining of lack of income. If the Navy managed to drive them into penury, how have the men here done so well? They're spending money like water.'

'So you don't plan that we should join your brother?'

Harry, who had lain back with his eyes closed, looked up at his servant. He'd been mistaken about the man's mood. The usual cheerful smile was missing. Pender was worried, that much was clear. Harry reasoned that he must be rattled by the unfamiliarity of the place. Harry, more accustomed to the perils of ports all over the world, even with what had already happened, felt less threatened.

Then he felt a slight pang of guilt as another ploy slipped unbidden into his mind. He'd sent James away with the excuse that he wanted to keep him out of harm's way. But he knew that James wasn't fooled. Nothing would convince him more of Harry's peaceable intentions than if he sent Pender away as well. He would, after all, have Broadbridge's crew to protect him. Best to find out that was possible before making a final decision.

'There are too many things need doing for that,' he said, finally answering the question. 'I may send you back with him. He'll need his sea-chest anyway, and I'll want you to take it aboard. He'll require a deal of care for some time yet. Mr Williams I trust, but not Barnes and the rest of the officers. If I decide against the *Principessa*, then I can rejoin you both aboard the next ship that comes into victual. That will be here in a few days.'

'You don't reckon that's a mite dangerous, bein' here on your own?'

'A few days will make little difference.'

Pender's face was now positively miserable. 'That depends on whether you take account how long we've been in Genoa, your honour. After what we've been through the last two days, it could prove mortal.'

Harry decided to ignore his drift. He couldn't leave on this afternoon's tide, and that had nothing to do with plans to attack the

French or pretend to apply to join the syndicate. There was, quite simply, too much to occupy him. Besides, too many people knew that they'd been aboard the *Principessa*. If he went off now it would be taken as a tacit admission of guilt once the bodies of those two seamen were discovered. To cap it all, he'd had enough of that pessimism from James for one day. He returned the conversation to Bartholomew, his ships, and their success.

'They must be covering some specific routes that the French merchantmen sail. Perhaps they have secret information about that. It's a pity we never really got a chance to talk with Broadbridge. I feel that in his cups he might have let something slip. I wonder if Sutton knows anything?'

'He might, for he's sharp,' said Pender, smiling again. 'You might say he has the nose of a good thief.'

'He'll be aboard the *Dido*.'

'Aye,' said Pender. 'He was only ashore 'cause they'd been out all night. His lot can't afford to stay ashore. They ain't got the price of a drink.'

Having towelled his face dry, he handed Harry a fresh shirt, and then laid out a clean coat. While he was changing, Pender waved his set of picks, and nodded in the direction of Captain Broadbridge's sea-chest. Harry thought for a moment, then nodded. The man was dead in mysterious circumstances. It would make no difference to him, and there might be something in there that would answer some questions. His servant had the chest open in a few seconds. He lifted the lid and stood back. Harry stepped forward and started to rummage through the contents.

What was revealed came something of a surprise. Firstly the items you would expect to find. An oilskin pouch holding some papers relating the ownership of the *Dido*. These were wrapped round a heavy decorated latch-key, which fell out and lodged in the small amount of clothes the chest contained. Harry flicked it over, giving it a cursory glance, noting that it had some form of heraldic device on the grip. Then he turned his attention to Broadbridge's clothes. These included the late captain's best coat and a pair of rather worn pistols. But underneath these lay a mass of elaborately scripted documents: bonds relating to a variety of enterprises, from mining concessions to shares in a scheme to promote a flying contraption, and finally, most numerous, share certificates for participation in an corporation set to dig a navigation canal. He selected one or two and passed them to Pender, standing behind him.

'What the devil's all this?'

Harry was leafing through the rest of the papers. They were all new, with the portion for the name of the certificate holder left blank. Harry thought back to the way Broadbridge had dunned them for a hundred guineas. 'I'm not sure. Pender. But I would say that there's more to Captain Broadbridge than meets the eye. I had half wondered if we'd find some money, but there's not even a brass farthing in here.'

Apart from all the papers the good captain had been a man of few possessions, and fewer pleasures, apparently, save the bottle.

'He was hard up and no mistake.'

'You saw James and I advance him a hundred guineas. There's no sign of that either.'

'Perhaps he had it about his person, Captain. Or maybe it's aboard his ship.'

'That's possible. Mind, only a fool would be parted from their valuables around these parts.'

Harry closed the chest and asked Pender to relock it while he finished dressing. His buff coat was too heavy for the climate, but it was all he had. Another look in the mirror confirmed that he had once more returned to decent society.

'Happen it's at the bottom of the harbour,' said Pender.

'I searched him before we wrapped him in those flags. He may well have had the money with him when he set out.'

'What now?'

'Get my brother's things together. I shall go and call on Bartholomew. See if you can locate Crosby. I want a word with him. Then we'll go aboard the *Dido*. Once we've done that you can carry on to *Swiftsure*. I want you to afford me a proper introduction to Sutton. We can then find out if he knows anything.'

Harry banged on Bartholomew's door, perhaps a shade too heavily in his impatience. But there was no response. He went back down to the side entrance and reluctantly sought out Ma Thomas. Daylight did nothing for her appearance or her temper, and she coldly informed him that other people's movements were none of her affair. This was followed by a few more imprecations at the nature of captains conspiring to impoverish her, leaving Harry no wiser. He was half-way back to the room to fetch Pender, when he ran into Bartholomew coming down.

'Why, Captain Bartholomew. I have just been looking to find you.'

Bartholomew favoured him with a half-smile. 'Then you have achieved your purpose, Ludlow.'

'I wonder if we could return to your rooms; I would like to speak with you alone?'

The other man nodded, and turned round to make his way back up the stairs. Harry followed, his nose wrinkling as he was engulfed in the odour of Bartholomew's freshly scented body. He'd obviously been at his toilet when Harry knocked. As he opened the door, Harry recalled his heavy banging, and apologized for it. Bartholomew turned quickly and looked at him, causing Harry to pull up sharply. But no words followed the look, and Harry was left wondering why he had the impression that he had alarmed Bartholomew, rather than angered him. He was shutting the door behind them when Harry spoke, and the words made him freeze with his hand still on the doorhandle.

'Broadbridge is dead.'

Bartholomew turned slowly, looking at the ground. He said nothing for a few seconds, then lifted his hooded eyes to meet those of his guest. 'Dead?'

'Murdered, along with a couple of local sailors.'

'Where?'

'Aboard a ship called the *Principessa*. She's moored outside the harbour.'

Bartholomew said nothing, so Harry kept talking, outlining how he had found the body, and the subsequent attack on them in the cabin, his discovery of the two local sailors, and his continued suspicions of French involvement. Bartholomew didn't move throughout. Nor did he interrupt. He just stood, one hand on his chin, his eyes focused on a point behind Harry, listening.

'If my suspicions are correct, you must ask yourself, Captain Bartholomew, what action they will take next.'

'I can see that it's a matter of some concern. Does anyone else know of this?

Harry shook his head, curious at the man's detachment. 'Not yet. I thought that you ought to be the first to be informed.'

That mocking half-smile came back on his face. It was as though he had dismissed the matter from his mind. 'Is telling me first in any way connected with the conversation we had the other night?'

Harry didn't blink. The lack of feeling for the death of one of his partners was telling. They looked at each other in silence for a few moments, as Harry waited for any further response. Bartholomew seemed in no mood to give anything away. Harry knew that it would be wise to adopt the same tone. Yet he felt he ought to register some disapproval of the lack of even the faintest sign of grief.

'I was rather hoping to discuss with you what action to take against Captain Broadbridge's murderers before discussing business matters.'

Bartholomew's smile widened, for to him, Harry's words spoke volumes. 'I just wondered if you'd thought on it.'

The frown that appeared on Harry's face did nothing to dent his smile. 'If you are waiting for expressions of remorse, Ludlow, I will not play the hypocrite and oblige. You may have seen Broadbridge as a rescuer. Indeed you may have esteemed the fellow. I saw him as a liability.'

'The man is dead,' said Harry coldly.

For the first time the other man's voice betrayed a hint of emotion. As he spoke he rubbed his fingers gently across his brow, as though troubled by an unwanted thought. 'And I am sorry for it. I would wish him still alive, but out of my way.'

'Yet you agreed to advance him the money to buy that ship.'

Bartholomew was genuinely surprised. He shook his head slowly, looking Harry in the eye, as he thought about what to say next. 'Sit down, Ludlow, and stop frowning at me so.'

Harry paused, then turned round and sat in one of the deep armchairs. It faced the open door of the bedroom, dominated by a great four-poster of dark carved oak, the made-up bed covered in a lace counterpane. That room was panelled as well, heightening the atmosphere of life in an earlier age. He noted also that the suite was clear of any signs of habitation. Obviously his host, pacing up and down before him, was a man who liked his rooms cleaned early.

Bartholomew didn't speak for a while, marshalling his thoughts.

'When Broadbridge first arrived he led me, and my compatriots, to believe that he was a real tyro. He had money in his pocket, and a tall tale of exploits he'd undertaken in half the oceans of the world. And he'd heard about us. The man was afire to join, and prepared to pay good money to buy his way in.'

'Is it that simple?'

'We are in a strange business. Care must be exercised to ensure that we're dealing with the right sort. Anyway, Broadbridge kept on at us. Said he'd settle for a share of the inn, and a chance to prove his mettle when the time came. So after some discussion, we agreed.'

'We? I have been told that you decide.'

Harry hadn't meant to sound disapproving, but he must have given that impression, for Bartholomew bristled slightly. 'Lovers of Classical Greece speak of the benefits of democracy, Ludlow. But if you've commanded a ship, you'll know that such notions are useless.'

'Forgive me. I thought we were talking about a syndicate of businessmen.'

'We are, but their assets float.' Bartholomew smiled at his own pun. 'Let's say I'm the senior officer. Broadbridge showed right away that he was useless. The plan was for one of us, once we'd got him the right to sail out of here, to take him on a short cruise, to see what he was made of. We were out of the port for near six weeks. Despite my instructions to wait, he set off on his own, telling all and sundry, it seems, that he was going to return with his fortune made.'

'But it wasn't a success.'

'And no wonder, Ludlow. The man could barely read a chart, and he would brook no interference from anyone aboard, even though some of his hands have spent their lives at sea. And what did he do? He sailed right in the direction of a fleet of the King's ships, and that with half his crew deserters from the very same. Only a fool's luck saved him from losing the lot to the Navy.'

Bartholomew stopped, and shook his head slowly, wearing the smile of a parent amused at some childish misdemeanour. 'He sailed right through them in the dark, you know. And he was so drunk he held his course, singing at the top of his voice, and forcing even the biggest warships to sheer off.'

'Then why advance him to the money to buy the *Principessa*?'

Bartholomew sat down, and looked Harry right in the eye. 'But I didn't. I point-blank refused to do so.'

'Did you mention your offer to me?'

'I think it was somewhat less than an offer, Ludlow.'

'But it is that now?'

Bartholomew shrugged. 'It's not that simple. First off there needs to be a vacancy. And before you mention Broadbridge, let me say he doesn't count.'

'And if there was a vacancy?'

Bartholomew made a dismissive gesture with his hands. 'There are terms.'

'And profits. You are getting ready to set sail now, I hear.'

'Word spreads quickly.'

'You have a rendezvous arranged, I believe.'

Bartholomew pursed his lips and remained silent.

'Perhaps if you were to outline that I would have a better idea of what's on offer,' said Harry, well aware that somehow the invitation to join the syndicate had been watered down, if not withdrawn.

'That information is vouchsafed only to members of the syndicate.'

'That sounds remarkably like a blind investment.'

'Half blind.' Bartholomew waved his arm to indicate the tavern. 'They get a share of this too. When I first heard your name, I had a feeling I'd come across it before. Did you have a father in the Navy?'

If Crosby hadn't already told him that, Harry would have been amazed. But he nodded anyway. 'To return to Captain Broadbridge's death. Did you take my point about the French?'

'I'm not convinced your theories are correct.'

'Do you have any others to put against them?'

'No. But then I don't have your burning wish to speculate.'

Harry felt slightly angry. It all seemed plain enough to him. 'You don't feel threatened?'

Bartholomew shook his head slowly. 'Not in the least. Besides, I have more pressing matters to attend to.'

'I wonder that your patrons allow that French ship to stay in the harbour in any case.'

'Patrons?'

It was now Harry's turn to smile. 'I know little about Genoa, but

I doubt you could support this, and your activities, without powerful local interests combining to aid you.'

If he'd hoped to dent the man's assurance, he signally failed. 'I flatter myself that the contacts we have here are adequate.'

'Merely adequate?'

'Sometimes the exercise of power has the contrary effect to that which is intended. I have often observed that when interests compete, mutual respect achieves more than belligerence.'

The way that Bartholomew admitted his own connections was wonderfully succinct, while acknowledging that there were others equally powerful.

'Can you rely on those who favour France to show such restraint? And with all the pressure from below, can you be sure that the Genoese Republic will still be in the hands of those people next week?'

Bartholomew's mocking smile looked very like pity. 'I should not attach much importance to rumours of popular uprisings. They are much exaggerated. And if we're going to discuss the politics of this part of the world, we should fetch an abacus.'

Bartholomew's refusal to accept his conclusions was merely a minor irritation, for it left him with the one option to achieve a solution, and that was the one he favoured all along. But he couldn't help feeling that he'd been on the receiving end of a degree of condescension.

On first sitting in these rooms, Bartholomew, having spoken to whoever came to the door, had definitely hinted that joining the syndicate was possible. Now, by his manner and his words, he was virtually telling Harry that if he chose to apply it would not even be considered.

They had both been playing the same game, Bartholomew dangling a carrot to see if he could find out what Harry was after, and his guest pretending an interest for his own purposes. Neither had achieved much success, but Harry couldn't help feeling that, left as it was, Bartholomew would see himself as master of the game. That mocking look was still there. The man still saw him as a supplicant. He hadn't smoked that Harry Ludlow had no desire to join his damned syndicate in the first place. There was no purchase in letting on, but he didn't want to leave this room with Bartholomew hanging on to his smug air. Time to wipe the mockery out of that smile.

'I'm glad we understand each other, Bartholomew, for I feared you would seek to enrol me. You have saved me some embarrassment, for a blunt refusal often offends.'

Nothing in the man's demeanour changed, so Harry decided it would do no harm to let him know that Harry Ludlow was no fool. 'One thing I did wonder at . . .'

'What's that?'

'I wondered where it is you land your cargoes and dispose of your captures. And I wonder that you get away with it. There must be those in Genoa who would dearly love to see you pay something, if only to exercise their abacus. Should I decide to sail from here, I must put some effort into finding out how it is done.'

It was very smooth, for Bartholomew's voice didn't really change. But a look into his eyes, no longer hooded, was enough to tell Harry he was angry. He stood up abruptly.

'I normally avoid giving advice. It's very rarely accepted, however well intentioned. But I will make this exception and observe that you may find another harbour more profitable than Genoa. And if you truly ascribe to your theories it will obviously be less dangerous. Now, if you will forgive me, Ludlow, I do have other business to attend to. And since we are preparing to sail, I doubt we will have an opportunity to converse further.'

Harry stood up as well. 'Come, Bartholomew. Perhaps we'll meet again, either here, or at sea.'

He frowned at that, for he knew what his visitor was implying. And if Crosby had told him anything about Harry Ludlow, he would have guessed that any monopoly he enjoyed could soon be challenged.

He fixed Harry with a cold stare. 'Perhaps we will, Ludlow.'

CHAPTER SIXTEEN

Pender hadn't been able to locate Crosby, so he grabbed a couple of boys from the quay and took them off to fetch James's chest, while Harry bespoke a boat, this time with a couple of oarsmen, to take them out to Broadbridge's ship.

Everything Harry had heard about the *Dido* was true. It was no vessel to go privateering in, rather the kind of craft that plied the coastal trade, with the exception that it had been altered to carry a few cannon amidships, though even the gunports cut in the bulwarks looked as though they didn't suit. And the comparison with what should be was made worse by the proximity of the other ships in the syndicate's little fleet.

They had dirty grey salt streaks down their sides, which only served to tell Harry that they moved easily through the water. *Dido* had salt streaks all over her hull, stem to stern, evidence that she shipped a good deal of the sea through the planking. Judging by her shape, which reminded Harry of the doggers that fished the North Sea shallows, that would pale beside the quantity of water she'd take in over her bows in any kind of sea. He was left wondering how anyone could have been persuaded to buy such a boat for such a purpose.

'Avast there,' said a voice from below the bulwark. 'Sheer off.'

'Is Carey Sutton aboard?' shouted Pender, indicating to their boatmen that they should ship oars.

'What if he is? Who's asking?'

'Tell him Pious Pender wants a word.'

The voice growled threateningly. 'You stay clear till I see what he says.'

As if to emphasize the point, one of the gunports creaked open, and they found themselves staring down the muzzle of a four-pounder cannon. The two boatmen went white, but Pender just smiled at them. They were not reassured. The four of them sat, rocking gently on the filthy water of the harbour.

'Is that you, Pious?' Sutton's head peaked over the side. He treated Harry to a hard look, before asking Pender what they were about. Pender indicated to the boatmen to pull closer, so that he could speak quietly. They shook their heads. Pender, turned, and looked meaningfully at the gun muzzle, giving a sharp gesture to indicate that they would be safer out of its way. Reluctantly the two Genoese pulled on their oars and brought them within talking distance.

'We've come for a word, Carey, about Captain Broadbridge.'

'He ain't here. He went out to look at that ship yesterday afternoon and he's yet to return.'

'I said I wanted a word about him, not with him.'

Sutton's tongue was suddenly between his lips, and his brow furrowed as he tried to read into Pender's words what the man wasn't saying.

Being closer, Pender kept his voice down. 'It'd be best if we come aboard, Carey.'

A long pause, before Sutton spoke. 'Aye. Happen it would. I'll ask Lubeck.'

'Who's Lubeck?'

'Sort of master's mate. Bastard's from the Hanse, and I'm damned if I can make out half of what he says.'

Sutton was back in a trice, a huge blond man with a craggy face beside him. Pender went through another ritual of persuasion to get the boatmen to pull alongside. Climbing aboard, he had a quick word with Sutton. Then Sutton, with a deal of arm waving, had a word with the blond man before leaning over the side and beckoning Harry to follow. Harry looked meaningfully at the boatmen, and a hurried conversation ensued on deck. After a minute two men appeared, leaning over the side, muskets in hand, deliberately not

186

looking at the two frightened oarsmen. Harry, sure that his brother's possessions were safe, clambered aboard.

The deck was, to a naval eye, a disgrace. Dirty, streaked with grease and tar, and covered in all manner of filth, especially the scuppers, casks, and bales lying strewn about. The rigging was all ahoo, with loose ropes and badly clewed-up sails very evident. It would have taken half a day to get the boat properly ready for sea. And amidships on the forecastle, not tied off, lay a pile of brand-new guns. Harry walked over for a closer look, and counted ten twelve-pounders and four twenty-four-pounder carronades.

He couldn't think what they were doing aboard. The twelve-pounders were bad enough. The *Dido* might just stand them if they were rarely fired, and one at time. But the carronades? The recoil from them would, on their fixed carriages, spring every joint on a ship like this. He looked down into the waist. Slings full of shot for both types of weapons covered the lower deck. And they were surrounded by enough barrels of powder to satisfy the captain of a first-rate.

Sutton stood talking to Pender, watched carefully by the rest of the crew. Harry, walking up the larboard gangway, counted about thirty of them. There would be many more, men off the *Swiftsure* and other ships that had revictualled here. But they wouldn't show their faces while he was around. He walked over to join Pender, Sutton, and the big German by the mainmast.

'So,' said Sutton sharply.

'He wants to know what's up, Captain,' said Pender. 'I'm not sure I know what to tell him.'

'Who has charge of these men while Broadbridge is away?' asked Harry.

Sutton aimed a dismissive thumb at the blond giant. 'Lubeck here runs the boat, but he's left me in charge of the hands, especially if'n we go ashore. You could say I'm the captain's right-hand man.'

Harry noticed that Sutton had turned slightly and spoke softly so that the German couldn't quite hear. 'I need to talk to you alone, Sutton, is that possible?'

The other man nodded, and said a few words to Lubeck, who frowned at Harry but went away nevertheless. Once he was out of earshot, Harry spoke again. 'Is there somewhere we can talk?'

A long silent stare, then Sutton spun on his heel and made for the cabin. To call it such was to elevate it. It was small, dark, low-ceilinged, and extremely cramped. It smelt of tallow, bilge water, and unwashed humanity. The only air and light came two round holes, one on either side. It was really just a place to sleep, convenient for the deck, whilst affording the owner a modicum of privacy. Sutton, bent double, indicated that Harry should take the only chair, seating himself on the unmade cot.

'Make sure we're not overheard, Pender,' said Harry, as he shut the door behind them. He took the seat just as Sutton indicated.

'Captain Broadbridge is dead,' said Harry, without preamble.

Sutton must have guessed at something like this from Pender's reluctance to speak. Either that, or he was a man so used to others dying that it had no effect on him. He sat silently, waiting for Harry to continue.

'He was murdered aboard that ship he went to see. We found his body last night.' Sutton looked past Harry to the door as he continued. 'Hard to be certain, Sutton, but we think it was the same lot that attacked us the night before.'

He could see Sutton trying to work this out in his mind. If he drew any conclusions he wasn't going to pass them on without prompting.

'We thought you might have some ideas.'

'I'd best tell the lads. They'll be needing another berth.'

Sutton stood up abruptly and made for the door. He opened it and whispered to Pender. Harry's servant replied so that both could hear. 'You can talk to the Captain, Carey. I told you to take my word on it.'

Sutton half turned so that his reply was also addressed to both. 'It's not for me to take it or leave it, Pious. I've got to eat, and so has the rest of them poor buggers. An' we've done precious little of that the last few weeks, since Broadbridge was so set on owning that ship that he practically stopped buying victuals. Man's dead. Don't matter how, since it's not my job to care. Not that he wasn't a good enough type, in his own way, though he talked a damn sight more than he did. But he was no sailor, an' I know that even if I've only been afloat a few months. Him putting all his money into the syndicate was more like robbery than anything else. And as for buying this tub, he never had a hope in hell of keeping abreast of the likes of Bartholomew, and the bastard knew it when he sold it. It's my reckoning that they only did it cause they had spare mouths to feed an' it suited them for someone else to pick up the cost.'

Harry frowned. He put aside the question of all these 'spare' hands for the moment and gestured with his arm to indicate the ship. 'Bartholomew sold him this?'

'Not Bartholomew as such. The syndicate. Least ways that's what they call it. But it's Bartholomew really. The others do pretty much what they're told.'

Harry wondered if Bartholomew had misled him deliberately, for he had certainly given the impression that Broadbridge had bought the *Dido* himself. 'Shut the door, Sutton, and sit down.'

There was a moment's hesitation. Pender turned just enough to deliver a reassuring nod before Sutton obliged.

'Did he sell him those cannon as well?'

'No. An' that's likely another reason we've been on short commons. He had those guns delivered when we came back from that bloody cruise. Said they was going to surprise Bartholomew. God only knows if he's paid for them yet. There was a bloke here yesterday, a sort of local tipstaff, waving some papers and threatening all sorts, though I couldn't make out a word he said. Damn me if Broadbridge, who's been living on credit for weeks, don't produce a purse full of gold, and fob the bastard off with a part-payment for whatever he was after. Thank God the rest didn't see it, or there would have been a mutiny.'

Harry now knew where his loan had gone. The money which was supposed to feed his hands had probably gone to buy guns Broadbridge would never have been able to use. He hadn't taken to Bartholomew much, but the man was right about the late captain of the *Dido*. He reached into his pocket, taking out some gold coins. 'If it's food you need, then I can help. As for a bed, I don't think anyone is going to claim this tub.'

'That's all you know. If Broadbridge is dead, this reverts to the syndicate. That's the rule, no matter how much you're worth. And if'n we can't get ourselves on another boat, we might as well hand ourselves back to King George, for they won't take us on the other ships.'

Another question mark against Bartholomew. That was probably what he meant when he mentioned terms. Harry felt that Sutton knew a great deal more than he was saying, but to question him now would only court a refusal. In time, the man might come to trust him. That would be the moment for a proper talk. 'I intend to buy the *Principessa*. If I do, I need to crew it.'

Sutton looked at him with surprise. 'You don't look like the type to crew a ship with Navy deserters, which most of the hands here happen to be.'

'Take this money, Sutton. Purchase some food, and keep everyone aboard the *Dido*. Can you do that?'

'Ay, ay, Captain,' said Sutton, clasping the coins, suddenly respectful.

'Now tell me about the hands, I want to know who the sailors are.'

Sutton was happy to oblige, though as he talked his inexperience about life afloat became apparent. Yet Harry formed the distinct impression, confirmed by Sutton himself, that he'd been Broadbridge's right-hand man. Odd to elevate a person like Sutton when what he really needed was someone who could handle a ship. Harry's mind wandered to that chest full of documents and share certificates, none of them signed. And all these guns he'd bought and, it seemed, hadn't paid for. Pender had said that Sutton was a good thief. Perhaps Broadbridge required those services more than he needed the help of a proper sailor.

At least Sutton had identified the big German, Lubeck, as the most experienced man aboard, and Harry was pleased to hear that there were a number of proper tars in the crew. 'Right, Sutton, I need to talk with these men, alone. But say nothing to anyone else, about Broadbridge or my plans.'

He passed over the slip of paper that the victualling agent had pressed into his hand on the *Swiftsure*. 'Take a party ashore and go to this address, which is at the far end of the quay. Purchase some victuals, enough for two days, and ask Signor Brown to expect me before noon.'

Sutton nodded. He looked at the door again, as if trying to decide to say something and needing the reassurance of Pender to do so. The look in Harry's eye made such a consultation impossible.

Sutton shrugged, as if what he said was of no account. 'Seems to me that you're taking the same chance as Captain Broadbridge. Which is daft, seein' as how you're a lot brighter than him.'

Harry stood up, crouching low to avoid hitting his head on the deckbeams. 'What chance is that?'

Sutton looked guilty for a moment. He gazed at the money Harry had given him. 'Truth is, Captain Ludlow, that I've been trying to shift my hammock ever since I came ashore. Nice enough man, as I say, but Broadbridge was no more a ship's captain than I'm a blue fart, and that were proved on his so-called cruise. That was a right fuck-up and no mistake. I had no mind to sail with him again, not just 'cause he didn't know what's what about ships. Worse'n that, he knew bugger all about the Navy. And with him at the helm, in this barky, we stood to be pulled up by the first one of the King's ships we came across. How we got away with it, last time, I'll never know. It's one thing to walk back after being ashore, tippin' the hat and beggin' your pardon. A floggin', yes, but not enough to keep you from taking up your duties. To be taken out of a privateer, forced like, is more like a floggin' round the fleet.'

Harry indicated those outside, with some difficulty since he was still bent over. 'Did that apply to the rest?'

'Them that's got any sense worked it out. I keep my own counsel. But it don't alter things, do it? That's why I'm surprised at you. Mind I'm only speakin' out 'cause you're vouched for by Pious there. You know that what I've been sayin' is true, and though you might be a better seaman, it applies to you just as much as it did to Broadbridge.'

'I do know, Sutton, and you impress me by pointing it out.'

'So we'd be better off handin' ourselves in.'

'No. You see, Sutton, I will have Admiralty exemptions to man a ship larger than this.'

If Sutton noticed there was an element of prayer in that, it didn't show. His jaw dropped, and he looked happy for a moment. Then his face clouded again. 'Not much good for deserters are they, Captain?'

Harry laughed out loud. 'Sutton. You're right about being a novice afloat. There's hardly a man jack in the Navy that hasn't run at some time, and not a privateer at sea who don't depend on ex-Navy men to crew his ship. Now alert those men and line them up to see me in here.'

Sutton opened the door and Pender turned to face them. They looked as though they were about to speak when Harry stopped them, telling Sutton to carry on and asking Pender to come and shut the door.

'I think, if I move quickly, I have a crew.'

Penders response was correct, but the tone was rather flat, as if the man was reserving judgement. 'I'm right glad to hear it, your honour.'

'My brother was less than happy about my remaining here in Genoa,' said Harry.

'Makes sense,' replied Pender.

'Then you'll be pleased to know that I'm afire to get out of the place myself,' snapped Harry. 'You will take my brother's chest to the *Swiftsure*, inform him of my intentions, and accompany him back to the Fleet. Once I've transacted my business, I will join you.'

Pender just looked at him, expressionless. Harry could not sustain the angry tone, for his servant's unenthusiastic response was prompted by a genuine fear for his safety.

'You'd best be on your way, Pender,' he said with a smile. 'Or the *Swiftsure* will sail without you.'

It was a direct command, for all the gentle delivery. Pender held Harry's gaze for a second, with a look that some would have felt to be insolent. But it was just Pender's way of saying that he wasn't fooled.

'Ay, ay, Captain,' he said formally, his fingers brushing his hat. Then he turned and left, leaving his master feeling like a proper scrub.

Harry cursed himself roundly. He stood in the wardroom door of the *Principessa* looking at the empty table. There was blood there in plenty. But no bodies. He knew he should have anticipated this. Yet as he reflected he was at a loss to know what he could have done to prevent it. Forced by necessity to get James to a surgeon, he would not have contemplated leaving Pender alone on board to look after the ship. He went back on deck to join the others. Their presence aboard and the reasons he'd brought them was a grave breach of the normal rules of business. But time, not to mention events, mitigated against adherence to principle.

Swiftsure was preparing to sail, the rigging full of men. By his reckoning he had a clear forty-eight hours, even with the most favourable winds, before another ship could take its place. No one man, regardless of his experience, could undertake the task of listing the ship's requirements in the time available. So he sorted out those on the *Dido* who could do the work with him, and fetched them over to the *Principessa*, sure that any fuss at this stretching of Toraglia's permission to view the ship could be overborne by his obvious desire to do business.

Lubeck was walking around, taking a purchase on the shrouds and trying them for tension. He muttered away to himself in a guttural voice, half cursing, half caressing the ship. In the boat coming across, Harry had established that he was an ex-master who had got roaring drunk one night in the pool of London, only to wake up two days later and find himself a volunteer in King George's Navy. Unable to make head nor tail of his name, he'd been entered into the ship's books in the name of his home town, which he kept repeating to the bemused first lieutenant.

Having spent nearly a year aboard a man-of-war, his English was much improved, though Sutton made a great show of not understanding him. Harry surmised, in the confused ranking system aboard the *Dido*, that there was a certain rivalry. Sutton might have been Broadbridge's right-hand man ashore, but he would have been useless in any position of authority afloat. On the way across the harbour Lubeck and Harry had a lively conversation about the limited time the German had available. As soon as he had enough money, he was on his way, by coach or on foot if necessary, back to his native town on the Baltic, and Lubeck raised a great fist to show what he would do to anyone who stood in his way.

The three other men, standing by the wrecked bulkhead, were all man-of-war to their fingertips, with their long well-greased pigtails sewn with coloured ribbons. The *Dido* might have been an untidy ship, but they had taken care of themselves. It was a pleasure to see them cut off their misdirected curiosity as soon as he appeared, for it denoted hands well versed in avoiding the attentions of zealous officers. In his experience, men such as these, who could dodge even the most stringent rules, and who were apt to be called work-shy, often made the best petty officers. For they knew all the tricks, and they would tolerate no one doing to them what they had so long practised on their own superiors.

In these four men, all rated able, who could hand reef and steer, he had the backbone of the crew for his new ship. He would command the ship, with Lubeck acting as his master, able to stand a watch and keep the ship safe on course. Each one of the others would head a division, captains of the forecastle, tops, and afterguard. Harry was strict in the way he manned his ship, adhering as closely as possible to the methods he'd learned as a youngster. He would brook none of the chaos that he'd seen on the deck of the *Dido*.

Amongst the others he'd find someone who'd worked long enough with a carpenter to make a fist at doing his job, a man with the natural authority to assume the duties of a boatswain, yet another who had an interest in cannon and would happily take on the responsibilities of a gunner. Anything he couldn't find he'd have to whistle for, or train himself.

Harry thanked the luck that had made him avoid mention of the bodies in the ward-room. In truth he would have be sorely shifted to find a way of explaining it, and had put it to the back of his mind as something to deal with once he had them aboard. Indeed he had gone below immediately with the express purpose of lashing the ward-room door shut until he could fathom out what to do with them. Now they were gone, probably over the side, and while he felt for their families there was nothing he could do about it.

But there was still the bulkhead and the state of the cabin. He wasn't fool enough to think that these fellows hadn't picked up some information aboard the *Dido*. No matter what precautions you took, sailors had a way of finding out things that beggared belief. They seemed to be able to pick up a whisper through a six-inch plank, though nothing in their manner would ever let you know that they'd heard. He gave them a bald outline of the facts, telling them that Broadbridge was dead, and what had happened when they found the body, alluding to an unspecified rivalry in the matter of buying the ship. This served two purposes. It told them that their new commander was a fighter and no fool, and it also warned them that there was danger about, and a man who didn't keep a sharp eye out could end up dead.

He had his own watch on the ship now but he needed to shift himself to legitimize his presence. He left Lubeck and his mates to sort out a sail plan, and tally off the yards that would have to be hoisted to carry the sails, and make their various lists while he had himself rowed ashore. The men in the boat wouldn't look at him, lest their eyes betray their deep curiosity. Not that they were worried. This man was prepared to feed them, and for the moment that was sufficient to ensure their undying loyalty.

Harry was free to turn his mind to what to do next. He was, by nature, a man who preferred to act quickly, and in this case speed was of the essence. The *Swiftsure* was now at single anchor, and the boats were out to tow her head round so she'd be away soon. Forty-eight hours before another warship arrived. Not much time to rig a ship, take a short cruise, finalize the details of the purchase, victual her, and get to sea.

For the plan he had in mind, to make a fuss about the death of Broadbridge would be a mistake, and any subsequent action, following so soon, would be directly linked to his murder. This left him with yet another problem. He'd have to concoct a tale about the two seamen that would hold water until he could get away from Genoa. They were working for Toraglia. But if they were only hired labour, then he could always say that he had taken them on as hands himself. God help him if they were family retainers. The main thing was to set in train the steps necessary to buy the *Principessa*, and to do that he had to get the ship to sea for a cruise. Only then, given his previous statements, could he safely bid for her.

He tried to work out what his opponents would do next. If they'd searched the ship, they'd know, that apart from a quantity of blood-stains and that damaged bulkhead, there was no real evidence of the events of last night. Yet they felt safe enough to row across the harbour in broad daylight and hoist those bodies over the side. If he showed signs of doing everything he could to get out of Genoa, then he might convince them that they had nothing to fear. And if he didn't report any of the murders, there would be no hue and cry, and no need for desperate measures to stop him. On all counts it made sense to stay silent. It would lull his enemies in a false sense of security, leaving him free to pursue a plan of which they could know nothing.

CHAPTER SEVENTEEN

People arriving at the house of Guistiani on foot were obviously a rare occurrence, since, for all their loud hammering on the heavy gates, Harry and the escort he'd brought from the *Dido* were kept waiting, while those responsible for the place made sure of them. Nor was it easy getting to Giacomo Gustiani himself. The anteroom was crowded, as it had been the day before, but the servants seemed to suffer from a form of professional deafness when it came to admitting supplicants to their masters' domain. Having been ushered straight in, he had not noticed the desk off to one side of the room. Here sat the fellow who'd led the way the day before. A fussy little man with rouged cheeks and an old-fashioned full-bottomed wig, he apparently acted as some form of appointments clerk. He clearly loved his job, and the power it gave him, for he treated all Harry's loud protestations that haste was essential with a silent shrug, and a gesture to the ledger on the desk before him.

Harry moved to the centre of the room and fumed quietly, then approached the desk again. The clerk favoured him with the same resigned shrug of the shoulders. It seemed absurd that he could not proceed for the mere want of an address, but he had no idea where Count di Toraglia and his wife resided. He realized that he would have to act or the man at the desk would delay him all day. Keeping a weather eye out for other servants, he made for the other side of the room, moving swiftly through the crowd without knocking into anyone. There he paused, waited until all the servants were too far away to stop them interfering, and barged in.

The Guistiani brothers, in conference with several other sleek-looking men, looked up in shock, and the doorway behind Harry was suddenly full of liveried retainers. But Harry was already talking. 'I require directions to Count Toraglia's house, and someone from here to take me. I can hardly call otherwise.'

'Signor Ludlow,' said Alfredo Guistiani angrily, but Harry kept talking.

'I apologize to these gentlemen, but I will not be kept waiting all day for such a simple matter.' Harry was watching both the brothers closely. He didn't know who to trust in this city state, and that included these two. He looked for any sign of alarm greater than that caused by shock of his sudden entry.

Giacomo recovered almost immediately, roundly cursed the ineptitude of his epicene clerk, and gave loud instructions that the gentlemen should be taken with haste to Count Toraglia's villa. The clerk, wilting under the gaze and words of his master, half stood and grovelled an affirmative reply. Harry, closing the door and going back to the desk, was gratified to see that the colour in the man's cheeks was not now solely composed of rouge.

An escort was provided, one of the fellows he had the day before, and with a posse of his own new hands in tow they set off. They made their way south through the town and out of one of the old gates in the imposing city walls. The place had long since spread beyond the old defences. Given the number of houses that rose above their heads, forming dark and shaded canyons crowded with bustling humanity, it was impossible to tell if one was outside the walls or not. But the Count's villa stood alone, surrounded by a high wall topped with sharp metal spikes. The gate, like that of all the large properties hereabout, was studded with bolts and made of thick oak. The knocker was a huge affair, bearing a heraldic crest on it, a bird of prey with a small mammal fast in its claws. Harry felt it vaguely familiar, but in a city awash with heraldry, it was by no means unusual.

The postern gate, off to the side of the main gate, was opened by a grave-looking servant, old and bent, who listened carefully to Guistiani's man before ushering Harry inside. But he would not allow in the three sailors Harry had with him, or the man from the Guisti-ani. With an emphatic shake of the head, he shut the postern gate in their faces and they were left to fend for themselves in the crowded street. The courtyard was a riot of colour and smells, each one pressing in on the other in an untidy abundance of plants and trees. He followed the servant down a winding path, heavily shaded and laid with old worn flagstones, catching the odd glimpse of the car-riageway that led to the main entrance through the trees.

This informal garden, encroaching as it was on the path, with the trees forming a canopy overhead, was oppressive rather than shaded, an impression strengthened by the overpowering scents of plants in bloom and the odour of rotting vegetation. Eventually they emerged at the point where the path and the carriageway met, and Harry could see the house. Again there were no windows on the ground floor, and at the top of the walls embrasures had been constructed giving the place a Gothic appearance, even more like a fortress than the Guistianis' bank. The general impression was of a house and grounds gone to seed.

The cool tiled hall was welcome after the heat of the streets and the garden. He could hear subdued voices, talking urgently, almost as if an arguement was in progress, except the tone was too restrained. The servant motioned for Harry to wait, and went through the hall into a inner courtyard, his presence bringing silence. Harry looked about him. The walls were white and practically bare, and with the tiled floor it was more like a Levantine residence than a Latin one. Some gilded and inlaid scimitars crossed on one of the walls height-ened the flavour of something eastern. It seemed a house designed for two things: sound defence and the need to nullify the heat of the world outside.

Apart from the swords, a single portrait broke the monotony of the white walls. Harry moved closer to have a look. The subject was of medium height and stocky, wearing a plain blue coat and white breeches, a feathered tricorn hat in his hand and a jewelled sword on his hips. It was the background, dotted with ships under sail, that told you he was a sailor. The face was handsome, and the eyes lively. It was hard to reconcile this image of sturdy health with the man he'd come to see.

The servant was gone some time, leaving Harry kicking his heels impatiently. He finally returned, bowed, and motioned Harry to follow him out into the shaded courtyard. He heard the sound of running water and as he emerged his eye was taken by the height of the jets streaming from the elaborate sculptured pond in the middle of the open space. The Count and his wife lounged on a pair of silk-covered divans by the side of the fountain, and between them lay a table laden with fruit. A hookah, bubbling merrily, and obviously in use, lay at the side of Toraglia's couch. Harry surmised that the man was asleep, for he did not react to the sound of Harry's footsteps.

But Harry's eyes barely noticed the Count, being dragged without protest to the vision on the other divan. The garment she was wearing could have been easily described as indecent, it was cut so low. Her hair was piled high on her head as before, leaving her graceful neck and her face, free of even the slightest trace of powder, to be admired. And Harry made no attempt to hide his regard. He thanked the Lord that the Count was blind as well as asleep, for he could not have failed to notice the reaction in Harry's features. He knew he had assumed the same inane grin that he'd carried on his face the first time he met her. No wonder half of Genoa was queueing up for this creature. To her credit, the Countess seemed not to notice. She carried her beauty lightly, with an overwhelming air of innocence.

She favoured him with a warm smile, indicating by dumb show both that her husband was asleep, and that he should avail himself of the other divan, which lay right by the side of the fountain, receiving the maximum benefit from the cooling air created by the streams of bright water. Harry sat down, his mind registering that the seat was warm, as though recently occupied. The servant reappeared again, bearing an elaborate Venetian glass pitcher full of pale silver liquid. He placed it, with a matching goblet, on the table, removing another half-full glass as he did so.

'We must wait, Signor Ludlow, for my husband requires rest.'

All thoughts of haste slipped from Harry's mind. The Count could sleep as long as he liked, Harry Ludlow was perfectly content to sit here in the presence of this girl and drink fresh lemonade. It was a measure of how smitten he was that, short of time and usually most careful for the welfare of his men, forgot all about haste and the trio stuck out in the hot and dusty street.

She spoke as if she read his mind. 'They are rarely of a long duration, but frequent. And I would not dare to give you permission to sail the *Principessa* on my own, since I presume that is why you have come. Anything else, yes, but that ship is closer to his heart than I am myself.'

'I cannot bring myself to believe that, Madame.'

'Are all Englishmen so immediately gallant, Signor? Your brother was very forward. The Count, I'm afraid, remarked upon it.'

She leant forward to pick a grape from a dish on the table, and Harry had to turn away to avoid being caught looking down her cleavage. Could she be so completely unaware of the effect she was having? She behaved as though the attributes that God had given her were of no account. He felt he must change the subject, lest his desire to be something more than gallant get the better of him.

'I was struck by the portrait in the hall, Madame.'

'How I would love to remove it,' she said, frowning. 'It does Alfonso no good, having his vistors gaze on an image of his former self. Some are so crass as to actually allude to the difference.'

Harry looked at the wasted figure asleep on the divan. He agreed with her. Yet he didn't want to say so, didn't want to seem incapable of independent thought. It was with a feeling of deliberate contrariness that he replied.

'Perhaps such reminders help to fortify him, Madame, to raise his spirits. Any sick man would long to return to his former health.'

For the first time Harry saw a trace of impatience. If anything she looked even more beautiful, with a definite hauteur sharpening her features. For all his previous intentions Harry continued quickly, not wishing to be thought of as her enemy. 'Mind, with you to sustain him, he needs little else.'

She bowed her head slightly in acknowledgement, but her features didn't soften. Harry spoke again, fearing that she would lapse into an angry silence. 'How did his illness come about?'

'Suddenly. Like a bolt out of the blue. One day the handsomest man in Genoa, surrounded by blushing maidens at every ball we attended. The next, near death's door, and only saved by providence. He lay in a coma for days.'

Harry had the slight feeling that she was mocking him. Perhaps it was just the rehearsed tone of an oft-repeated phrase. Her face softened again and her smile returned. 'But he has the constitution of a bull, Signor Ludlow. He could hold nothing in his stomach and he was reduced to a skeleton. Yet he survived. I only thank the Gods that I attended him myself, with the household servants of course.'

'And doctors?'

'Doctors!' she snapped. 'I wonder if they make more out of death than they do out of life. What would they have done? Bleed him? An already weakened man and a physician takes away that which gives him strength. And I was right. His attack would have killed anyone else. Not Alfonso. He lived, blind, and depending on me for everything. Now he wavers. Sometimes I think he will recover. At other times I am set to call the priest to administer last rights. But never will I entrust him to a doctor.'

The Count moved slightly, and in a flash his wife was up, crossing over to kneel by his side, a concerned look on her face. Gently she rubbed both her hands on his furrowed brow, then opened them to circle the prominent temples. The mouth, set in the relaxed posture of sleep, changed into a smile, as the Count, waking from his slumbers, raised his hand in the air. His wife immediately took it and squeezed, and Harry, in no way a sentimental man, felt a pricking at the back of his eyes to see such mutual regard in a situation in which one of the lovers was doomed.

'We have a visitor,' she said softly, placing her hands on his lips. The Count's head turned, a habit from when he had his sight. 'Signor Ludlow.'

The Count looked confused for a moment, his brow furrowing again.

'The Englishman we met yesterday, who wants to buy the *Principessa*.'

The man's face showed all his emotion, first the smile and nod at the mention of an Englishman, and the subsequent change to a glum expression when he recalled that his ship was for sale.

'Have you looked at her?'

'I have, Count Toraglia. And may I say that I like what I see. If she'd been rigged I think I would have upped anchor without permission.'

Toraglia smiled. 'You have a crew, Signor?'

'Yes,' said Harry softly. 'And I admit to a degree of impatience. I've taken the liberty of putting the leading hands aboard to look over the ship as well.'

That was somewhat less than the truth, of course. But it would suffice till he was on more intimate terms. The Count sat up, swinging his sightless eyes in Harry's direction. He sat silently for a moment, his face gloomy, which accentuated the premature ageing caused by his illness. Harry held his breath, wondering if he was about to receive a wigging for his effrontery.

'I realize that I should greet you with cries of anger, and seek to play the cunning vendor. Yet I understand. This is sad for me.'

Harry relaxed, letting his breath out slowly. 'Giacomo Guistiani told me how important she is to you, Count Toraglia. I too understand.'

The Count's face cleared again, but he could not bring himself to smile. His hand waved in a weak gesture, meant to ease Harry's concerns. 'Then perhaps you are a true sailor, Signor Ludlow.'

'I would esteem that a compliment should I ever be worthy of it.'

The Countess, who had been kneeling beside him, took both his hands in hers. 'It has to be, Alfonso. The longer the ship lies idle, the greater the cost.'

'I know my dear. But you have not stood on her deck with the wind on her quarter, and felt her cutting her way through the water, studding sails aloft and kites out, with the log showing fourteen knots. And now I must send someone to show this *Inglese* how to sail her. Will he buy? I know he will. No one could resist the purchase of that ship.'

Harry wondered for a moment if he was playing the cunning vendor after all, but then he cursed himself for a heartless wretch, and tried to remember how he'd felt when he'd lost his ship. There was no explaining it to a landsman, just as a man who never owned a horse or a dog could not see why the loss of them should be an occasion for real sorrow.

Harry had some trouble with the mixture of French and Italian as the Count continued. Talking about his ship had lifted his spirits, making him seem more youthful. The enthusiasm was clear in his husky voice as he started to outline her qualities.

'And she sails amazingly close to the wind, Signor. You must stow her a bit by the stern, of course, or she'll not answer her rudder right . . .'

His wife, with a worried look, put her hand on his cheek and he stopped talking, the face again falling into the visage of an old man.

'Alfonso, you must not tax yourself.'

He gave a rueful smile. 'I shall not do so because you do not wish it, but in truth, my love, what have I to save my energy for?'

Harry suddenly realized the implications of something the Count had said a few minutes ago. He mentioned sending someone aboard with Harry. That would never do, for he could not hide the missing watchmen, nor the condition of the ship, let alone the men he'd left aboard probably behaving as if he owned it already.

'Madame, I know your husband is a sick man, but can you not see how talking of his ship raises his spirits?'

Her features sharpened again. Plainly any interference in the care of her husband was unwelcome. Harry continued quickly. 'I'm no medical man, but I would strongly advise you to include the vital spark in his treatment, for I have often observed that a sick man can show amazing powers of recovery, given that they had something to care for.'

The Count gave his wife's hand another pat. 'I have something to care for, Signor.'

'Yet I observed just this very moment, sir, how your spirits lifted at the mention of rigging a ship. Why I would swear that to take part in the rigging of the *Principessa* again would raise you up no end . . .'

'Signor Ludlow,' said the Countess, with a look of alarm, but Harry kept talking quickly.

'I would esteem it an honour if you would accompany me back to the ship in person. There you could advise me on the best way to dress her, for I'm sure you'd want me to see the ship sail her very best. I realize that this is likely to cost me a pretty penny, but I'm bound to repeat, sir, that having already had a close look at the *Principessa*, I like what I see.'

The Count had brightened again, but his wife looked properly agitated. Harry kept talking still, as the best hope of getting through to the man. 'And I would also esteem it an honour if you would sail with me on my cruise, and we could then exchange our views on the way she handles. It would save time to have aboard the man who knows the way to coax the best out of her. And before you plead that it could prove injurious, I have often heard the greatest physicians recommend a sea voyage for the restoration of health.'

Now she was really angry. 'I cannot allow this.'

Harry was quite emphatic, and completely ruthless, for her husband was nodding in agreement. 'Madame, allow me to say that it's worth a try. Why, it may set your husband on the road to a complete recovery.'

The corner had been turned, for the Count could hardly contain his enthusiasm for the idea. His wife took Harry's arm and led him away slightly. She spoke quietly, using the sound of the fountain to cover her voice. There she objected that they had insufficient servants to carry the sedan chair. Harry, registering that they had indeed sunk to near penury, countered her objection with the fact that he had sailors waiting to perform that very duty, and that he would undertake to return the Count at the first sign of a decline in his health.

She spoke loudly now, so that her husband could hear. 'No, Signor Ludlow. I fear I must forbid it.'

Toraglia stood up, leaning heavily on his cane. His face was firmly set and though the words he used were addressed to Harry, they were aimed at his wife. 'Signor Ludlow. I will most happily do as you request.'

Harry turned just in time to see the look of flaring anger on the Countess's face as she bowed her head in submission. Regardless of his health, her husband was openly exercising his right to be master in his own house.

Aware that his action had bordered on humiliation, Toraglia set out to mollify his wife with repeated assurances that he would be in good hands. Her suggestion, one that alarmed Harry, that she attend on him, was overborne by the Count himself, who said that a ship being rigged for sea was no place for a lady. 'And as for the morrow, my dear, let us see how we fare today before undertaking a cruise.'

She mistook his meaning for she stated emphatically that the idea of a cruise held no pleasure for her, since she was a terrible sailor, constantly sick from the moment she set foot aboard until the time she left. In the end, it was the expression in her husband's face that finally won her reluctant approval. Harry had never realized how little the eyes counted when you wanted something badly enough.

CHAPTER EIGHTEEN

Another pair of hands was provided to add to Harry's three sailors, though there were sour looks when his men found they had to carry a double sedan chair. They tried to engage Toraglia's man in their general dissatisfaction, waving their hands and yelling scraps of the local argot. He merely met their moans with a blank stare which angered them even further. Opening his mouth wide, he pointed, and they observed that he lacked a tongue. Their angry tone immediately changed to one of embarrassed contrition, with murmured apologies.

On the way to the harbour, Harry tentatively mentioned Broadbridge, alluding to his interest in the ship. As far as he could tell, Toraglia's look of utter mystification was genuine as he made Harry repeat the name.

'The gentleman is not known to me, Signor. But I cannot speak for the Guistianis. He may well have approached them, though I doubt they would make the sale public so soon.'

'If they're acting properly on your behalf they should seek as many buyers as possible.'

Toraglia caught the drift of the remark and gave Harry a thin smile. 'Do not fear, Signor Ludlow. I will not stage an auction. If you like the ship, and we can agree a price that satisfies us both, I shall look no further. And by your actions so far I think you have demonstrated, perhaps unwisely, that you are taken with the *Principessa.*'

Harry answered rapidly, fully admitting that the liberty he'd taken of putting a few of his men aboard left him in a weak position to drive a hard bargain, whilst also reassuring the Count that there was a price beyond which he wouldn't go. He excused his actions on the grounds of haste, adding yet another lie to his tally by claiming intelligence of a rich French convoy that which would be at his mercy if he could get to sea on time. It sounded transparently false to him, but the Count was in such high spirits that he merely nodded with complete understanding. The man was so clearly pleased at the prospect of going to sea in his ship that he would have agreed to his guest stripping the copper off her bottom if he'd been asked. Toraglia began to recount some of his adventures from previous wars, talking as if they were old shipmates. Harry, engaged in dissimulation himself, tarred him with the same brush, wondering how much all this bonhomie was going to cost.

Toraglia was helped into the boat and rowed out to the *Principessa*, leaving the mute ashore to guard his chair until it was time to return home. They sat him in a captain's chair at the stern rail, and rigged a hammock in the sleeping cabin in case he should get tired. But the Count seemed to have taken on a new lease of life. All the way across the anchorage he had listed the *Principessa*'s little vices, talking about her like a doting parent. And Harry had listened carefully, for this was the experience of years distilled into hours. It would save him endless time, for he only had to check Toraglia's statements against the behaviour of the ship to know if they still held.

On board, Harry had positively puffed with pride at the way he'd handled things. Toraglia couldn't see the bulkhead, with its great gashes all round. Nor the deck. There was no hands as yet to priddy the planking and remove the black bloodstains from last night's affray. Lubeck had provided a list of requirements as soon as they came aboard. To that he would add his own. He sent his boat over to the *Dido* to begin the job of ferrying the men over, and had words with his leading hands so that they could sort out who they wanted in each division. That, he knew, was something that would require adjustment, but at this stage he was prepared to let them sort it out for themselves.

Luckily, Lubeck had some French and was able to communicate with the Count. Harry, on the cutter's first return with twenty of his new crew aboard, grabbed a couple of the more disreputable-looking types and had himself rowed to the quayside hard by the dockyard. Santorino Brown greeted him like a long-lost brother, and the length of the list in Harry's hand only served to raise his excitement. Harry dashed that by telling the man how quickly he wanted these stores.

Glumly Brown examined the two sheets of paper. 'But done it cannot be, Signor.'

Harry took back his own list, leaving him with Lubeck's. 'I'll settle for everything on this list by dawn tomorrow, plus rations and water for two days. And I'll need something better than this to provide a good dinner tomorrow afternoon. I want the rest of the stores and water ready to be loaded aboard the ship tomorrow evening. But most important of all, I need a cook.'

Brown threw up his hands, and the haggling started. Harry knew it was possible, just as he knew that Brown's objections were just a method of ensuring a high price for his chandling. Harry had done this in ports all over the world. It was a familiar dance, and if Santorino Brown thought he was driving a hard bargain, then Harry felt he should introduce him to some of the Indian traders he'd had to deal with in his time. The only point where he came unstuck was in the matter of ordnance.

Powder and shot were available, indeed plentiful. But the Council of State, no doubt fearing an uprising, had a tight grip on the Arsenal. You could only purchase guns from them. Brown told him mournfully that they charged extortionately and moved slowly. He would be lucky to get even two of the cannon he wanted within a month.

There was nothing Harry could do about that. He wondered about approaching Bartholomew regarding the guns on the *Dido*, but he knew instinctively that to do so would only court a refusal. He and Brown struck their bargain, with the victualling agent throwing in a berth at the quayside hard by his warehouse to speed the loading. Harry wrote a note for Brown's messenger to take the Guistianis, for the victualling agent did not repose enough trust in Harry Ludlow to act as chandler to his ship without money down on the barrel.

His final request was for the immediate dispatch of a pair of shipwrights and a quantity of the finest oak, both in boards and panel, for he had no intention of sailing out of Genoa, in what he now considered to be his ship, with the bulkhead to his cabin in disrepair. On the return to the *Principessa* he cast his mind to the other places that he might purchase some decent ordnance. The guns on the *Principessa* were too light for comfort. Nothing closer than Gibraltar came to mind, and he doubted that he would capture anything carrying the nine-pounder cannon he felt he required. In truth he was wary of approaching anything at sea that carried that calibre of gun.

Back aboard ship, he found that all his hands had come over, and after being afforded a decent, if cold, breakfast, were working away with a will. Toraglia and Lubeck were in their element. The Italian's face had a healthy look, with a colour in the cheeks more akin to the man in the portrait. He'd avoided the hammock all the time Harry had been absent. Sutton stood by the stern rail, his face unhappy as he cast his eyes about the rigging, full of men reaving and roving. Harry decided that forcing him to do that kind of work would only sour the man. He set him to putting the cabin to rights, with a kind of watching brief over the shipwrights, who'd come aboard in double-quick time, laden with prime seasoned oak, stain and varnishes, assured by Brown that they would be handsomely paid for their efforts.

Harry, who liked to toil as much as anyone, threw off his coat, and ignoring the effect that his labours had on his shirt and breeches, set to himself. Soon he was covered in grease, tar, and muck, and his hands, which hadn't hauled on ropes for an age, were raw. But none of this dented the pleasure he took in the work.

The yards were on their slings and the courses and topsails bent on. The outer jib boom was out so that the forestay could be hauled aloft at a moment's notice. Harry gave the orders that had the men rushing to the capstan. Not neat and tidy like a well worked-up crew. They bumped into each other, and stood on each other's toes. There was a deal of cursing and shoving, but also the sound of laughter. Harry had told them, that the sooner they got to the quayside, the sooner he could get a cook aboard to feed them a hot dinner. God help him if Brown had failed him there, for if he had, Harry Ludlow would find himself toiling over the coppers, cooking for the men himself.

The men in the tops undid the bunts and the reefed topsails fell open, stretching out as the lower booms where pulled taut. The familiar cries rang out as they raised anchor, sailing right over the bower anchor to pluck it out of the slime. Only a scrap of canvas was raised, enough to allow Harry to back and fill, so as to carry out these manoeuvres. Now, with a gentle breeze steady off the sea, he dropped the main and forecourse, also well reefed, and with the boats helping to control the head of the ship, he conned her into the crowded quayside.

As soon as the *Principessa* was under way, the Count finally wilted, and consented to use the hammock that Harry had provided for him. He slumbered peacefully, oblivious of the hammering, sawing, and planing of the shipwrights and the continual cries as the ship was steered and warped through the crowded anchorage, to finally bump gently alongside the fenders on the harbour wall.

Brown was there, surrounded by brawny loaders and piles of stores. He also, much to Harry's relief, had a one-legged fellow beside him who looked every inch a cook. He was the first aboard, closely followed by great bundles of wood, and the galley stove was lit in a trice, smoke billowing out of the chimney. Harry quickly ordered two vital casks brought aboard, one of rum, and the other of lime juice. The hands crowded round while he did the duty as master at arms personally, mixing the grog and dishing it out. He raised his eyes in surprise as he found himself filling a messkit for Count Toraglia's mute servant, who'd had the good sense to fetch the sedan chair to a spot by the ship. He grinned at the man, a miserable soul, who failed to reciprocate. Even the Count, awake after his two-hour nap, was glad of a pitcher of grog, though Harry wondered what that, added to the exertions of the day, would do for him.

Like a bad penny, no doubt attracted by the chance of a free drink, Crosby came aboard. Harry fought down the temptation to have him slung off the ship and poured him a measure. He then enquired what had brought him here, trying to sound as if he didn't know.

'Why, you're the talk of the port, Captain Ludlow.'

'And Ma Thomas'?'

'There too. I can't think that Bart is too pleased with you, but he's such a deep cove it's hard to tell. He's not one to shout when he's angered. Just the opposite. He goes ice cold when he's mad.'

'I'm not aware of having offended him,' replied Harry, untruthfully. By rights the hands he had aboard this ship belonged to the *Dido*, and with Broadbridge dead they were his. He was damn sure that Bartholomew was offended.

'Them that gives offence rarely are,' said Crosby, tweaking his bent nose. Then he saw the look that remark brought to Harry's face, and he continued quickly, 'Not that he ain't a touchy bastard. It don't take much to get on the wrong side of him.'

That sounded as though Crosby had some experience, which didn't surprise Harry in the slightest. 'He'll be getting ready for sea himself, I dare say.'

'He is that. Off the day after tomorrow, by all accounts.'

'Any idea where he's headed?'

Crosby looked at Harry, his soulless eyes wary. Then he drained his drink and offered his jug for a refill. Harry obliged. 'That's not the sort of thing he lets slip. I doubt even the other captains know, for sure.'

'I find that hard to credit, Crosby.'

'Perhaps Chittenden knows. He's like Bart's number two. He has the *Mercury*.'

Harry leant closer. 'He must have nice set of victims lined up. It's just occurred to me that there's a pretty penny going begging for someone who could beat Bartholomew to it.'

That was stretching the truth somewhat. It had occurred to Harry days ago. He knew, to some, it might smack of thieving, but to him all was fair in love, war, and privateering. He didn't owe Bartholomew anything, and in a game so loaded with chance anything that reduced the odds was welcome.

Crosby frowned. 'Beat him?'

'If he has a rendezvous, it wouldn't be too hard to guess where the shops he's after are coming from. Perhaps they could be taken up beforehand.'

'I wouldn't want to be close at hand if he discovered that.'

'Genoa isn't the only port around here.'

Crosby looked around the deck, his lip curling with distaste as he saw the amount of labouring being done. He tweaked his nose again, this time keeping hold of it to aid his thinking. Harry said nothing, content to let his offer work its way around the other man's mind. He didn't really want Crosby aboard, but if that was the price of easy success, so be it.

'A pretty penny is one of them sayings that don't seem to amount to much, especially when it's a way off.'

'Money on the barrel now, and five per cent of the captures.'

For someone with such dull eyes, it was remarkable how much expression such an offer generated. 'And a berth if you want it.'

The nod was almost imperceptible, and Crosby followed Harry into the cabin. The frame of the bulkhead was in place and the shipwrights were starting on the panelling. Crosby watched as Harry counted out twenty gold coins on to his desk, scooping them into his hand and out of sight in one swift movement.

Harry fixed him with a threatening look. 'I expect value for money, Crosby.'

'I don't doubt that, Captain Ludlow. Just as I don't doubt you'll get it.'

'Come aboard when you like,' said Harry as they walked back on to the deck. Again the man looked around the deck and it was plain he didn't like what he saw.

'Perhaps in a couple of days, Captain?'

When all the work is done, thought Harry, but he managed a bit of a smile.

If Harry had any doubts that he'd set tongues wagging, they were laid to rest quickly. As Crosby went down the gangplank, Doria came up, followed by his nephew. He had a confident manner, like a man who expected to be made welcome. This evaporated as he spotted Toraglia sitting in his chair by the stern rail, sipping the potent mixture of rum and lime juice from his jug. He stopped suddenly, looked at Harry, then back to the Count, his eyes narrowing as he sought to make sense of it. Then, almost as a way of recovering his dignity, the Admiral looked Harry up and down, alluding silently to the state he was in. Filthy, looking more like a tramp than a ship's captain.

'You have bought the ship?'

'Not yet. I intend to take her out for a cruise first.'

'Very wise.' Doria nodded slowly, but his eyes took in the stores being loaded. He frowned, no doubt thinking that Harry was lying. Then he wagged his finger as though what he was about to say had just occurred to him. 'You mentioned the other day that you may wish to sail from here. Indeed I remember you sought my aid in the matter.'

Harry snapped back at him, for it was a definite hint that he would need to pay a bribe. 'If I was to do so under the same terms as Bartholomew I might be interested.'

Doria was too long in the tooth to react to the anger in Harry's voice. He looked as though the name was new to him. 'Bartholomew? Ah, yes. Perhaps when you have had your cruise we had better have a talk.'

'So it's possible?'

Doria made a Latin gesture, hunching his shoulders and opening his hands. 'My friend, with care, anything is possible.'

With that he turned on his heel and marched back down to the quayside. His escort, and his nephew, fell in behind him and he made his way back to the Customs Fort. Harry walked aft. 'We have just had a distinguished visitor, Count Toraglia.'

The Italian lifted his face enquiringly, then he showed a flash of distaste as Harry told him who had been aboard.

'Admiral Stefano Doria,' he said, 'is distinguished for only one thing, and that is his venality.'

That was a sentiment Harry completely endorsed. 'Sup up, my friend. Once my lads have had a drink, I'll detail them off to take you home in your sedan chair.'

They would be the lucky ones, for the others would be working flat out with whips from the yards, cranes on the quay, and sheer brute force to get the stores aboard the ship.

The Count reached out, and Harry took his hand, ignoring the pain on his raw palms as the Count squeezed, for he was, through his disability, a tactile man. 'Thank you, Signor. I have had such pleasure from this. Why, I almost feel my old self again.'

Harry, looking at his grey, lined face, doubted the words. But he'd clearly enjoyed the day, for the sounds and the smells had taken him back to a happier time. 'I will fetch you at an hour before dawn, Count, and if the wind is fair we'll take her out into the bay and put her through her paces.'

'You must dine with me tonight.'

'I'm flattered, but . . .'

'Come, Captain Ludlow. I brook no refusal. I have worked on rigging a ship myself, and I can, even without eyes, guess the state of your dress. I am also a man who now tells a great deal by touch, and as you took my hand just now, I felt that it was raw. You are not a common seaman. Hauling on a rope is not your normal occupation, and I fear you have suffered for it.'

'I think you require sleep more than you need a guest, sir.'

'Be assured I shall rest. But my slumbers are short and frequent. And I have something to ease your muscles and take the sting out of your hands, for I spent most of my life trading in the east, and I incline, like them, to the efficacy of warm-water baths, frequently used.'

'A Roman tradition too, sir, to which I am much attached.'

'Then that settles it. You shall return with me, to my house, for the night. You shall bathe and have a soothing salve for your hands. And then we shall dine together. Please indulge a man who loved society, but has been forced into loneliness by this crippling affliction.'

Harry still hesitated, so the Count continued. 'And if you cannot see your way to indulging me, think of my poor wife, deprived of all pleasure because of an ailing husband. Your company would amuse her, I'm sure.'

Harry wondered if that was really true. He called to Sutton, fishing in his pocket for the key to Broadbridge's room. 'Light along to Ma Thomas's. My clothes are in Captain Broadbridge's room. Fetch them back here so that I can lay out something to make myself presentable.'

He saw the man's eyes flicker at the mention of Broadbridge's name and Sutton jerked his head to indicate the rest of the crew, who up until now had been left with rumour.

'Tomorrow, Sutton. I'll tell them tomorrow. For they will not be going ashore for a while once we sail. Speak to no one at the inn, d'ye hear?'

Sutton nodded quickly, and grabbing a pair of hands set off down the plank and along the quay. Harry called to Lubeck. The blond giant, his scarred face streaked with grime, ambled over to where Harry stood.

'I'm leaving you in charge of the ship tonight.'

Lubeck blinked, but made no reply. Perhaps he thought it some sort of test. 'Once the sedan chair party is back on board, no hands to go ashore. Can you do that?'

'*Ja*,' said Lubeck.

213

'There's food a-plenty, and work to do until the small hours. Another tot of grog at the end, and I want everyone to sling their hammocks and get some sleep. Just an anchor watch, with you in charge. I shall relieve you in the morning, and you can have a couple of hours then.'

Lubeck looked at him for a long time. The Captain was going ashore, to sleep in a bed for the whole night, while he was been left to do the work. Harry wondered if the man was going to rebel. But Lubeck's craggy face broke into a smile, showing the gaps in his teeth. And the way he said 'Ay, ay, Captain,' for all the heavy accent, left Harry in no doubt that he was flattered by the trust thus placed in him.

'Any trouble, Lubeck, tell the men that they are on wages for today, and double if the work's complete.'

'Dockyard vages,' said Lubeck, grinning, and Harry laughed, sharing the mariner's joke at the kind of money earned by the robbing bastards who built their ships.

Toraglia sat in the cabin, behind the desk, running his hands over the top like a man finding an old friend. If he wondered at the noise of the two carpenters, putting the finishing touches to the new bulkhead, he said nothing. Harry was up to his elbows in turpentine when Sutton returned, stripped to the waist trying to get some of the more stubborn streaks of grease of his body. His shirt, filthy and torn at the sleeve, lay in a corner. The sea-chests were brought in, and Harry sent Sutton off to the galley in search of hot water. The other two men were instructed to put his chest in the coach for now.

Harry was momentarily thrown when he saw two chests instead of one. Then, looking closer, he realized that one of the two belonged Broadbridge. Sutton returned as the men who'd brought them in went back on deck. He was about to say something about the extra chest when Harry, with a sharp flick of his head, indicated that Count Toraglia was present, and silenced him.

Quickly he opened his own chest and removed his mahogany dressing case. 'Sutton, I am to dine with the Count tonight, and I will spend the night there. I want you in charge of the party carrying the sedan chair.'

He saw Sutton's face register shock. 'I'm not actually asking you to carry the damn thing, but I want you to shepherd our hands back to the ship, then see them there in the morning. Now light along to the cook, and find out what time he reckons the men's dinner will be ready.'

'How the fuck . . . Beggin' your pardon, your honour, how can I do that, since the bugger don't talk no English?'

Count Toraglia laughed, and the action shook his body as much as it cheered Harry's soul. For here was a man who'd not laughed in an age, and it didn't matter a damn if it was pleasure or grog. It was a good sound to hear.

'Tell your man that I shall accompany him, if need be.'

He'd said this in French, but Sutton had protested in English. 'My dear Count Toraglia, am I to find I've been struggling away in French with a man who speaks fluent English.'

'No, my friend, I have a few words, that is all, and most of them the less polite examples of your language.'

The Count having found his tongue was talking away, the drink making him garrulous. Like any man his thoughts wandered and so did his subject. He talked again of the ship and his exploits, of his life before his illness which seemed to exist of an endless round of balls and entertainments interspersed with occasional trips to sea. He recalled women he'd known, not boasting in any way, but leading Harry to suspect that Toraglia, married and single, had put a few noses out of joint. He spoke less cheerfully about his illness which had struck without any prior warning, not even a feeling of tiredness. He praised his wife and the care she gave him, though the lament for a former life was there, in the tone of his voice, if not the words he used.

Harry, busy with his toilet and really only half listening, cleaned himself, put on a fresh shirt and stock, then donned his good buff coat, carefully packing the other things he would need to be presentable. He took Count Toraglia's hand and led him on deck, still talking away. Harry locked the cabin door, glancing at the heavy key before he put it in his pocket. It bore the same heraldic device as Toraglia's door knocker. A bird of prey with a small mammal in its claws. He was just about to ask about it when the mute servant appeared to assist his master. The look he gave the freshly built bulkhead put all thoughts of keys and heraldry from Harry's mind. Harry took Toraglia's arm and between them they helped the blind man down the gangplank. Sutton called out to those he wanted for the sedan chair, which produced a furious bellow from Lubeck, who saw his authority being challenged.

Harry kept out of the subsequent exchange, as Lubeck told Sutton, haltingly, but in no uncertain terms, that he would decide who undertook which duty. He knew if he interfered he'd undermine the man who would be his second in command. And right now he needed Lubeck a damn sight more than he needed Sutton. Once in the chair, the Count was off again, chattering gaily. Harry could see that he was happy, and that in turn pleased him. Yet he knew that they still had, at some point, to agree a price, and the thought entered his head that, added to the false position he already occupied, every piece of knowledge, and each laugh at every sally, was going to cost him money. God forbid they should finally disagree. He'd have to unload all those stores he'd taken on board. Harry shrugged at the thought. He'd made a decision, and time did not allow for any other course.

He was tired himself when they arrived at the Count's villa. Harry leant out to repeat his instructions to Sutton, and was quite shocked at how pale the man looked. Harry had to call his name twice to attract his attention. Surely Lubeck's wigging hadn't upset him that much. He listened silently to Harry's orders, nodding absent-mindedly. Soon they were through the gate and being lowered to the ground, the curtain, which hitherto had kept out the dust and smells of the road, was thrown back, and the Countess, her face anxious, leant in and examined her husband. She saw before her a man content, and her worries evaporated. Harry found himself on the receiving end of the most engaging smile.

CHAPTER NINETEEN

Harry lay in the scented water, eyes closed, and let the warmth soothe his aching limbs. He had not laboured so hard for years, using muscles that had seemed to creak alarmingly before he got into this huge bath. Sunk into the floor, with room enough for ten men, it lay at the centre of a collonaded room. The water was heated on the Roman model, using hot stones, and so the temperature stayed high as it flowed in and out of the bath.

The Countess had been an anxious woman when they returned, fussing over her husband and carrying him straight off to his bedroom to rest. She had then returned, and, no doubt on Toraglia's instructions, set about rubbing a soothing ointment into Harry's hands. It had been hard, being so close, and in physical contact. But again that air of innocence that she carried took any suggestion of sensuality from her actions. That and her questions about how her husband had coped with the strain of the day.

The meal they ate, seated on their divans, in the cool of the inner courtyard, was light for a man of Harry's appetite, prescribed as it was for the normal needs of the Count and his wife. Small spiced dishes alternated with cool pulses, and plentiful fruit. The wine was Toraglia's own, a crisp white which bubbled somewhat in the glass. The flagon lay behind Harry, cooling in the spray from one of the fountains. On the table, the candles which lit the scene smoked gently, keeping the insects at bay.

After the exertions of the day, Count Toraglia had great difficulty in keeping his eyes open. He struggled manfully to fulfil his duties as a host, and Harry knew he would not appreciate any suggestion that he retire. They conversed quietly, speaking of voyages they had made, of sights seen, and of the strange and exotic peoples they'd met. Toraglia talked gloomily of the decline of Genoa and Venice into little more than satrapies of their more powerful neighbours, Austria and France, and of the problems associated with running the Republic. Harry declined to be drawn, since it would have been impolite to express a derogatory opinion on the state of Genoese politics in the house of one of its nobles. But he could not help thinking, that if all his peers had an ounce of Toraglia's nature, then the place would be better for it.

Throughout, his wife ate steadily if sparingly, contributing little, and mainly seeing to her husband's needs. Harry could smell her perfume, mingling with the odours of the flowers and trees. It was a heady scent, musky and eastern, and he often found that he had to drag his mind back to listen to the quietly spoken Count, having missed a great deal of what he'd said. Eventually, the blind man lay back on his divan, still talking, but his voice faded and was no more. He was asleep in seconds, his lined face relaxing, taking years off him. Now it was easier to see the man whose face adorned that portrait in the hallway. The Countess stood up, taking an embroidered blanket from beneath her divan. She covered him over, moving the candles from his side of the table.

Then she fetched the wine from the fountain, and leant over Harry to pour him a glass. Her body brushed against his and he felt a sudden surge of feeling, that seemed to reach to his very fingertips. She was deliberately leaning into him, and as if to reinforce this, she gently laid her hand on his shoulder to support herself. She must have felt him stiffen, for she laughed very softly.

'I think my husband likes you, Signor.'

'Mutual, Madame,' croaked Harry.

'There are not many people that he would invite to dine with us, nowadays, on such a short acquaintance.'

'I realize that it has been a strain for him.' Harry was wondering if he could stand the strain himself, for she had made no effort to move. Even now that his glass was filled, she stood with the flagon in her hand, her thigh pressed against his arm.

Again she laughed, softly with a low timbre. 'My future troubles him greatly, for he realizes that his illness could carry him off before he has seen that I am safe.'

'Safe?'

'Wherever we go, men surround us. Alfonso listens to them carefully, and always tells me afterwards, which one would be suitable, and those he would disapprove of. I'm afraid your brother scored very poorly.'

Harry tried to be ingenuous, but realized that he struck completely the wrong note. 'Suitable?'

'Alfonso wishes to have a hand in the selection of my next husband. It is the aristocrat in him. As he says, given good health, he would wish to ensure that I was not foolish in my choice of lover. As he is now incapable of performing what he sees as his duty, he becomes quite obsessed by present needs, as well as my future welfare.'

Harry was no stranger to the lax morality normal amongst the upper reaches of society. After all, he was, if not an aristocrat, rich enough to be a member of it. And this would not be the first time he'd set out to seduce another man's wife, with the husband absent, indifferent, or colluding in the act. Much hypocrisy was talked by the English, citing the looseness of European morals, while adjuring fidelity in the poor, as they swapped partners with dizzying rapidity. All was well if things were kept within the bound of accepted decency, which was that a wife, taking a lover, should not embarrass her husband. He could hardly mistake the drift of the Countess's words, nor could he claim a lack of desire. It wasn't from any overwhelming sense of propriety that Harry hesitated. The Count, even if he'd contrived at this, was clearly dying, and that circumstance troubled him.

'Pray that the need will not arise,' said Harry quickly, looking at her and shifting away slightly.

'But it is arising, I think.' She leant forward as she laughed, this time amused by what she'd said, her eyes flicking towards his breeches. Harry wondered what had become of her air of innocence, for it had entirely evaporated, to be replaced by an atmosphere of salacious innuendo. 'Few meet his high standards, and even fewer have been invited to dine with us.'

She rubbed her hand over his shoulder, giving it the slightest squeeze, and her voice was husky as she spoke. 'How fortunate that I share his taste.'

Harry, a man who prided himself on his competence, positively stammered. 'Madame, I cannot allow you to talk this way.'

Suddenly she sat down on the divan, looking Harry in the eye. But she spoke without urgency, as if realizing that she risked scaring her quarry.

'Come, Signor. Do you not realize that my husband has arranged things in this way? He is aware of his shortcomings as a man, caused by his illness, just as he is aware of my needs as his wife. Ask yourself, would you invite a man, someone you'd only just met, to dine and spend the night at your house, knowing that you would inevitably fall asleep and leave this stranger alone with your young wife?'

'The servants,' said Harry, well aware that he was beginning to equivocate.

'Are few, and be assured they will remain silent.' She stood up, and reached down for his hand. When she spoke his name, her accent made it sound new to him. 'Come, Signor Ludlow, 'Arry, is it not? I think if you decline, Alfonso may take grave offence.'

Harry allowed himself to be pulled to his feet by the gentlest of pressure. After all, who would not want to believe such a beautiful creature? She led him up the broad staircase to the gallery which ran right round the inside of the building. Harry had another moment of doubt, seeking to hesitate as they reached the top of the stairs. But she turned swiftly and pushed her body against his, pressing her hips into him urgently. What little strength he had to resist evaporated instantly and he leant forward to kiss her.

She skipped away from his proposed embrace and dragged him towards an open doorway. Once inside she turned again and threw her arms round his neck, kissing him full on the lips and forcing her eager tongue between his teeth. Harry put both his hands on her soft buttocks and pulled her violently towards his groin. She moaned and ground her hips, then gasped, tugging to remove Harry's coat as his hand encircled her breast, teasing the erect nipple.

Through the thin garment every contour of her body was plain to the touch. Harry pushed himself away, throwing off his coat. He felt her hand run over his breeches. Her eyes were fixed on his and he saw in the faint moonlight her tongue run round the lips of her partially opened mouth. Whilst he ripped off his shirt she sought the buttons that held his breeches. He reached down, pushing her hands out of the way, and in one swift movement he lifted her flimsy dress over her head and threw it into a corner.

The huge four-poster bed was several feet away, and they clasped at each other and they staggered towards it. He could feel her finger-nails digging into his back as they thrust at each other. Finally her knees gave way and she fell backwards on to the bed. Harry, breeches undone, was inside her almost before she touched the counterpane. Months at sea, with no female company, told rapidly, and it was with a slight feeling of shame that he stopped moving, his head buried in the nape of her long neck.

She laughed softly and her muscles contracted around him as she did so. 'Why, 'Arry. You are just like a young boy.'

He was about to apologize, to plead long abstinence, when she pushed him violently on to his back. She looked down into his eyes, still smiling. 'Boys recover quickly, I'm told. And when they do, they are extremely patient. You will be patient too, 'Arry?'

She kissed the nape of his neck. Then her lips drifted down to encircle the nipple on his breast. She didn't linger for long. Her tongue next flicked in and out of his navel, before drifting down, slowly and deliberately to replace her hand, which had been busy from the very beginning, trying to arouse him again so that she too could experience the pleasure she so patently craved.

She lay, face down, her hips arched as Harry entered her for the third time. The slight groan she emitted spoke equally of pleasure and anticipation. As he began to move within her she murmured words he couldn't understand and raised her hips further until his penetration was complete. She licked his finger before slipping it greedily into her mouth. Then she started to moan softly, her whole body rotating to increase the pleasure she took from Harry.

He pushed harder, raising his head as he did so. The shadow on the wall, caused by the moonlight, made him stop abruptly, bringing a soft protest from the woman beneath him. He turned his head, then his body quickly, but the figure had ducked out of sight, leaving just the sound of a hurried scuffling as evidence of reality. He would have gone to investigate if Lelia di Toraglia had not pushed him backwards, straddling him urgently and using her hand to place him back inside her.

Her hands rubbed his chest and her whole body rocked back and forth, with her loose hair swinging as she tossed her head. The moans were not soft now. They increased in volume and in frequency. Harry responded as her pulsating muscles gripped him, thrusting upwards to meet her. One last cry and she fell forward, her mouth covering his. He rolled her over on to her back, still inside her, feeling her teeth sink gently, and gratefully, into his shoulder.

The slight scuffing sound woke him. That and her fingers pressed on his lips. The Count stood framed in the doorway, the light from the moonlit gallery silhouetting his body. His voice was husky as he spoke.

'You should not have let me fall asleep, my dear. What will Captain Ludlow think of me as a host.'

Her fingers pressed a little harder on Harry's lips. He looked sideways at the Count's shadow on the opposite wall, the knot of fear in his stomach easing as he realized that it was an entirely different shape to the one that had appeared there before.

'You were weary, Alfonso, it seemed for the best,' she replied softly.

'You saw to our guest?'

She smiled at Harry before replying. 'Yes, Alfonso.'

'Thank you, my dear. He seems an excellent fellow. Less barbaric than the last of his fellow countrymen we had as a guest. I shall retire again. You have given instructions when I am to be woken?'

'Of course. Now go to bed, Alfonso. You must get all the rest you can. Do you wish me to help you?'

'No. I can manage. Goodnight, my dear.'

He left, using the walls to guide him. Harry lay as rigid as a board, doing all he could to avoid contact with her naked body. Either she sensed this, or she was sated. She removed her hand from his lips and lay down without a word. He waited until her breathing was even, before getting out of the bed and gathering up his clothes. He stood, conjuring up in his mind the image of that first shadow. Not the Count. A woman by the long hair, perhaps? Yet in truth the vision had been so fleeting that he could not be sure what he saw. He gave her a last, wondering look, so beautiful in this light, with her black hair spread across the white bedding. Then he turned and made his way back to the room he had been given when he arrived.

'You seem rather silent this morning, Captain Ludlow.'

They were back in the sedan chair, jogging along in the early morning light of the pre-dawn. Harry was silent because he was trying to justify his behaviour to himself. He could easily forgive Lelia di Toraglia, excusing her actions as those of a woman frustrated by the need to live with a such sick man. In truth, you could go so far as to praise her discretion in the way that she kept such longings from her husband. But that did not justify his behaviour, and as soon as the Count spoke he was back to thinking himself the worst kind of scrub.

'Forgive me, Count Toraglia. I was merely running everything through my mind to ensure that nothing is forgotten.'

'Then I shall not disturb you, my friend.'

Harry cursed under his breath, wishing that his companion would speak so as to interrupt the train of uncomfortable thoughts that chased each other through his mind. But the other man kept his peace, gazing straight ahead with his sightless eyes, his face wearing a contented smile. He sat, fingering the key in his pocket as the silence lengthened. Harry could abide it no longer and, in a bid to take his mind off his behaviour, pulled the key out and asked the Count about the provenance of his heraldic crest.

The Count, rather surprisingly, laughed. 'It is an ancient device, of course. But there is, it seems, a great deal of difference between the intention and the impression. Family folklore has it that the bird of prey that you see is really rescuing the poor creature in its talons. That is supposed to denote the protective nature of my distant ancestors.'

He laughed again and leant forward to touch Harry on the knee, his voice dropping to a confidential tone. 'I rather think that is an invention to suit these gentler times. The history of my family may be pure in recent ages, with the Levantine and Black Sea trade to sustain the family fortunes. But, if one goes back far enough, they achieved prominence for the very reason that they, as strong men, preyed upon the weak. So I think my arms, when they were created, served as a warning to beware of the house of di Toraglia.'

Harry was examining the device closely. He could see no gentleness in the bird's hooked beak. And the animal in its claws looked to be in distress. He was thinking of his own father, who'd shown an acquisitive tenacity that had shocked some of his contemporaries, though he'd never allowed avarice to interfere with his proper duty.

'I dare say we'd all blush with shame at our families' exploits, if we had any inkling of the truth.'

'Truly, Signor Ludlow. I comfort myself that they were no different to the ancestors of anyone else with a noble name.'

They came out on to the cobbled quayside, and Harry pulled the curtain back, craning his neck to get a view of the ship. The *Principessa* was like an anthill, with a steady stream of men marching aboard carrying stores, while other items, like water casks, were being hoisted aboard with whips from the yard. Buckets of shingle, the extra ballast that would keep the vessel trim, were being hauled out of the hold and dumped on the quay, where men with barrows stood ready to take it away. The rigging was full of topmen, making perfect the things that they had rigged hurriedly the day before. All thoughts of Lelia di Toraglia left his mind at the sight.

It was only then he realized that Sutton hadn't turned up outside the villa with the other hands, but his thoughts on this were interrupted by the sound of bellowing. Lubeck stood in the middle of the deck, issuing a stream of orders, keeping half a dozen different activities under control. Harry led Toraglia up the gangplank, and placed him in the chair by the stern-rail, his mournful servant now taking station behind him. He saw Sutton coming up the gangplank, a cask on his shoulder. He'd obviously decided being a servant was beneath his dignity, and had taken to work to avoid it. Or perhaps the German giant had collared him. Whatever, it was none of Harry's concern.

Brown, having extracted a fair price from Harry, had hired extra men, and by the time the sedan chair arrived the loading of the ship was nearly complete. Coat off, he was up in the tops in a flash, checking that blocks wouldn't foul and that the pulleys were well greased. He tried the chains which held the yards, hauled on ropes to see they were secure. He had slowly made his way up to the crosstrees, above the topmast yard, when he spotted something interesting in the busy harbour.

Harry called down for a telescope, and one of the more nimble topmen raced up the shrouds to fetch it to him. There is a clarity to the light of early morning, especially in a hot climate, that quickly fades with the heat of the day. He blessed this as he adjusted the telescope, for what he saw clearly now would have been a hazy blur in an hour. The French sloop, large in his glass, was a fair way off. A hooded figure had just gone through the entry post, hunched over, to be greeted by the much taller figure of Tilly. They made quickly for the cabin before Harry could see the identity of the cloaked visitor. But he'd been followed aboard by two men clad entirely in black, and they lingered on at the side of the deck, still in sunlight. One of the men turned and leant over the rail. Harry's heart gave a little jump as he saw the fellow was wearing a matching black bandanna wrapped round his head in the same manner as the man he'd killed two nights ago. He wondered what he might find aboard, if he did manage to take the sloop. But if he'd had any doubts about the desirability of attempting to do so, they completely evaporated now. Harry was grinning from ear to ear as he slid down a backstay to the deck, which earned him a suspicious look from Lubeck. But now was not the time to tell them of his plans, not with visitors aboard.

The gangplank was inboard, and the command 'stand by to unmoor ship' rang out. The warm wind was swooping down from the hills, steady in the open, but rushing through the narrow alleys that ran every twenty paces from the quayside up into the town. They braced the reefed topsails round to catch it, and swung the rudder. The *Principessa* hauled away from the quay on her own. Harry took the wheel, and with a man in the chains, yelling a furious warning to any boat silly enough to get in their way, he conned the ship out of the harbour without assistance. Even at this snail's pace he could feel that she answered her rudder well, the slightest turn on the wheel altering her course. They were out past the mole, into clearer waters. Harry nodded to Lubeck, who yelled out the orders to drop the courses.

Lubeck was shouting commands, getting the last bales and casks off the deck, to tidy up badly looped falls, and generally to turn the *Principessa* from a mess into what it should be, a sleek fighting ship. Harry glanced over his shoulder at Alfonso di Toraglia. His head was arched back, with his nose in the air, as he sniffed the wind. The flag behind him, which his servant had rigged, showed his coat of arms on a red and white background. With the wind nearly dead astern, the flag whipped forward over his head, and the sound of it flapping no doubt added the patent joy apparent on his face.

The ship was pitching slightly now in the increasing swell of the outer roads. Harry trimmed the yards, and brought her round so that the wind was more on her quarter. He could feel her through the wheel, as he spun it over to hold his course. The ship was vibrating ever so slightly, not an indication of any danger, more a sign of life flowing freely. He handed the wheel to Lubeck.

'Would you care to take the wheel, Count Toraglia?'

The man positively leapt up, and his servant led him over. Harry wanted to give him the wheel, for they were sailing easy, with not much set, and courtesy demanded he offer some time. Later, if this wind stayed true, they would have a whole suit of sails aloft, and the *Principessa* would be racing along, her deck canted like a pitched roof, with more than one man needed on the wheel to hold her course.

Toraglia was delighted. Harry stood behind him, issuing the odd quiet instruction to take them round some of the shipping still waiting in the outer roads. Lubeck, without waiting for Harry's instructions, yelled at the hands to trim the yards as necessary, pushing those suffering from sea-sickness to their stations, despite their feeble protests.

They were clear now, with only the odd fishing boat to bar their way. The sun shone, the wind held, a steady topgallants breeze, and the land, with its smells, was fading behind them. The tang of the sea filled their nostrils, and it seemed to Harry, just by looking at Toraglia's face, that a few more trips like this would return him to health in no time.

CHAPTER TWENTY

With land out of sight, Harry detailed two of the more willing hands to steer, while he, trumpet in hand, called the orders to make more sail. Nothing sudden, for he wanted to see the effect of each addition on the ship's performance. And what he saw he liked. Every new sail gave a little something extra. He shook the reefs out of his courses and topsails, set his staysail, and brought the *Principessa* round a touch more so the wind was coming in slightly further forward. The yards were braced round, sheets and tacks adjusted to take the best advantage of the steady breeze.

Then it was topgallants yards aloft and the sails bent on, while the outer and flying jibs were made ready. 'Stamp and go' came the order, and these too were up. Harry watched the masts carefully, for they had been out when the ship had been refitted. If they were not properly seated in the kelson, this was the moment he was going to find out. The wind was singing through the taut backstays, music to his ears.

It would have been wonderful to send the royals yards aloft, and rig extra booms from the yards to carry studding sails. But this was not the day for such things. Not that it mattered, for she flew along. Harry took the wheel again, and felt that she was jibbing a bit. The hurried stowing of the hold was to blame, since that, affecting her trim, manifested itself more at speed. And speed it was, though Toraglia was not impressed by the nine knots that they read off on the log. Harry sailed on through the morning, mixing the combination of sails and logging in his mind how the ship behaved. The glass turned for the umpteenth time, and the hands were looking to their new captain to be fed, so he brought her up into the wind and hove to.

The brand-new cutter was over the side and he had himself rowed round with Lubeck as the hands ate their dinner. The German had discussed restowing the hold with Toraglia, and was keen to take his advice. Harry agreed, for that would trim her more by the stern. Back aboard he gave instructions for the officers' meal to be prepared, keeping just enough sail on the *Principessa* to control her drift. He made sure he had a man aloft as a lookout, for if a warship came on the scene he would not wait about to see its flag. Harry Ludlow would be off like a shot, heading back to Genoa and safety.

He set her under easy sail again once the hands were fed, and handing the deck over to the captain of the afterguard so that he too could get to know the ship, he took the Count below to the main cabin. Toraglia's nose twitched, for it still reeked of fresh varnish. To a sighted man the new bulkhead would have stood out like a sore thumb, but the blind Alfonso was content to accept Harry's explanation, made out of earshot of his mute servant, that some dolt had tipped over some shellac that his brother used for his canvas.

Brown's cook had prepared a wonderful spread. Toraglia's servant tasted everything before his master, obviously a matter of long habit since Toraglia made no effort to explain, leaving Harry to wonder at the incidence of poisoning in this part of the world. The wines had been selected without tasting, and also without agreement on price, so Brown, a businessman before anything, had chosen to load him with some rare and expensive vintages. Harry looked at the list which had come aboard with his personal stores, and reflected that haste was proving expensive. The talk, convivial, was all of the *Principessa*, though not of the price, and Harry wondered if this atmosphere of cameraderie would still exist after they'd enjoyed a good haggle. Toraglia retired to the sleeping cabin after lunch.

Harry returned to the deck to see how she handled now that they'd shifted some of the water. The improvement would have seemed slight, or even non-existent, to a landsman, for the addition of half a knot on her speed was hard to spot. But Harry could feel that she moved through the water with much greater ease. She also answered her helm more readily and he knew that in stronger airs that would mean the difference between twelve knots and the fourteen claimed by its present owner, plus the ability to outsail most vessels afloat. Most important of all, it meant that he could run if he needed to, and more telling, catch whatever he fancied, given a wind.

He changed course in mid-afternoon, and headed for home, sailing right into the wind. Now the yards were braced hard round, to an angle of twenty degrees to the keel. Harry pushed her head round as far as he could, pleased to see that she still answered a shade over six points free. They sailed on tack upon tack, the working of the crew improving with each operation, sighting land as the sun dipped below the horizon.

He gave instructions to Lubeck to bring her back to the quayside, there to load the remaining stores, and to take her out of the harbour once that was completed. The cutter was over the side waiting to take them ashore, for conning the *Principessa* through the busy harbour once more would take an age. Sutton was nowhere to be seen when he called for the hands needed to carry the sedan chair, and he could not waste time searching for him. He had Toraglia lowered over the side in a chair, and they rowed ashore in darkness.

Harry would have preferred to talk about the price elsewhere, but Toraglia had asked that they do so at his house, insisting that since his wife was his true partner she too must be involved. Now that they had reached the point of discussing terms, Toraglia seemed more willing to talk of his reasons for selling the ship, putting himself at some disadvantage as he did so, for he admitted to certain financial constraints. Then he tugged with great force at Harry's capacity for sympathy by alluding to his death, pushing aside the dismissive responses, insisting it could not be long delayed.

He wanted whatever he got from the sale to go to his wife. It seemed there were rapacious nephews in the offing, waiting to inherit his property. And it had become clear at the start of his illness that these nephews cared little for the future comfort of his wife, going so far as to hint that she vacate the property at the height of his illness. Harry blushed unseen when the Count assured him that she would readily find another husband. But her case would be enhanced with a dowry. Since he'd recovered sufficiently to transact business on his own, they had been busy converting what assets they could, lodging the money with Guistiani's in his wife's name, against the day when she would be on her own, very likely turfed out of the marital home on the very day he died.

'Yet what right have I to burden you with all this, which is surely none of your concern? Odd how I have come to esteem you on such a short acquaintance,' said the Count, leaning forward again to touch Harry's knee with a degree of intimate familiarity.

Harry felt tears prick the back of his eyes. 'Would that I had the power to make you well, Count Toraglia. Should what you say come to pass, I feel I will be losing a friend.'

Toraglia laughed. 'And all this before we contest a ducat. I fear we are poor merchants, Captain Ludlow.' A minute pause, before he continued. 'But I would ask you one thing. If it is in your power to do my poor wife a good turn after I'm gone, it would reassure me to know that you would oblige.'

'Of course,' Harry croaked. If he then wondered at Harry's immediate and vociferous objection to staying the night, it didn't show. Soon they were back in the sedan chair and heading for the Toraglia villa, and to Harry's mind an encounter he would rather avoid.

His fears that there would be some kind of awkwardness were proved groundless. The Countess had returned to her previous impeccable demeanour. Neither by look nor gesture did she refer to the events of the previous night. She was attentive to her husband and polite to Harry, with no trace of tension in her voice as she asked him about the events of the day. Once more they retired to the courtyard, there to drink wine and eat. And this time, after the food, to haggle. Yet it was good-humoured affair, for even Toraglia's wife gasped at his opening price. He was not angry with her for letting him down, treating it as a jest himself. He soon named a more realistic figure.

Harry offered a hundred ducats less. The Count, throwing up his hands, would not budge, singing the praises of the *Principessa*. Harry offered a shade more. Still he wouldn't be shifted. The argument went back and forth, with Harry conceding little and the Count refusing to budge. Time was passing and Toraglia was tiring. Deep in the pit of his stomach Harry feared that he might be forced to sleep here, with all the attendant risks that included. He, trying to emulate the Latin gesture of his host, threw up his arms and conceded the price, comforting himself with the thought that he was paying for it out of profits he'd already managed in another ship.

Toraglia was plainly disappointed, for his face showed the first trace of real anger that Harry had seen. 'I do hope that my disability is not affecting your judgement, Captain.'

Harry was aware his quick surrender looked like condescension, but he really didn't think he had any choice. Perhaps, in his haste, he answered the Count a shade more pointedly than was necessary. 'It has not, sir. But she is a fine vessel, and if I think her worth every penny of that amount. I cannot see why you should seek to dissuade me.'

'He will not do that, Signor. You may take my word on it,' said the Countess.

Her husband frowned at that interruption. But he must have realized the game was over, for his shoulders drooped slightly. Toraglia had been looking forward to the cut and thrust of continued barter, which would complete the pleasure of the last two days. But it was not to be.

His wife produced ink, a quill, and paper so that the contract could be drawn up. Harry wrote a letter instructing the Guistianis to transfer the required funds. The business was complete, with Toraglia near collapse, though he stayed manfully awake till Harry made his hurried apologies and prepared to leave. Despite his protestations, the Countess walked with him to the hallway, stopping underneath her husband's portrait. The old bent servant stood by the door, waiting to escort him to the postern gate. They were out of her husband's hearing when she spoke.

'Do I take it that I was included in the price?'

James would have said something gallant. Not Harry, he didn't know how. Yet he knew he made a hash of the truth, his voice harsh. 'It was to avoid a repetition of the events of last night that it was so high.'

He saw a flash of anger, and hurt in her eyes. Then, in a gesture that he meant kindly, but somehow performed insultingly, he bent down, kissed her hand, and left.

He came out of the gate to find his three escorts gone. Harry cursed under his breath, and for a moment contemplated knocking at the door and begging re-admittance. But after what he'd just said that was impossible. Perhaps the men had spied somewhere to get a drink on the way. Hard to say, since he didn't know them very well. Lubeck was the one who had picked them. He had no way of knowing if they were reliable or not.

Having little choice he set off through the now darkened and deserted streets. At some point he would have to turn down towards the harbour. He tried hard to recall the route he'd taken yesterday in the company of Guistiani's messenger, but quickly realized he'd have to rely on pure instinct. How could he recognize any of the things he'd seen in daylight in this stygian darkness?

It was neatly done. The cold steel of the pistol was at his temple before he could open his mouth. Hands held him from behind, and a voice he vaguely recognized spoke. 'Someone wants to see you, Ludlow.'

Harry, expecting a French voice and certain death, was surprised. The man had spoken in English. They threw a blindfold round his eyes and tied it tight. He had the absurd thought, as they bustled him away, that it was unnecessary to blindfold a man on such a night. Sounds echoed off the walls of the narrow alleyways as they pushed him along. The creak of a door, again familiar, and suddenly Harry knew where he was, and who had spoken. It was the voice of the rat-catcher, Beldeau. And by that distinctive creak of the door he knew he was in the rear warehouse of Ma Thomas's inn.

Was it just Beldeau, taking revenge for the humiliation Harry had meted out to him in the tap-room? If it was, that would mean a beating. But why fetch him here? Something like that could be done in the streets, and in a town like Genoa the chances of anyone taking any notice were slim. Then Bartholomew spoke, his voice harsh, as though he was straining to control it. 'Take off the blindfold, Beldeau. I need to look this bastard in the eye.'

Harry blinked in the candlelight, before looking round to see his captors. All three of the men he'd knocked down were there, plus two others, their faces vaguely familiar. Both Beldeau's eyes were black and his nose was swollen to twice its normal size. Then he turned back, and found himself looking into Bartholomew's eyes. There was none of that amused air about the man now. His eyes were as hard as stone, and directed at him. Suddenly Bartholomew stepped forward and fetched him a slap with all the force he could muster. Harry spun away, too late to take the sting out of it. Habit had him half-way to returning the blow but Beldeau and the man called Tinker grabbed him.

There was a slight taste of blood in Harry's mouth, and a numbness in his jaw as he spoke. 'Is that how you fight, Bartholomew?'

'I dare say you'd prefer my men to let you go?'

'I promise you a bout if you do.'

Bartholomew snorted derisively. 'A bout, Ludlow? What are you, a prizefighter?'

'Ask your friends.'

He heard Beldeau growl, right by his ear, as Bartholomew responded. 'What a sporting fellow you are. Odd that I asked my "friends" what to do with you, since my first instinct was to string you up. No, said Beldeau, for he too has a score to settle. He reckons to have some sport with you, and he has persuaded me that I shall enjoy it.'

'You will, Bart, take my word on it. An' so will I,' said Beldeau.

Harry was searching his mind, trying to think what he could have done to cause such a reaction. Surely sailing as a privateer, purloining a number of hands, or making insulting references to the syndicate didn't warrant all this. Had he heard of Harry's attempt to question Crosby? Or had Crosby come straight back here and told him everything, plus a bit more – for he was given to exaggeration. Beldeau taking revenge he could see, for the way Harry had knocked him out must have rankled. But that was meat for a thrashing, perhaps a severe one if Beldeau was as mad as Crosby said. But to string him up. What for?

'I am at a loss to know what I've done to offend you.'

Bartholomew stepped forward and hit him again. 'Are you, by damn? Shall I tell you what we have decided?'

Harry didn't reply, since there didn't seem any point.

'It's Beldeau's notion, and I have to say when he told me, I was impressed. I dare say you have spied his hat, and had a good look at his face, so you will know what he does.'

'Rats, Ludlow.' This was said by Beldeau, softly, almost caressingly, in his ear. 'I rear 'em as well as fight them.'

Bartholomew continued, his voice carrying an almost jesting tone.

'He catches his own, you know, and breeds them special. Feeds them up, and crosses the ones that grow the most. So what he ends up with are the biggest rats he can manage. But to make them fight, that's hard. You have to feed them, then starve them. You know when they're hungry, for you put one of the little ones in with them. When they eat it, you know they're ready. It was his rats that the negro was fighting the other night, so you can see how successful he is in making them big.'

'I seem to remember the negro finished well within the time.'

'He did too. Beldeau was upset. But the man is a champion at the sport.'

'We should have made him fight ten instead of six, with a reputation like his,' growled Beldeau.

'One a minute. I think I would have backed your rats at that, Beldeau. What do you reckon a novice could handle?'

Harry felt his blood chill, for he knew what was coming. 'Not more'n two, Captain.'

Bartholomew smiled now. 'Let's show him what's in store, shall we?'

Harry was pushed towards one of the larger barrels. Tinker opened a door half-way up, then pushed Harry's head through. He'd heard the sound of scrabbling rats all his naval life, but even before Tinker shoved the lantern into the barrel, he knew that he was going to see more rats in one place than he'd ever seen before. And he was right. He looked down into a sea of gleaming eyes, as the rats froze for just a second. Then they panicked and tried to get away, but in the confines of the barrel there was nowhere to go, so they just ran in circles, climbing over each other, biting and scratching, squeaking in their high-pitched way. Some tried to climb the walls, but Beldeau had lined it with a circle of grease so they fell back amongst their mates. The larger rats started to attack the smaller ones, and in one corner some of them had gone into a frenzy, literally ripping a half-grown creature apart.

Harry was pulled out again, and the door was slammed, plunging the rats back into darkness. Beldeau pushed his swollen face close up. Harry could smell his breath as he spoke. 'Mustn't get 'em too worked up, eh, Ludlow. Else there be nowt left for you to fight.'

Bartholomew laughed. 'Are you a novice, Ludlow, or did you indulge in this sport as a youngster in the West Indies?'

Harry fought to keep his voice even. 'I'm not frightened of the odd rat, Bartholomew, if that's what you mean. Just as I'm not frightened of you. Just untie me, and I'll show you. I'll take all of you if you like.'

That amused the man even more. 'The odd rat? He offers us the odd rat, then says he'll fight us all. I fear you see yourself as a tyro, Ludlow. Put his nose close to theirs, Beldeau, and let's see what kind of hero he is.'

They flung the door of the barrel open again, and this time, as they shoved him through the opening, they lifted his legs so that his head was pointing to the floor. Tinker shoved the light in again, and Harry fought to shrink his body away from what he saw. His head was within inches of the bottom of the barrel, practically amongst the teeming rodents. As the light panicked them again they started to run, but sensing this intruder as the cause of their distress they all tried to bite him. Beldeau and the other man holding him pushed him down till his head hit the floor. Harry felt the teeth start to sink into his neck, head and shoulders. He screamed out in fear, and they hauled him up and out again. Bartholomew was laughing, and as he looked around the grinning faces of the others, Harry's heart sank. There was no mercy in any of the eyes.

'A novice, I think, Beldeau, don't you?' said Bartholomew.

'Ay, ay, Captain.'

'We'll start him on four.' He waved an elegant arm to his rear. 'We've got a special arena prepared for this, the largest barrel we could find, cut in half so that we can watch. We'll be just above your head if you stand up. I wouldn't do that if I were you, of course, since I for one will almost certainly fetch you a buffet if I can.'

Bartholomew's voice went suddenly ice cold. He was full of hate for Harry Ludlow, though he and God alone knew why.

'Shall I tell you the terms, Ludlow? We shall put you in the barrel with four rats to start, and you will be allowed the ten minutes to kill them. If they are not dead in the time, I'll string you up from the first hoist I find on the quayside.'

'And if they are?' Harry croaked.

'Then you shall have a rest. And after your rest, you shall fight five. Then another rest, and you'll fight six. Then seven, eight, and nine. And if you can still see and are still alive we'll try you on ten.'

'Why should I bother, since you intend to kill me anyway?'

'You'll bother, Ludlow,' he snarled. 'It is in the nature of man to cling to life. And perhaps I shan't kill you. Perhaps Beldeau's rats will win.'

Bartholomew's voice was filled with mockery. 'A promise, Ludlow, that I swear I'll keep. If they do win, and you are blinded, I shall let you live. You've had your sport, you bastard. Now I intend to have mine.'

CHAPTER TWENTY-ONE

They'd slung him in another empty barrel, his hands still tied, while they prepared for their sport. Harry sat in the dark searching his mind for a motive in Bartholomew's behaviour. Perhaps the man was mad. And what did he mean when he said he would string him upon the nearest hoist? That was what had happened to Howlett.

He had tried to find the door of the barrel as soon as they put him inside, but with his hands tied behind his back that was difficult. Also, in the darkness, he could go round and round the thing without ever knowing when he'd gone full circle. What had happened to the men he'd had with him? Where were they? And what about those on the ship? Would they wonder where he was, or would they just assume he was still at Count Toraglia's villa? They didn't know him well and he hadn't taken them into his confidence about his plans. If he didn't show up, they'd just sit there, eating their way through his stores, and waiting for him to return.

No one else had any cause to realize he was missing, since he'd transacted his business with the Count. Perhaps if he hadn't sent Pender away. But then, if he kept him around his servant would have been with him tonight, and possibly killed before he came out of the villa. Or worse, captured and in the same predicament as his master.

Reluctantly he turned his mind to the immediate future. Harry had seen rat-fights on board ship. The usual practice was for a man to poke his head down the hawse hole, and try to do them one at a time as they climbed the cable. Only once had he seen it done the way they operated in the tap-room, and that had been in the West Indies. Bartholomew's slight twang sounded as though it could be his birthplace. That set off another train of thought. Harry's father had held the command in the West Indies for three years, and had enjoyed a degree of success in suppressing the actions of the Caribbean privateers, who, out of sight of authority, behaved more like pirates. Was Bartholomew one of them, for he was of an age with Harry, who'd been a midshipman when his father held that post?

He tried to remember every word that Bartholomew had said, every look and every gesture. He could recall no overt enmity. But then would Bartholomew expose it if it was there? He'd been rude to James, much more than he had to Harry. Was that because he disdained to be polite to an obvious lubber, or was it the Ludlow name?

It was too much of a coincidence surely, that someone Harry's father had harmed twenty years ago should be seeking revenge on the son. Then his mind turned to Broadbridge. Did Bartholomew think Harry had killed him? Again Harry ran the events of the last two days through his mind, desperately searching for a motive, for if he could find it, he could plead his innocence. Then, perhaps, he could persuade them to let him go.

Sounds outside the barrel forced his mind back to the rats. It was the kind of thing youngsters talked about in the midshipman's berth, pretending an ability they didn't possess. But he'd had it from some of the older hands. He knew, hands tied, there were only two ways to kill them. One by tossing them like a terrier, thus breaking their necks. The other needed sheer brute strength to crush them between your teeth. Neither prospect was very inviting. Yet, for all Beldeau's boasting, rats were timorous creatures unless cornered, preferring to run rather than engage anything larger. Harry had caught enough of them as a lad. He'd fattened them up and eaten them. Sometimes he'd sold them to his messmates, to assuage the endemic hunger that afflicted every youngster aboard a man-of-war. But trapped rats could be vicious, and he was sure that Beldeau knew, from experience, how to make a rat feel that sole means of escape was to fight.

The door, which turned out to be right by Harry's right arm, was flung open. As the head came through Harry butted the man. He felt a sharp pain, and wondered if he hadn't done himself more damage than his opponent. But the other fellow yelled, grabbed his head, and pulled it back out of the barrel, leaving the door ajar. Harry was through in a flash, scrambling out, tripping over the step at the bottom. He fell heavily and rolled, trying to get to his feet. The boot caught him just behind the ear as he got to his knees, and he was knocked sideways, his head reeling. Another boot caught him in the ribs, before hands got hold of him to drag him to his feet.

'Let's not be too violent, gentlemen, or we will deny our rats a worthy opponent.'

Bartholomew's words calmed the men holding him, and they pushed their charge towards the sound of the voice. Harry shook his head to clear his brain, before looking up. Bartholomew, along with a dozen others, was standing on a raised platform which ran round the outside of a huge wine barrel. They pushed him up on to this step, so that he could see inside. It had been cut in half, and the bottom formed a compact arena.

'We have provided you with a good quantity of sand,' said Bartholomew. 'After all, we would not wish you to suffer from pained knees.'

Everyone else in the room laughed at this, and Harry heard the sound of coins as they placed their bets on him succeeding or dying. He looked at Bartholomew, whose eyes had returned to their half bored, half amused way of drooping indifference.

'Why?'

'You don't know, Ludlow?'

'No, I don't. And I would dearly like to.'

The place fell silent, as though Harry wasn't the only one waiting for an answer. Bartholomew leant forward, and spoke to Harry alone. 'No, Ludlow. Now now. But rest assured, just before you die, I shall whisper it very softly in your ear.'

He raised his voice. 'Now come, and have a good look at your opponents.'

Harry looked down into the arena. Four large rats scurried about, fruitlessly looking for somewhere to hide. Their panic seemed to increase with the noise around them, as all those in the room crowded on to the step to see.

'Beldeau assured me that they're famished. You can of course refuse to take them on. I shall start my watch and give you the command to jump in. If you don't and the ten minutes elapse, I shall, regardless of how it disappoints my fellows, take you out into the street and hang you.'

Harry pushed himself up on to the edge. Hands still held him and he pressed back against them, using that to keep himself upright. He saw Crosby across the other side of the barrel, and the malignant grin that he gave in return was enough to convince Harry that he was looking at the cause of his misfortune. Crosby made a show of exchanging money with his neighbour. Harry's own money! Fairbairn stood behind him, making no attempt to peer into the arena. He looked ill, but, there again, he always did.

The men behind, still holding him, were grinning, sensing his fear, and were quite happy to hold him there for a while. But they wouldn't do it once Bartholomew started his timing, and if Harry didn't jump, they'd probably push him. He looked down at the rats. Two of them had stopped running, and instead were scrabbling in the sand trying to find a place to hide. Perhaps they sensed danger too. Who could tell?

'On the count of three, Ludlow.' Bartholomew tallied off the number, and Harry, after he had said three, hesitated for a fraction of a second then leapt into the barrel, straight for the burrowing rats. He tried to get two of them but one was too swift, scurrying away from his foot. But the other, intent on digging, sensed his approach too late and he landed on it with his right foot, the entire weight of his body crushing the creature beneath him. He knew he had to be bold, to take the initiative, for it was a major challenge to kill three rats in ten minutes, and he didn't doubt Bartholomew's words. The man would hang him. Staying alive was imperative. There was always the chance of escape, but the end of a rope was no way out of this. He dropped to his knees and went straight for the rat he'd missed, calculating that it was the least ferocious, since it had tried digging to escape the noise above.

The barrel was a problem, because he really needed a corner where he could box them in. The others had got as far away from him as possible, and he dived across the sandpit to try and pin his target, cracking his head on the side of the barrel. He felt the fur of the animal slip through his teeth, but he just managed to get a grip on its tail as it tried to escape. The rat spun round and bit at his cheek, but Harry pulled himself up and swung the rat at the side of the barrel trying to stun it. It took him four attempts and he suffered four painful bites before he got it right. The rat went limp, dazed but not dead. He could hear the yelling of the crowd in his ears, some egging him on, others braying for the rats to go for his throat. He stood up and stamped on the dazed rat as it lay in the sand, crushing its head. Almost at the same moment he was boxed around the ears, only remembering as he fell Bartholomew's strictures about standing.

As Harry crawled across the pit on his knees, towards the two remaining rats, they didn't run. They stood their ground, their small glittering eyes holding his. He went for the one on his left, thumping his head on the barrel again as he missed. It didn't try to escape. Instead the rodent bit into his chin and held on. Harry shook his head like a terrier, trying to dislodge it. He managed at cost of half an inch of skin, and as it fell he followed it down, his mouth closing around its neck. Again he shook his head like a dog, and he heard the bone break and the animal go limp. A perfect kill.

There was no time to feel triumphant. He set off after the other one. It ran around the barrel, occasionally turning to confront him, but always slipping away as he attacked. He made a false lunge, and as it ran off he threw his whole body at it, trying to trap the creature between his back and the wood. Success, but at the cost of more flesh and blood, as the rodent trapped beneath him sought to escape. He pressed hard, forcing his body against the barrel despite the pain. Then he rolled over to attack. The rat, weakened by the crushing it had endured, was too slow to get away. It was in his teeth, but he'd missed the vital neck. Harry bit down hard, and he felt the warm blood run over his mouth and the rat struggled frantically in its death agony. When it was still, he stood up, and spat the creature at Bartholomew.

If he'd hoped to dent the man's malice he was sadly disappointed. Bartholomew merely looked at his watch, and pronounced that Harry had seen off the four rats in six minutes. Some cheered, others groaned. What upset Harry, as he looked through the haze that covered his eyes, was the way Beldeau was smiling at him. That lopsided grin told him that the rats he'd just fought were not his best. He would have stronger, bigger, and perhaps hungrier rats to come.

'I think decency allows for a short break, Ludlow. We shall return you to your abode, while we go and have a wet.'

Harry was back in the dark again, and he heard the sound of voices fade away. He dragged his mind away from thoughts of the wounds he'd suffered, though they nipped like the devil, trying instead to think of ways to get out of this trap. But on another level his mind was also working on ways to kill rats, for he had no doubt he'd be back in the pit before long, and this time with five rats to fight. He wouldn't get the chance to kill the first one in the same way. He knew they wouldn't allow him the opportunity. But that action with his body had proved a success, and if he could get them by the tail he had the chance to dash their brains out.

Again he cast his mind back, trying to recall if he'd ever heard anyone telling him how to do this. People talked of such things without ever having experienced it, so their information was, at best, second-hand. But it was generally held that there was a way of fixing rats with a stare, a method that froze them just long enough to give the man a decided advantage. But he had a vague memory that this was accompanied by a serious risk, for if you fixed the rat with your eyes, when they attacked, that's the part they went for. So be it. For he had to survive, and however many rats he fought and killed, and however many bites he sustained, that was paramount.

The sound of voices coming back alerted him, and he wondered how long they'd been gone. Not long enough for him to achieve anything in the way of an escape. He had no way of calculating the time. But it must be the middle of the night. It had been after midnight when he left the di Toraglia villa. Surely that was a couple of hours ago? These men, regardless of how much they liked this sport, had to sleep sometime. If he could just get through to that point, it would at least give him a longer period of peace. Then he might be able to do something about getting away from here. A slim hope, but in such a situation you grasp what you can.

The door was opened again, this time cautiously. Harry waited for them to come and get him, resisted them as they dragged him out, and made his way as slowly as possible towards the pit. He was glad to see that his audience was in no hurry. They were still drinking, placing their bets, examining him, then looking into the pit before exchanging odds. Bartholomew stood in the same place, his watch in his hand. Harry climbed up on to the step, making a great show of weariness.

'I insist upon a fair contest,' he said.

Bartholomew raised his eyebrows in surprise, as though Harry was in some way insulting his integrity. Given what he was about, Harry wondered if the man was sane. 'I have no way of knowing if you watch is accurate.'

Bartholomew gave a small laugh. 'If I didn't despise you, I'd admire your effrontery, Ludlow. I wonder how Mr Hunter of Bond Street would take it, hearing you questioning the accuracy of his timepiece.'

'You say it's a Hunter?' snapped Harry.

'Do you doubt it?' Bartholomew shoved the watch under Harry's nose, which allowed him to see that it was near three o'clock. At best, he calculated that the first fight, from taking him out of his confinement, to the start of this one, must run at near an hour. If he could drag them out, it would be daylight before he had to fight seven rats. With the drink and the smoke in the room, plus the time, there was some hope that his audience would tire. Then he realized with a shock what that meant. He would have to fight one more rat than the negro, and that fellow, an expert, took eight minutes to dispatch six of them.

'Given your undoubted talents at this sport, Ludlow, we've decided to bring matters forward a little.'

Harry turned away from Bartholomew's smile and looked down into the pit, which had been cleared of the dead rats, and raked over to hide the blood. Now it contained seven rats, much bigger than the ones he'd already killed. Was his imagination exaggerating their size? More to the point, they were still, watching each other rather than the crowd above. It was the stillness of a threatened attack, not of fear, and Harry knew that these were some of Beldeau's finest. Large, vicious, and already cannibals of their own kind. He also knew that protest would be useless.

The level of sound was rising as the wagers were agreed. Harry was hoisted on to the barrel this time, and thrown in as soon as Bartholomew gave the signal. He went straight down on to his knees to avoid the blows being aimed at his head by those who'd bet against him. That wasn't the only thing different. These creatures didn't wait. Three of them, starving and smelling blood, went for him right off, one catching him in the arm, and another on the back as he bent forward to engage the third. This rat froze and stared at him. Harry could feel the pain as the other rats bit him repeatedly, but he ignored it and held the gaze of the one he was facing. Two seconds can seem like a lifetime at a moment like this, and they gazed, the man and the rodent, into each other's eyes. The rat suddenly leapt for his left eye. Harry jerked his head, and with what could only have been luck, caught the animal. He didn't stop moving and the jerk of his head that broke its neck was one continuous action.

No time to congratulate himself on finding the true method of successful rat fighting. He slammed sideways trapping the rat on his arm against the barrel, slamming it repeatedly. It fell into the sand and Harry stood, ignoring the blows aimed at his head, and stamped on it before it could recover. The third rat was still clinging to his back, and he fell away from a particularly vicious swipe and felt the creature go into a frenzy of biting as it was crushed against the side. He rolled his body to and fro, trying to get extra purchase with his feet in the sand. It stopped biting, and as Harry pulled himself away it fell to the ground, twitching. It wasn't dead, but it was hurt enough to leave while he fought the others.

The other four had stayed out of the battle, and as luck would have it, two of them were now fighting each other, trying in their starvation to make a meal of their fellow creature. Harry ignored them and threw himself towards another one which adopted the same pose as the first, freezing in its position as it stared him in the eye. Again that pause before the rat leapt. This one was quicker, or he was slower. No matter, Harry felt the thin skin of his eyelid tear as he jerked his head to get rid of it. The rat landed on all fours and turned to face him again. He saw out of the corner of his blooded eye that the two others were still fighting. He tried to locate the last one but he couldn't see it. Then he felt it running up his back. He ignored that and faced his opponent again. This time, when it leapt, he was the quicker, but he didn't get it right for its head went right into his mouth. He bit hard through its neck until he felt the bone, keeping up the pressure till it went limp.

It was still in his mouth, its blood running down his chin, when he stomped on the two who were fighting each other. The last rat was savaging the back of his neck and he spun and twisted to dislodge it. The sound outside the pit had reached a crescendo, mingled cheers and cries of unfair. Finally he managed to jerk it off and Harry dropped back on to his knees, following it down as it twisted and fell. He didn't go for it, knowing that if he did it would simply scurry away, wasting valuable time. He waited, inching closer and looking it in the eye.

This one was not to be tempted so easily, and they stared at each other for several seconds. Harry reckoned that if he blinked it would attack, trying to get him in the fraction of a second his eye was closed. Time? How much had he left? He went for the rat quickly, and this seemed to surprise the animal, for it was slow to try and get out of the way. But it did succeed in leaping sideways and attacking his exposed cheek. Again Harry had to raise himself and shake his head to dislodge it, losing another half an inch of skin. Then he was on his knees again, holding its gaze. This time the rat didn't wait, but went straight for him. Harry caught it beautifully, and in one sweeping movement dispatched it. It went limp, but he held its fur in his teeth while he killed off the other rats that lay wounded around the arena. Again he stood up and looked Bartholomew in the eye, thinking there was a neck he like to get his teeth into.

'Seven minutes for seven rats, Ludlow.' There was no admiration in the voice, more irritation. He looked over the pit towards Beldeau. 'I think you claim too much for your creatures, Beldeau. You'd better sort out something more ferocious for the morrow.'

Bartholomew turned his attention back to Harry, glancing at his watch. 'We shall begin earlier tonight, Ludlow, and rest assured that we shall carry on until the game is done. For I must sail on the ebb the day after, and when I do, you shall be either blind or dead.'

CHAPTER TWENTY-TWO

Harry's head ached abominably, both from the blows he'd received
and those he'd inflicted on himself by bashing his head against the
side of the barrel. At least they'd untied him, although that had led
to a painful period as the blood rushed back into his hands. He was
drifting in and out of sleep as he tried to think of some way out of
this prison. Nothing came. The sound of voices made him jerk himself
into life and his heart sank. Surely his time hadn't elapsed so quickly?
Harry pressed his ear against the staves. Voices yes, but not the
sound of a crowd. Two people, perhaps three, in quiet conversation.
The thud was quite audible, and Harry heard the scrabbling sound
as someone tried to open the door. He braced himself to attack, and
as the door swung open his fist was half-way to Fairbairn's face. By
the time Harry had pulled his punch, the strength was out of the
blow. But it was still sufficient to knock the skeletal surgeon flat on
his back. Harry, carried forward by his momentum, followed him
out through the doorway, landing right on top of the man and driving
the wind out of his body. Looking sideways he found himself staring
into the sightless eyes of a sailor, no doubt placed to guard him. His
body was sprawled untidily on the floor, the back of his skull a bloody
mess. A cooper's hammer lay beside him.

Fairbairn was trying to get to his feet, and Harry instinctively
grabbed at him to help. He then picked up the hammer, looking
around to see if there was a more potent weapon laying about. The

surgeon was shaking like a leaf, and as he pointed towards the sailor on the floor his finger trembled alarmingly. He spoke in short bursts, gulping great breaths of air as he did so. 'Couldn't let it pass. Barbarians. I fear I've killed the poor fellow.'

He was no poor fellow to Harry; more likely he was one of the people who'd stood on the step and swiped at him in the pit. He grabbed Fairbairn, who seemed to have frozen, staring at the corpse, and dragged him towards the doorway that led into the alley. Pulling it open, he pushed Fairbairn through. Hands grabbed him immediately. So did Harry, catching the surgeon by the collar and attempting to drag him back into the warehouse. Fairbairn became the object of an uncomfortable tug of war which Harry, in his weakened state, was bound to lose.

He swung the hammer, knowing that he was as likely to harm his rescuer as those holding him. He caught one of the hands gripping the surgeon, causing the man to let go with a cry of pain. But he was still being hauled out into the alley. He would either have to surrender Fairbairn, or take his chances in the open. The choice was taken from him. Another, much larger, pair of hands grabbed the surgeon, and gave him such a powerful tug that Harry was catapulted out through the door, tripping and falling to his knees.

'Christ Almighty,' cried Pender. 'Let the poor bastard go!'

He grabbed Harry and hauled him to his feet. No time for words to explain what his servant was doing here. Lubeck, who had pulled both of them out of the doorway with apparent ease, hoisted Fairbairn easily and then ran off down the alley, not stopping till they were well away from the warehouse. Harry, gasping for breath counted the rescue party. It was still dark but he could see their faces in the moonlight. Ten men. Where were the rest of his crew?

Pender must have guessed what was in his mind from the look in his eye. 'That's all we could muster, Captain. The rest were swayed by Sutton.'

'Sutton?'

'Ay. He said that what happened to you was none of their concern. You worked them hard for a couple of square meals. It took more'n a bit of grub to get him courtin' a row with Bartholomew.'

'What the devil are you doing here?'

'Mr James Ludlow's instructions, your honour. He said, begging your pardon, that you were safe enough at sea, but that you was like a child ashore, and shouldn't be let out of sight. He told me to keep an eye on you, an' only to make my presence known if you seemed about to leave.'

Harry gave a rueful smile, and silently thanked his brother. He looked round as his eyes lit on the surgeon, who was still being held up by Lubeck. 'Fairbairn, are you all right?

'No, sir, I am not,' the surgeon gasped, for the big German, not sure what was going on, still had him round the throat.

'Gently, Lubeck.' The blond giant looked at him, then let Fairbairn go. He dropped to his knees holding his throat, and Harry staggered over to help him to his feet.

'The *Principessa?*'

Pender pointed to Lubeck. 'This fellow took her out from the quayside after she'd finished loading stores. That's why it took so long to get a rescue party together. She's anchored outside the harbour.'

'Do we have a boat, Pender?'

'We do.'

'Come, Mr Fairbairn. I fear that Ma Thomas's inn is not a place you should return to.'

'The cutter is moored near the Customs Fort,' said Pender.

'Let's go.' He led the way north along the quayside, stumbling as he ran, for Harry was on the verge of collapse. His head was throbbing, and each bite and scratch seemed to have a painful life of its own. Pender, who must have wondered at his condition, took him by the elbow to help him, and Harry turned to give his servant a smile. He saw the teeth flash in the moonlight, and that one sign that Pender was confident made him feel that the situation could be rectified.

They were in the boat, pulling hard out of the harbour with the first hint of dawn in the sky. Pender, now that he had time, was anxiously examining what he could see of Harry's face.

'I damn near missed you. When you went off in that sedan chair, I took my time, thinkin' I knew where you was goin'. These alleys all look alike, specially in the dark. I got well lost. And then when I found that villa there was none of those hands outside like last time, it seemed that you set off back to the ship. I was just deciding to make my way back to the quay, when you came out.'

Harry leant over and touched Pender's arm. 'You saw them take me?'

'Ay, though I heard more'n I saw. But there were too many to tackle, even though I had pistols. I stood as much chance of hittin' you as them.'

Tired as he was, Harry was thinking of what he needed to do next. That he was going to kill Bartholomew, he didn't doubt, and everything else would take second place to that. How was he going to accomplish it was a mystery. He didn't have enough men to attack Ma Thomas's or Bartholomew's boats, even if he could personally muster more than Pender and Lubeck had managed. If he waited until Bartholomew put to sea, he would be facing odds of five to one. Lightly crewed they might be, but with his four-pounder cannon, it would be suicide to try and take them all on. If only he had those twelve pounders sitting uselessly on the *Dido*. And what about those carronades?

'Lubeck. Put the cutter about and head for the *Dido*.'

There was a moment's pause while the German slowly translated this. Another while he considered it. Then he did as Harry asked.

'Whatever for, Captain?'

'We're going to steal her, Pender.'

'What, that useless tub?'

The boat lost some of its speed, as the rest of the men pulling on the oars exchanged looks and murmurs. They hadn't signed up for this when he took them on as crew, and they'd already done more than their share. Harry felt that, as his rescuers, they were entitled to an explanation. But ingrained habit made him contrive an excuse. 'Two ships are better than one, even a hulk like the *Dido*.'

They weren't satisfied, for the cutter's speed dropped even more. Harry cursed softly. 'I'm going to take and destroy Bartholomew. If I have to fight them all, I intend to. But him I want more than anything. I can't explain everything to you all right now, but I know I can do it. And I also know that he's heading for a rendezvous with some prizes. I intend to take those as well, and since there will only be one ship's crew, I dare say each share of the booty will amount to a tidy sum.'

His little speech hadn't quite done the trick. Money excited them. Death didn't. It was Pender who supplied the words that tipped the balance. 'One thing at a time, lads. Let's do as Captain Ludlow says for now, 'cause that looks easy. Then we can put our minds to the future in the light of day.'

The speed of the cutter increased immediately, and they sped towards the side of the *Dido*, racing past the other ships of Bartholomew's little squadron. No one was awake as yet, and if they had a man on watch, he wasn't paying much attention. Bartholomew hadn't bothered to put anyone aboard to guard the ship. He knew, as did Harry's boat crew, that it wasn't worth stealing. It wallowed in the gentle well, creaking alarmingly, and smelling of tar and rotting timber.

Harry was first aboard, his energy restored by necessity. The others followed. The men who'd volunteered were the best of his new crew, and they ran quickly to carry out Harry's whispered instructions. There would be no time for hauling up anchors, and Harry gave Lubeck an axe and told him to stand by to cut the cables. A scrap of canvas was all Harry needed at this point, and he called out to the men to let the maincourse fall.

The *Dido* strained on her anchors, with the sound of protesting wood coming from beneath Harry's feet. He called to Pender to organize the sailors who'd come down from setting the sails. 'Get some turpentine, some big wads of tow, and a couple of flints and tapers. Put two of them with axes to stand by on the stern anchor. As soon as Lubeck cuts through the bower, tell them to go to it. And fenders! We'll need fenders. Use the capstan bars if you have to.'

Harry nodded to Lubeck, who stood by the bows. The German swung the axe with all his might. The noise seemed to thunder out across the whole harbour as the man hacked away. Ten times he swiped at the heavy cable before it parted. The *Dido*'s head swung round, and Lubeck ran down the deck to join the others hacking at the other, smaller, cable. It gave way with a loud crack and whistled into the water. The ship was clear, and Harry spun the wheel to take her out past the stern of the nearest of Bartholomew's ships. He had to lessen the odds, and he intended to start that right now.

'Lubeck, take the wheel.' The German rushed to his side. 'Steer me across the hawse of that polacre.'

'That's the *Bella*,' a voice said. 'Captain Freeman!'

A pity it wasn't Bartholomew's, but that couldn't be helped. Harry grabbed a hefty bunch of tow and lashed it to a capstan bar, calling to the others to do the same. He then stove in the cask of turpentine that Pender had fetched from below. The tow was dipped in the turps, soaking it up. By the time that Lubeck had them close to the *Bella*, they had a dozen of these missiles ready.

Harry lit a taper with the flint, then a lantern. He knew he was taking a risk, for turpentine from the barrel had spilled all over the *Dido*'s deck. But it was risk he was prepared to accept with a ship he didn't really want. As they sailed by the little flotilla, Harry lit the first bundle of tow. It flared up immediately. He stood like a Greek athlete with a javelin, aimed it at the *Bella*'s rigging, and threw. It caught in the mizzen shrouds. These, covered in tar, and dry as tinder in this climate, flared up. Pender and the others followed his example. Soon the ship was covered in pricks of light. As they sailed by the stern, they snagged through the anchor cable with the *Dido*'s bows. Harry and Lubeck leapt out on to the bowsprit. Straddling it, they hacked at the *Bella*'s cable till it parted. Then it was fenders out to avoid the two ships colliding as the *Dido* drifted past the *Bella*'s sternlights. Harry threw his final missile through the open window of the main cabin.

He could hear the cries of panic, for sailors feared fire aboard their ships more than anything else. It would have pleased Harry greatly if one of his missiles had gone down the main hatchway and set the magazine alight, but that was asking too much. The *Bella* was nevertheless beginning to burn merrily, and in enough places to cause those trying to fight the fire a lot of trouble. Reduced to one anchor, the burning ship swung round on her single cable and crashed into its neighbour.

'Whose ship's that?' he called out as he eased himself back on to the deck.

'Frome's. The *Ariel*.'

'What's Bartholomew's ship called?'

One of his hands reeled off the names. '*Daedalus*. The others are *Mercury*, Captain Chittenden, and the other is *Cromer*. That useless sod Pilton has her.'

He saw the flames licking their way out of the *Bella*'s main cabin. He must have landed his burning wad on some furnishings for it to ignite so quickly. It might not burn the ship to the waterline, for they'd likely put it out before that. But this polacre, damaged, would not sail with Bartholomew, reducing the odds by twenty per cent. Men from the *Ariel* were fending off the burning threat, ignoring the cries for help from their mates on the *Bella*.

'Steer for the *Principessa*,' he shouted to Lubeck. The *Dido* wallowed across the harbour, with Lubeck struggling to hold a course as it threatened to fall off with the leeway. Harry made his way to the small cabin.

'Are you all right, Mr Fairbairn?'

The surgeon looked at him with his pale blue eyes. 'Where's Broadbridge?'

'Dead, Mr Fairbairn. But I don't have time now to tell you of the circumstances.' The surgeon was still staring at him. 'I was not the cause, sir, my word on it.'

'Bartholomew?'

'I don't rightly know. But after what happened tonight, it certainly wouldn't surprise me.'

Harry ran back on deck. 'Lubeck, as we come alongside, I want you to go aboard the *Principessa*. All hands about ship and get her out to sea. I'll need a dozen more men to sail this. That is if she doesn't sink on us first. I doubt you'll have much difficulty in catching us up.'

He turned to Pender and explained in English what he'd just told Lubeck in French. 'Some of the crew might not like it, your honour.'

Harry turned back to the German. 'Any signs of dissent from the crew, Lubeck, you have my permission to sling them over the side.'

The blond man grinned, his scarred face lighting up in the morning sky. The sun had yet to appear over the top of the mountains, leaving the port still in shadow. Harry looked back to where the *Bella* still blazed; it looked as though the crew were winning. He suddenly felt utterly exhausted, and he had to hold on to the bulwark to stay upright. Pender took his arm and led him towards the small cabin.

'You'd better lay down now, Captain, afore you fall down.'

Fairbairn stood up as they entered. Harry flopped on to the cot, and the surgeon leant over him to examine the cuts, bites, and bruises that covered his face, shoulders and neck.

'Barbaric,' he said. 'Fetch me some clean water and some cloths. If there are any spirits about fetch them too, we must clean up these wounds.'

Pender disappeared to search the ship. Harry passed out, and slept through Fairbairn's ministrations, just as he slept through the arguments on the deck of the *Principessa* when the *Dido* came alongside. Lubeck threatened to throw a couple of the least willing over the side, but it was the moment when Pender floored Sutton that turned things, for he'd been the most vocal in his objections.

They got the *Dido* under way again, heading out for the open sea. The *Principessa* was up with them in no time, and the two ships headed out into deep water. The land dropped away behind them and they sailed on through the morning, at no great speed for their pace was set by the slower ship. Harry slept on, unaware that Fairbairn, having raided the sailmaker's locker, was busy stitching him up. Pender, seeing the needle in the surgeon's hands, was no happier to watch this being done to someone else, so he removed himself.

Harry woke just before noon. His throat was as dry as a bone, and when he tried to speak no sound emerged. Fairbairn must have heard something for he came into the cabin. He held a cup to Harry's lips, letting him drink slowly.

'We're at sea?'

'Yes. We lost sight of land about an hour ago.'

Harry started to sit up. 'Is anyone in pursuit?'

The surgeon, his hands on the patient's shoulders, shook his head. 'You need to rest, Captain Ludlow. I have rarely seen anyone in such a state of collapse. You didn't even move when I stitched the skin over your eye. There are others to take care of the ship.'

Harry pushed the surgeon's feeble arms aside. 'Rest? I've no time for that, Mr Fairbairn.'

As he moved to get out of the cot, all the aches and pains seemed to well up together. Forcing himself to sit up, Harry swung his feet on to the floor with a look of pain and ran his hands over his face and neck. He felt the stitches that Fairbairn had used, touching them gently.

'Thank you. I must have been quite a sight.'

'You were at that. In fact you still are.' Fairbairn almost smiled. Funny how the attempt made him look sad.

'I owe you my life,' said Harry.

'Had I known those fellows were about, I could have safely left you.' Now he did look miserable, shaking his head slowly. 'I didn't mean to actually kill him, you know.'

Harry put his hand on the surgeon's arm so as to pull himself to his feet. 'It was no more than he deserved, sir. I wouldn't give it a second's thought.'

'But then you're not me, Captain Ludlow. My job is to save life, not take it.'

'Then the slate is even, Fairbairn, for as I say, you saved mine.'

Harry made his way out of the cabin on to the sunlit deck. He looked over the rail and saw the *Principessa* sailing easy on the larboard quarter. If he needed anything to raise his spirits that was it. That and some sustenance.

CHAPTER TWENTY-THREE

The two ships were lashed together, with the pumps clanking away on the *Dido* to rid her of the water in her hull. They shifted most of her stores into the *Principessa*, especially the powder and shot. That had raised her slightly, but she was in such a state she was making water whilst stationary. Harry had been down in the hold to have a look at her knees and cross bracings. They were so rotten that he could poke his finger through the wood. It made what he proposed to do both a necessity and a pleasure.

Shifting the guns took till mid-afternoon. They struck the four-pounders down to the hold, replacing them with the *Dido*'s twelve-pounders, and located the four carronades amidships. Given the weight of metal proportionate to the *Principessa*'s hull, too many broadsides could damage the ship. But Harry had in mind a more staggered form of attack, never firing more than one carronade at a time. Yet he knew if he got close enough to Bartholomew he'd let the whole lot go and damn the consequences. Every time Harry conjured up that face in his mind his blood boiled and he had to divert himself with something physical to calm down.

Did Bartholomew and his fellow captains know about these guns? If not, he would have a distinct advantage, for the carronades, known as smashers, fired a large ball over a small distance. At the right range they were lethal to a ship the size of those he intended to engage. He would soon know by the way they behaved. His first priority was to weld his crew into a half-decent fighting machine. They cast off the *Dido* and let her drift away to leeward.

He was short of hands, but Bartholomew was shorter still; even distributing the hands from the *Bella* left him with fewer men per ship than Harry mustered on the *Principessa*. Each of the twelve-pounders, nine feet long, required eight men to fire them. One side alone took up forty men, with five men each to man the two carronades, leaving precious few people to sail the ship, supply the guns with powder and shot, carry out emergency repairs, and remove the wounded. If Harry had been sailing fresh from home, he would have more than doubled the crew.

First he had them run the guns in and out, and practise loading them. This allowed each man to become familiar with his team, and by moving men about Harry took what started as a farce and produced some semblance of order. The nimblest men were on the carronades, since he had one simple plan. To get close to his enemy, do as much damage with his cannon as possible, disable the others, then board and take Bartholomew's ship.

Men get bored with pretence; they like to hear the sound of real gunfire. Harry obliged, letting them fire away as much as they pleased. With what he'd loaded himself, added to the large quantity of shot he'd taken out of the *Dido*, he had more than he could decently store. Only in the balls for the carronades did he need to show caution. But he'd put the best men on those, and they needed the least practice.

The guns roared out one at a time, and Harry watched the men as they reloaded, stepping in to advise them of ways to speed it up. Having done this with each gun he moved on to rolling broadsides. It was no good expecting people to manage this by sound, because in battle they wouldn't hear any shouted orders. The gun captain had to time his fire to the man before him, with Harry or Lubeck giving the order for the first gun to fire its second shot.

The sea around the *Principessa* boiled as round after round was fired into it. Harry then made up a target on a raft so that they would have something to aim at. After a period of firing from a stationary position, he tried firing on the move. The men were now black from head to foot and smoke rolled over the ship as she bore down on the raft and fired. It wasn't perfect, for the target still floated, but they had got close enough to satisfy him. Harry hove to, for it was time to make a speech.

'Gentlemen. We don't know each other. But I've watched you today, and you've had a proper chance to look me over. I expect rumours are flying about because of what happened last night, so I'd better tell you what I intend. For reasons I can't fathom, Gideon Bartholomew wants me dead. He chose a way of doing it that lacked any Christian feeling. Any of you that have spoken to the lads that got me out will know what I mean.'

A shudder of fear and disgust rippled through the assembled hands.

'I don't know what Bartholomew is about. All I know is that he's making a mint of money. I intend to take it off him, and I won't lie to you, I intend to kill him as well. It would be nice to pretend that the odds mean nothing, but that would be a downright falsehood. I will say this, though. I'll take a wager that I'm as good a sailor as any in that little fleet, and I'll also wager that this ship, the *Principessa*, can outsail the lot of them.'

'So you intend to fight them all?'

Heads turned and Harry looked to see who'd spoken. It was Sutton. He had a badly swollen black eye where Pender had clouted him, and Harry's servant made to move forward again. Harry couldn't understand what had happened to Sutton to change him so, for he'd seemed willing enough to join early on, though he'd proved work-shy. Now he seemed to be making every effort to undermine him.

'I won't fight them all at once, Sutton.'

'They might not give you any choice.'

Harry smiled. 'I'm not fool enough to leave them the option.'

'So you say,' Sutton sneered.

Harry looked slowly around the assembled faces, full of doubt. 'What if we can take just one of them, and find out what they're about? If we could get to their rendezvous before them, we could steal their money from right under their noses.'

That pleased his crew, for there was much grinning and digging in the ribs. But Sutton wasn't to be mollified. 'Seems to me that you're more bent on gettin' Bart. Seems to me that you'll get us all killed just for that.'

Harry decided it was time to gamble. They were either with him or they weren't. If not, he'd rather have them off the ship. 'Anyone who wants to, can leave the ship. The *Dido* is over there. She might be a tub, but she'll float long enough to get you to where you want to go.'

It was subtle, for in truth they had nowhere to go but back to the Navy. Harry made his final pitch. 'Those who're going get over to the entry port. Those who are staying best get below for their dinner.'

There was much murmuring and quiet argument, as people traded the prospect of Harry's offer. Money and the risk of death, against what they could expect from the Navy, which was the risk of death and no money. Harry could see that he was winning. Sutton looked set to speak again. Harry called to him to cut him off, swinging his arm to indicate the *Dido*.

'I think your ship awaits you, Sutton.'

The man walked towards the entry port. He'd boxed himself into a corner which no one wanted to share, and Harry admired the way that, left with no choice, he didn't plead or whine, but took the only decision he could. Time to get the poor sod off the hook.

'You'll have a devil of a job sailing it by yourself. And I better warn you that I intend to use it for target practise in about half an hour. And if it's any help to you, Sutton, I would like you to stay.'

Someone laughed, but it wasn't derision, for a couple of other grabbed him, jostled him playfully, and dragged him below. Pender smiled at him. 'Neat, your honour. Very neat.'

They put the *Dido* under topsails and lashed the wheel. Harry stood on the deck of the *Principessa* as the ship came about for its run in. Not the real thing, with no return fire. But it would cheer up the men no end, and when they came to face a real enemy, he hoped that their spirits would be as high as they were at this moment.

The *Principessa* bore down on the *Dido*. Harry gave the order to open the gunports, load, and run out. All went smoothly, and the men leant over their guns with a keen air. As they came abreast Harry gave the order to fire on the upward roll. The nearest gun went off, and there was loud cheer as the ball smashed into the side of the *Dido*. Then the second gun, which missed its timing. Cries of derision erupted as it sent a spray of water over the *Dido*'s side. This was followed by the first carronade, and one of the *Dido*'s gunports disintegrated. The ball carried on, just missing the mast, and taking out the bulwark on the other side of the deck as well. The second carronade put a ball clean through the hull. The *Dido* staggered as though some great hand had grabbed it, and they could hear the sound of tearing timbers below decks, even at two cables. Wood flew off the mainmast from the next shot, more of the side was damaged by the next, and the last one, poorly aimed, went past the bows.

Harry put the ship about once they'd headreached the *Dido*, and the men rushed to the other side to repeat the manoeuvre. Shot after shot went home. Holes appeared in the side, and after several passes the bulwarks were a jagged mess. Next he had them shooting bar shot at the rigging, and that was in tatters after two passes. The *Dido* wallowed in the swell, with no way left on her.

No more carronades, she wouldn't stand it. He kept up the firing with the twelve-pounders, pass after pass, shot after shot. The *Dido* started to settle in the water, every shot into her hull opening a dozen seams. The guns were hot and the men were tired, with the sun dipping into the western sea. Still she floated. He decided on one more pass. Then he would house the guns for the night.

He bore down, bringing his ship in close. This time he did include the carronades. The rolling broadside was now well practised, though far from the perfection he loved. But what he had was enough. The balls crashed into the other ship sending wood flying in all directions. Then the carronades spoke. This time they must have hit something mortal, for the *Dido* split in two. The men cheered as if they'd just won a great fleet action. Harry ordered all to be made secure, as he put his ship about, and leaving the wreckage of the *Dido* littered across the ocean, headed back for the approaches to Genoa.

'I wonder if it would be possible for you to put me ashore somewhere?'

Harry looked up from his plate at Fairbairn. The surgeon was in a terrible way. He hadn't touched his food. His gaunt face had a hunted look, and every so often he would clutch at his stomach as if in the grip of some deep pain. He was desperate to feed his opium habit, and the means to do so lay back at Ma Thomas's. Harry would have been reluctant to let him go anyway, for he was heading into a fight, and a surgeon aboard was a great comfort to the hands. But he had no intention of putting him ashore so that he could head right back to the inn, driven by his habit. For a man like Fairbairn, in the grip of something so cruel, secrecy would be sold for a taste of opium. But it wasn't just that. He owed Fairbairn his life. The man had killed to save him, causing himself great distress in the process. Perhaps there was something Harry could do to return the compliment.

'No, Mr Fairbairn. I cannot put you ashore. I don't have either the time, nor the inclination.'

'You must,' he gasped.

'No. I have a fight on my hands, Mr Fairbairn.' The surgeon grabbed his stomach again, and his lank fair hair fell over his face and he shot forward in pain. 'So it seems do you. Let's pray that we both win.'

Harry sat with him that night, holding his hand and talking to him. He gave him some tobacco to chew, which helped a little. At times Harry had to hold him physically on the cot, and for someone so thin and wasted he showed surprising strength. In the end, much against his will, he had to strap him down, so that he could get some sleep himself. As he came into the main cabin, Pender poured him a cup of coffee.

'It will get worse. I don't want to restrain him, but I'll have to tonight. From now on we take turns.'

'God forgive me for saying it, Captain, but what he needs is something to do.'

Fairbairn lay in the coach tortured by his obsession, screaming for relief, while Harry in the sleeping cabin dreamt of rats trying to tear out his throat, and the unholy cries from his nightmare were every bit as unnerving as those of the surgeon.

Yet Harry Ludlow was clear-eyed enough at sun-up the next morning. He sat on the foremast crosstrees, his telescope trained on the distant harbour of Genoa. They beat to and fro all morning, watching ships heading in and out of the port, speaking none, and ignoring all enquiries. They'd have to risk Bartholomew picking up news of his presence. But Harry reckoned if he had a rendezvous, then he would keep it. After all, he outnumbered Harry Ludlow by five to one.

They'd just turned the glass on the afternoon watch when he spied his quarry, all five of them coming out of the roadstead in an untidy line. He turned his glass on to the *Bella*, easy to spot with her single long mast, genuinely amazed that she been made ready to sail. Harry had the impression that she was labouring. He took them in turn, watching each ship for a while to see how they handled. Bartholomew's ship *Daedalus* was in the centre, for all the world like a commodore, and ably handled. The wind was foul and they had to tack out of the bay, a manoeuvre Bartholomew carried out better than his consorts. Looking at the sails, he could see that *Daedalus* was the fastest ship. He had reefs in his courses and topsails where some of his fellows had none, sailing more slowly than he needed to to maintain the line.

It was plain to see that the *Bella*, second in the line, was keeping them back. She had sails going in and out every few minutes, as she sought to increase her speed a fraction, and a steady stream of water shot from her side, evidence that the pumps were working flat out. The ship ahead of her was not faring much better, despite being undamaged, and Harry, looking at her lines, and the setting of her sails, marked her out, for she was capable of better. It was her captain that let the ship down, for his ship-handling was a mess. He guessed, from what he'd been told, that she must be *Cromer*. Apparently her captain, Pilton, was a buffoon. The ones astern of Bartholomew, *Mercury* and *Ariel*, looked to be much better sailors, and much better ships.

They were well out of the lee of the land now, and as they turned south the wind favoured them and they increased speed. Harry, knowing he would now be able to see them from the deck, slid down the backstay and gave the orders to set more sail, bringing his ship round on to a converging course. They must have had a lookout on him, for Harry heard the sound of a gun, and he saw a puff of smoke from Bartholomew's ship. They edged closer together, to afford each other more protection.

Harry grinned. Bartholomew couldn't realize how much he had revealed. They weren't going to commence any action, leaving him the initiative. Bartholomew would reckon on Harry going for the slowest ships, which is why he'd placed them ahead. As Harry engaged he could come up to assist, helped by those astern of him going wide, hoping to catch Harry in a trap from which there would be no escape.

But Harry didn't want to attack his slowest ships, and that was another thing Bartholomew had inadvertently told him. If he'd brought out the *Bella*, slowing his whole line to accommodate her, that meant that he needed the ship for some reason. Very well, let him keep her, for the very lack of speed would be to Harry's advantage. These men sailing in convoy was one of the things that had nagged at him.

Whatever they were about to do required all their ships. And if that need was strong enough, Bartholomew would stick with it. If he did, Harry Ludlow would have an easier task picking off his best ships. For one thing was certain. If those two lead captains tried to come about to engage him when he attacked the rear ships, they would probably miss stays. Given their rate of sailing compared to Harry's they would most certainly miss the battle. The odds had fallen from five to one down to three to one. Harry fully intended that before the day was out he'd have reduced them further.

CHAPTER TWENTY-FOUR

Harry sat a mile away from his quarry, sailing along on a parallel course. The wind had swung round into the north-west, gusting slightly, and being colder than the southerlies the day was clear and bright. The five ships were silhouetted against the rocky coastline. Bartholomew had decided to stay close inshore, as an added security measure. It was a shrewd move, and somewhat confounded Harry, who needed room to manoeuvre for the best chance of success. He realized that he could not hope to cripple more than one ship at a time, and even that would pose problems, for if he hesitated they would be down on him in a trice, outnumbering him and nullifying any advantage he had. There was the other consideration, that as soon as he fired his guns the level of his armaments would be revealed. You can only surprise an enemy once in such circumstances, so the first time had to count. What he really needed to know was where Bartholomew was headed, and that without them knowing that he had gained the information.

Chittenden, who as the second most senior captain was bringing up the rear, was sailing along very comfortably. Given that their leader had slowed the whole flotilla to accommodate one ship, Harry was left to wonder how far Bartholomew would carry this. Could he, over the course of the afternoon, so damage one of Bartholomew's ships that he would be forced to leave it behind? And how would they behave in battle? Harry knew it was attitude and training that produced a good crew in a fight. He always worked up his crews with the idea of fighting a ship that would shoot back, and do so with enough power to win. The richest prizes were the biggest, and they always sailed with a large crew and a lot of cannon. Most privateers avoided them like the plague. Indeed, most privateer captains couldn't even see the sense in practising gunnery, since they only ever envisaged themselves as being in action against a small merchant ship. They relied on speed, a few wild shots to unnerve their opponents, and a lot of shouting and screaming as they boarded. He couldn't wait to find out how this lot would behave.

Harry gave the orders to bring the *Principessa* round. He had tried this several times, and on each occasion the result had been the same. He watched as the three rear ships, *Mercury, Ariel,* and Bartholomew's *Daedalus* made more sail, moving up to cover their slower consorts. He called to Lubeck and the three leading hands to whom he had given command of their sections. Pender stood beside Harry as they gathered on the deck, behind the wheel.

'What I want to do is take out the last ship, the *Mercury*, the main advantage being that if they want to support her they'll have to bear up and reverse their course, and given that they're close inshore, they'll try to tack rather than wear. Coming right up into the wind will slow them even more. Chittenden knows that as well as we do, so at the first sign of attack, he'll come abreast of the next ship in line, which is Frome's ship, the *Ariel*.

'So we must fool them. Bartholomew might not think it odd if we seem to go for him. Foolish, yes, for I'd be playing right into his hands. But given what happened in that warehouse, he may think my anger has got the better of my judgement. So we must favour that thought, get within range, bear up ourselves in a flash, and get between the bows of the *Mercury* and the stern of the *Ariel*. They don't know how fast we are on a bowline. If we can do it quick enough we can force Chittenden away from the land, away from his friends and any immediate help.'

He could see that this had them worried, for the crew was new to the ship and each other. 'If the manoeuvre looks to be going wrong, I'll come back round and bear away. We only go into action if the odds are in our favour.'

'You don't reckon on him having a go at us?' asked Pender, articulating what must have been in everyone's mind.

'No, if he was going to do that, he would have sought to engage us before now.'

The captain of the tops spoke up. 'Seems daft, for he must know we can't fight them all.'

'Look at it from his point of view. What man in his right mind would take on odds of five to one?' The speed with which they all looked away amused Harry and he gave them a wide smile.

Pender spoke up, his voice full of supportive confidence, though the look he gave Harry had a strong element of hope attached. 'If he'd bothered to get to know you, your honour, he'd never have doubted it.'

'But he doesn't know me. He'll expect me to act like he would himself. He thinks that I'm going to shadow him, not attack him, hoping for some kind of opportunity to present itself. And opportunity is a two-edged sword, for he might find he has the chance to take me by surprise, or get away from me one moonless night. One serious attack, even if it's not completely successful, will throw that plan out the stern windows.'

'And how does that aid us?' asked the captain of the topmen. He didn't ask what he must indeed be wondering. How, in the name of hell, could Harry Ludlow be so sure of all this?

'The first rule of war is to force your enemy away from his own plans, then impose your own.' Harry looked out over the larboard side. They were coming closer. His guns had been loaded as soon as he spotted them. 'Gunports shut until the last moment, I don't want them to see those carronades until it's too late.'

Harry took the wheel himself, while Lubeck took station amidships, trumpet in hand, ready to yell the orders. It was a tricky affair right enough, for most of the men would have to be involved in the change of sails. Then, once they had braced the yards round, they'd have to run for their guns.

Bartholomew's ships were now sailing with their bowsprits practically brushing the stern of the ship ahead. There was the chance of a collision if Chittenden didn't sheer off. Again Harry was relying on this need to maintain their fleet. Preservation of their ships intact must be their overriding motive, so Chittenden would not ram Harry. He'd do everything in his power to avoid it. Harry smiled, and for the first time thought of James, who, in a situation like this, would have accepted that his brother knew what he was about, and not indulged in any of the carping criticism that had so annoyed Harry in Genoa.

He pulled his mind back to the present. The flotilla had their gunports open, and as the *Principessa* came within range they commenced firing. Harry handed over the wheel, and raised his glass to get a good look at their cannon. It was as he thought. They were as lightly armed as the *Principessa* had been before he'd exchanged the guns. They would have to be very lucky to do him any serious damage with those weapons at this range. What he must avoid at all costs was a close-range fight with more than one of them. Four-pounders, if there were enough of them, could still cripple him, especially if he was caught between two arcs of fire.

'Stand by to go about,' he shouted. The wind was coming in over the larboard quarter, and he'd increased speed to aid his manoeuvre. When he gave the order and spun the wheel, the *Principessa* began her turn. The ropes holding the yards were released, those on the other side taken up, and they hauled like heroes, bracing the yards round to catch the wind now coming at the ship just behind her larboard bow. The *Principessa* staggered slightly, but with her hold restowed, and steering right, she didn't miss stays. And once round she took the wind like a champion yacht, and Harry aimed her straight at the small gap between Frome and Chittenden.

Frome held his course. He had to, for they were too far inshore to do otherwise. It would be fatal for him to bear away. Chittenden maintained his too. Harry looked over the stern. Bartholomew had let fly his sheets and was getting ready to tack to come back to aid the *Mercury*. There wouldn't be much time. In fact if Chittenden didn't do anything, there would be no time at all. It was a game now, to see who would give way. Harry reckoned he had no more than a minute before he would be so committed that he could not get out of the way. That was not a situation he could really risk. The crew, half-way between the guns and the yards they'd just braced, stood with bated breath as the gap closed at an alarming rate.

Harry was about to haul off when he saw movement on the deck of the other ship, as Chittenden's crew rushed to release the yards and let fly the sheets. He also saw Frome's men heaving their guns round to take him as he passed. He'd have to ignore that, for he couldn't fight both sides.

Frome's guns spoke just as the *Mercury* bore up with the wind dead astern, his bows swinging towards the rocky coastline. Being hurried the mizzen sails took the wind out of the mainsails and they flapped uselessly. The ship lost way. Harry yelled for his men to man the guns, ducking down as shots whipped over his head. Frome had fired on the uproll and though he'd holed the main and mizzen courses, he'd done little real damage. The *Principessa*'s speed was barely checked. His men had the gunports open, and they stood poised. Harry shouted to one crew who were set to try and bring their gun round to bear early, telling them to let him do the aiming, and to fire as they saw the *Mercury* through their gunports.

Chittenden was in difficulties. He'd worn round in the most lubberly way, with some evidence of panic on his deck. His gunports were closed with everyone busy trying to put right the trouble they'd made for themselves. He was therefore defenceless. Worse than that, he was still swinging round, presenting his stern to the *Principessa*. Harry shouted to the few remaining men on the sails to let fly his mainsail sheets. They released the braces and the *Principessa*, down to topsails only, slowed immediately. Those upper sails kept some way on her, but with the extra time gained by slowing the ship, the *Mercury* had swung right round. Frome was now right astern, his guns useless. Bartholomew was half-way round, and Frome couldn't turn until they'd passed each other, for fear of running right across Bartholomew's bows.

And Harry was drifting by his quarry, giving each gun captain plenty of time to pick their moment. The first gun spoke, and a great chunk of the decorated sternrail disappeared. Harry called to Pender to hold the wheel steady, and ran forward to aim the carronades himself, for he'd never get a chance as good as this again. Sporadic musket shots were being returned from the *Mercury*. The second twelve-pounder was high, but it served to keep heads down as the ball whistled across the deck, smashing into the boats bowsed tight above the waist.

Harry was bent down, the slowmatch in his hand. He touched the hole. And the carronade fired. The great ball went right through the sternlights, smashing its way through the whole length of the *Mercury*. Harry was at the next gun just in time to fire that. The *Principessa* had rolled into a trough caused by the inshore swell, and the ball from the second carronade went into the hull below the windows at a downward angle. The *Mercury* shuddered, and Harry knew that he'd done real damage. He stood up, calling to the hands on the forward guns to haul on the mainsail braces. The rear guns fired, now on the up-roll, with two balls going through the cabin, and the last knocking the mizzen mainsail yard right out of its chains.

Harry took the wheel again. Lubeck was yelling through his trumpet as they reversed the angle of the yards to bring the *Principessa* round so that the wind would favour her. She was handling beautifully, and as soon as she had the breeze on her starboard beam she took off like a hare.

Bartholomew was coming up as best he could, sailing into the wind. Harry couldn't spare all his men, but he called to the carronade guncrews and invited them to send their regards to the *Daedalus*. They rushed to their stations, and as the *Principessa* passed Bartholomew's ship they took two great chunks out of her bulwarks, which ruined the aim of all but one of *Daedalus*'s cannon. Harry saw his enemy as they went by, standing on the deck, his long curly hair whipping in the breeze, just like the feathers in his hat. Bartholomew raised a musket, aimed it at him, and fired. But his deck was pitching too; it was more of an insult than a threat.

The *Mercury* was dead in the water. Everything had worked out much better that Harry could have hoped. Bartholomew had obviously told Frome to keep his heading to provide protection to the two slower ships in the van, *Cromer* and *Bella*. Harry went full speed after him. With his sails now set and drawing well, he had the guns reloaded and run out. He was in high spirits, laughing and exhorting his men.

He was head reaching on Frome. But the two other ships had started to tack in unison, so by the time he came up it would be three to one. He brought her head round slightly. Frome would have to wait, but the lead ship, the *Cromer*, with Pilton at the helm, would have to take station on the outside flank of his consort. For even an inept sailor such as he had come round quicker than the fire-damaged *Bella*. Harry could see Frome waving his arms, trying frantically to signal *Cromer* to stay in line astern of the *Bella*. But Pilton either didn't see or didn't care to be told what to do. As he caught up with the *Bella*, he put down his helm to pass by on her larboard side.

Harry adjusted his yards, and trimmed his wheel to take Pilton on his starboard side, one to one.

Pilton must have suddenly realized the danger he was in, and tried to bear up. He shoved his helm down and his bowsprit ran straight aboard the *Bella*, fouling the mainmast shrouds. Frome had to pack his topsails to avoid running into the pair of them, and the little fleet was now in complete disarray. The slower speed of the other ship swung Pilton's stern further out, and Harry had to perform a quick manoeuvre to get clear of him. Only the carronade crews were at their guns but they went by at such a pace their shooting was wild. One ball struck Pilton just on the waterline, and he had a hole that would ship a lot of water. But it was nowhere near mortal, while the other ball disappeared without trace.

Bartholomew had made another mistake. He came round again to pursue Harry, leaving the *Mercury* exposed once more. Bartholomew, who could not hope to come up with his lead ships before Harry wore round himself, now presented himself as a lone target while the *Principessa* returned to re-engage the *Mercury*.

Harry came round neatly, despite his damaged sails. Bartholomew was in an impossible situation. If he came on he would face Harry's guns and probably sacrifice the *Mercury* to boot. Chittenden's ship was too light to withstand the weight of shot, and alone presented an easy target, given the confusion on her decks. If the *Daedalus* wore round again to protect her, his lead ships, two of them fouling each other's rigging, would face the same fate. He chose to come on, for that meant saving four ships instead of endangering one.

Harry had his starboard guns loaded and run out, with the twelve-pounders loaded with grape. He gave Bartholomew a thorough drubbing as he went by. The carronades, heaved round to aim forward, fired first, opening up the side of the ship. The twelve-pounders crews did their best to pour their grape through the gaps provided. Harry was gratified to see that Bartholomew had flung himself to the deck. There was no insulting gesture with a musket this time.

Chittenden knew what was coming. He could see the effect of the grapeshot on Bartholomew's ship, and he'd already had a taste of the carronades. But he had to hang on, for Bartholomew had changed his course and tacked again in pursuit of the *Principessa*. Harry cursed the man, who'd done the right thing for once. Had he kept his heading Harry could have boarded and taken the *Mercury*. He stood, desperately trying to calculate the time he would have alongside Chittenden before Bartholomew came up to engage him on the other side.

It all hinged on whether he abandoned his original plan, and went for complete success now. At all costs he mustn't endanger his own ship, and he knew that, even if his opponents were lightly armed, he'd been lucky. The *Principessa* had suffered no real damage, and he hadn't lost a single man. With what he'd achieved, these men would now follow him to the ends of the earth. They were so fired up he knew they could take the *Mercury*. Yet if he risked it all on one throw, he might find himself outnumbered, with Bartholomew boarding on one side of him, and his men fighting the *Mercury* on the other. The combined crews would at least keep him occupied till Frome came up. He alone had shown himself to have the ability to stick to a prepared plan, and Harry didn't doubt that, as part of that plan, he'd have to fight the *Ariel* as well.

Discretion being the better part of valour was an expression Harry hated, since it flew in the face of his nature. But this was the time to exercise it. He left his sails set, called for the twelve-pounders to be fired off and reloaded with bar shot, and as he went by the *Mercury* he gave her the same kind of rolling broadside that they'd given the *Dido*, and with much the same result. The rigging was torn to shreds, and the carronades smashed into the hull, going clean through above the waterline.

Harry sailed on until he was out of range, then hove to, giving rapid orders for the men to given drinks and food. Bartholomew had come alongside the *Mercury*, and was yelling at Chittenden to get some way on his ship. Harry watched through his glass as Chittenden waved his fist at Bartholomew, obviously angry. No doubt his commodore had told him he was a fool. Yet it had been Bartholomew himself who'd made all the errors. If he'd even made a feint at attacking Harry this morning as he came out of port, he would have sown some doubt about his intentions.

Bartholomew was now hove to himself. Harry, handing his cup back to the ever attentive Pender, called to his men to get a move on, and was pleased to see them abandon the remains of their food to continue the fight. Fairbairn, with the physical appearance of a corpse, had come on deck, and was looking listlessly in the direction of the small dispersed fleet.

'Was he asleep?' he asked Pender, for he'd quite forgotten about the man.

'No, Captain. As soon as I said we was going into battle, he asked me to show him where the ship's surgeon should be.'

Harry called to him. 'Come, Mr Fairbairn, and observe that we have done well today. All of us.'

Harry bore down again. He didn't want to leave them any time to regroup, though he had little hope of achieving anything, with all five ships now bunched together. Lightly armed they might be, but they presented a formidable arc of fire if he was fool enough to sail into it. He elevated his twelve-pounders and with their greater range indulged in a little target practice. It was enough to interrupt the frantic work being carried out above deck to repair the rigging, but the men below carried on, repairing the shot holes in the hulls of the damaged ships.

It wouldn't stop them. Nor did Harry really want to. But if he sat and did nothing he would die of frustration, and having handed the wheel to Lubeck, he took to aiming the guns himself, concentrating on the *Daedalus*. Not that he wanted to hit Bartholomew. Killing him was something he needed to do at close quarters. Eventually they got the mizzen yard back up and new sails, blocks, pulleys, and ropes in place. Harry could see that they were about to make sail, and with the sun dipping on the horizon, he watched them drop their courses and head out to sea, away from the land which had provided them with such poor security.

There was no line ahead now, more a sort of star formation which afforded some mutual protection, with Bartholomew in the middle so that he could personally co-ordinate the actions of all the ships. If anything they were slower than they had been this morning, making no attempt to leave Harry behind. Were they trying to lure him on, hoping to ensnare him in a trap? He brought the *Principessa* in closer as night fell, though the moon, now full, made it seem like blue-coloured day.

Harry sent the hands for a hot meal, and then with half a watch

271

on deck he had the men sling their hammocks and get some sleep. He realized that, successful as the day had been, he'd failed in his primary task. He still didn't know where they were headed, and by tomorrow night there might be no moon by which to observe them. If it was at all cloudy Bartholomew would have a chance to slip away. While Harry had a shrewd idea he was making for the Straits of Messina and points east of the toe of Italy, he couldn't be positive. Tonight, or to be more precise, in the small hours of the morning, before daybreak, he must go in and cut out one of those ships.

Attacking at night was tricky at any time. With this star formation Bartholomew had placed all his ships within easy reach of each other, and there being no attempt at speed, the minimum amount of manoeuvre could bring Harry into battle with three ships in minutes. He pondered what to do. Ideas of dropping off the cutter, full of men, as he sailed by, so as to take one of his enemies by boarding while he engaged, wouldn't be possible. He simply didn't have the resources. Whatever way he sought to tackle them would mean he would be facing three ships. Then he had an idea. It wasn't much of one, but he had a good notion of what they expected him to do, so doing the opposite seemed an appropriate choice.

They'd kept a sharp lookout, for as soon as Harry increased sail he heard the cries that brought the crews tumbling up on to the decks of all five ships. He kept his bowsprit pointed towards them, and saw in the moonlight that the two rear ships, *Cromer* and *Bella*, had swung round to present themselves broadside on. Bartholomew backed his topsails and the *Daedalus* dropped back into the gap between them, while *Ariel* took up station on the larboard flank, and *Mercury* did the same on the starboard. Again a defensive manoeuvre, underlining once again the point that they needed their ships more than they needed the defeat of this single attacker.

What Harry should have done was either shear off out of danger, or if he was desperate to indulge in a fight swing round to make his way down the line, taking on each enemy in turn. But that would expose him to grave danger, for the flanking ships could then come round and trap him. What Harry actually did was to keep his bows pointed firmly in the direction of *Daedalus*. He'd loaded his guns on both sides before he'd increased sail, opened his gunports, and heaved his guns round to aim forward. Harry intended to go through the line, having fired his guns only to spoil his enemies' aim. Once through, he would again eschew the obvious, for they would expect him to come round to assault them on their unguarded side. He intended to confound them by going after the *Mercury* again. After that, it would be down to the sailing qualities of the other ships. If he was left alone long enough he would board her. If not, tomorrow was another day.

Bartholomew must have thought that Harry was after him again, for the *Principessa*'s bowsprit was aimed directly at his quarter-deck. He increased sail, which opened up a slight gap between him and *Cromer* astern. Harry put his helm down, fired off a broadside at *Daedalus*, and headed straight for Pilton in the *Cromer*. Pilton did the opposite of Bartholomew, reducing speed and increasing the gap considerably. Harry spun the wheel again and headed straight for it. His starboard guns now raked Pilton's ship. True to his salt, the *Cromer*'s captain put his helm down to turn away.

It was a pity to sail by Bartholomew without giving him a hammering. Especially since Harry had stolen his wind, and was right athwart his hawse. Once through the line they would have the weather gauge, something he'd enjoyed most of the previous day. But he could outrun them all so he was not really concerned. Pilton, having sheered away, kept coming round, his larboard guns firing erratically and ineffectually at the *Principessa*. Harry held his fire, even though his guns were reloaded, and sped past him, put his helm hard down, and headed straight for the *Mercury*.

Chittenden, who'd suffered a great deal earlier in the day, was not in the mood to try a contest. He'd taken a real pounding in the afternoon, and watched while his fellows did nothing to help him. He turned the *Mercury* to get the wind on her quarter and make a getaway. Harry literally whooped with joy. He could not have hoped for more. And behind him Pilton was causing chaos, for he'd cut across Harry's stern, making it impossible for the others to come round in pursuit.

Still aimed forward, Harry's guns opened fire much sooner than Chittenden expected. He sheared away from the fire, for the carronades had hit his hull again. The gap between *Mercury* and his consorts was increasing by the minute. Harry was coming alongside, his guns firing in a regular rolling broadside that seemed almost leisurely. And he was inflicting damage, which was more than could be said for Chittenden's reply. His guns were going off individually, aimed wildly, doing no harm at all.

Harry touched the helm to shorten the range. Chittenden tried to edge away, but in so doing cut his speed. He was forced back on to his original course. Bartholomew was still trying to get round *Cromer*, and the only ships that had even a hope of coming to Chittenden's aid were the fire-damaged *Bella* and Frome in the *Ariel*. But Frome was the most distant, and though he was round, he showed no sign of coming on, no doubt obeying Bartholomew's rigid orders to keep his station.

Harry edged closer and closer, his guns firing without hindrance. He could see Chittenden, standing by his wheel, issuing instructions to the man at the helm. The forward carronade went off again, and they were quite simply no more. There was no wheel, no helmsman, and no ship's captain. The *Mercury*, with no one to steer her, and no pressure on the rudder, simply spun round broadside on to the wind. There was panic aboard, as the hands, now leaderless, rushed in all directions. Harry took the way of the *Principessa* and glided alongside, his every gun now aimed at his opponent. One of the men, with perhaps more sense than the others, took an axe and cut away the ship's Genoese colours.

Harry grabbed the speaking trumpet and shouted for all the hands to go below. His men were throwing grappling irons to bring the two ships together. Dispirited, outnumbered, and outgunned, they were only too happy to oblige, and they headed for the companionways. Lubeck and a party of men jumped aboard as soon as they touched, muskets at the ready, willing to shoot anyone who'd had a change of heart. More men were hauling a cable up from the bowels of the *Principessa* and a line was passed over the shattered bulwarks of the *Mercury* and led forward. The line was nipped on to the cable, and that was passed over to be attached to the *Mercury*'s bows.

Harry looked anxiously over his shoulder, but the four ships were a mile away. He gave the orders and the *Principessa* got under way again, pulling the *Mercury*'s bows round and heading due south. Lubeck organized some of his prisoners to man relieving tackles so that the ship could steer, and it wasn't long before Harry cast off his tow. Now under their own sails, both ships opened the distance between Bartholomew and the others. Their pursuit, which had been half-hearted anyway, soon petered out.

CHAPTER TWENTY-FIVE

Harry sat in the *Mercury*'s sleeping cabin, studying the charts he'd found in Chittenden's sea-chest. The main cabin was wrecked, with the sternlights in tatters and great gashes in the bulkhead where his carronades had smashed through. He also had a list of courses and he was busy figuring out Bartholomew's destination. He was truly surprised to find that it was just a couple of landfalls. The first one was an island off Southern Dalmatia, the other on the coast of Asia Minor. He'd expected their rendezvous to be somewhere out at sea, on one of the trading routes from the east. The kind of profit they enjoyed could only be achieved if they took a large convoy. He was at a loss to know how they made any money where they were going.

Questioning the hands produced nothing. Harry didn't expect them to know any details, for Chittenden would not have bothered to tell them their destination. But he was not prepared for their total silence. They clammed up to a man, behaving as if he was a King's officer intent on hauling them into a man-of-war. He had never encountered such a surly bunch anyway. They were less communicative than any sailors he'd ever known. And now he had to decide what to do with them. He could give Lubeck the *Mercury* to command, but could he rely on these men if they got into a fight with their late compatriots? They could just take over the ship again and either surrender or attack him. He could mix the crews, but he was loath to do that, since his men had performed well, and were likely to become the kind of working unit that every captain dreamed of.

Harry didn't think it was worth the risk, and he called Lubeck in from the quarter-deck.

'We'll continue south, Lubeck. At the first suitable inlet, preferably one with some rocks close inshore, we'll run this ship aground and burn her.'

'The men?' asked Lubeck.

'Can walk ashore. Where they go from there is not my business.'

The German nodded and followed Harry out into the dawn. Harry went over the side and was rowed back to the *Principessa*. Half-way across the water he could hear Fairbairn's screaming. His agony seemed to come in waves, receding for several hours, then coming back worse than before, like a woman in labour. Harry had no idea how long this would go on, but he was determined to rescue the man from himself, and at least give him the chance of leading a full and satisfying life again.

Daylight found them off a suitable cove, with a reef near the sandy beach, and a small fishing village behind. Harry raided the *Mercury* to replace his powder, then ordered Lubeck to proceed. The German set his sails, and ran the *Mercury* into the bay at full speed. As she struck the reef, her main and mizzen masts toppled over the forepeak, taking all the ship's rigging down with them. Chittenden's hands were hustled into the water, forced to wade ashore chest high. Smoke appeared from the hatches, and by the time Lubeck was pulling back to the *Principessa*, the ship was ablaze from bows to stern.

Harry was still troubled by the references on those charts, so he sailed north looking for Bartholomew. By noon he knew that he'd missed him. The man had changed course to avoid contact. It didn't matter, for he knew his destination, and there was no reason to suppose that he wasn't still making for it. He couldn't know that Chittenden had been killed before he had a chance to dispose of his charts. So Harry put the *Principessa* about and headed south again. With luck he'd fall in with them before they got there. But it would need to be luck, for Bartholomew, having changed course once, could do so again. The chances of two ships meeting in the vast expanse of the open sea were remote.

The weather going south was blissful, warm and dry with steady winds that rarely troubled them. Harry had time to relax and time to reflect on the events of the last four or five days. A chance to talk to the men he'd taken command of about matters other than sailing and fighting the ship, though they exercised the guns and their sail drill daily and nursing Fairbairn was an on-going duty. But he realized that chasing Bartholomew had diverted him from his initial intention. That French ship would still be sitting in the harbour at Genoa, free to murder whoever they wished while he was sailing without exemptions. If he came across an English warship now, in circumstances that precluded flight, he'd lose every man jack aboard. Bartholomew first, but as soon as he'd dealt with him, Harry would need to return to Genoa and cut out that sloop.

Having weathered the Straits of Otranto and entered the Adriatic they had a few periods when the wind turned foul, requiring them to beat up into it, tack upon tack. Delay was compensated for by the pleasure Harry took in the increasing competence of his crew, with the operations gradually improved to the point where Lubeck's speaking trumpet became an accessory, rather than a necessity. Despite this, it was more like a cruise for pleasure than anything else, attended by fine weather, with the exception of one day when the slate-coloured sky, with the choppy vicious cross-sea, was more reminiscent of the English Channel than the Mediterranean. The sun shone, the wind was fair, and they reeled off the miles at a pleasing rate, leaving Harry plenty of time to quiz the hands.

His enquiries served a dual purpose, for he became acquainted with his men as well, turning them from mere faces into individual personalities. Pender was quick to sort out those who might be able to help, the kind of men that kept a sharp eye out for everything going on around them, as distinct from the mass of the crew, who knew nothing and cared less, content to fight or sail, as long as they were fed. Harry was interested to begin with, but by the time he had questioned the crew he was wildly curious. It was plain that Broadbridge's moods had veered from fear to euphoria around the time of Howlett's murder. And the more he heard about Broadbridge the less he liked the sound of him.

He had terrible trouble with Lubeck, who got confused between the names Bartholomew and Broadbridge with dizzying regularity. He'd had high words with both Bartholomew and Broadbridge that day. The former, taxed to provide better food for the crew of the

Dido, had told Lubeck to save his strictures for his captain. Broadbridge had blustered as best he could, then assured the big German
that he was going ashore to sort the matter out this very second, that
their needs would be met by King George himself, and food would
be plentiful from now on.

'King George?' asked Harry, wondering if Lubeck had made an
error in the language again.

Lubeck thumped the desk again, this time to prove he knew what
he had said. 'King George feed us, and no mistake. Those words he
used.'

Harry was at a loss to see where this led him, so he changed the
direction of his questions. Lubeck knew all about the murder of
Captain Howlett, which had been the talk of all those who could
speak even a modicum of English in the harbour. And it did appear
that Broadbridge might have seen something that night. He'd come
aboard in the morning smelling of more than drink, with his eyes full
of fear as well as the pain of a hangover. Broadbridge had brushed
aside Lubeck's questions about victuals. But he'd then asked the
German to tell anyone who enquired that he'd come aboard hours
ago.

Harry questioned the other men closely to confirm this, particularly those he'd put in positions of authority, since they were the
ones with the sharpest eyes. Their stories tallied, for Broadbridge,
desperate to communicate with Lubeck, had been forced to repeat
himself several times, and in his anxiety, had forgotten to keep his
voice down. Sutton had been ashore too but had returned well before
Broadbridge, stone-cold sober and in a foul temper. The captain,
coming back just before dawn, had the odour about him of a man
who'd lost control of his bowels. Yes, he'd had a look of fear in his
eyes and had, in the following days, reacted angrily to any mention
of Howlett's body swinging on a gibbet. The whole of that day and
the next had been spent skulking in his little cabin, with a warning
that he was at home to no one.

He'd gone ashore on the third day, answering an instruction to
attend upon Bartholomew and the other captain and explain himself,
again taking Sutton with him. They'd been gone all day and half the
night. On his return Broadbridge exuded a new air of confidence,
assuring all about him that their troubles were over, and that sailing

with Captain Broadbridge would be as good a berth as Fiddler's Green itself. Sutton, pressed by the others to tell what had caused this change of mood, declined to let on.

'Fiddler's Green,' scoffed Pender, having heard the name for the umpteenth time. 'There ain't no such place.'

'Allow a sailor his vision of a personal heaven, Pender. I for one will not have a word said against it. A land of milk and honey, where a tar is never short of money, rum, or female companions, is just the thing to sustain him when things are looking bad.'

'Life is better looked straight in the eye, Captain. You knows that as well as I do.'

'Time to look Sutton straight in the eye, I think,' said Harry. Pender nodded and went off to fetch the man. Sutton had avoided Harry Ludlow like the plague, no small feat in a compact ship. If he couldn't quite duck Harry's physical presence, he'd certainly seen to it that their eyes never met. Harry had let him be until he'd finished questioning the others. Sutton knew a great deal about Broadbridge, certainly more than the others aboard. But did he know anything about Howlett and the naval captain's death?

'The night Captain Howlett was murdered, Sutton. Where were you?'

'Howlett?' said Sutton. 'Who's he?'

Harry looked at the man before him, slouched in the chair with an insolent air. 'You must be the only man aboard that doesn't know that name.'

'Perhaps my nose is a mite shorter than most. I don't go poking it where it's none of my business.'

'Why did you murder Captain Howlett?'

That made him sit up. 'Who says I did?'

Harry was no tipstaff or magistrate, but he was sharp enough to see an opening when it presented itself. 'You're not well liked, that is obvious. Mind, I'm not sure I believe everything that I've been told about you.'

'That bastard Lubeck . . .'

Harry smiled. 'There's not a man aboard that hasn't put you ashore on the night of Captain Howlett's murder.'

'What does that prove? I never went near the poor bastard.'

'A moment ago, you didn't even know the poor bastard's name.'

Sutton leant forward, fear in his eyes. 'You couldn't avoid his name. He was the talk of the port.'

Instinct made Harry change the subject, the feeling that Sutton needed time to gnaw on the accusation of murder. 'Lubeck did say something that made me curious.'

'Don't know how, since he can't speak the tongue!'

'It was to the effect that King George would provide food for the hands.'

'News to me,' said Sutton.

'I just wondered if Broadbridge had arranged to hand all the deserters back to the Navy, as a way of saving himself from the need to feed them.'

'He'd never have done that,' snapped Sutton. 'An' if he'd even hinted at it, you'd have found him swinging from a hoist instead of Howlett.'

It was said with such conviction that Harry believed him. Sutton would know that a man set on betraying the crew of the *Dido* would not stop to save one sailor. He adopted a knowing air. 'It would explain why Captain Broadbridge went to see Howlett.'

Sutton shook his head, missing the trap. 'He didn't go to see Howlett.'

Harry leant forward quickly. 'Then who did he go to see, and why?'

Sutton realized his error. But he had dealt with the law all his life, and he was still alive. 'How should I know?'

'Because you went with him, Sutton. Hard to believe that you had no idea who you were going to see.'

'Happen the Captain didn't see fit to inform me.'

'I don't think he'd have had to. You're the sort who would know without being told.'

'Well I didn't, so that's that,' Sutton snapped.

'The Genoese reckon that Howlett was killed by English deserters. How would it be if I handed them you, with the information that you were ashore that night?'

'So were a lot of folk.'

'I dare say those folk would be happy to say what they were about. Just as I imagine that the Genoese have some novel methods of extracting the same information from you.' Sutton blanched, afraid to ask the obvious question. 'And I shall hand you over to them, just as soon as we return.'

Sutton was scared now. A flogging round the fleet was preferable to the methods of Italian interrogation. 'What's Howlett's death to you?'

'I'm curious, Sutton. And it's to my advantage to disprove the theory that he was murdered by Englishmen. Pity that you will have to suffer to establish that I'm correct.'

'I had nothing to do with it.'

'I believe that you're telling the truth. Something our Genoese friends may, or may not, find out eventually. But if you will not tell me what you were really about, I'll be left to conclude that you're lying.'

'If I tell you?'

'Then you have nothing to fear.'

He paused for several seconds, weighing up the odds. Sutton shook his head slowly when he finally spoke, acknowledging that he was taking the lesser of two distinct evils. 'We went ashore to see a fellow called Gallagher.'

Harry frowned, for he'd heard the name, but he couldn't place it.

'He was the Crown victualling agent in Genoa.'

'That fellow.'

'He and Broadbridge had done some business before. The Captain had arranged to meet him to get some more money.'

'More money?'

'You asked me what I was about, Captain Ludlow, an' I've told you. I'll say nowt else. Gallagher didn't show. We went round to his place, but it was all locked and barred, so we went back to Ma Thomas's place. The Captain sat there pouring rum down his throat, gettin' angrier by the minute. All he afforded me was a tankard of ale, and I had no mind to sit there and watch him gettin' drunk while I had an empty cup so I came back aboard the *Dido*. What Broadbridge did after that was none of my affair.'

'One more question, Sutton. Could Broadbridge have murdered Captain Howlett?'

For the first time since he'd entered the cabin, Sutton laughed. 'Broadbridge! By the time I left him he could barely stand.'

'Everyone said he was a frightened man when he came back aboard. And he hid in his cabin for two days. Could he perhaps have seen something?'

Sutton shrugged. 'He might, I suppose. Don't see that it makes much odds now.'

'Oh, it does, Sutton. Remember, Captain Broadbridge was murdered too.'

Sutton's face suddenly went blank and the eyes that he aimed at Harry were deliberately out of focus.

'Land ho!' The voice from the masthead was faint in the cabin, but Harry was on his feet immediately, making his way out of the cabin. 'Go back to your duties, Sutton. Perhaps we will talk further.'

Harry was out of the door, so he didn't hear Sutton's soft reply. 'Not if I can help it, we won't . . .'

Harry stood on the quarter-deck, his glass trained on the distant island. Half his mind was still on his recent conversation. There was much he still did not understand, but being in no position to improve his knowledge he dismissed it, concentrating instead on that before him; the island off the coast of Southern Dalmatia which had been Bartholomew's first landfall.

Not one to avoid a chance of playing a trick, Harry hoisted Genoese colours as soon as he'd raised the island. He sailed through a narrow entrance into a broad, and empty, horseshoe-shaped bay. A small walled town, seemingly deserted, sat at the centre, surrounded by steep hills rising step upon step. A difficult place to get to, and by the look of the soil and the terrain, not one to support much life.

Fairbairn, whose periods of health seemed to be more stable, was on deck with Harry. Good, plain, and plentiful food had filled him out a bit, and he'd begun to shave regularly. Not one to take the sun, his face was still red. But at least it was the red of a healthy man.

'No sign of Bartholomew?' he said, shading his eyes.

'I'm not surprised. He'll be days yet, even if he's had more favourable winds than us.'

'You intend to wait here for him?'

'No,' said Harry, shaking his head. 'I intend to go ashore and see what I can find, though in truth I don't expect much. Once I've done that we'll head back out to sea.'

'Am I correct in assuming that this is his destination?'

'One of them, yes. Why is a mystery. But I wouldn't want to be caught at anchor when he arrives, and with the odds the way they are, I don't want him to anchor either.'

'Would he not be at your mercy if he did?'

'Quite the opposite. He could adopt a defensive position that would be near-impregnable, especially in a bay shaped like this. With the number of hands he's got, we'd be outnumbered three to one. No, I intend to stand off the island, and attack him before he ever gets near the bay. With luck, he'll never drop his anchor.'

'And if you fail?'

Harry grinned. 'He's got to come out again sometime. I shall attack him again when he does.'

'At the risk of sounding too pessimistic—'

Harry interrupted him, his face set, for he knew what the surgeon was driving at. 'I know where he's going. I shall follow him there, fight him on the way if I can. Failing success I'll fight him all the way back to Genoa, and if needs be, I'll kick in the doors to his room and kill him there.'

The surgeon had gone quite pale, for in his anger Harry had looked as if he was about to assault him in lieu. 'Forgive me, Captain Ludlow. Although it's not something I could undertake myself, I do understand.'

CHAPTER TWENTY-SIX

The jetty seemed in good order for a harbour that had no shipping. Lubeck brought the cutter alongside, and Harry climbed out, followed by a party of armed men. The small walled town was silent, apparently without life. Harry walked towards the gateway searching the top of the walls, and the embrasures, for any sign of life. Nothing stirred. He had his men stand well back from the walls as he hammered on the gates. There was no response.

'Let's go round the walls and see if there's another entrance.'

'I go one side, you go other,' said Lubeck.

'Best if we stay together, Captain Ludlow,' growled Pender.

Harry smiled and nodded. 'If you only knew how much faith I have in your instincts, Pender.'

They made their way around the outer walls, stopping suddenly as they heard a cry, straining to hear it again. It was repeated, but it couldn't be called a threatening sound, more of a high-pitched squeal, followed by another. Harry signalled to his men and they made their way round to the rear wall of the town to find another gate. The sound was clearly audible now, and a very peaceful one at that, for it was the noise of children at play. Harry tried the gate and it swung open easily. He stepped through cautiously, and found himself in an alleyway with whitewashed and ochre-coloured buildings, in some disrepair, rising on each side. Pender immediately pushed the door of the first building open. The men took the hint, and started to search each doorway they passed.

Pender emerged and shook his head to indicate that his was empty. So were the others. They walked on, following the sounds of the voices, until they emerged into a decent-sized square. A whitewashed building, larger than the surrounding dwellings, stood alone in the centre. Nondescript, it looked, if anything, like a place of worship. Perhaps an Orthodox church. They made their way over to the entrance. There was a lion's head carved in stone above the doorway, with a Latin inscription underneath. It was the Lion of St Mark, the symbol of the power of Venice. Harry was no Latin scholar and had some trouble with the inscription. When, eventually, he made sense of it, he froze. They were in a leper colony.

He was just about to order them to get out of the place when a young boy, blond haired and very healthy, ran into the square. He stopped when he saw the party of armed men. Other children, boys and girls squealing with pleasure, rushed into the square in pursuit. They too were all fair haired and pale skinned. What's more their complexions were unblemished. Not inmates of a leper colony, more the pupils of some privileged school.

Seeing the new arrivals they stood for a second, gazing fearfully, before racing off. The boy who'd come into the square first didn't stay to ask questions either, but headed after his companions down the side of the building. One or two of Harry's men looked set to pursue them, but he called them back. There was no need for heavily armed men to go in pursuit of children. He was debating what to do next when an extremely fat fellow, wearing a Turkoman's headdress and a long loose garment, came waddling into the square. He stopped when he saw them, hesitated for a moment while he worked up his courage, and then addressed them in a high-pitched voice.

Harry didn't understand a word of what he said. He looked around to see if anyone else had, but his companions were equally mystified. Harry motioned for his men to stay still, so as not to alarm the fellow, and walked over to him, addressing him in French.

'You must have seen our ship come into the harbour?'

The man just shook his head, uncomprehendingly.

Harry decided on a lie, and this time he spoke in English. 'We're with Bartholomew.'

The man beamed and threw up his hands, repeating Bartholomew's name, though the consonants where all ahoo. Harry tried to ask him another question, but it was plain that the only thing he'd understood was the name Bartholomew. He gabbled away in his high-pitched voice, in the same incomprehensible tongue that he'd used originally. Harry stood there trying to make sense of what was going on. By his voice and figure he suspected that the man was a eunuch. But how that, and the sign for a leper colony, fitted in to this place being Bartholomew's landfall escaped him completely. He turned his thoughts to the other one in Asia Minor, then he thought about the fair-haired children who'd run into the square.

With a sudden gesture he signalled to his men to follow, and overriding the objections of the fat man they made their way down the side of the main building. No sounds of laughter now, but by an open doorway at the rear, Harry heard the sound of gentle sobbing. The fat man tried to bar his way, but Harry pushed him aside. He went into the room, which was like some kind of dormitory in a parish workhouse, only twice as wide and five times as long.

Narrow cots lined the walls. Another two men, bald headed and similar in shape to the one Harry had already met, stood before a crowd of children. There were hundreds of them, all shapes and sizes. The girls seemed generally taller than the boys, and some of them looked mighty close to maturity. But they all had one thing in common. They were fair skinned and glowing with health. Pender, Lubeck and the rest of Harry's men had crowded in behind him, and were mouthing astonishment at what they saw.

'Beggin' your pardon, your honour,' said his servant, 'what the devil is goin' on here?'

Harry didn't answer the question, and his voice was full of anger as he spoke. 'Pender, back to the ship and fetch Mr Fairbairn. The rest of you outside.'

Pender knew Harry's moods. That tone brooked no delay. He dashed out of the door. The men were slow to react. Harry snapped at them and hustled them out into the sunlit square. He posted them round the building, with instructions to stop anyone from getting away.

'And for the Lord's sake, if it's one of the children, be gentle.'

'What if it's one of 'em fat blokes?'

Harry snarled. 'You treat them to a powerful kick up the arse.'

He paced up and down outside the door until Pender returned with Fairbairn. Then, after a few quiet words, they went inside. The children were still crowded up one end of the room. The three fat men were now sitting down, looking disconsolate. Indeed one was crying copiously, using his sleeve to wipe his eyes. Harry ignored them, and tried to address the children direct. They looked at him with deep suspicion, and refused to come when he beckoned. He walked towards them. They shrunk away. But being hemmed in by the wall there was a limit to how far they could go. Harry pushed his way amongst them, patting them in a friendly manner and looking them in the eye. Some of their fear evaporated, and as Harry took one of the boys gently by the arm, he allowed himself to be led over to Fairbairn.

Harry then stood back while the surgeon examined him. It was a slow process, for the boy was not co-operative. The others watched silently. Fairbairn led the boy back to join the crowd and selected another. Feeling safer, this one was more willing. The surgeon then selected one of the girls. All the time he tried to talk to them, using English and French. Nothing, just silent stares.

Fairbairn walked over to Harry. 'They seem well enough. In fact, they're full of health. Do you want me to examine them all?'

'I doubt it's necessary. They will have been well cared for.'

'What is it all about?'

'Can't you guess, Mr Fairbairn? Girls and boys, all young, all healthy and all of fair countenence. If you were to examine the girls you would find that they are virgins.'

Fairbairn was surprised at that. 'Virgins!'

'Oh yes. Innocent girls and boys, taken from their homes. Brought here in dribs and drabs until there are enough to warrant a trip to their final destination.'

'And where would that be?'

Harry turned away, but Fairbairn saw the look of disgust, and heard the cold anger in his voice. 'Asia Minor was Bartholomew's next destination, Fairbairn. Can you imagine how much these children would fetch in an Ottoman slave market?'

'Slaves?'

'Yes. The brothel keepers would be lining up to buy them, boys and girls.'

'African slaves to the Americas, yes,' said Fairbairn. 'But here in the Mediterranean! I was not aware that it still went on.'

They were out in the sunlight. Harry stood looking around him, a worried frown on his face. 'It's proscribed, of course. Every Catholic country has banned the trade, and the Genoese and Venetians put a stop to the pirates from the Barbary Coast, who made a mint out of Christian slaves. Not that slaving doesn't still go on. The brothels of Spain depend on the North African coast, and they lay claim to being the most pious nation in Europe. I suppose they justify their activities on the grounds that their captures are not Christians, just like the African slavers. But this is anathema, especially to the Roman Church. Anyone caught in this trade, operating from a papist country, would face the gallows or the garrotte.'

'I cannot believe that Bartholomew is involved in this.'

Harry rounded on him. 'There is nothing too base for that bastard. The profits are enormous, Fairbairn, and that's all he cares about.'

'I didn't mean that I don't believe, only that it is hard. I rather saw him as a dashing figure at one time.'

'Don't be fooled by the way he dresses. All those plumes in his hat count for nothing.'

'I'm not one to be fooled by plumes,' snapped Fairbairn, in a rare display of strength. 'I had time to observe him long before the events of that night in the warehouse. And trust me when I say that I could not believe him to be so cruel.'

His shoulders seemed to sag, as though the effort had been too much. 'He had, on occasion, shown me some kindness.'

'By financing your habit?' The look in the surgeon's eye confirmed that Harry had guessed correctly. 'I wonder that you call that kindness.'

'Many times I've refused a beggar a coin, for fear that he would waste it on drink. I doubt I'd do that now. I cannot believe that Bartholomew's generosity was prompted by malice.'

Harry put his hand on Fairbairn's shoulder to reassure him, for he knew he was still in the grip of his addiction. 'All I've witnessed is the malice.'

'He was not the same man, Ludlow. I have never seen him like that. Reserved, yes. Cold even, for he seemed to exist without friendship. But not evil.'

Harry waved at the building, his voice angry again. 'Yet he's involved in this. If this does not qualify to be termed evil, what does? Please do not plead Bartholomew's virtue to me.'

'Perhaps I was questioning my gullibility.' Fairbairn shook himself, as if trying to rid himself of a bad dream. 'What do you intend to do?'

'God alone knows. But I can't leave these children here.'

'You mean to take them home?'

Harry laughed. 'Would that I knew where home was, Fairbairn.'

'That's the first thing to find out, your honour,' said Pender, who was leaning against a wall, in the shade, close enough to overhear their conversation.

Harry turned and looked at him. 'If you've any ideas on how that can be achieved, I appreciate hearing them.'

Pender put his head down and sucked on his teeth. 'How much time have we got?'

'Hard to say, Pender. If Bartholomew kept to the speed he showed us, it could be weeks before he turns up.'

'Seems to me that these here nippers would take a lot of feeding.'

'And this place doesn't look too fertile,' said Fairbairn, looking at the barren hillsides.

Harry acknowledged the point. 'Which means one of two things. Either they are supplied from somewhere on the mainland, or there is a limit to the time they're supposed to stay here.'

Harry made his way towards the doorway again. 'Those eunuchs will know.'

'How can you be sure they're eunuchs?' asked Fairbairn, for he hadn't heard the first one speak.

'They are,' said Harry as he went through the door. 'Who else would you leave on an island with all these virgins. If you hear a sound like a woman screaming, pay no heed.'

Getting the three eunuchs out of the main room was a task in itself. They didn't want to go, either out of fear for themselves or fear for their charges. That there was a bond of affection between them seemed plain. The children's anxiety increased the more Harry pressured them.

Eventually he got them into another room, theirs by the look of the three comfortable beds. He tried every language he knew. Half-forgotten words from a seafaring past that might just work. It was a slow process, with much sign language, but eventually Harry was led through a series of corridors to a storehouse. He could see that it was only a a quarter full, and by the folded sacks that lined one wall, he could also guess that the place had once been packed to the rafters.

There was a small cell off the main storeroom, no doubt a place where some monk had contemplated salvation, and prayed for the souls of his diseased charges. He called to one of his men, pushed the three eunuchs into the cell, and told him to guard them. Getting hold of Pender, Lubeck, and Fairbairn, he went back to talk to the children. That was an even slower process, for though they all seemed to share the basis of a tongue, there was a fistful of different dialects and it was not one any of the adults had ever heard before.

Added to that, their lack of trust was a severe hindrance. Lubeck had the most success. He had children of his own, and being near white haired like most of these youngsters seemed to encourage their trust. Harry noticed that neither his nor Fairbairn's colouring, both fair, achieved anything like the same result. Lubeck liked children, and they could sense it. Over the rest of the day they built up a picture. Some of the older children, taken out to the bay and asked to point, confirmed that they came from somewhere to the north.

The biggest breakthrough came when Lubeck took two pieces of stick and made a crucifix. They all seemed to recognize this, which meant they were from a Christian country. But which faith, Orthodox or Roman?

'Fairbairn, you must know a good bit of Latin?'

The surgeon nodded. 'Do you know any parts of the Roman Mass?'

'I'm no papist, but the High Church service is somewhat similar.'

He began the Lord's Prayer. That did the trick with one or two of the boys, who had, no doubt, served at altar. Harry listened carefully to what they said, drew several maps in the sand, then ordered them fed while he went back to the ship to look at his charts.

It was clear that the children were not Italian, for their tongue had no Roman derivations. They would be unable to read a map. But they knew that they'd come from the north, and they'd gone some way to describing the nature of their landscape, indicating that they resided within sight of a mountain range. They had also apparently, in their journey, crossed these high mountains, which put them as coming from somewhere on the northern side of the Dolomites.

That didn't really answer what he was going to do with them. They couldn't stay here, and he'd have a hellish job to get them all aboard the *Principessa*. Being that they were papists, the best solution would be to hand them over to the nearest priest. But the nearest priest was in Italy, as far from the homeland of these children as he was now. And he still had Bartholomew and his consorts to contend with. He couldn't leave his crew here in case they turned up.

He went below decks and looked at the available space. It would be nip and tuck, and they'd have to use the deck as well as the hammocks, but he could probably get the girls and the younger boys down here. The older boys would have to sleep on the deck, as would the crew. That would be no problem if the weather stayed fair, but with autumn approaching, there was no guarantee that it would remain so.

Harry called to the cook. He ordered him to bake as much bread and biscuit as possible. Then he went ashore again, taking all the ship's boats this time, and shifted the remaining stores of flour from the storeroom to the *Principessa*. The cook groaned when he saw the quantity. Harry called the men still ashore back to the ship and gave the whole crew a lecture about looking after their charges, promising a hanging for anyone who so much as touched a hair on the head of these children.

The galley, with the cook sweating profusely, was alight all day and half the night. Harry, with the aid of Lubeck, managed to convey to the children that they were going home. A couple of the older children seemed to be some kind of leaders, or at least they had the respect of the others. Once they'd convinced these two the rest followed like sheep.

After a good night's rest, Harry had them brought aboard in the boats. They were excited now, gabbling like a flock of geese, larking about and touching things they shouldn't. Stern words seemed to do little to contain them, and Harry thought by the time they were all aboard that he'd rather sail with a crew of right hard-nosed buggers than raise anchor with this crowd of irrepressible youngsters.

The *Principessa* was low in the water with such a load, and she was unlikely to set any records for her speed. They wallowed along, heading due north. Harry would dearly have loved to drop his charges on the nearest part of the Italian mainland, but there was little point in dropping them off in some southern Italian port. Further north, at the head of the Adriatic, there might be people who were aware of this trade, and who would know whence these children came.

The weather held, and the hands seemed happy to sleep on the deck, for the nights were warm. And their routine, on such a crowded ship, had become less arduous, for there was no room to swab the decks, and any idea of fancy sail drill or firing the guns was out of the question. Fairbairn had his hands full, not surprising given the number of children in his care, so he had no time for a return of his own ailment.

The older girls were more of a problem than his own men, since they would insist on flirting with the crew. Harry threatened to confine them below decks. The other children could not avoid being restless. Lubeck found the solution. He organized games, got the hands to teach the nippers to tie knots, broke the boys and girls into parties of a manageable size, and taught them how to survive while climbing the rigging. Then set the teams against each other, with prizes for the winner made by the sailors, with boarding nets rigged and boats over the side to catch anyone who fell. Full she might be, but after a few days of this skylarking the *Principessa* was a happy ship.

Harry tried to avoid all other shipping, but the further north they sailed the closer they came to Venice, encountering a vast increase in traffic. He knew that many a glass would be trained on him, wondering what the hell he was about, with his rigging full of capering youngsters. Polite signals to heave-to were much in evidence but he ploughed on, making for the port of Trieste.

It took a week and half, by which time the children, Harry, and the crew, were all one big happy family. Some of the girls wouldn't get home in the same condition that they'd left, for a sailor's ingenuity was never more evident than in the presence of a willing girl, crowded ship or no. But no one complained, so Harry, despite his lecture, let it pass.

He left the ship well off land and went ashore in the cutter. Once he'd landed Harry headed for the nearest church, and having found the priest, explained in halting Latin the problem he faced. This fellow was of little help, sending him off in search of a nunnery. He found it, and he discovered, to his mind, a saint. The Mother

Superior, once the situation had been explained, threw up her hands and thanked the Lord that these children had been delivered from evil. Yes, she would take them. There would be someone here in Trieste who would speak their tongue, and when Harry offered her a large sum of money for their upkeep, she took it gratefully, swearing on the cross that the money would be used to get these children back to their homes, though she knew, as well as Harry, that they would not all be welcomed back, some of them having been sold by their parents to the slavers in the first place.

He brought the *Principessa* into the harbour. Word of his cargo had got round the town and a large crowd had gathered. Harry noticed that while most cheered there were those who eyed some of the youngsters in the most salacious way. But the nuns were like sheep-dogs, harrying the children away with their bundles. Some of them turned, boys and girls, to wave to the hands lining the side of the ship, and Harry observed that some of his most hardened tars had a tear in their eye. He had a catch in his own throat. Time to put an end to all this nonsense.

'Right, swabbers on deck,' he yelled, 'let's get this damned ship cleaned up.'

Fairbairn had a run ashore, heading for the apothecary shop to top up his medicine chest. Harry left him to it, knowing that in purchasing the things he needed to perform his duties as a ship's surgeon, he would be exposed to the opportunity to purchase opium. If he did, then Harry would have to try and stop him taking it. But in the end, only Fairbairn could control his habit. No outside agency would be anything other than temporary. Fairbairn, knowing full well that Harry was concerned, reassured him when he came back aboard that, while he had looked at the cause of his downfall, he had suffered no desire to purchase any. His face, pale and drawn, gave the lie to such easy assurances. But he'd resisted temptation. Perhaps he was completely cured.

Harry cast off as soon as he'd topped up his water and taken on some fresh meat and vegetables. The *Principessa* was clean and clear of bodies and she sailed like the ship he remembered. Harry just prayed that in rescuing these children, and delivering them to safety, he had not missed Bartholomew.

CHAPTER TWENTY-SEVEN

As he headed back south, Harry cracked on, driving the crew and the ship relentlessly. Rarely off the quarter-deck, he had no time for anything other than speed, and although he still wanted to pursue the threads of what had happened in Genoa, he wanted Bartholomew dead at his feet much, much more. With Sutton still avoiding him if he could, there was no time to continue his questioning before they raised the island again.

Bartholomew's squadron was restored to five ships once more, sails clewed up, and their masts stark against the sandy white of the beach. Harry turned his glass to the newcomer. It was a merchant ship, broad-beamed in contrast to the sleek shapes of the rest of Bartholomew's flotilla. Harry looked above the town at the tall hills that dominated the island. They knew he was coming. A lookout up there, on such a day, would be able to see for miles.

It was clear to him by the way they were moored that they'd been at anchor some time. The ships had a settled air, as though they were in a home port. They were strung across the bay, with four privateers forming a line to cover the single merchantmen. Bartholomew would have taxed the eunuchs. Presumably he knew how to communicate with them. Why wait, when there was no longer anything to keep him here? Unless they were waiting for Harry Ludlow, knowing that he would return. And perhaps, given his previous behaviour, they surmised he would attack. He didn't doubt they'd be after revenge.

Harry toyed with the idea of obliging them, but the odds were too great. He could of course sail into the bay, sit off, and bombard them from a greater range, but they had men in abundance if they didn't have to sail. He, in their place, would have hauled some guns ashore to place on either side of the narrow entrance to the bay. And just in case that failed he'd have loaded some cannon into the ship's cutters to turn them into gunboats, a deadly weapon when fighting in a confined space, with manoeuvre impossible. Harry had the good sense not to underestimate his enemy. After all, they'd had plenty of time, it seemed, to ponder on the question.

He steered for a point in the middle of the opening to the bay, and hove to just out of range of land, content to sit there studying the four fighting ships. They'd either been here a while, or they'd stopped off somewhere on the way, for he could see fresh paint on all of them. Any damage that he'd managed to inflict south of Genoa had been patched up. Even the *Bella* looked as though her fire damage had been put right. He could imagine them sitting there, willing him to fall into a trap they'd carefully prepared.

It came as a bit of a shock to see men racing up the shrouds of the fighting ships. They were getting ready to make sail. He watched as they cast off their anchors, and dropped their topsails to carry them out of the bay. Surely they weren't trying to escape, for they seemed intent on leaving the merchantman? But why come out to engage, when all they had to do was to sit at anchor and frustrate him, and forcing him to fight on their terms? It made no sense to come at him right off. No sense, unless you included anger.

Harry slid down to the deck, and ordered Lubeck to make sail. The ship had been cleared for action the minute they sighted the island. There was little more to do. Knowing that the day would be long and hard, Harry ordered a hot meal prepared. Then they doused the galley fire. They made all possible sail away from the shore. To a jaundiced eye it might have looked as if Harry was preparing to flee, but if he was going to have a fight then he wanted plenty of sea room.

Once clear Harry shortened sail again. Would it be a repetition of the last engagement, with them all bunched up defensively? He stood at the stern rail, his glass on them, looking for some sign of their intentions. They dropped their courses once they cleared the

lee of the land. The four ships formed up in line ahead with Bartholomew in the van, Frome in the *Ariel* next, then *Bella*, with Pilton in
the *Cromer* bringing up the rear. With the wind south-easterly Harry
turned north. It was his best point of sailing and he wanted to see
what they would do. At the sound of a gun, like a miniature fleet,
they all turned after him. Bartholomew wasn't saving his ships any
more. Their cargo was gone. He had come out to fight. This time
Harry wasn't the hunter, he was the hunted.

The prospect of fighting four ships, all attacking, presented a whole
new set of problems. He could not best all of them if they sought to
engage. No ship was that nimble. How determined were they? It was
of primary importance to find out. He put the *Principessa* about and
beat up towards them. On they came, clear to the naked eye now.
This time, they were going to try to force battle, and if they continued
to do so he would have to turn away.

Harry watched them for a good ten minutes, judging their rate of
sailing. He reckoned he could get a shot off at Bartholomew with his
twelve-pounders, on the turn, before he'd have to make all sail to get
away. And it would be close, especially if the two fastest sailers,
Daedalus and *Ariel*, decided to crack on. But he reasoned that only
Daedalus would outrun her consort, so he'd only face a single-ship
action, with him having the legs of her if he felt endangered. Providing
Bartholomew didn't get in a lucky shot and wound one of his masts.

They were converging at speed when the oddest thing happened.
Harry had to look twice to make sure he wasn't seeing things. The
three rear ships turned away on a more southerly course. But Bartholomew came on alone, heading straight for the *Principessa*. Harry
nearly turned away immediately, for he sensed a trap. But seeing
that he was only facing a single ship, he decided to wait, and have
a careful look. His enemy's gunports were still closed, and Harry
wondered if Bartholomew had acquired some heavier guns with
which to surprise him. Or was he really proposing to take on Harry
alone, in a fight to the finish?

The *Ariel* had now detached itself slightly from the other two, and
was coming round on to a parallel course with *Daedalus*, but far to
the rear. She was also sailing easy, making no attempt to close the
distance between her and Bartholomew. If anything, the gap was
increasing. She was no threat unless he was engaged so close that he

couldn't get away. Harry had to admit they had him foxed. He couldn't figure out what they were about. It didn't make sense to fight alone when you had odds of anything up to four to one to choose from. Unless Bartholomew was determined, at all costs, to revenge himself on the man who'd stolen his business. Harry couldn't believe that. The man was as cold as ice. Harry had rarely met someone who so lacked passion.

Harry ran through a whole host of possible explanations. Had he had a falling-out with his fellow captains? Had they refused to support him? Did Bartholomew feel he could achieve more success on his own? He then realized that his action in repatriating the children had done more than deprive Bartholomew of one cargo. His whole livelihood, perhaps his life, would be forfeit if Harry Ludlow returned to Genoa. He had to be stopped.

Whatever, he had no need to change his tactics. He would still give Bartholomew a broadside on the turn, but he would slow his getaway, allowing *Daedalus* to come up with him when it looked safe to do so. Then they would have a bout, just the two of them, for none of his friends would be close enough to help. Harry issued his orders, and watched his approaching enemy carefully so as to time it right. The *Principessa* swung round. To Bartholomew it would look as though she was just changing course. But pretty soon they would see her swing round, gunports open, and they'd know what they were in for.

If they did, it didn't check Bartholomew's speed. Harry fired off his long guns, and saw one ball strike the hull, bouncing harmlessly off, while another went through Bartholomew's jib. Then Harry was round, taking the wind on his larboard quarter and heading away. He looked back at the other ships. The *Ariel* was coming on, but still at no great speed. The gap between her and Bartholomew was still increasing. The other two were still heading south. The *Daedalus* ploughed on, and would soon, if he didn't set more sail, steal Harry's wind. If he wanted to disengage, this was the moment to do so, for if he waited much longer the decision would be taken out of his hands.

Harry felt uneasy. He searched the deck of Bartholomew's ship, trying to see if he had anything extra aboard. Nothing showed, and as the gunports opened Harry could see that he still carried the same ordnance as before. He wondered if Bartholomew had stripped some hands out of the other ships so that he could board in numbers. Harry gave quick orders to load with grape and hold their fire after the next round had been fired. He might have more men aboard now, but he wouldn't by the time Harry Ludlow was finished with him.

He felt the *Principessa*'s speed drop as the *Daedalus* took some of the wind out of his sails. The distance, which had been closing slowly now seem to disappear in the wink of an eye. Bartholomew came alongside in a few seconds. The four-pounders, heaved right forward, fired one by one, each gun carefully aimed at the side of the *Principessa*. And this time they struck home. Wood flew in all directions. Harry fired off his rolling broadside to disrupt this careful aim, and it was pleasing to see that his guns did more damage than Bartholomew.

Coming abreast of each other, Harry held his fire, prepared to suffer the shots of the four-pounders. He could see that Bartholomew was edging closer, intent on boarding. The man stood where he had before, his feathered hat on his head. Harry raised his glass, and looked at him close to. The bastard was smiling. It was as if all was going according to his plan. Having taken Harry's wind he decreased sail himself and still he edged in towards the side of Harry's ship. Then he called the men from his guns and lined them up. Harry did a quick head count. There were no more than his usual complement. Unless he had more men hidden down the hatchways out of sight, Bartholomew was proposing to fight Harry knowing he was out-numbered!

Harry yelled to Lubeck to shorten sail. Bartholomew, seeing him checking his speed, did the same. The two ships slowed together, coming closer. Harry shortened sail even more, leaving only his topsails drawing. Bartholomew followed. Harry, still prey to his suspicions, made a quick decision. If there were more men down that hatchway, the way to fetch them out and neutralize them was to attack. If they came out early he could still decimate them with grapeshot. If they kept their place, he would make it his first job to close those hatchways off and trap them below decks.

He called for all hands to stand by to board, leaving just the gun captains standing by their weapons. The two ships had now slowed to a near standstill, barely keeping steerage way. Harry's men, with

Lubeck in the middle, started to crowd the starboard rail. No crowd from the *Daedalus* gathered to oppose them. As the ships crunched together, Harry gave the orders and his men jumped on to the deck of Bartholomew's ship unopposed.

It was all wrong. Some kind of trap. Harry spun round and saw that the *Ariel* had raised everything she possessed and was cracking on. He was right, they'd set out to snare him, but while the plan was sound, the execution was lamentable. *Ariel* had left it too late. Either that or Bartholomew had got too far ahead. It didn't matter. Here was a chance to get Bartholomew, and he might just have enough time to do it.

Lubeck and his men stood on one side of the *Daedalus*'s deck, Bartholomew and his crew on the other. There was an abundance of threatening looks, but little action. Harry yelled at the top of his voice as he jumped the gap himself, Pender right behind him. His men picked up the cry and battle was joined. But all the aggression was on the side of Harry's crew. They attacked with venom, but Bartholomew's men seemed content to just hold their line. What Harry needed, indeed expected, was a mêlée; something that would break up the enemy and allow his superior numbers to tell.

He worked his way to the centre of the line to get near to Bartholomew. The man smiled at him from behind a line of sailors holding a fearsome array of boarding pikes. If Harry tried to get him he would die before he even got close. Pender spotted it right away, and grabbed Harry's arm in case he should be tempted.

'Come on, you bastard,' his captain shouted. Bartholomew must have heard him above the din because, if anything, his smiled widened. Then he gave Harry a small, insulting, slightly effeminate wave. Harry's blood boiled, and damning the consequences he charged the line of pikemen. His flailing sword was no match for them. If they had, at that point, decided to counter-attack, he would have been in trouble. Beldeau was the only one to break ranks, coming forward despite Bartholomew's shout to desist. He tried to spear Harry, but his pike was knocked in the air by a vicious swipe. Harry's sword took him under the chin, half severing his head as it came out of the side of this neck. Beldeau screamed and fell to the deck and Harry stepped in to finish him, ignoring the other pikes that surrounded the dying man. But he couldn't follow through.

Pender, who had him by the collar, saw the danger, and hauled him back.

It was a measure of Pender's own frustration that he addressed Harry like a common seaman. 'What the fuck are they about, Captain?'

'They'd planned to trap us,' gasped Harry.

Pender looked over his shoulder. 'They might just do it at that.'

'That's their plan, man. Can't you see? They just want to hold us here.'

Harry swore heartily and pulled out of the crowd to look back towards the *Ariel*. She was coming up hand over fist, and at this rate she'd be alongside before Harry achieved anything. The fight, if you could call it that, was slackening even more as his men lost their enthusiasm. Lubeck was trying to do something, swinging an axe mightily, but it was being parried by any number of men. He heard Bartholomew shout, and the line of men in front of him abandoned defence and suddenly thrust forward to engage. The crew of the *Principessa* were happy to oblige.

The clash of metal on metal filled the air, interspersed with the cries of wounded men. Bartholomew was trying to hold him till *Ariel* could join. Harry looked further south expecting to see that the other two, *Cromer* and *Bella*, had come about and were also heading to join in the battle. Not so, they were still heading away at a steady pace.

'The man's a damn fool,' cried Harry, some of the spirit returning to his voice as he pointed to the oncoming ship. He had no time to give an explanation to Pender, who looked as though he was hoping for one.

Ariel was heading for Bartholomew's larboard side to reinforce him, instead of attacking the *Principessa*. That was the final mistake that made Harry decide to stay where he was. Frome was as much of a dunce as the others, giving up the chance to catch Harry between two fires in favour of the security of landing his men on the side of the ship that Bartholomew occupied. The crew of the *Principessa* would be outnumbered, sure. But if the worst happened and they looked like being overwhelmed, Harry still had an ace up his sleeve.

'Pender,' he called urgently. 'Get back aboard the *Principessa*. Those cannons are still full of grapeshot. If we start to fall back, wait until we're clear, and let Bartholomew and his men have the lot.'

Pender grinned, and ran off to obey. Harry kept his eye on the *Ariel* to make sure that he had judged correctly. She made no attempt to steer for his ship, and he could see clearly that the starboard side was lined with men ready to come to the aid of their friends. Harry threw himself into the fray, calling to Lubeck to redouble his effort. Axes swung harder, pikes jabbed with more venom, and Harry himself swung his sword to deadly effect, going after Tinker, since Bartholomew was still safe behind his pikemen.

He heard, rather than saw, the *Ariel* crunch alongside. The yells seemed to increase for a moment as the two crews united. Then the crowd of sailors before Harry's men just melted away. They dropped their weapons and leapt on to the deck of the *Ariel*. Suddenly Harry found he had no one to fight. They had all gone and Frome's ship was fending off. He hadn't shortened sail at all, just loosened his braces to take away the force of the wind. Harry had missed that. He hauled them tight again, and with the wind coming in on his quarter, and his helm hard down, they started to draw away immediately. The *Ariel* quickly opened the gap between herself and the *Daedalus*.

Harry was dumbfounded. He could see no reason for this, for it flew in the face of all logic. Bartholomew leant over the side of the *Ariel* and shouted to him, 'I can't give you my life, Ludlow. But I leave you my ship. I hope you enjoy your capture.'

Then Bartholomew laughed, and he was joined by the combined crews of the two ships as the *Ariel* pulled further away. Harry was rooted to the spot, for Bartholomew had achieved the one thing that Harry Ludlow praised above all others in battle. Complete surprise. So total that no one uttered a sound.

He woke up quick enough. He saw the cutter rowing away from the stern, trying frantically to catch the *Ariel*. They were desperate to get away from the *Daedalus*, having jumped out of the sternlight windows. Why had they been in there and why had they waited until everyone else had departed to make their escape? Harry's nose twitched at the familiar smell, knowing it had, indeed, been a trap. Bartholomew had brought him on, using his own ship to do it, sensing that the mere sight of him would blind Harry Ludlow's judgement. He yelled for his crew to get back aboard the *Principessa*, wondering if, in his torpor, he'd left it too late. Men, bemused, were slow to follow. As a matter of course they'd lashed the two ships together as they came alongside. Harry picked up a boarding axe on the run, reached the side of the *Daedalus* and started to hack at them with all his might.

'Pender. Get everyone below,' he screamed.

Lubeck, not sure why, was hacking at the lashings as well, and they were soon parted. Nothing was happening and Harry looked aloft. Some of Bartholomew's men had lashed the yards together. He screamed again, this time at the topmen to get aloft and cut them free, and they rushed to obey. His crew behaved quickly, obeying a man they trusted, a man who didn't think he had time to explain. They might just make it. He was aboard the *Principessa* himself now, and his heart lifted as he saw the ropes aloft part and the blue water appear between the two hulls as the ships drifted apart.

'Make sail,' he yelled, and again he was promptly obeyed. More men rushed up the shrouds to loosen the clewed-up sails. Harry was to regret that command more than anything. For as they reached their stations he heard the first dull boom. He only had time to yell an incoherent warning before he flung himself to the deck. The remaining barrels of gunpowder went up. The side of his ship by his head disintegrated. The blast, coming from below decks on the *Daedalus*, took the force of the explosion, and all the things it had destroyed, upwards. The *Principessa* nearly turned turtle as she was blown over on her beam ends. She righted herself, but the counteracting swing was just as bad. Harry had to grab on to a ringbolt in the deck to avoid going over the side. Barrels of gunpowder were still going off. The world was a mass of explosions and flying wood. Blocks and pulleys rained down and the ship was rocking back and forth. Then a sudden silence. Harry hauled himself to his knees. Bodies, and bits of bodies, lay everywhere. His carronades had been blown across the deck and had gone clean through the bulwarks on the other side, leaving huge gaps.

He looked forward, still dazed. His jib and staysails had gone, so had his courses, blown clean out of their bolts and now a tattered mass of holes. He looked up. There was nothing left of his masts above the cap. His topmasts and all the rigging were gone. The men sent up there to set the sails had gone with them. He looked over the side. Not difficult, for there was no side to speak of. The *Daedalus* was no more, just a hollow hull, like a canoe, slowly sinking into the foaming sea.

Then, as bits of wood continued to fall into the sea and rain on to the deck, the screaming began. Men who'd been stunned by the explosion regained consciousness. Harry looked beyond the remains of the *Daedalus* to the *Ariel*, sailing away to the south to join the other ships. The sound of cheering came across the water. He was too wounded to curse Bartholomew. Not physically, for the explosion, going upwards, had passed over his head. But he felt his heart would break to hear some of the screams coming from his mangled crew. And as he looked at his poor ship, he was near to weeping. Standing, he saw Lubeck's trunk, the axe still tightly gripped in his hands. His head was nowhere to be seen, and Harry, remembering his dream of home and how he played with the children, felt the tears coursing freely down his cheeks.

CHAPTER TWENTY-EIGHT

They were lucky to make the bay. The *Principessa* was taking a lot of water through a great gash in her side. Harry steered her in towards the sandy beach, conning her round so that she would broach to on her undamaged side. He felt her grind sideways, siding gently into the soft sand. She would settle here if he wasn't quick. The air was rent by an unholy scream. Fairbairn was down below, up to his elbows in blood, as he tried to treat the wounded. The bodies of the dead had been left where they lay. Saving the ship was paramount. Pender had been sent ashore with a few able-bodied men and a cable, running from the stump of the mainmast, to attach to the nearest thing that would hold the ship in place. Once secure, Harry got two cables out from the stern and the bows, running at an angle to hold her fast.

The pumps clanked constantly, fighting hard to keep the level of water down. Harry's first priority was to heave her over so that the gash was above the waterline. Once that was covered, by a tarred sail if necessary, she could be dried out, raised up the beach if she floated, heaved over again, this time with her stores shifted, and the hull properly repaired. And there was always the chance that the *Principessa* had suffered serious structural damage. A check on that would have to wait until the hold was cleared.

His main problem was a lack of hands. He'd lost a third of his men, and some of the most nimble at that. Most of those remaining had some kind of wound. He found the three eunuchs still ashore, and despite their squeals of protest, he put them to labour on the pumps. To get the *Principessa* half over, he attached the original cable to a point higher up the broken mainmast, ran it ashore round the base of a well-greased tree, then brought it back to the capstan. Everyone heaved: Harry himself, the three eunuchs, and anyone whose wound had left them with one good arm or leg. The only upright person not involved was the surgeon, still toiling below.

When Harry looked over the side, he realized just how lucky he'd been. With his holds full, the blast had stove in the side, but the planking had run up against a packed shot locker. The metal had held, preventing the water from forcing the seams even further apart, something that would have sunk his ship well out in the bay. A temporary repair was all he wanted for the moment. With the ship further up the beach he could careen her properly, and then, using planking from the squat merchantman still sitting in the harbour, he could effect proper repairs.

The men were exhausted. They needed rest and medical attention. Harry set off for the merchantman, taking the jolly-boat and Pender. He'd rushed below when ordered and had escaped with nothing more than a few bruises. They climbed aboard the deserted vessel, and immediately went below. The whole ship reeked of powder. Blankets, which when the ship had been loaded hung wet between the barrels, flapped drily in the warm air. This was where they'd acquired the means to make their bomb vessel. By the look of the decks and the cabin, the ship had been taken by force, for they were marked with dark bloodstains. Bartholomew must have cleared his hold to accommodate the amount of gunpowder this ship could carry.

But he hadn't bothered to clear the normal stores out of the merchantman. The sail locker was half full, and there was a good supply of spare timber. They'd taken the food, the drink, and the cargo, but left everything else. Harry went back on deck and looked at the masts. They were not like the ones he'd lost, being shorter and rather stubby, but they would suffice. The *Principessa* wouldn't handle like her old self, but she would sail, and right now that was what he required.

Pender had been silent all the while, knowing that his captain was not in the mood to answer questions. But his curiosity finally got the better of him. Being no sailor, he was at a loss to know what their true situation was. 'How're we doin', your honour?'

Harry looked across the bay at the copper, showing clean on the bottom of his stricken ship. 'He damn near did for us that time, Pender. I underestimated him. If we hadn't got that bit of air between us and the *Daedalus*, we'd have ended up at the bottom of the ocean alongside her.'

'What about now?'

Harry waved his arms to indicate the ship they were on. 'A choice. We can sail out of here in this. But she's a bit of a tub, and if we wanted to catch up with Bartholomew . . .'

Pender couldn't keep the surprise out of his voice. 'Catch up!'

'Why, yes,' said Harry, as if any other conclusion was impossible.

His servant sounded like a man trying to control his anger. 'I'm not one to question your orders, Captain . . .'

Harry smiled as he interrupted, for the first time since the explosion. 'Yes you are, Pender. And I'm grateful for it.'

Pender smiled too, showing that set of perfect even teeth. 'Sometimes you are. But what if I was to question them now?'

'I still have a score to settle with Bartholomew. If the damage to the *Principessa* is too great, then we will have to settle for this. But if she can be repaired she'll get us back to Genoa with more speed. I have to assume that's where he's headed.'

'Seems to me our ship took a right hammering, your honour.'

'She did. But you'd be amazed at how resilient a wooden ship is. And remember, she'd just had a refit before we bought her, so everything below decks was as sound as a bell. We can rip this ship apart to provide the necessary timber, and though the yards ain't perfect, they'll do for a jury rig.'

Fairbairn was bent over Sutton when Harry went below to see him. He'd lost his right arm. The surgeon had removed it and slung it in the barrel to join the other limbs he'd been forced to amputate. Sutton lay, white faced and sweating, and Fairbairn tied up the ends of the stump.

'I'm sorry, Sutton. Truly sorry,' Harry turned to Fairbairn. 'How many more?'

'This is the last of the serious ones. I left him because I thought I might save it. But it was shattered completely. As to the rest, we've got no end of splinters and other wounds to deal with. I was going to ask if I can get the casualties ashore. That dormitory that held the children looks like just the place to set up a hospital, and being off the ship will help a lot.'

Harry needed as many men as he could muster. But he could not deny that his wounded deserved attention. With a genuine element of compassion he agreed. 'Make it so, Mr Fairbairn. The boats are at your disposal, as a priority.'

Sutton spat out the leather strap from between his teeth, put there to stop him biting his tongue off in his agony. His voice croaked as he spoke. 'Not much use now, am I? No bloody arm. I can't be a dipper or a sailor!'

Harry didn't know what to say, so he said nothing. He made his way to his cabin for the first time since the battle. It was in chaos and Pender had just started to clear it up. Papers lay everywhere. Harry saw that Broadbridge's chest, which had been in the coach, had been blown apart, scattering his bogus share certificates all over the place.

'What do you want me to do with these?' asked Pender, holding up a sheaf.

Harry looked at the copperplate writing, and the inviting drawing of a busy, profitable canal. 'They'll do to heat the tar. Burn the damn things. And his chest.'

Pender bent down and picked up the pistol and a key. 'What about these?'

Harry, tired and somewhat dispirited, was quite short with him. 'Do what you damn well like, man. Throw them over the side for all I care.'

Then he saw the key in Pender's hand as his servant turned to toss them out of the hole where the sternlight windows had been.

'A second, Pender. That's the key to the cabin door.'

'It ain't,' said Pender, with genuine surprise. He looked at it closely, recognizing the heraldic crest on the grip. 'How the hell did it get over here?'

Harry took it off him. 'Strange things happen in an explosion, Pender. Look at me, I was on deck, right by the bulwark, and I haven't even got a scratch.'

Harry walked across to the cabin door. He bent down to replace the cabin key, but it was still in the lock. He stayed bent, casting his mind back to Ma Thomas's inn. 'Pender, when we opened Broadbridge's chest, it had a key in it. Do you remember?'

'Can't say I do, your honour. I don't recall ever looking in his chest after I opened it.'

'It did, I distinctly remember, though I didn't pay it much heed.'

Harry stood upright and held up the key in his hand. His servant looked towards the door. 'So it's not the door key after all?'

Harry took the key out of the cabin door, laid them both in his palm, and pushed his hand towards his servant. They were of a different size, but not by much. In all other respects they were identical.

'It's not this door key, but look. Do you recognize the device?'

Pender nodded doubtfully. 'Only 'cause I've seen it here in the cabin. I'd no mind to give it attention otherwise.'

'Did you ever get a look at the knocker on the door of Toraglia's villa?'

His servant looked totally mystified, so Harry explained. 'It has the same crest as the key to this cabin.'

Pender and Harry looked down together. Both keys had the heraldic crest of a bird of prey taking a small mammal in its talons. 'What would Broadbridge be doing with a Toraglia key in his chest?'

'Does it fit any of the doors in here?' asked Pender, looking round.

'Only the main door has a lock, Pender. And look at them. They're not the same shape. They were made for different locks.'

'Well if'n it's the bloke who owned this barky, then he must have given it to him?'

'They never met. I asked him about Broadbridge. He didn't have the faintest idea what I was talking about.'

'So where did it come from?'

Harry was silent for a moment, as a whole host of thoughts filled his mind. Sutton's words rang in his ears. 'Did you know that Sutton had lost an arm?'

Pender was surprised by the change of subject. 'Sutton? Has he, poor sod? Mr Fairbairn had some hopes of saving it.'

'You said he was a good thief.'

'Aye. Very nimble fingers. But it's a dangerous game, that. You stand more chance of getting caught dipping than any other form of thieving. Stands to reason since you're standing right beside your mark.'

'He was a pickpocket?'

'I thought you knew that,' said Pender.

Harry just shook his head, and put the keys in his pocket. 'Fairbairn wants the wounded ashore. He's going to set up a hospital in that dormitory. Let's leave this and muster who we can. The sooner we get them ashore, the sooner we can get to work shifting the stores.'

Pender gave Harry another wide smile. 'This being marooned on a desert island lark ain't all it's cracked up to be.'

They started the water out of its casks and pumped it out, lightening the ship considerably. Harry took a spell on the pumps himself. The three eunuchs had collapsed, not being used to performing any kind of physical work. But they'd shown concern for the casualties, and an ability to tend their wounds, being gentle souls, for all the nature of their trade. Harry had passed them over to Fairbairn to help run the hospital.

The next job was back-breaking, for with few fit hands clearing the holds was punishing work. Harry couldn't remove everything, some of it would have needed a full crew on the capstan, but he shifted enough to satisfy himself that the *Principessa* was still reasonably sound. She had taken a nasty jolt, and some of her copper bolts were looser than they should be, especially in the forepeak. But he knew that given a complete hull she'd sail, though it was inevitable that she would take in a lot more water through her seams than she had before.

They carried out a temporary repair on the gash in the hull, using a tar-covered sail. Harry righted her again, pumped her out some more, and had her hauled up the beach as far as possible, taking care to place her at low tide. Then, having shifted as many of the remaining stores as possible, he heaved her right over so that half her hull was out of the water. They beached the merchant ship beside the *Principessa*, at an angle to act as a breakwater, then started to cannibalize the timbers from her hull. It wasn't neat, for neither Harry nor any of his remaining hands were true carpenters. But it was enough, and they sawed and planed and hacked with their adze, sometimes up to their knees in water as the tide rose enough to flood the temporary staging, until the hole was repaired. Harry coated the timbers with several layers of tar, and four days after the battle, having worked every daylight hour, he was ready to float her off again. He waited until the tide was high. Not that it made much of a difference in the Mediterranean. But the extra couple of feet sufficed, for she was great deal lighter now than when he'd beached her.

They eased her hull down, very gently, into the rising water, in order not to dig her keel into the sand. Harry had his fittest men in the cutter, with a cable to the bows, with the others aboard the merchant ship standing by to push with the capstan bars. As she started to lift he yelled an order. They began to push and pull like the devil, and with a sucking sound, the *Principessa*'s head came off the beach. The water flowed under her stern as she righted herself, and quite suddenly the ship seemed to bounce and she was afloat. Those who had the energy let out a ragged cheer.

He had everyone sleeping ashore in proper beds, though he himself used the storeroom, since some of the wounded screamed terribly in the night. The three eunuchs seemed tireless in their efforts to treat their charges, and they fussed around with buckets of cool water and sponges from the bay, dabbing at the sweating brows of the wounded men, and dosing them with herbal remedies of their own devising. In the evenings, after a decent meal, Harry had time to try and communicate with them, for there was nothing he could really accomplish in the dark.

It was a slow process, which of necessity started with the word Bartholomew. It progressed from there, using sign language and drawing in the soft earth with a stick, through 'yes' and 'no', to a graphic description of their home, which seemed to be somewhere on the Black Sea coast if their pointed fingers were to be believed. They drew a ground plan of a large building, some sort of palace, indicating that this was the place they'd come from. It had many servants and a powerful master. Mention of their master led them into some kind of joke which involved chopping motions with their hands around their mouths and their groins. When Harry had tempered their giggling he managed to establish that this master, whoever he was, had been dead for some time. Then it was the number of suns and moons to establish that they'd been on this island for the past two years.

On the fourth night, Harry, for once wearing his coat, reached into his pocket for a handkerchief. As he pulled it out, the key that had been in there since the day of the explosion fell out also. One of the eunuchs bent to pick it up, and as he saw the crest, he beamed with pleasure. But his face froze when he saw Harry's reaction to the one word he'd said. Harry quickly composed his features, smiling again, as though the mere dropping of the key had been the thing to cause him annoyance. He took it back, made his excuses, and left.

He went through to the hospital. Fairbairn had set up home in the eunuchs' room, taking one of their beds so that he could be near his patients. He looked up at Harry as he approached, and the dark circles under his eyes, plus the stubble on his chin, made him look as he had when Harry had first clapped eyes on him. But the cause this time was genuine exhaustion, not opium.

'How is Sutton?' he asked.

Fairbairn pushed his lank hair out of his eyes. 'He doesn't answer, Ludlow. It's not the wound. That is healing well, and he doesn't want for attention from your eunuchs. His spirit, or the lack of it, is killing him.'

Harry had seen a steady trickle of men returning to duty over the past few days, some seeming to make remarkable recoveries. He knew that he was in the presence of an exceptional surgeon and physician, and pleased that even at the low ebb to which his tiredness had reduced him, he had shown no desire to return to his former habit.

'Have you spoken with him?'

Fairbairn nodded.

'Why is he so low?'

'The man sees no future for himself. And can you blame him? If he'd still been in the King's Navy, he would at least been entitled to set up shop selling spiritous liquor. But he's not. He talks of Botany Bay, wishing that he refused the Royal bounty and gone there.'

Fairbairn rubbed a hand over his brow, then tried to squeeze the exhaustion out of his eyes. 'I have often noticed that in the criminal class. A compulsive desire to start anew.'

Harry thought how with his help Pender had done just that. He went and sought him out now, taking him away from a game of dice.

'Sutton's all right deep down, your honour,' said Pender, once they were out of earshot of the other players. 'Leastways, I think he is.'

'Then why did we have all that trouble with him?'

'Not at first. I seem to recall he was willin'.'

Harry looked at the clear night sky. 'Yes. So do I. How honest is he?'

'I told you, he was a thief.'

'Pender, you were a thief. I would trust you with everything I possess.'

Pender was slightly abashed, then smiled at the compliment. 'To my mind there're two sorts. There's those that does it cause they're too bone idle to do owt else, and there's others that refuse to buckle under. But they don't feel inclined to starve.'

'Sutton's not the type to buckle under. He would have left the ship alone that first day out. And I had a hell of a task getting him to admit to anything when I questioned him.'

'That's right. He came to thieving to avoid hunger, I reckon. Much like me. An' like me, seeing he found he was good at it, he didn't see no reason to do any other work.'

'So if I offered him a place, say on my estates, you think I could trust him?'

Pender was wary; he didn't want the responsibility, even although he knew Harry would never blame him. 'That I cannot say for sure. Just as I can't say if'n it's a good idea to go filling your property with villains.'

'Would you trust him?'

The was a long pause. Reluctant he might be, but Pender wasn't the type to let a mate down. He'd regretted belting Sutton in Genoa, but that was a case of higher loyalty, and no time to mess about. And Sutton hadn't forgiven him for that, staying well out of his way ever since.

'Let's say I'd be willin' to give him a chance, though I'd keep an eye on him for a while.'

'So the answer is yes?'

Pender nodded, but he made sure that it carried reluctance as well as agreement.

Harry laughed, though he didn't have much to be amused about.

'That, my friend, was like extracting a healthy tooth with my fingers.'

'It's not everybody that can afford to be certain, your honour.'

Sutton looked away as Harry sat down by his bed. He shook his head when his visitor enquired after him. But Harry spoke to the back of his neck.

Harry decided he might as well start with a pure guess. 'The night we met, on that quayside, where had you come from?'

That brought his head round, slowly for sure, but round nevertheless, to look Harry Ludlow in the eye.

'I wondered at Broadbridge making you his right-hand man. When I opened his chest.' Sutton's eyes showed a flicker of reaction. 'I had Pender open it the morning after we found his body. As I was saying, I wondered at your position. After all, if Broadbridge was intent on being a privateer, he needed good sailors, not good dips. Then we found all those certificates he had. He wasn't a sailor at all, was he?'

'That was plain enough,' croaked Sutton.

'What was he up to?' Sutton didn't reply, so Harry continued. 'Those share certificates were no good to him in Italy. But they pointed to the kind of man he was. Is that how he got those guns? Did he persuade the Navy victualling agent to invest in one of his schemes? You said that you went ashore the night Howlett was murdered, to see Gallagher and get some "more" money. So that wasn't the first time Broadbridge had met him, was it?'

Sutton gave a single shake of his head.

'He had involved Gallagher in some scheme. One that cost the man dear. That would explain why he ran away. Admiral Hood said he'd absconded with the money entrusted to him to purchase stores. How much of that money had Broadbridge already dunned him for?'

'How the hell should I know?'

'Broadbridge was on his uppers, yet a few days later he was talking about turning the *Dido* into Fiddler's Green. What happened to elevate his spirits to that degree?'

Sutton didn't reply. 'The night you rescued us from those men on the quayside, had you been up to something?'

Sutton still didn't speak, but he did turn to look at Harry. 'An odd direction to come from, that. That's not the place to catch deserters. You do that on the quayside or the beach?'

'I don't know what you're driving at.'

Harry took the key out of his pocket. Sutton looked at it and tried to keep his eyes from showing any reaction. 'We found this in Broadbridge's chest as well.'

'So?'

'So? It has the same crest as the key to the cabin on my ship. Odd that, wouldn't you say?'

Sutton had become more animated, in fact near angry. Harry felt that this loss of listlessness was caused by his feeling threatened. 'Can't see that it was. He was after buying the fucking ship, weren't he.'

'Count Toraglia said they'd never met.'

'Then he must be a lying bastard. They all are in those parts.'

'The first night we went there, in the sedan chair, you seemed scared of something. So scared you avoided the duty the next morning.'

He turned his head away. 'Can't recall.'

'In fact, you've behaved oddly ever since. This key was in Captain Broadbridge's chest. The captain, dead, was in the cabin of the *Principessa*. But this key doesn't fit my cabin. It was made for another door, though for the same owner. You just happen to be a dip, a man adept at pinching a purse. I would reckon a key is easier to lift from a pocket than a purse. Especially from the pocket of a blind man.'

Sutton spun his head round sharply. 'Look. I don't know nothin', leave me be.'

'Mr Fairbairn says that you're going to die.'

Fear filled the man's eyes at that. No one had said anything to him. All he heard were the normal sounds of medical reassurance.

'He maintains that you're not fighting hard enough, that you've lost your vital spark, and that if you don't want to live there's nothing he can do for you.'

Sutton settled back on his cot, leaning against the wall and closing his eyes. 'What's to live for?'

'I asked Pender about you.'

'I'll not say nowt against Pious, even if he did clip me one. You have a good 'un there.'

'That's more or less what he said about you.'

'Then I thank him kindly.' Harry saw Sutton's eyes turn watery, then he blinked and turned away again.

'He said that if I was to offer you a future, you could be trusted to take it, and not repay me by stealing my possessions. I have large estates and there's work even for a man with one arm. The offer is there if you want it, and if you live.'

Sutton was confused. He knew he'd caused Harry a lot of trouble. 'Why?'

'Because I want to know certain things, or perhaps I just need them confirmed. You'd been to the Toraglia villa before. You were involved in some scheme with Broadbridge to make money, and it wasn't out of sailing as a privateer. The source of funds from Gallagher had dried up, but he found something else to provide his keep. He was a crimp, and you were to be his accomplice.'

Harry held up the key. 'I asked where you came from the night you rescued us. You'd been somewhere in the town. Was it to try this perhaps, and see if it fitted? Or did you already know the answer to that? What was the idea? Did you plan to rob a blind man? Or was it something to do with the syndicate?'

That scared him. He pushed himself on to his elbows and glared at Harry. 'How do you know all this? Not that I'm saying you're right, mind.'

'Because I just dropped this key next door. I was with the eunuchs, and one of them picked it up. He recognized it right away.'

'So he recognized it. They can't tell you anything, they don't speak English.'

'They speak enough, Sutton. Just enough. You see when he picked it up, he said the one word he does know.'

'What's that?'

'He said Bartholomew. Is that where you got it from?'

Harry came back into the room where the three eunuchs sat lounging on cushions. He had Pender and a brace of pistols with him, for he had no illusions about the difficulty, and the capacity for confusion, in asking three men who didn't speak English to take their clothes off.

As it was, the amount of sign language was excessive, as was the quantity of giggling. Pender's pistols didn't scare them at all. But if they'd been looking into Harry's eyes when he examined their backs, they would have stopped laughing damned quick. His eyes were diamond hard and full of hate. For they all had that crescent-shaped mark and the badly deformed skin, with the strange lettering down the side, in exactly the same place as the black-clad villain Harry had killed aboard the *Principessa*.

CHAPTER TWENTY-NINE

'People who've lived on the wrong side of the law can spot one another right off.'

Sutton had been sitting up when Harry returned, and some of the waxy grey colour had gone from his skin. Harry doubted that it was because of his offer. More likely Sutton had revived because of the attention being paid to his every word. 'Not that Broadbridge ever said he was a felon. For he'd never tell a truth where a falsehood would serve.'

'Do you know where he came from?'

Sutton shook his head. 'No. But he had money to spend, at least to begin with, and he was free with it.'

'Someone else's most like,' said Pender, unaware of the connection between Broadbridge and Gallagher.

'Too right, Pious. Anyway, he cottoned on, right off, that I was no sailor. That was when he was beggin' to get a slice of the syndicate.'

'Bartholomew told me how hard he badgered them.'

'But he'd not tell you why. Broadbridge knew they was up to no good, 'cause I tell you he could smell it.'

'I never liked the set-up, I'm bound to say,' said Pender. Harry gave him a sharp look, pleading that he shut up and let Sutton speak.

'I don't even know how long he'd been around, or if he'd come out straight from England. But he had a hound's snout for money. He could smell a profit a mile off.' Sutton shook his head again, smiling a bit this time. 'He was a bit of a card, old Broadbridge.'

Harry conjured up the ace of spades. 'So you think he'd already found out what the syndicate was about before he asked to join?'

'Not the sort of thing he'd let on to the likes of me. But I take leave to doubt that he knew. He spent an age trying to find out where they got their money, for they never seemed to bring any stuff ashore. He just knew it wasn't on the up an' up. He'd had a sniff around before I ever met him, and he'd spotted that Bartholomew was forever skulkin' out the back way. That he did tell me about. So we followed him and saw him going into that villa, sneaky like. That's when he set me to get the key.'

'When was that?'

Sutton put his tongue between his lips, deep in thought. 'Not long after that Captain Howlett was murdered. Three or four days.'

'Everyone I spoke to said that he was scared witless after that happened.'

'An' no mistake.'

Harry spoke gently now. 'Yet you don't think it was him?'

Sutton's voice was filled with scorn for that notion. 'He didn't have it in him, drunk or sober.'

'Could he have seen who did it?'

'I told you, he was arseholed drunk. If'n he saw anything it would be double.'

'He told me he'd had words with Bartholomew the night you rescued us.'

A slight frown at the change of tack. 'Ay, that's right.'

'Do you think he threatened to expose him?'

'Expose what? He still hadn't cottoned on to what they was about. Besides, Broadbridge wasn't the sort to threaten. No, he wanted a slice of what was goin', that was all.'

'But if Bartholomew threatened him . . . ?'

'Then I dare say he'd give warning in return.'

'So what else did he find out?'

'Nothin'. That night we came across you and Pious, we'd picked up some deserters, more for an excuse than because we needed 'em, and with Lubeck asking how the hell he intended to feed 'em. Captain Broadbridge was afire to have a look inside the place. Near got caught by some right slippery bastards and we had to scarper. Broadbridge headed off in the wrong direction, 'cause he couldn't tell left from right, and we was making our way back when we heard you shout.'

'These slippery bastards wouldn't be dressed entirely in black by any chance, would they?' Sutton's eyes opened wide and he nodded slowly as Harry continued. 'That's why they attacked us in the dark. They mistook us for your party.'

'I didn't reckon that at the time, Captain, 'cause I didn't get a proper sight of them on the quayside. But I did after.'

'After Broadbridge was killed?' asked Harry. Sutton just nodded. 'And outside the villa?'

'I got the fright of my life, an' no mistake.'

'You thought I'd killed him, so as to take his place.'

'I didn't know what to think. All I wanted was to keep my own counsel and stay alive. If'n there'd been a King's ship in the harbour I would've given myself in. But I was stuck. On the one hand there was Bart, and on the other was you. I'd heard enough tales of Gideon Bartholomew to see you as the safer bet.'

Harry questioned him some more, but Sutton seemed to dry up, partly through exhaustion. He knew there were still things the man wasn't saying, for the inconsistencies in his tale were obvious. Broadbridge might not have told Sutton what he knew, but he must have a good idea what Bartholomew was up to. Given that the crew of the *Dido* had been on short commons for some time, he would have had to tell Sutton something to get him out looking for deserters. And Sutton must have known, that night on the quay, that those men were after him, not Harry Ludlow.

But he also knew that no amount of interrogation would get them out of him. Sutton was well versed in the ways of his trade. He might be willing to assist Harry, but he'd would do nothing to incriminate himself if he could avoid it. Besides, he had enough. Toraglia and Bartholomew were connected. The Count had been powerful once, and it seems he was still. He'd arranged for the syndicate to sail under Genoese colours so that they could pursue his interests. Privateers coming and going raised no eyebrows. Profitable merchantmen without cargo certainly would. And the French? Harry could see no real connection, but Toraglia must be on their side. Perhaps he'd promised to occupy the English privateers in a way that would leave French commerce be.

The men in black, with their strange brand marks, had been his, laying in wait on the quayside to catch Broadbridge, then sent out to the ship because they'd failed. Bartholomew must have had a hand in that, removing the threat that Broadbridge posed. It didn't explain Howlett, of course, and Harry wondered whether that might be an unsolvable mystery. His mind went back to that first night aboard the *Principessa*. No wonder Toraglia'd had too few men to carry his sedan chair. Harry and Pender had killed them.

'You need to rest, Sutton. Right now I have to get our ship ready for sea.'

She was not the same ship at all, and it was never more obvious than it was now, as she beat up into the northerly wind through the Straits of Messina. She wouldn't lie as close as she had before, and with the kind of gimcrack top hamper that Harry had aboard she kept falling off, especially on the starboard tack with the stronger leeway. It was hard work to make any headway at all. He fought on with a grim determination, for even though they had been at sea for a fortnight, Harry's desire for a confrontation with Bartholomew and Toraglia had not abated. The wind had brought upon a stubborn determination, which was quite unusual in so affable a man.

They'd made remarkable speed up until now, and Harry had half a thought that if Bartholomew was in no rush, they might just catch him. But this wind, even if the three ships were just over the horizon, would favour them against the *Principessa* in her present state. There was no one else up to steering her in these conditions, and Harry had been on deck for over two full days. His eyes were red-rimmed and his face was caked with salt, and he stared ahead with a fixed expression, only occasionally glancing at the sails to see how they drew. He'd long since given up trying anything new. She wouldn't answer to innovation and that was that.

Everyone else aboard fervently wished he would just lie to until the wind changed, but if Harry could gain a mile then he would do it. He would not brook a sideways glance of protest from the men he called on deck every hour or so to change tack.

Even Pender, who could say things to Harry Ludlow in a way barred to others, kept his silence. Fairbairn, who had tried to tell

Harry that he was driving himself too hard, had been threatened with a keelhauling if he interfered. He'd been bluntly informed to mind his patients and leave the running of the ship to the owner. They were short of hands and short of masts to sail her properly. She was leaking substantially more than she had, which meant that sailing into the wind the pumps were never still. And they hadn't experienced anything like a severe blow.

Harry had gone slowly crazy after he made the connection between Bartholomew and Toraglia. It worked on him like a drug whose dose increased naturally. He'd driven everybody to get the ship ready for sea, and worked through the night with lanterns rigged to get what he needed across from the merchantman. Stepping the upper masts had been a sore trial. They'd rigged and rove, and bent on sails to see if they fitted. Pender, who hated a needle, had been set to sew with all the others. Harry had even shipped canvas to the hospital so that the men there, who couldn't walk, could at least contribute something.

And his crew knew that something had changed him. But no one dared broach the subject. For all his hatred of Bartholomew, Harry had slowly come to loathe Count Toraglia more. He'd actually liked the man, had warmed to him and cursed himself for what happened with his poor wife. And all the time the cunning little Italian had been sucking him into a trap. Greed was the key. They'd heard that he had money to spend. How convenient to sell Harry Ludlow a ship he'd never take delivery of. After Broadbridge's death they must have known he was a threat, but instead of attacking him, as James had feared, Toraglia had flattered him, sailed with him, and timed his naps to perfection.

And that last night, when he'd been in such a rush. The Count must have known death awaited him. If not the manner of his death then certainly that it was about to happen. He'd had been made fool of, and that hurt more than everything else.

Even though he'd thought of it night and day, Harry couldn't believe his eyes. He even rubbed them to make sure he wasn't dreaming, for he'd gone short of enough sleep to warrant it. But the sails were unmistakable, for he'd spent so much time looking at them they were as familiar as his own.

With *Ariel* in the lead, the ships were sailing along easily, not risking spars or canvas. Harry, now that the wind had swung round, had set everything he could, and was making around five knots. If they had a glass on him, they didn't react. And no wonder, for it would take a clever eye to tell that this was the same ship they'd nearly blown out of the water. Her masts were different and her sail plan was more likely to be a subject for humour than fear.

Harry sailed on through the morning, coming up slowly on his three quarry. They hadn't smoked it was him, and he wondered what they would do if they did. Harry doubted if he could even fight one of them with his ship in this condition, and he was now blessed with fewer men than any one of them. But still he held his speed and there was no one aboard to question the wisdom of what he was doing.

He handed the wheel over to Pender, who in the last weeks had become quite a proficient helmsman, and made his way up the mainmast to the cap. He couldn't go any higher, since the topmast he'd rigged was too flimsy to lend itself to the weight of a man perched right on its top. But even this small increase in height afforded a more advantageous view. He was still there when the commotion started on the decks of the three ships. Someone had taken a closer look at this strange fellow overhauling them, and looked at the hull and the figurehead, rather than the odd set of the sails.

Arms waved, and Harry could see much hailing going on through speaking trumpets. He found he was biting his lip, for if they came round to engage him, he'd have to run into the wind. But if the spectre of Harry Ludlow, risen (to their minds) from the dead, worked on their imagination, he might achieve something yet.

Suddenly the *Ariel* set more sail. The others followed, but being the better ship she shot ahead. The *Bella* was still labouring after all this time, and Harry guessed that the repairs he thought she'd had were just a superficial coat of paint. He was still gaining on her, but the other two were drawing away, *Ariel* more than *Cromer*. Bartholomew was abandoning Freeman to his fate.

Then Pilton put his helm down and bore away from the land. He might be a buffoon, but he must have known Harry was after Bartholomew and given the choice he'd leave the *Cromer*. And he was right. Harry blessed the man for acting in character, though God knew what he would do if *Ariel* turned. And she'd have to, because there was no way he could catch her now.

He turned his glass back on to Freeman. If he'd had any sense he would have taken the same course as Pilton, for Harry couldn't care less about the *Bella*. But either out of loyalty or stupidity, he was holding his course, putting himself between Harry and the *Ariel*.

They sailed on through the next three hours, with *Ariel* sinking in the distance while *Bella* had come within hailing. Harry kept shifting his helm to try and pass her, but Freeman wouldn't have it, forever coming round to stay in his path.

Harry lifted his speaking trumpet. 'Let me pass. You have my word I shall not attack you.'

For answer, Freeman fired his stern chaser, sending a ball close to the *Principessa*'s side, covering her deck with a spray of water. It would have been so easy before. He could have slipped round the *Bella* in no time, and he would then have caught the *Ariel* with Bartholomew aboard on his own. The thought spurred him on. Harry trimmed the wheel so that his bowsprit was aimed right at the *Bella*'s stern.

Then he closed up. Freeman's stern chaser fired at regular intervals. Harry had everyone down the hatchways except those he needed. Pender stood beside him, helping him con the ship, for Harry was forever darting forward to shout a warning to the *Bella*. Several of the balls struck the *Principessa*'s hull, but Harry ignored them. Shots to the hull he could live with, as long as Freeman didn't go for the sails, because it wouldn't take much to bring them down about his ears.

The *Principessa*'s bowsprit was now edging towards the *Bella*'s stern rail. Harry held her there, decreasing his speed a little by loosening his braces. He made his way forward and called for a crew to man the bow chaser. He was going to try and blow the bastard out of his path, or at least scare him enough to get him to move over.

The gun was run in, loaded, and run out. Harry was just about to give the order to fire, when Freeman let fly his sheets and put his helm hard down. The Bella swung broadside on, and the *Principessa*, still going full tilt, ran straight into her. Harry heard the sound of wood tearing into wood, and also the crack of it snapping. But worse than that he felt the grinding vibrations of his own hull beneath his feet. The *Principessa* juddered and swung round. Harry just had time to fire off his cannon while it would still hit something. Pender had been quick, calling all the hands from the hatchways to board the *Bella*, and they ran forward to where the two ships joined ready to attack over the bows. But Freeman had lowered his boats, and his men were piling into them.

Harry yelled for them to get back aboard. He had no time for Freeman or his crew. He wanted to get his ship clear so that he could continue on after the *Ariel*. He'd fouled the Bella's rigging so the boarding axes now turned to slashing at that. As she pulled clear, Harry heard a groaning sound from his own hull, and he knew that the ship was sorely wounded. He rushed below, heading for the forepeak, and there, underneath the prow of the ship, he could hear the water sluicing around. Then it started to cover his feet. Hitting the *Bella* had cracked the already damaged *Principessa*'s hull right open, and water was pouring in through her bows.

He ran back on deck and ordered everybody aboard the still floating *Bella*, which was now drifting away on the tide. He hoped and prayed that Freeman hadn't set him another trap with powder. The *Principessa*'s boats were over the side and men were throwing everything they possessed into them. Fairbairn was helping those whose wounds made it difficult for them, including Sutton, and the three eunuchs were running around in a state of panic. Harry had to slap one of them in the face and heave all three bodily into the boats. He went into his cabin one last time. Pender had got all his things into his sea-chest and was carrying it out of the door.

'The key, Pender?'

'In my pocket, your honour,' his servant replied. Harry took the other key from the cabin door, had a last look round, and walked out. The bows were settling into the sea. Soon the guns, cast loose to fire if needed, would break lose from their breechings, crashing forward to smash their way through the figurehead.

Harry stepped into the cutter, which was now level with the bulwarks, and ordered his men to pull for the *Bella*. Then he saw Freeman's men doing the same. They had seen that the *Principessa* was going down, and had decided to try and return to their ship. Harry yelled furiously and grabbed an oar himself. If Freeman caught them in the water, in boats like these, he could easily sink them by cannon fire. His men, who'd been looking fondly at their ship, spotted what was happening and started to pull like the devil. They won by a short head, and Freeman, realizing that he wasn't going to succeed, ordered his boats to turn away for fear that Harry would be tempted to do the same to him.

They came aboard the *Bella*, and before they'd had to time to settle Harry was at them to set some sail. He looked out to where Freeman and his men were pulling heartily to get as far away as possible. Harry put his helm down and sailed away from them. Looking back, he saw men collapsing over their oars.

The *Bella* was, of course, slower than the *Principessa*, and given the distance to Genoa, Bartholomew would be there a whole tide before him. Harry didn't care. He had more than Bartholomew to see to, and when he went ashore, he intended to set the whole Genoese Republic on its ears.

CHAPTER THIRTY

Harry sailed right in, forcing several boats to haul out of his way, calling all the while to ask about the *Ariel*. Eventually he found someone who'd spotted her. She had sailed into the outer roads, dropped off her pinnace, and headed out to sea again right away. Harry set the *Bella*'s head straight at the quay. As soon as he reached the harbour area, where the shipping was too crowded to force a swift passage, he hailed a boat crew, with Pender in charge, and he had himself pulled ashore at speed.

'Straight for the Royal George, lads!' he shouted. Pender, ever thoughtful, handed him two more loaded pistols, which he stuck in his belt. The boat bumped into the quayside and he leapt out, guns in hand, running for the entrance to the inn. A shay sat outside with a driver dozing on the box. Harry dashed past it and into the darkness of the interior. Crosby, who was sitting nursing a tankard with a worried look on his face, leapt up, startled, as Harry rushed in. He tried to block him but was too slow to move. Harry swiped him with the pistol as he went by, knocking him to the ground.

He crashed through the door to the back. Ma Thomas stood in the hallway, her moon-like face alarmed at all this commotion. She opened her mouth to ask Harry what he was about, but he pushed her, with some difficulty, out of his way, and shot up the stairs three at a time. Bartholomew's door was locked, and Harry crashed into it. It didn't budge, being heavy oak. He aimed the pistols at the door and fired, splintering the lock. A mighty kick with his foot and he dived through the door, the other pistols up and ready to use.

Bartholomew sat in the same deep armchair as he had that first night they'd met. No mocking smile this time, his eyes had a startled look. His body was twisted, and his screwed-up face testified to the death agony he'd suffered. He had bitten through his swollen tongue, and the blood had dripped on to his shirt front, where it was now drying. Both rooms were in a mess. Through the door Harry could see the unmade bed. Chests lay, lids thrown back and half packed. A strongbox stood open and empty where it had been taken out from behind the panelling.

'What the fuck—' Ma Thomas stopped as she saw Bartholomew, putting her hands to her mouth in an uncharacteristic gesture. Harry walked slowly over to the table. A Venetian glass, blood red in colour, was the only thing on it. It was half full of red wine. Bartholomew had been drinking too. His glass, of the same type as the one on the table, lay at his side where he'd dropped it, the wine long since drained into the cracks in the floorboards.

Harry picked up the half-full glass and sniffed. It had the smell of a good claret. Then he lifted the one that Bartholomew had used, and sniffed at that. An odd smell to that, like almonds. Harry guessed he'd been poisoned, and touching the blood on his shirt with his fingers, he realized that it had happened some hours before.

'Harry. Where the hell have you been?' He spun round. James was in the doorway, with Pender right behind him. His brother's jaw dropped open as Harry turned to face him, for in doing so, he'd revealed the body.

Harry looked past James to his servant. 'Pender. Go out to the ship and ask Fairbairn if he will join us.'

James opened his mouth to say something, but Harry put up his hand to stop him. 'Not now, James. I must attend to this first.'

'He came rushin' in, calling for me to fetch a shay, then he sent Crosby off to deliver some message. That's the last I saw of him till now, though I'm bound to say I heard him banging and crashing about.'

Ma Thomas was upset, though Harry doubted it had anything to do with Bartholomew's body. She was probably wondering how this was going to affect her future. 'Not that he was any good to me. I never saw a shilling of his money.'

'Did Crosby come up here when he returned?'

Ma Thomas was all belligerence again. 'How should I know?'

'Crosby is lying in pool of his own blood on the tap-room floor.' said James, a note of deep disapproval in his voice.

'Could you see if you can revive him, James?' His brother looked set to protest. 'Please James. I wouldn't ask if it wasn't important.'

'I would be more willing if you told me what's going on here.'

'I don't have the complete answer, James, and even if I did, I don't have the time. For if I don't move quickly, brother, then this man's murderer, and very likely Broadbridge's, is going to get away.'

'You know who killed Broadbridge?'

Harry's voice showed his uncertainty. For this body had shocked him. 'I think I know who ordered it, James.'

'You only think so? You'd better make certain before you go accusing anyone.'

James was feeling excluded again. Harry knew that his brother had probably been worried sick. He knew nothing about the things which had happened since they last met. It would have been so easy to blast him for his obvious pique, but Harry felt that, if anything, he should apologize. Yet he could not do so, for such an act would open him to a discussion of the mystery, something he was not ready to undertake. He was thrown back once more on an inadequate response.

'James. I know that I'm not making things clear to you.'

His brother's face was like granite. 'Understatement, Harry.'

Harry smiled suddenly. 'I'm alive. Pender's alive, and thank God you seem to be well. Everything in my world is near perfect. But if I was to try now to tell you all that's happened in the past weeks, we'd be here for an hour at least. That's an hour I don't have to spare, but I look forward to having it very soon. An hour when you, at your leisure, can tell me what has been going on in the world.'

He must have seen the strain in Harry's face, for recent events had taken their toll. James walked over and put his mended arm round Harry shoulder. 'Sorry, brother. I must stop standing on my dignity.'

'How's the arm?' asked Harry

James, close to, was examining his face, looking at all the little scars which had not yet healed. 'What happened to your face?'

'That is another thing that will have to wait, brother. And you'll need a strong drink when I tell you.'

James nodded. 'I'll go and see if I can revive Crosby.'

He was just going out the door when Pender came in with Fairbairn. The surgeon was now the picture of health, and it was such a startling contrast to what James had seen before that he had to look twice to be sure it was the same man.

'Fairbairn?'

'James,' said his brother impatiently. 'Crosby.'

James went down the stairs, calling over his shoulder, 'Ay, ay, Captain.'

Harry took another sniff at Bartholomew's glass then passed it to Fairbairn. He sniffed in turn and his nose twitched. 'Poison?'

Fairbairn looked at the position of the body then he stepped forward and lifted Bartholomew's eyelid. Finally he sniffed at the glass again and nodded. Harry handed him the full glass. Fairbairn sniffed that in turn, dipped a finger in the wine, and touched his tongue.

'This seems fine,' he said.

'So whoever shared a glass of wine with him, put poison in his.'

'It looks that way.'

Harry was still for quite a while, thinking. Then he started knocking on the walls looking for a secret entrance. Sutton said that Broadbridge had spied the dead man coming and going out of the back entrance. And that day, when Harry'd knocked on his door, he'd been out of the room. So there had to be another way in and out. Ma Thomas was by the doorway watching him. Something in her eye made him suspicious. 'Where is it?

'Right by the fireplace, on the left. Just push.'

'I would have appreciated it if you'd told me.'

She scowled. 'I would've, if you'd asked.'

Harry went down the spiral staircase to a passage that ran for about twenty yards. At the end there was a doorway which opened out on to the alley. The key was still on the inside, and the door was slightly ajar. Harry looked at the key carefully, but it was a plain affair, with no crest or anything to identify it. He went back upstairs to find James there, but no Crosby.

'You hit him too hard, Harry. It will be a while before he talks to anyone. Fairbairn has gone to have a look at him.'

'No matter. I know the answer to the question I was going to ask him anyway.'

'So. Do I warrant some kind of explanation?'

Harry changed the subject quickly. 'What brought you back to Genoa?'

'Harry, I've been here for weeks. I came back as soon as Williams assured me my arm was on the mend. I really do think you should tell me where you have been.'

'I have been to a leper colony, brother.'

'Indeed,' said James, testily. 'I try to avoid lepers, so I'm not over-familiar with the effects of the disease. But I know that is not what has caused those blemishes on your skin.'

'No, James, that was rats.'

That shocked him. 'Rats!'

'You see, brother, it is too complicated to explain now. How did you get here so soon after I arrived?'

'I've had the place watched. Guistiani hired me some excellent fellows.'

Harry was looking about the room again, as if hoping some clue would leap out at him. 'What did Guistiani say about me?'

'Only that you'd bought the ship, and that you had disappeared on a cruise without informing him of your destination. Count Toraglia told me you were in such a hellfire hurry to get to sea that you left without saying farewell.'

Harry's head snapped round, and he barked the name. 'Count Toraglia?'

'Yes. Is that so strange?' Harry didn't reply, so James continued. 'I went to see him, to find out if he knew your whereabouts. We shall go and visit him. I must show you the portrait I've done of his wife. I am immoderately pleased with it.'

But Fairbairn came back into the room, followed by Pender. Harry told his servant to fetch their boat crew. He saw that James was about to ask something. 'Please, brother, no more questions.'

Yet he knew that would not do. James deserved some form of explanation. He turned back to look at Bartholomew's body. 'I came here to kill him, James. But someone beat me to it. Time to find that someone, and bring all this to an end.'

'All this?'

He was saved from answering by the appearance of his boat crew. Harry immediately led the way down the secret staircase and out through the passageway into the alley. He walked confidently ahead, forcing the others to a fast pace to stay with him. The party of armed men cut a swath through the crowded streets.

'Were are we headed, Harry?'

'Can't you tell, James? You must have come this way a few times.'

James looked confused, then angry, and finally he lapsed into a thoughtful silence. They were out of the town gates now and heading along the route to the Toraglia villa. As they approached the high white walls that surrounded it, Harry could hear his brother give a soft curse under his breath.

'Wait and see, James. And I assure you this time I'm not being impetuous.'

Harry strode ahead, produced his key, and quickly opened the postern gate. The whole party filed through with Harry in the lead, and James, somewhat dragging his feet, now bringing up the rear. Harry heard the noise of the man coming through the undergrowth and spun to face him, but Pender was there before him with a club raised and his foot out. The fellow tripped and sprawled across the path. Pender fetched him a blow behind the ears and he went limp. Harry bent and turned the man over. His mouth was wide open, and the missing tongue was plain to see. He was entirely dressed in black, and wearing a black headscarf.

Harry turned to look back at his brother, standing rigid in a state of shock. 'A mute, James. Recognize the clothing? I dare say you didn't spy this fellow when you came here to do your portrait, brother.'

James couldn't answer. He was just staring at the man on the ground.

Harry turned him over and ripped the shirt from his back. The crescent-shaped brand mark stood out, stark against the man's olive skin.

'Keep your eyes open, there may be others,' he said.

'How many, your honour?' asked Pender.

Harry treated him to a smile, thinking there were not enough to carry a sedan chair. 'Certainly less than four.'

Pender shook his head to indicate he didn't understand. They continued towards the house, with the captive dragged along behind them. He came to and wriggled in his captors' arms, but made no sound.

They were in the hallway, their feet echoing on the tiled floor. Harry stopped and looked at James's portrait, which hung alongside Count Toraglia's own. His brother had caught her well, seeming with his brush to be able to portray her beauty, and in some way project her lack of vanity. She sat dressed in a loose-fitting gown of pale blue silk with a hooded black velvet cloak just covering her shoulders. At her feet sat a bird of prey, holding a small mammal in its claws.

'When we see them, James, not a word, d'you hear.'

James was quite shocked at the commanding tone of Harry's voice, and still somewhat confused by what had happened in the garden. 'If you say so, brother.'

She'd heard them and come to investigate. So had the tall mute servant who'd attended Toraglia on the *Principessa*. The old servant who'd shown Harry in that first day appeared dragging a sword which was far too heavy for him, showing great loyalty, if no practicality, in the face of this party of armed men. Leila di Toraglia stood framed in the doorway to the inner courtyard. Harry, still quite taken with her beauty, glanced from her to the portrait and back again. A wonderful likeness.

'Madame. I have come to see your husband.'

'Indeed, Signor.' If she was frightened by all these weapons it didn't show. 'He has only just returned from the city. I know he must be tired. I will see if he feels up to receiving you.'

'Forgive me, Madame. I've come too far to stand on ceremony.'

Harry pushed past her. Toraglia had heard the voices and his nose was in the air, almost like a sniffing hound. 'Leila. What is it?'

Harry spoke before she could. 'Harry Ludlow, Count Toraglia.'

There was a moment's confusion. James spoke up. 'My brother, Count. The one to whom you sold the *Principessa*.'

Toraglia's face lit up with a smile. 'Ah, Captain. How good to hear from you. A successful voyage, I hope?'

There was no warmth in Harry's response. 'You might like to know that the *Principessa* is at the bottom of the Ligurian Sea.'

The smile disappeared, and he turned his head slightly as if seeking reassurance from his wife. 'I am not sure I like your news. And if I may say so, Signor, your tone. It seems rather rough.'

'The night I dined here you said that I was less barbaric than the last English sailor you'd entertained.'

His wife stiffened at that. He looked confused. Harry surmised he'd be trying to remember not only if he said it, but where.

'You remarked upon it to your wife.'

'Did I?' His head swung round the room, for he didn't quite know where she was. 'Then it was less that polite of you, my dear, to say anything to Captain Ludlow.'

'Was his name Howlett by any chance?'

James stiffened and gasped. The Count maintained his aristocratic air. 'That is the fellow. A rather harsh man, in the manner of your naval officers. We met at a ball in the city. I have to say he rather forced himself upon us.'

'And you have often entertained a privateer captain called Bartholomew. Another Englishman?'

The Count frowned. 'Occasionally would be closer to the truth. And not of late. As you may remember, I enjoy the company of sailors. May I ask the purpose of your sudden arrival at my house, and the meaning of all these questions?'

'And why the need for all these armed men,' snapped the Countess.

Harry spoke quickly, for Toraglia was alarmed at that information. 'Captain Howlett was found hanged down in the port.'

'A very sad affair, Signor. Some deserters from his own ship, I believe.'

'Had he been here to dine that night?'

For the first time Toraglia showed a trace of genuine anger. He must have heard of the various speculations on the death of Howlett and the inference in Harry's words was too obvious to ignore. His aristocratic demeanour quite evaporated. 'No, Signor, he had not. He came to us the previous week.'

'You've just returned from the city, Count Toraglia.' A sharp nod. 'Did you call on Bartholomew while you were there?'

'How could I, since I don't have any idea where to call?'

'I asked you once about a fellow called Broadbridge. You said you didn't know him.'

The voice was even, showing no trace of emotion. 'Did I? I don't recall.'

Harry deliberately followed suit, keeping his voice calm. 'He was murdered in the cabin of the *Principessa*, the very day you first offered to sell it to me.'

Toraglia frowned. 'Murdered, you say? How do you know this, unless you were responsible?'

His wife finally spoke up. 'Captain Ludlow. I really think that my husband is too tired . . .'

Harry cut right across her, and anger flashed over her husband's face at the way Harry addressed her. 'Be quiet, Madame.'

Toraglia struggled to his feet, his hand looking for support. 'I will not allow you to talk to my wife in this way. Please leave my house.'

James spoke too, his voice worried. 'Harry.'

'Count Toraglia. Before I leave this house I am going to find the answers to some questions. As your wife has told you I am at the head of a party of armed men. You, sir, are in no position to refuse me an answer. What do you know of the sale of Christian children to the slave markets of the Ottoman empire?'

Toraglia waved his hands impatiently as though the question was a distraction. 'I know that it is forbidden in all Catholic states on pain of death.'

'Yet it still goes on?'

Toraglia shrugged. 'Where there is profit. But it is a dying trade . . .'

'Your servants, Count Toraglia, are they all mute?'

He nodded, thrown by the change of subject. Harry pressed on.

'They are not local men?'

'No.'

'And are they all Musselmen?' Toraglia nodded. 'They came as part of your wife's dowry?'

'Yes,' he snapped angrily, and his voice rose. 'Now will you please go.'

Harry raised his voice to drown the blind man out. 'And they all have a sign on their back, a brand mark. A crescent with lettering beside it.'

This time his wife answered. 'Yes. It is my father's brand mark.'

Harry turned to face her. 'You were born in Anatolia, Madame, on the shores of the Black Sea?'

'Her father and I were old trading partners,' snapped the Count. 'Which is the kind of information you can find in any salon in the city. This is most impertinent, and I will answer nothing more. Neither will you, my dear.'

'I think we should go, Harry.' said James.

Harry spoke without taking his eyes off the Count. 'You promised, James. I came into port today ready to accuse you of murder, Count Toraglia. The murder of Thomas Broadbridge.'

Toraglia mouthed the word and the name as Harry continued, 'Not personally, but by using these mute servants that came to you as part of your wife's dowry, at least one of whom also died aboard the *Principessa*. In fact, I killed him. That is where I first came across that brand mark. The second place I saw it was on the backs of a trio of eunuchs at an abandoned leper colony off Southern Dalmatia.'

The Countess tried to stop him from going any further. 'Who do you think you are, Signor, to come into our house and bandy about such accusations?'

Harry ignored her. 'I came to accuse your husband of murder. Madame. Indeed I have spent the last three weeks thinking of little else. I also intended to kill Gideon Bartholomew.'

Toraglia lifted his nose again, in that canine way, but he didn't follow the movement with a question.

'Bartholomew tried to kill me. Indeed, we had just struck a bargain and signed the papers transferring the *Principessa* to me, and a large sum of money to you. He abducted me outside this house the minute I left.'

Harry paused for a moment to let these words have their effect. 'I came to kill Bartholomew but when I got to his rooms he was already dead.'

The Countess gasped, looked at her husband, put her hand to her mouth, and sat down suddenly on the divan behind her.

'Bartholomew was poisoned. I regret not being the agent of his death myself, though I had something less devious in mind. But his death confused me. At the very least it eroded my certainties. I had to look at things afresh, only to discover that I had been wrong. Yet the real solution to it all lay with him, even though he was a corpse.'

Again Harry paused, this time to see if his words would provoke a reaction. No one spoke. 'His glass of wine was poisoned. There was another glass, the one he poured for the person who killed him. That didn't contain poison.'

Harry reached into his pocket. 'I have in my hand a key, Count

Toraglia. It fits your postern gate. It was stolen some time ago from the pocket of a visitor to your house. That visitor was Bartholomew.'

Toraglia's face remained a mask. Harry gave him a chance to speak, but he declined to use it. But all eyes were on him, even the sightless ones of Count Toraglia.

'Mr Fairbairn. Could a physician identify the poison that killed Bartholomew?'

'It may be possible, given time.'

'And tell me. Is it possible to survive a dose of a fatal poison?'

'Yes.' Fairbairn replied doubtfully. 'It depends on the poison itself, the quantity administered, and the constitution of the person taking it.'

'And what would be the effects of that?'

'I don't know, Ludlow. It could be anything. It would depend on what was used.'

'Could it blind you?'

The courtyard seemed suddenly to have an echo. Or was it the silence that followed that question. Fairbairn spoke hesitantly. 'Yes, it could.'

'And what would then happen if you administered small quantities on a daily basis?'

'There would be a general deterioration in the person's health, leading eventually to death.'

Toraglia was stiff as a board, his face set, and his eyes for once shut tight. No one else in the room seemed able to breath.

'When I discovered Bartholomew's body, Count Toraglia, I thought you'd killed him out of jealousy. I surmised that you had arranged the death of Broadbridge because he threatened your association with the privateers. But that left Captain Howlett's death unexplained. Yet the motive for his death was jealousy too, but not yours. With this key in his pocket, I fear Bartholomew was a more regular visitor to your house than you knew. It is your blindness that has saved you from a false accusation. One glass containing poison, the other a harmless glass of wine. I had to ask myself how a blind man could do that. And, of course, the answer is that he can't, for he doesn't know when the potential victim isn't looking.

'You may wonder where I heard the words you spoke about Captain Howlett, labelling him barbaric. You uttered them the night I came here. I was in your wife's bedroom, sir, and you were standing in the doorway having just woken from a deep sleep.'

Toraglia looked as if he'd been slapped. Harry continued without mercy. 'Captain Howlett was going back to his ship from this house the night he was killed, though I doubt you were aware that he had called.'

'Leila,' he croaked, sitting down.

'Jealousy is a terrible thing. It soured Bartholomew. He killed Captain Howlett because of it. He also tried to kill me for the same reason. I dare say that it's the primary cause of the fact that you are blind.'

Harry turned to face her. 'And you played it to the end, Madame. You would happily have let my accusation against your husband stand. Tell me, Countess, how much was it worth, supplying the brothels of Turkey with that which they valued most? Did you have some arrangement with the French, or were you just visiting another lover when you went on board that sloop in the harbour?'

Harry leant forward and laid the key on the table. 'I return your key. I cannot say that I envy you your wife, Count Toraglia, though there was a time I did. Nor do I envy your situation, for all this begs the question of how long you will survive. There must come a point when your wife no longer requires the cover of a husband to cloak her activities, a time when she will have sufficient of your family wealth to dispense with you altogether.'

'Signor, I beg you to allow me some time with my wife,' he croaked.

'I must act upon this matter, sir, for I have no choice. Yet my esteem for you as a man, and as a fellow sailor, is such that I cannot deny you the right to put the affairs of your own family in some order. To that end I will lock up your servants and leave my crew to protect your person.'

Toraglia fought hard to attain the aristocratic mask that he saw as essential to his position.

'I am obliged, Captain Ludlow,' he croaked.

His wife sat still, looking neither right nor left, staring at a point between, for all the world as though it was she who was blind. After a pause James leant forward and laid another key on the table. It was the exact match of the one that Harry had placed there a moment before.

POSTSCRIPT

'I believe Bartholomew came upon us the night I stayed at the villa. I saw a shadow on the wall, thinking with the long hair that it was the silhouette of a woman.'

Harry gave his brother a wry smile, then looked wistfully out of the open window. James poured another glass of wine, but stayed silent, content to let Harry air his thoughts. They stared silently at the distant harbour, the ship's lanterns twinkling against the blue-black sea and the great light of the *Lanterna* casting enough of a glow to challenge the streak of moon on the water. The parlour overlooked the harbour, though as part of a villa in the hills it remained aloof from the odours of the port. Painting and sculptures lay about, for James had not spent all his time in Genoa fretting about his brother.

Harry swirled the wine in his goblet. 'I would dearly love to know if she would have finally killed Toraglia. She had most of his money and I dare say Bartholomew was pressing her to finish him off. Yet the poor man, once disabled, provided her with a shield for her promiscuity. Having discovered freedom, I doubt she was afire to be chained to another husband, especially one as jealous as Gideon Bartholomew.'

He gave an impatient shrug. He was a man who loved certainty. 'Impossible to know, of course. But I feel that their relationship was stormy and getting worse. Perhaps Fairbairn was right; there may well have been a decent man inside. He was surprised when I told him of Broadbridge's death. I half sensed that he was upset. Did she do that on her own? Perhaps as a response to his murder of Howlett? Or even, God forbid, as a threat to him?'

'She's the only one alive with the answer.'

Harry shoved his goblet forward for a refill, even though he'd hardly touched the contents. 'Then we are likely to remain fog-bound, brother.'

'Perhaps she'll confess,' said James.

Harry smiled and shook his head. 'I rather fancy she inclines towards the Koran, not the Bible.'

'Pender mentioned those unfortunates who died with Broadbridge, the men you found aboard the *Principessa*.'

That cracked the veneer, for Harry Ludlow was more on edge than he cared to admit. He was drawing breath sharply and unevenly, and his free hand moved in a gesture full of frustration. 'Not a word, not a frown, brother. I told Doria, particularly.'

The hand was making a tight fist. 'What was his response? Dockyard idlers, workshy layabouts.'

'No one cares?'

'Dammit, James. Someone, somewhere cares!'

The ruddy face was lined with exhaustion. Harry's movements seemed uncoordinated, shocking in such a competent man.

'I think you need rest, Harry. Badly.'

Harry shook himself visibly, drained his goblet, and put it out to be refilled. 'I need another drink, brother.'

When Harry spoke again, James, in the act of obliging his brother, could tell that he wished to change the subject. 'One thing I must particularly thank you for—'

James raised a quizzical eyebrow.

'You sent Pender back. I'm not sure I'd be here if you hadn't.'

James now had both eyebrows raised, and an uncharacteristic look of surprise on his face. 'I didn't send him back. He insisted on returning ashore himself, though I own I agreed with the sentiments he expressed.'

'What sentiments?' asked Harry.

'He alluded, in his way, to your pig-headedness, brother, to your desire to poke your nose into affairs that don't concern you, as well as to the devious streak in your nature which was a threat to all and sundry, not just yourself. I have, of course, précis'd his remarks, and removed the cursing, for the sake of clarity.'

He watched Harry's face cloud with anger. 'Mind, I was under the influence of laudanum, so I may have imagined the swearing.'

Harry and James Ludlow sat on the harbour wall, Pender behind them. They watched as the French sloop slipped her mooring and headed out of the harbour. It was the conclusion of a hectic few days during which Leila di Toraglia had been confined to a nunnery for her life's duration. With Count Toraglia's grateful assistance, Tilly, the French chargé d'affaires, had been deemed *persona non grata*. Toraglia himself, freed from his daily dose of poison, was beginning to gain weight, though his sight was lost for ever.

'I should feel elated, James, but I don't.'

'You'll have your exemptions, that is if Admiral Hood keeps his word.'

Harry smiled ruefully. 'To tell you the truth, I'm not sure if I really want them.'

'What about the hands?' asked Pender, who'd picked up the drift of Harry's thoughts days ago and was ever mindful of the fate of those less fortunate.

'They will be safe enough, if not fêted, in Leghorn.' Harry turned round to look his servant in the eye. 'And I shall of course provide for them in the mean time. There is the matter of Sutton, I know.'

'Don't you go frettin' about Carey Sutton, your honour. Mr Fairbairn's set to take him on as a servant.'

'Is he, by God?' said James.

'Ay. And he says that Sutton don't need to worry about only having one arm, for in the medical lark, you only need a smile to rob folks.'

'If we're not going privateering in the Mediterranean, Harry, where are we going?'

'I wondered how you felt about going home, brother?'

James smiled and put his arm round his brother's shoulders. 'Home holds fewer terrors for me now. For all her criminality, Harry, that damned woman had some uses after all.'

341